EDGE OF SANITY

AN EDGE NOVEL

SHANNON K. BUTCHER

A SIGNET ECLIPSE BOOK

SIGNET ECLIPSE
Published by New American Library, a division of
Penguin Group (USA) Inc., 375 Hudson Street,
New York, New York 10014, USA
Penguin Group (Canada), 90 Eglinton Avenue East, Suite 700, Toronto,
Ontario M4P 2Y3, Canada (a division of Pearson Penguin Canada Inc.)
Penguin Books Ltd., 80 Strand, London WC2R 0RL, England
Penguin Ireland, 25 St. Stephen's Green, Dublin 2,
Ireland (a division of Penguin Books Ltd.)
Penguin Group (Australia), 250 Camberwell Road, Camberwell, Victoria 3124,
Australia (a division of Pearson Australia Group Pty. Ltd.)
Penguin Books India Pvt. Ltd., 11 Community Centre, Panchsheel Park,
New Delhi - 110 017, India
Penguin Group (NZ), 67 Apollo Drive, Rosedale, Auckland 0632,
New Zealand (a division of Pearson New Zealand Ltd.)
Penguin Books (South Africa) (Pty.) Ltd., 24 Sturdee Avenue,
Rosebank, Johannesburg 2196, South Africa

Penguin Books Ltd., Registered Offices:
80 Strand, London WC2R 0RL, England

First published by Signet Eclipse, an imprint of New American Library,
a division of Penguin Group (USA) Inc.

First Printing, December 2012
10 9 8 7 6 5 4 3 2 1

PUBLISHER'S NOTE
This is a work of fiction. Names, characters, places, and incidents either are the
product of the author's imagination or are used fictitiously, and any resemblance
to actual persons, living or dead, business establishments, events, or locales is
entirely coincidental.
   The publisher does not have any control over and does not assume any responsibility for author or third-party Web sites or their content.

ALWAYS LEARNING   PEARSON

For April Fowler,
who has done more for me than I'll ever deserve

Chapter One

It was the blood that woke him.

Clay Marshall's fingers were glued together, sticky and itching where the blood had dried. The heavy, metallic smell of it clogged his nose, choking him with the stench of violence.

He stared at his dirty hands, disoriented and numb from shock. Fatigue dragged at his bones. Pain pounded deep inside his skull, worse than any hangover.

The water stain on the ceiling was a familiar comfort, telling him he was in his own bed. Now, if he could only remember how he'd gotten here.

As the fog of sleep cleared, the meaning of the blood began to take hold. Concern gnawed at the edges of his numb haze, nibbling away at the false sense of calm. Reality squeezed around him, shoving out his breath like a giant boa constrictor.

Clay sat up, trying to control the fear before it became full-blown panic. His clothes were stiff and dark with drying blood, as if someone had splashed a bucket of it down his front. He searched for the source of the blood, seeking out the kind of physical pain this much blood loss would create.

He ripped off his shirt and jeans, only to find the skin beneath whole. His sheets were stained, but there was no pool lying where he'd been. Those smears were only from contact with his clothes.

Clay rushed to the bathroom on shaky legs and peered into the full-length mirror on the back of the door. No cuts. No gashes. Only a collage of bruises of varying ages and a body that was so thin he barely recognized it.

The blood wasn't his, and yet he could find no relief in that knowledge. It had to belong to someone.

The need to scrub it away arose, compelling him to stumble into the shower. Cold water hit him hard, driving the air from his lungs before it slowly warmed. He lathered himself from head to toe, watching in disgust as the rusty suds spiraled down the drain.

Even though the hot water stung, he still felt detached from the world, as though he were covered by a thick layer of foam, preventing anything from really reaching him. His head was clouded with confusion—so much so that he was only just now realizing that he was confused.

He dried off and headed for his kitchen, where the coffee lived. After three cups and twenty minutes, Clay's brain finally began to function. And with that relative clarity of thought came fear.

There were stains on his floor in the shape of his boots, leading from the kitchen door all the way to his bedroom. He followed them to where the bloody pile of clothes lay on the rug.

There was even more blood on them than he'd imagined. So much, he knew someone had to be dead. The question was who? And whether Clay had been the one to kill them.

A sick sense of dread settled over him, making the coffee in his stomach churn.

He had no memories of last night; he couldn't remember anything since lunch yesterday. The sun was streaming in through the windows, but as hard as he tried, there was simply a gaping black hole where the missing time should have been, as if he'd been asleep since then.

The blood proved otherwise.

Clay turned on the local news and barely breathed as the anchor moved from one story to the next. He wasn't sure what he expected to hear—reports of a building collapse or a giant pileup on I-35, maybe—but he knew what he feared: murder.

His hand shook as he surfed from one station to the next, seeking some sign of what he'd done. When they started repeating the same stories, he wasn't sure whether he was more relieved or scared. Maybe he hadn't hurt anyone. Maybe he'd saved someone's life and gotten them medical attention. Then again, maybe they just hadn't found the body yet. Or bodies.

This wasn't the first time Clay had woken up with blood on his hands, but he had no way of figuring out how to make it be the last time. The only person he could trust was his best friend, Mira. She was like a sister to him, and he couldn't stand the idea of burdening her with his problems.

Still, if anyone could help him solve the mystery, she could.

Clay dug his cell phone out of his bloody jeans and wiped it clean before dialing Mira.

Her voice was so cheerful and bright, it hurt his head. "Good morning, Clay. You're up early."

"Heya, squirt. I need a favor."

"Sure."

"I need to know if anyone in the area was killed last night."

The line went silent for a minute. "Uh . . . what?"

He hated lying to her, but there was no other way. "I

saw a ton of blood on the sidewalk outside a club. I was wondering if anyone was murdered. Can you find out?"

"Where was it?"

Shit. He hadn't been thinking clearly enough to consider even such a simple question. He was even worse off in the mental department than he'd thought. "I don't remember. I was drunk."

"Clay," she said in that voice that told him she knew he was lying. "What's really going on?"

"Can you find out or not?"

She let out a heavy sigh. They'd been friends a long time—since they were kids—and he was not easy on his friends. Especially Mira.

"Hold on." Disappointment weighed on her voice.

Clay heard the clicking of keys in the background before she came back on the line. "There was a drug-related shooting that killed three. One fatal car accident. Three deaths from natural causes. That's all I could find."

"Any John or Jane Does?"

"You want me to hack into the morgue? That's a little dark, even for you. What's going on?"

"Nothing. Really. Don't worry."

"How can I not worry? You sound awful. Did something happen?"

The lie nearly choked him. "No. I'm sorry I bothered you."

"You're not a bother, Clay. You know I love you. Whatever you need, I'm there, okay?"

An unexpected spurt of emotion clogged his throat. She was the only person in the world he really cared about. He didn't know why she stuck with him when he was such a mess, but he was glad she did. "I love you, too, squirt."

"Then let me help you. The headaches, the blackouts—you need help."

The pile of bloody clothes popped into his mind, staring at him in accusation. Until he figured out what was going on, he wasn't safe to be around. "I'll be fine. But I'm not feeling so great, so I'm taking a sick day. Will you let Bella know?"

"Sure. Get some rest and call me if you need anything, okay?"

"I will," he lied.

Mira hung up the phone feeling sick to her stomach. Clay was getting worse. The bruises, the split knuckles, the dislocated joints. And now he wanted her to check death records? Even if her IQ had been cut in half, she would have been able to figure out what that meant.

He thought he'd killed someone.

Clay kept pushing her away, making up reasons why they could no longer hang out together. The more she tried to help, the harder he pushed.

If he wouldn't let her help him, she had to find some-one who could. And there was only one man Mira knew who had even a chance at getting through Clay's thick skull.

What she was about to do would piss off her best friend, but that was just too bad. She owed him her life—even if he didn't remember—and if she had to suffer through his anger, so be it.

With her decision made, she picked up the phone.

Chapter Two

Clay had just shoved the last of the bloody fabric into a trash bag when his doorbell rang. He took his time washing his hands, hoping whomever it was would just go the hell away.

The chime rang again, followed closely by a sharp knock.

"I know you're in there," came a man's calm voice. "Mira called me."

Payton Bainbridge. His boss's right-hand man and an all-around buttinski.

"Go away," called Clay.

"Not going to happen. Open the door."

"I'm sick." He forced out a fake cough to add texture to the lie.

Payton's disbelieving tone said he wasn't buying Clay's story. "I'm immune. Open the door."

The sooner he got this over with, the sooner Payton would leave and shove his nose into someone else's business.

Clay unbolted the triple-locked door and let the older man in.

Payton was in his late fifties, with the suave kind of good looks that made younger women take notice. Or maybe it was simply his ridiculously expensive suits that spoke to them. He walked in, spine straight, hair perfect, suit without a single wrinkle, looking as if he'd just come from one of those celebrity makeovers. His pale eyes moved over Clay's rumpled clothes and mussed hair, but rather than disdain for Clay's lack of grooming, there was guilt in his eyes—as if he were somehow responsible for the way Clay looked.

"You need a doctor." Payton shut and locked the door behind him, dimming Clay's already dingy living room.

"I'm not that sick. Nothing a bit of rest and some chicken soup can't cure."

"You're favoring your left knee and hunching over as if your ribs ache. No amount of soup will fix that. You need to be X-rayed for broken bones."

Payton had looked at Clay for all of ten seconds and seen that? Shit. That meant he was going to have to take more time off work than just a day.

Clay straightened up, ignoring the throbbing pain in his ribs and shoulder. "My bones are fine."

Payton pushed past him and walked into the kitchen like he owned the place. "Mind if I make coffee?"

"You won't be here long enough to drink it."

The older man ignored him and went about searching Clay's cabinets, putting a pot of coffee on. "Mira says you're in trouble."

"Mira is wrong. Everything is fine."

"Your bruises say you're lying. Judging by the color palette you've got going there, you've been injured at least three times in the past two weeks."

"I joined a fight club. I would have told you, but you know the first rule of fight club . . ."

Payton turned around, his face tight with anger and something else Clay couldn't name. "This isn't a joke. She said you were asking about dead bodies."

"Mira and I are clearly going to have to have another talk about oversharing information."

"She trusts me. You should, too. I'm not here to judge."

"Then why are you here?"

Payton's direct gaze slid away to the empty mug he was holding. "We all make mistakes, Clay. If you've made one, I can help set things right. All you have to do is tell me the truth."

The truth wasn't going to help him any more than it was going to help the person whose blood he'd been wearing when he woke up. "I've got it under control."

"Do you?"

"Yeah. So you can take your coffee to go. Keep the mug."

Payton stared Clay right in the eyes, daring him to lie. "Did you kill someone last night?"

In that moment, Clay's world began to close in around him. The panic he'd felt since seeing the blood exploded until there was no room left to breathe. The edges of his vision began to fade out into gray nothingness. Sound became muted until all he could hear was the rapid, out-of-control beat of his own heart.

He needed help. He needed to find someone who could make sense out of the chaos his life had become. Mira was too vulnerable and precious for him to fuck over with his problems. As far as she stuck her neck out for him, one of these times, she was going to lose her head.

Payton stood there silently, patiently. He didn't move a muscle or blink a lash. There was no hint of reproach on his face, only the faintest lines of regret.

Clay swallowed, barely able to work up enough moisture to move his tongue. His choices were simple: continue on alone and wake up covered in blood again, or grab ahold of the lifeline Payton offered.

He didn't want to hurt anyone. He knew he was completely capable of killing and not remembering much. The mission in Arizona a few months ago had taught him that. Even now, he had only vague flashes of images, like dreams fogged over by time.

What if he killed again? What if this time he hurt someone he cared about? What if he hurt Mira?

That couldn't happen. He'd eat a bullet before he'd take that risk.

And yet he took that risk every day, never knowing when he'd lose another chunk of time and wake up bruised and broken, with no memory of what he'd done or where he'd been.

Today had to be his wakeup call. Mira was still alive and safe. That could all change so fast. She was the only family he had, and he couldn't gamble with her life.

Clay met Payton's stare and told him the truth. "I don't know."

"How can you not know? Either you killed someone or you didn't."

"I don't remember anything about last night. That's how. I remember grabbing a burger at lunch yesterday. After that . . . nothing. Until this morning, when I . . ." He couldn't even say the words. If he did, they would make this whole bizarre nightmare real.

"What happened this morning?" asked Payton, his voice gentle but insistent.

Rather than reply, Clay fetched the trash bag and dumped it out on his kitchen floor. Bloody sheets and clothes tumbled out in a stiff clump. The meaty smell nearly gagged him.

"This happened," said Clay.

A look of panic that mirrored Clay's brushed over Payton's aristocratic features. "Are you hurt?"

"Not enough to make this mess. It's someone else's blood."

"Or some*thing*. It could be animal blood."

Clay hadn't even thought about that, and it brought him a sense of relief so heavy his knees buckled under the weight. He collapsed into a kitchen chair, dizzy and swaying. "You think?"

"It's possible. I'll have it tested."

"I don't want anyone else involved."

"I understand. I'll make sure the test is anonymous."

Clay's head was suddenly too heavy to hold up. He propped his elbows on the table and let it sag into his hands. "Things are all fucked-up, Payton."

"I know. I'll help you sort it all out. But you've got to be completely honest with me. No more evasion. No more lies. Agreed?"

Clay hesitated. As much as he liked the man, he didn't trust anyone as much as he'd need to if he was going to spill his guts about everything. Instead, he let out a grunt that could be taken as agreement.

"This has been happening for a while, hasn't it?"

"The bloody clothes? Hell no. At least not like this."

"No, I mean the lost time—the blackouts. This isn't the first time you lost your memory."

Clay debated lying, but Payton didn't seem too freaked-out by the possibility, which gave him the boost he needed to say what needed to be said. "It's been going on for months now."

"How often?"

"Not very, at first. These past few weeks . . . at least four times that I know of."

"What do you mean by that?"

"There were a couple of times that I woke up and things weren't where I thought I'd left them. Once I was wearing clothes when I was sure I'd stripped down before going to bed." He lifted his head and forced himself to confess. "I think I'm going insane."

Payton's mouth turned down and a haze of regret dulled his eyes. "You're not. I won't let that happen. I'm going to see you through this. If you do what I say, everything is going to be fine."

"I don't see how. Once Bella finds out, I'm going to lose my job."

"Bella won't find out. We're going to fix this. I swear it."

For a glittering, hopeful second, Clay believed him. He clutched onto that hope and held on tight. "How?"

"First, you need to give me your phone."

"What?"

"Your cell phone. If I'm right, then it's dangerous for you to carry one."

Clay had no idea what to make of that, but he shoved his hand into his jeans and pulled out his phone. He set it on the table.

Payton stowed it in his pocket, his demeanor changing to one of all business. There was no more emotion showing through—just the get-it-done attitude that Clay had come to recognize. "I'm going to send you someplace safe. Isolated. I want you to take my car and go there right now."

"Why?"

"I'll explain everything once I'm sure, but for now, I need you to trust me."

"Why send me away?"

Payton pulled a key from his ring and wrote an address on the back of his business card. "The farther you are away from here, the better. Don't tell anyone where you're going. Don't speak to anyone along the way—not even a clerk at a gas station."

"Payton, you're freaking me out here. Why go to all the—"

"When you get there, unplug the phone. Don't bring

any electronics with you. No laptop, no games, no GPS. Nothing—understand?"

"No. I do not."

Payton shoved the key and the card at Clay. "I need a couple of days to gather some information, but you shouldn't be alone. I will send someone to stay with you."

"I don't need a babysitter."

"You do. If you don't want to hurt someone else, you do. Trust me."

"I don't want anyone from the Edge to know I've gone off the deep end. I have to work with these people."

"It won't be someone from work. I'll have your guardian show up at the back door at exactly six thirty-two. If anyone but me shows up at any other time . . ."

He trailed off as if debating his options, leaving Clay hanging.

"What? What crazy thing do you want me to do along with all this other cloak-and-dagger bullshit?"

"If anyone else shows up at any other time, kill them."

Payton waited until Clay was behind the wheel and on his way before he left in the other man's car.

First order of business: Burn the evidence. He didn't need to keep a sample to see whether it was human blood. He knew it was. The things Clay would be used for had nothing to do with animal control.

The suggestion about it being animal blood had been a strategically timed diversion to keep Clay from breaking. The man was already on edge. There was no way to know how long he'd been suffering with his secrets. He'd said months, but chances were even Clay wouldn't remember everything.

Payton was counting on it.

After a quick stop at one of the houses Payton kept

set aside for extreme circumstances, the clothes and sheets were no more than a burning ball of ash. He watched the glowing embers while he made the call.

Dr. Leigh Vaughn answered on the sixth ring, leaving Payton biting his nails.

"This had better be good. I'm in the middle of something."

"I'm sorry for the interruption, but it's important."

"It always is," she said on a sigh. "What is it this time? Another secret gunshot wound I can't report?"

"No. It's a much bigger favor than that."

"Spit it out. I don't have all day. Patients are waiting."

"Send them home."

"What? No way. If your emergency is that serious, then go to the hospital."

"If you do this, I'll get you in to see Garrett."

The line went silent for too long.

"Leigh? Are you there?"

"Yeah," she said, her voice thick with emotion. "I just . . . You're not joking, are you? Because if you are, you should know that I'm really good with a scalpel, and you have to sleep sometime."

"No jokes. I wouldn't do that to you."

"Okay," she said. "Whatever you need. Name it."

"Be sure. Because once I drag you into this mess, you're in it for good. Understand?"

"I don't care. If you can promise me a visit, then I don't care."

"Good." Relief poured over Payton like cool rain. Until now he hadn't been sure exactly how he was going to keep Clay safe while Payton took care of his own mistakes.

"What do you want me to do?"

"Pack as fast as you can. Bring your medical supplies. And a gun. Make sure you pack a heavy sedative. Chances are you're going to need it."

Chapter Three

Clay watched the clock all day long.

As posh as Payton's vacation home was, done all in pale blues and greens, it did nothing to soothe the restless itch on the back of his neck. He couldn't turn on the TV and distract himself. His mind was too scattered to read a book. When he'd tried, he'd read the first sentence sixteen times before finally giving up.

He was too nervous to eat, despite having gone all day with no food. If he shoved anything in on top of his anxiety, he knew it would come right back up. He couldn't stand the thought of doing that to Payton's plush carpet.

At six thirty-two and six seconds, a quiet knock sounded on the back door.

Clay had been waiting for it—wishing for that knock to come even as he dreaded it. And now that the moment was here, he felt glued to his seat, unable to stand.

His Sig sat on the little round table in the breakfast nook, next to a cold cup of coffee and a lace doily. He picked up the weapon, letting the cold steel ease his nerves.

Whoever was behind that door was going to know

what a head case he was, and as much as he hated that, he knew Payton was right. Someone needed to keep him from slipping out at night to do whatever it was he did. If that meant letting some dude handcuff him to a bed, so be it.

Clay eased the door open two inches, letting his weapon ride along his thigh, out of sight. Standing under a yellow lightbulb, huddled inside a jacket, was a woman he'd never seen before.

He was so shocked by her presence—that she wasn't a man—that he stood there like an idiot, staring. She had dark, reddish hair she wore pulled back from her face in a high ponytail. Small, fine curls escaped at her temples, springing away in defiance from the rest of the carefully smoothed strands. Freckles decorated her nose and cheeks, and the cold wind had rubbed a deep pink color over her skin.

"Clay?" she asked.

He nodded, mute.

"Payton sent me. I'm Leigh." She didn't offer to shake his hand, which was just as well, considering his hand was full of gun.

Her dark gaze drifted down his body and back up again, as if assessing him in a single glance. While there was a no-nonsense air about her—a directness in her stare that surprised him—he found himself relaxing.

He'd been expecting a confrontation—some big, burly asshole who was going to try to bully him around. He hadn't considered that Payton would send someone Clay could easily overpower.

"Are you going to let me in?" she asked, her tone as brisk as the wind.

He stepped back, sliding his weapon into the back of his waistband as he moved.

Leigh stepped inside, brushing so close to him, he

could smell her skin. Muscles along his spine began to loosen up, and he realized just how tightly he'd wound himself as he'd waited for six thirty-two.

She set two overnight bags on the counter. "Do you talk?"

"Of course I do."

"Good. My sign language is rusty." She stripped out of her jacket, making the buttons on her modest blouse strain to confine her breasts.

Clay froze, unable to look away, despite what manners dictated. He was completely captivated by the sight, marveling in how easily his brain switched from red alert to blunt male interest.

The pain in his ribs faded away, and all the tiny muscles lining his skull eased up their death grip. Until now he hadn't realized just how much pain had been running in the background, shoved down where it wouldn't distract him.

He was definitely distracted now.

"Do you have anything else to carry in?" he asked, looking for some excuse to leave her presence and get his shit together.

"No, I got it all." She wasn't looking at him as she spoke. Her gaze was on the kitchen, taking in the rich cherry cabinets and granite counters. "Swanky place Payton's got here."

Clay hadn't noticed how nice the kitchen was until he'd watched her notice. He didn't give a shit what the kitchen looked like so long as it had a coffeepot and a microwave. But he didn't want to be rude, so he grunted at her so she'd know he'd heard.

Leigh turned and lifted an eyebrow at him. It was slightly darker than her hair, but with the same warm coloring.

He'd always had a thing for redheads. Especially ones

who were stacked. It was predictable and clichéd, but there was no help for it. The hormones wanted what the hormones wanted.

And Clay's hormones were going to continue to want. No way was he going to hit on this mystery woman when he had no clue who she was or what Payton had told her.

What if he'd warned her that Clay was a potential nut-job, blacking out and slinking around at night, hurting people?

Even worse, what if he hadn't warned her?

Her gaze swung back to him, and he was struck by how pretty her eyes were. Big, conveying an open kind of innocence, but also dark, glittering with keen intelligence. She was watching him closely, but he couldn't tell whether she was trying to figure something out or making sure she could get out of the way if he took a swing.

"You look hungry," she said. "Have you had dinner?"

"No."

"Good. That'll give us something to do while we get to know each other."

She opened the bottom freezer drawer and leaned over to rummage inside.

Clay's clichéd hormones had a predictable response when presented with what was possibly the finest ass he'd ever seen. Her slacks molded to her curves, hiding more than they showed. And yet it was more than enough for Clay's dormant libido to sit up and stretch.

His mouth watered and a slow burn began heating his skin as he stared in helpless fascination. He was like some kind of hypnotized, drooling idiot, his eyes following where she led. Each minute sway of her hips pulled him along for the ride, leaving him standing there, too dumbfounded to realize she'd been speaking to him.

She turned around, frowning at him. "Did you hear a word I said?" There was no heat in her tone, only gentle curiosity as she crossed the big kitchen to where he was standing.

"Sorry. I'm not myself lately."

Leigh was close enough now that he could touch her if he so much as swayed forward. Too close. He could smell a trace of vanilla and something sweet he couldn't identify. Beneath that was the scent of heat and woman — something he hadn't noticed for a long time.

When was the last time he'd so much as gone on a date? Like so many other details, it was something he couldn't remember.

A starburst of golden green radiated from her pupils, brightening her dark brown eyes. On her right cheek was a cluster of freckles that were thicker than the rest. There was a slight dent in the center of her chin that seemed almost too masculine for such a soft, pretty face.

She reached up toward his head. Clay grabbed her wrist, riding along on a wave of pure instinct. Her delicate wrist bones shifted inside his grip, shocking him back to something resembling rationality.

He let go of her fast, but the heat of her skin clung to his palm all the same.

To her credit, she didn't flinch away or cower, even though he was much bigger than she was.

"I wasn't going to hurt you," she said, her gaze fixed on his.

Clay almost laughed at how ridiculous the thought was. If his laugh hadn't been rusted shut from disuse, he would have. "I know."

"Are you going to let me touch you or not?"

He wasn't sure. Part of him wanted her to stroke him from top to bottom and back again, but the rest of him screamed out a warning of danger. She wasn't going to hurt him, but he couldn't guarantee the reverse.

Leigh waited, giving him time to decide. The fact that

she didn't push relaxed a few more of those muscles that had been tied into cramped knots.

He gave her a tight nod and braced himself for whatever it was she was going to do.

She moved slowly, as if he were a wild animal she wanted to tame. Her hand settled on his forehead, as light as the touch of a butterfly. Her fingers were cool, drawing away some of the heat she'd ignited beneath his skin.

Clay closed his eyes and let his world contract until it consisted solely of the few square inches of skin that connected her to him.

A fine trembling fluttered through her hand. The faint beat of her pulse flickered along his brow, barely perceptible. Her skin warmed, soaking in his heat.

Clay had held himself apart from his friends for the past few months, slowly retreating inward. He'd spent less time with Mira and more time alone, his instincts telling him that he was becoming a danger to her. It had been so long since someone had touched him that even something as simple as this brush of skin on skin had the power to rock him to his core.

The pressure of her hand on his head eased, and he knew instantly that she was going to pull away. He didn't want that. Couldn't stand the thought. Not yet.

Panic took over his body, hazing out the edges of reality a bit more. He grabbed her arm, instantly realizing his mistake. He didn't know this woman. He shouldn't be touching her at all. And yet there wasn't a force on the planet strong enough to get him to let go.

Leigh wasn't sure what she'd expected when Payton had asked her to come here, but it wasn't Clay's hyperobservant state of relative calm. He wasn't raging or out of control. In fact she felt the strands of control vibrating through his touch, pulled taut but not yet breaking.

Even though he'd jerked into action when she'd tried to move away, his grip on her arm now was careful, if no less insistent.

At least his reflexes were still excellent. He hadn't reached that sluggish, fevered point that Hollis had right before he died. And there was no rage, nor was he dripping with paranoia—wide-eyed and twitchy.

His pupils were a bit dilated, but maybe that was simply an illusion created by his eyes' striking amber color. Vibrant, like sunset, almost glowing in their brilliance, his eyes pulled her in. There was pain there—something beyond merely physical. And fear. She wasn't sure what a man his size had to fear, but that latent terror was unmistakable.

His clothes were too big, as if he'd recently lost weight. Deep grooves of fatigue were carved around his mouth. Shadows sagged under his eyes. He hadn't shaved in a couple of days, and his messy brown hair was in need of a good brushing. Still, as disheveled as he was, something about him called to her.

Maybe it was the desperation that radiated out from him as he clung to her wrist, as if he was certain that she could save him.

She hadn't been able to save Hollis, a fact she needed to remember before she let Clay and his hopeful gaze go to her head.

"You don't have a fever," she said. "That's good."

Leigh tugged against his grip, hoping he'd take the hint and let go. Grudgingly, he did, releasing her so slowly it felt like a caress.

The skin where his hand had been tingled with warmth. She could still feel the rough slide of his fingertips across the inside of her wrist. As closely as he was watching, she didn't dare rub the feeling away, as much as she wanted to rid herself of that tingling so she could think straight.

This job of watching Clay was dangerous. Not only to her, but also to him. She had to remember that above all else.

Professional distance. That's what she needed with this man. She'd known him for less than ten minutes and he'd already pulled her in, making her curious and all too aware of his presence. She had to find a way to shove a wedge of space between them—one that included no more touching.

Squaring her shoulders and donning the mask she wore at work, she took a long step back. "Are you hungry?"

"Not really," he said, but the look he gave her—the scorching heat of his gaze as it traveled up and down her body—told another story.

"Well, I am. There were some chicken breasts in the freezer. I'll make us some."

Leigh went about finding pans and spices, trying hard to pretend she was ignoring Clay while tracking him closely. He hadn't moved from where he stood, simply watching her as she cooked. The mix of blatant male interest and desperation sliding off him had her on edge, fumbling as she flipped the chicken in the skillet.

"You can help if you want. I saw some canned veggies in the cabinet."

He was still for so long, she wasn't sure he'd heard her. Finally, he crossed the space, passing so close behind her she could feel the disturbance of air he caused.

With her back to him, she couldn't see what he was doing. She heard the clink of glass on the counter, an electric can opener, the sound of metal pans tapping together, and then water running.

The hair along her arms lifted in awareness a second before his lean arm reached past her, setting a pan of water on the stove. His heat blanketed her left side, and his voice rumbled low, close to her ear. "I found a box of mac and cheese, too. It's easier on my stomach than meat."

She turned to face him, finding him only inches away. She could smell the scent of dryer sheets clinging to his plaid flannel shirt. The sleeves were rolled up, revealing sinewy forearms layered with lean muscle.

"Have you been having trouble eating?" she asked.

His shoulder twitched in response, leaving her to interpret that as a yes.

Before she could think better of it, she slid her hand along his ribs, feeling them easily. He flinched as if she'd hurt him, making her snatch her hand back to where it belonged.

He was too skinny for a man his age—especially one who did the kind of physically demanding work that was necessary at the private security company the Edge. Instead, what greeted her was the hard, ridged contours of a man who needed more food—very similar to what she'd expect on a bottomless teenage boy. The width of his shoulders and depth of his chest were all grown man, which meant his twitchy shrug was a huge understatement.

He definitely needed to eat.

She turned away as if finding nothing of interest, when in fact she was far too interested. "Mac and cheese sounds good. Will you see if there's anything to drink in the fridge?"

Clay left her side, giving her room to breathe again. She wasn't sure what it was about him that captured her attention so completely, but she wasn't used to feeling off-balance. Hers was a world of routine and logic. She was a mechanic for the body, troubleshooting and repairing whatever was broken. There was no room for emotion beyond sympathy for her patients' pain and determination to fix it.

The way she felt about Clay went well beyond those limits.

Payton needed to get here soon and release her from her guard duty before she did something stupid and forgot how dangerous Clay could be.

They sat down to eat, and while she'd been starving, she found her stomach too fluttery for food. She toyed with her chicken until the silence was too much to take.

He watched her the whole time, his gaze so intense it was almost palpable against her skin. She tried not to look like she was watching him, worried that her scrutiny would stop him from eating. As it was, he seemed to be making a dent in his pasta, and she didn't want to mess that up.

Leigh forced herself to eat, feeling him watch every time the fork went to her mouth. Finally, after several minutes, the strain of his silent, intense interest was too much.

"What do you do at the Edge?" she asked to break the silence.

"How did you know I work there?"

"Payton told me."

"How do you know Payton?"

"I know most people at the Edge—at least those who don't refuse to come and see me the way you have. I figured you knew who I was, even though I've never seen you as a patient before."

His gaze lifted from his half-empty bowl, narrowing on her. "Patient?" He said the word as an accusation, his body shifting from relaxed to tense in a heartbeat.

Dangerous vibes tumbled out of him, setting off

Leigh's instincts. Adrenaline kicked her stomach and made her heart lurch in her chest. She clutched her fork in her hand, even though it was a paltry weapon against a man like Clay.

"I thought you knew who I was, or at least what I do," she said.

"Which is?"

"I'm a doctor. That's why Payton asked me to come here tonight—to make sure you were okay."

Clay shoved away from the table so fast the dishes rattled. "I'm outta here."

Leigh sat there for a second, too stunned and confused by his violent reaction to even figure out what had just happened. "What? Why?"

He whirled around, and his face was twisted with vivid hatred. "I cannot fucking stand doctors. I'm sure as hell not going to sit around and let you toy with me."

"*Toy* with you? What are you talking about? I'm here to help you."

"That's what they all say." He stomped into the living room, leaving Leigh no choice but to follow.

"I have no intention of doing anything other than making sure you stay safe."

Clay grabbed a duffel bag from where it sat by the front door.

"You're leaving?" she asked, outraged that something as simple as her day job would drive him away.

His expression was hard. His amber eyes glowed with rage. His rigid posture warned her to stay the hell away. "Tell Payton I don't want his help anymore. If he thought I'd hang out alone with a fucking doctor, clearly his judgment is flawed."

Leigh patted her pocket, making sure her self-defense syringe was still there. Payton had told her she might need it, and she wasn't stupid enough to ignore him. He knew the risks at least as well as she did. "So . . . what? You're just going to leave? Who will watch out for you?"

"I will. I don't need any help. I'll figure this out on my own."

Before he could leave and get himself killed, she flattened herself against the door, blocking his path with her body. "You can't do that. It's not safe."

"You have no idea what you're talking about. You don't know me, and you sure as hell don't know what I'm going through."

"I know more than you think. If you'd give me half a chance—"

He reached past her and pulled the door open, moving her weight as easily as he would a small child's. Her shoes slid across the floor, proving how outclassed she was in the strength department.

Leigh no longer had a choice. If she let him walk out, the chances of him surviving were slim, and she would not let another man die the way her brother had. Not while there was still something she could do to stop it.

She pulled the syringe from her pocket, flipped the protective cap off, and jabbed the needle into his shoulder.

He spun on her, his amber eyes bright with anger. A roar poured from his mouth. He reached for her, but the tranquilizer set in and he started to collapse.

Leigh shoved her shoulder under his and eased his bulk to the floor. He was a lot heavier than he looked, and she had to strain to keep him from hitting his head.

Once he woke up, there was going to be hell to pay.

Chapter Four

Dr. Richard Sage eyed the acne-scarred tech in the rumpled lab coat. "What do you mean you can't activate him?"

"The subject isn't answering his phone."

"For how long?"

The tech tapped his electronic tablet. "Last contact was at one p.m. yesterday. His phone has not moved since ten a.m. today."

That was more than twelve hours ago. Clay Marshall was never without his phone, which made it the perfect tracking and activation device. "Where is it now?"

"At his office."

"Put an alert on that phone. The moment it moves, notify me."

"Yes, Doctor."

Richard pressed a button to summon his assistant. Ruby Rypan entered the room a moment later. Her blond hair was smoothed back and restrained in some kind of elaborate twist. Her high heels clicked on the floor and pushed her from merely tall to Amazonian proportions. She was pretty but never let that get in the way of professionalism, which Richard appreciated. Her suits were always modest, showing no hint of cleavage or thigh, and she'd never once spoken of her personal life. She left for exactly eight hours each day, returning fresh and renewed, wearing a different suit. If it weren't for the bottled water that always resided on her desk, she could have been a robot.

"Yes?" she said, standing just inside his doorway, a tablet poised in her hands as she awaited his instructions.

"One of my subjects has gone missing. Put the word out to our contacts that I'll offer fifty thousand to any man who brings in Clay Marshall."

"Yes, sir." Her fingers flew on the tablet. "Alive or dead?" she asked, without any indication of her preference.

"Alive. I won't pay them anything for Marshall's body. Make that clear."

"Yes, sir. Anything else?"

Richard considered asking her to do the rest, but that was best left to him. Maybe it wasn't the best option to use thugs and killers to do an operation as delicate as finding and subduing one very dangerous man, but Richard had few options. And those thugs were expendable. There were always more waiting to fill the ranks so long as the money was good.

"No, thank you. Close the door behind you."

He waited until Ruby left the office. He typed a few keystrokes, bringing up the live feed displaying his daughter's work area at the Edge. She trusted Clay, making it easy for him to install several cameras without her knowledge. Or his. At least he had no memory of the act, making it impossible for his guilt to set off any kind of suspicion in Mira.

She was far too perceptive—a by-product of the alterations, no doubt.

Mira wasn't in her workspace. All of her monitors were black.

A moment of alarm streaked through him. If she was missing as well as Clay, whatever they were doing could not be good news.

And then he remembered. It was nearly midnight. She wouldn't be at the office this late.

In his windowless facility, Richard had little connection to the flow of time. He often worked until he was no longer able to stay awake, regardless of what time of day it was. Circadian rhythms meant nothing. Only his work mattered.

He switched over to the cameras hidden in Mira's home, flipping between feeds until he found the right one.

There was his little Mira—not so little now—all curled up in a blanket, working at her laptop. The TV was on, casting a flickering blue glow over her face. The deep resonance of a cable news anchor droned on in the background, interspersed with lighter voices of others. Occasionally, she'd look up at the TV, multitasking as usual.

She looked tired, worried, and so much like her mother, sometimes it was hard for Richard to watch her. She had the same tilted green eyes and softly rounded face. Even the way she sat, curled up like a child, was the same.

An ache so old it was as much a part of him as his own skin flared to life. Mira's mother was long gone—a victim of her own small mind. Mira refused to speak to him, leaving him to reach out to her in the only way he knew how. Illegal, but necessary. She was one of his greatest successes.

One day she would see that everything he'd done had been for her. All the experiments and long hours in the lab. The missed holidays and family dinners. None of that lost time mattered. His work had been a success, and the only thing left was for him to prove it. After almost twenty years of being looked at as a failure, Dr. Richard Sage was finally going to be vindicated.

All he had to do was find Clay Marshall and make him finish his mission. Once that file was obtained, Norma Stynger—his previous partner turned professional adversary—and all the others would see that his way was best. Slower, certainly, but far more effective.

But unless Clay was located, Richard's years of effort would be wasted. Clay was close to finding the file now. Richard could feel it.

Unless the thugs Ms. Rypan contacted failed.

Clay was too important to leave to chance, so Richard began the protocol for contacting one of the few men capable of capturing Clay alive. Someone Ms. Rypan didn't even know existed, just in case Richard had to have her eliminated one day. While most of the men in Richard's employ had been hired for their minds, Mr. Grady was not one of them. For hire to the highest bidder, Mr. Grady charged a fortune, but so far, he'd been worth every penny.

Richard had to jump through a ridiculous set of security hoops to send Mr. Grady his marching orders, but ten minutes later, he got the confirmation code that Mr. Grady was on the job.

Clay Marshall was as good as found, and once Richard had him back under his control, he wasn't letting him go again until he'd proven just how wrong Norma and the others had been.

Leigh was waiting for Payton when he walked through the door. She'd had several hours to work up a heaping helping of anger, and she was more than ready to let it fly at him.

She didn't wait for polite greetings. Instead, the moment

he stepped through the door, she blasted him with, "You tricked me."

"It's lovely to see you again, too, Dr. Vaughn." He slid out of his coat and draped it carefully over the back of a chair.

"Cut the bullshit. You sent me here knowing how much Clay hates doctors. You could have at least warned me."

"You might not have come. I couldn't afford to let that happen."

"Damn right I wouldn't have come. It's bad enough to be faced with a dangerous man who might crack at any second, but giving him a nice, juicy target for all that hatred was way out of line."

"I knew he wouldn't hurt you."

"How? You said he was like Hollis and needed my help. If you'll remember right, Hollis broke my arm before he finally . . ." She couldn't say the words. Her brother had died more than two years ago, and yet she still couldn't utter the truth aloud.

Payton cupped her shoulder. "I knew Clay hadn't gotten that bad yet. If he had, I would have sent him somewhere safe, where he couldn't hurt anyone."

Just like he'd done to Garrett.

She hadn't seen her oldest brother in months, and the ache of missing him never seemed to fade. Payton handed out visits like cookies to a child, ensuring her cooperation. And like a child, she went along with it, unable to resist the temptation.

Garrett was so lonely, kept in solitary confinement so he wouldn't hurt anyone or himself. She had to do whatever she could to see him as often as possible, so he'd know he was still loved.

Her anger faded, replaced by grief and loneliness for her brothers. "Why take the risk with Clay? Why risk my life?"

"Because Clay may be the key to stopping this for good. For everyone."

"Everyone who? Are you saying there are more men out there like Clay and my brothers?"

Payton turned away from her, pretending to be interested in the angle of the watercolor hanging on the wall. "Possibly. Clay will help us find out for sure. I may have been using you. I'm certainly using him. But I'm doing so in order to save others from suffering through what your family has. You're the only person I know who completely understands the risks."

It was tough for her to argue with that, as much as she wanted to. She and her two brothers had gone through a hell she wouldn't wish on anyone. She knew just how bad it could get and exactly what was at stake.

Leigh let out a long breath, searching for a sliver of calm. "Clay tried to leave once he found out that I'm a doctor. I had to sedate him to keep him here."

Payton nodded. "You made the right choice."

Sarcasm hung in her voice. "I'm sure Clay will see it that way—all nice and reasonable—when he wakes up."

"Where is he?"

"On the living room floor. He was too heavy for me to move."

"How long until he wakes up?"

"A couple more hours, maybe. It's hard to say. He looks like he hasn't been getting much sleep, so it could be longer. It would be best if he slept through the rest of the night."

Payton went to where Clay was sacked out on the floor. She'd put a pillow under his head and covered him with a blanket, but that was the extent of comfort she had to offer. As lean as he was, he still had at least fifty pounds on her.

"You should check him out while he's unconscious."

"Why?"

"To make sure he has no serious injuries. He's the type of man who would hide them rather than seek help. I've caught him sewing up his own cuts before rather than getting medical attention after a mission."

Wow. He really did hate doctors if he went that far. Most men were babies about pain, happily accepting whatever painkillers she was willing to offer.

Payton picked him up and carried him upstairs to a bedroom.

"You're stronger than you look," she said.

"Vanity has its benefits." He stripped Clay down to his boxers right in front of her, with no concern for his privacy.

She had to fight the urge to look at Clay, had to force herself to turn away to give him at least a small measure of respect.

"This is a bad idea," she told Payton, keeping her eyes on the carpet. "He already hates me because I'm a doctor. He'll hate me more once he knows I drugged him. How can I help him if he won't stay in the same room with me?"

"He can hardly hate you more for giving him a quick look, can he? It'll be our secret. Once you're done, I'll dress him again and he'll never have to know."

"Not only is that a huge violation of trust; it's illegal. I need consent to treat."

Payton offered her a knowing smile. "Since when have you let the legality of something stop you from doing it?"

A flash of anger surged and she spoke through gritted teeth. "Only when someone's bribing me with visits to see my imprisoned brother."

Payton let out a weary sigh in the face of their old argument. "He's not in prison. He's being held for his own safety. It's not even against his will. Garrett wants to be there."

"Because he knows what could happen if he's left to roam free. More people could be hurt."

"Unless we help Clay find out who's doing this and how. If that happens, then perhaps we can figure out how to undo it, and Garrett can go free without risk."

Leigh went still, worried that if she so much as breathed, that fleeting wisp of hope would disappear. "Do you really think that's possible?" she whispered.

"If Clay is well and at the top of his game, I do. Which is why I think you should take a look and make sure he's not in need of medical care while he's still too unconscious to refuse it."

It was then that Leigh realized that this was the trap Payton had set all along. He knew that if he dangled her brother's future in front of her, she would have no choice but to do as he wanted. "You're a son of a bitch, Payton. You know that?"

A sad smile lifted his mouth but didn't reach his eyes. "I do. Luckily, I don't let it stop me from doing the right thing. And neither should you."

He left, returning a minute later with her medical bag from downstairs. He set it on the carpet and then shut the bedroom door on his way out.

Leigh stood there for a moment, collecting her wits. She wasn't going to do anything to harm Clay. She'd already broken the law and drugged him against his will, so what was a little look-see going to hurt? If Payton was right and they needed Clay to find a way to help her brother, she really had no choice. Restoring Garrett's freedom was worth invading one man's privacy.

She sucked in a deep breath and sat on the bed where Clay lay.

His skin was covered in bruises of varying ages. From

fresh dark purple to aging yellowy-green. Several were the size of a man's fist, but a few were larger and longer, as if someone had kicked him or beaten him with a bat. His ribs had taken the brunt of that abuse.

No wonder he'd flinched when she'd touched him.

She moved his dog tags aside and ran her fingers lightly over his skin, feeling for signs of broken bones as gently as she could. He didn't twitch or make any noises of pain, allowing her to finish her exam without her stomach twisting with guilt.

Clay wasn't as skinny as she'd thought. There was no fat on him, and he really could use a few more pounds of it, but he was far from skin and bones as she'd imagined. Dense, lean muscles hugged his frame and were likely the reason he wasn't lying in a hospital with broken ribs. She couldn't guarantee they weren't cracked, and they were definitely bruised, but she didn't think any had been severely broken.

She donned her stethoscope and listened to his heart and lungs. Everything checked out—his pulse as slow and strong as that of an athlete in his prime.

There were several scratches and a couple of healing cuts that probably should have been sutured but weren't. One of them was a bit red and inflamed, indicating a minor infection. She cleaned it well and added some antibiotic ointment, forgoing the bandage for fear of him freaking out when he saw it.

With a heave of effort, she rolled him over enough to inspect his back, seeing more of the same. Lots of bruises, plenty of scratches, and a couple of cuts.

She picked up his hands one at a time, noticing the rough calluses along his knuckles and palms. There were a couple of small lacerations, but nothing that would have raised any red flags. He just looked like a man who worked with his hands.

Her gaze skimmed down his body, purposefully ignoring the bulge in his boxers. There was no professional reason for her to peek under there, no matter how curious she might be.

His wrists were thick, his forearms hard and ropey but not bulging with muscle. Inside his clothes, he would have easily passed for an average, athletic guy. Without that disguise, she could see the truth: Clay was a man who possessed the strength of steel and the resilience of rawhide. A lesser man would not be walking around after taking the kind of beating that would leave behind marks like these.

Some antiquated part of her found the notion exciting, while the clinical, detached part of her rolled its eyes.

He was just a man. The fact that he had a nice body under all those bruises and made her want to feed and pamper him had nothing to do with reality.

She started to get up, but Clay's arm wrapped around her hips, pulling her back down to the bed.

Leigh let out a startled squeak and clutched his hard arm.

There was no grogginess in his eyes—no sign of lethargy at all. Which meant . . .

"How long have you been awake?"

"Long enough to enjoy you petting me." His gaze was hot as it slid from her face, down over her breasts, and finally to where his arm crossed her hips, pinning her to the bed. She couldn't tell if that heat came from anger or something deeper she refused to acknowledge.

"I thought you hated doctors."

"I do, but even I'm not strong enough to turn down a chance to have the hands of a woman as beautiful as you on me. Now, if you'd pulled out another needle . . . let's just say I wouldn't have cared how beautiful you were."

His flattery surprised her, leaving her floundering for

how to handle it. In any other situation, she would have been irritated, but she couldn't seem to rouse the appropriate level of indignation—not when his words sent such a thrill sliding through her.

She lifted her chin and stared down her nose at him, searching for some kind of armor to wrap around herself. She was feeling things for this man she had no right to feel. Sympathy? Sure. Worry? Absolutely. But interest? Inexcusable.

Leigh forced her tone to come out frosty. "I'm not sorry about the tranquilizer. Keeping you here may have saved your life."

He sat up in a move that made muscles in his shoulders and arms flex. His face was only inches away from hers. She had to tilt her head back to keep looking him in the eye, and she knew if she looked away, he would take it as a sign of weakness.

With this man, weakness could be dangerous. Even if her heart was racing out of control, she had to pretend that nothing he did affected her. If he thought he had the upper hand, he would be more likely to get himself into trouble, thinking he no longer needed the help of one weak woman.

"Don't expect me to thank you," he said. "This was a violation of trust and you know it."

"You don't trust me, so I don't see how I could have violated anything."

"If I hadn't trusted you, I wouldn't have opened the door and let you in. But don't worry. I've learned my lesson. I'm leaving, and if you try to stick me again, you won't like what happens."

Chapter Five

Clay used every bit of acting experience he had to deliver that bluff.

He couldn't stand the thought of hurting her, but he didn't want her to know that. It was better if she was afraid of him. Maybe then she'd keep her distance and he wouldn't have to keep fighting the hard-on threatening to give his real feelings away.

It pissed him off that she had the power to disarm him so easily, without even trying. Even now, just sitting next to her on a bed, as angry as he was that she'd drugged him, he couldn't help but imagine laying her down and seeing what she had hidden under all those proper clothes.

Mussing her was high on his list of things he wanted to do before he died. Too bad that was never going to happen.

Even if he could overlook her being a doctor, he'd never trust her enough to relax, which was a shame. Between the moment he laid eyes on her and the moment he found out who she really was, his whole body had begun unknotting a little at a time. It had felt good, and for a second, he'd thought that maybe he'd found someone who really could make things better.

What an idiot.

He was back to being a mass of tension and worry, which, while no fun, was probably the safest bet. At least now he knew the truth.

She looked pointedly down to where his forearm barred her from getting up. "I think we're done here. You can get dressed."

"You undressed me. I think it's only fair if you do the honors."

Leigh smiled, showing off a mouth that was far too sweet and plump for Clay's peace of mind. "Actually, Payton was the one who stripped you. I'll ask him to come *do the honors.*"

Payton was here? Good. Finally Clay could get to the bottom of this mess and find out what was going on. And how to stop it.

Pushing Leigh's presence from his mind was impossible, so instead he simply pretended to ignore her while he threw his clothes back on. He turned his back and shoved his stupid, semihard cock into his jeans, zipping a sturdy layer of denim over it to make it behave. No way was he fucking a doctor, no matter how stacked she was, or how easily he could imagine the way her red hair would look spread across rumpled sheets. It was time his dick accepted the facts and left him the hell alone.

Payton was sitting at the kitchen table, sipping wine and eating the food Leigh had cooked.

A bizarre sense of jealousy reared up in Clay, making him angry that Payton was benefiting from her efforts when Clay hadn't been able to convince his stomach to cooperate. It was a stupid little thing, but one more to add to the growing pile of irritations.

Even this late in the day, Payton still had a perfect, polished appearance that made Clay feel like he'd been dragged backward behind a truck halfway across Texas. Normally, the comparison didn't bother him, but he was acutely aware of Leigh's presence a step behind him, and what she might think.

Clay sat down across from Payton and simply said, "Start talking."

"Did you have a nice rest?" Payton asked.

"You know she drugged me, so don't pretend we're having fucking high tea here. I want to know what's going on. Now."

Payton glanced at Leigh, who was searching through cabinets for something. "It's complicated."

"Good thing I'm not an idiot, then, huh?"

"Of course you're not. You scored higher than most on the tests we gave before we hired you."

Clay had forgotten all about those. He'd been at the Edge for most of a decade now, and his green years seemed so far away they were like memories of something that had happened to another person.

"Just start at the beginning. I'll try to keep up."

Payton smiled like that was some kind of joke. "I'll start with what you need to know."

Frustration raged through Clay, and he had to control his tone so his words wouldn't come out as a growl. "Fine. Whatever. Just start somewhere. Maybe with why you sent me here."

"You needed to be somewhere away from all means of communication. No phones or email. This place is too far out for most of that, making it safe."

"From what?"

"You're agitated. I think you need more rest. This can wait until morning."

Clay leaned forward, no longer willing to hold anything back. He let every ounce of frustration and rage spill into his words. "If you don't start talking, there will be no morning for you. I'm sick of the games and the delays. What the fuck is wrong with me?"

Payton paused for only a moment before he gave a slow nod of acquiescence. "You're being used against your will to act on the orders of another person."

Denial slammed a brick wall down, blocking off even a remote chance that Clay would believe something so ridiculous. "That's impossible. I would have known."

"No, you wouldn't. It's a sort of hypnosis—mind control. Whoever is doing this says a trigger word or phrase and it puts you into a kind of trance. They tell you to do things, and then you do. When they tell you to forget, you forget."

No way. There had to be another explanation.

Payton went on calmly, as if talking about the weather. "Whoever is doing it has to have some way to contact you. My guess is via phone, but there are other ways. As long as you're near any means of long-distance communication, you're in danger of being triggered again."

Clay sat in stunned silence, waiting for Payton to crack a smile. "This is a joke, right?"

The man's face was stony, without a hint of amusement. "I wish it were. I'm sorry."

Clay scrubbed his hands over his face, hoping it would wake him up from this bizarre dream. "You're wrong. You have to be."

"Why?"

"Because I'm stronger than that. I don't let people fuck with my head."

"This wasn't something you chose. This was something that was done to you by some unscrupulous scientist."

"Who?"

Payton's mouth flattened. "The better question is who is pulling the trigger now."

As hard as he tried, Clay couldn't make Payton's explanation fit within the constraints of what he knew to be real. "How could something like this even happen? How can someone hijack my body without me remembering how it happened?"

"It happens. You're not the first case like this I've seen. Unfortunately."

Clay held on to denial because it was the only thing keeping him sane. Even as he shook his head, niggling doubts began to trickle in between the cracks in his refusal to believe. "No. You must be wrong."

Payton's voice was gentle, like he was talking to a mental patient. "It explains the blackouts and the bruises. It explains your lost chunks of time."

The smell of coffee filled the air—so normal, like nothing had changed, even though Clay's whole world had just been tipped sideways.

"This kind of thing isn't even real." It couldn't be. Clay couldn't be that fucked-up. He couldn't be the puppet of some mad scientist willing to screw with people's minds.

"It is," said Leigh, her voice so soft and sweet in this sea of bleak confusion. "I've seen it before."

Clay looked to where she stood, her hips propped against the counter next to a gurgling coffeepot. She was shaking so hard he could see it from across the room. Sadness darkened her eyes, and she was so pale her freckles stood out in stark contrast.

"Seen it?" he asked. "Where?"

Her face crumpled with anguish, as if she was fighting off a sudden surge of tears. Clay was on his feet, heading toward her before he could stop and think about what he was doing.

"You don't have to talk about this, Leigh," said Payton.

She pulled herself together before Clay reached her,

but his feet kept moving. He wrapped his fingers around her biceps, being careful not to squeeze. He wanted to shake the truth out of her, but her pain was so vivid and real, all he could do was stroke the inside of her arm with his thumb. "What have you seen? I need to know."

Her bottom lip wobbled, but she held herself together. "My brothers. Both of them went through what you're going through now. I didn't know what was going on until it was too late."

"That's enough, Leigh," said Payton.

But it wasn't enough. Clay still had no idea what to do, but he didn't want to make Leigh cry. She was barely staying in control.

It pissed him off that he cared enough to worry about some paltry tears. His whole life was a mess, with the pieces he'd thought had fit now scattered all over the place. It shouldn't have mattered that she cried.

He let go of her and stalked over to Payton. "How do I fix it?"

"You don't. I do. You stay here where it's safe and don't let anyone contact you. Leigh will stay here with you and make sure you don't try to leave again."

Like hell. Now that he knew who and what she was, there was no way she was slipping another needle in him.

"How are you going to fix it?" Clay demanded.

"I have connections. I'm going to track down the people responsible and deal with them."

"Connections? Really? You think that whoever did this to me hangs out at political fund-raisers and country clubs?"

Payton's face darkened with anger, and something shifted in his posture. He went from giving off the relaxed vibes of a pampered socialite to screaming hardcore badass in the blink of an eye. Whoever this man sitting at the table was, he wasn't the soft, amenable businessman Clay had come to know. This man was dangerous. "I said I'll deal with it."

"How?"

"That's not your concern."

"The hell it isn't. You can't tell me that someone who has control over me isn't my concern."

Payton stood. Determination was evident in the angle of his shoulders, but there was regret lingering in the creases around his pale eyes. "You have to let me do this. It's too dangerous for you to be out there where you can be found. Hiding is the only way to keep them from triggering you again. Do you understand?"

"I understand that two people looking for the fuckers who did this to me are better than one."

Leigh touched his arm, so light he almost thought he'd imagined it. "You're wrong, Clay."

"Why?"

"You've been out of contact for too long."

"What do you mean?"

"You've been away from your phone. They'll know something's up."

"It's only been a few hours."

"You're a valuable asset to them. Do you think they're not going to keep tabs?"

"She's right," said Payton. "You're never without your phone, are you?"

"No. Bella's policy is for all of us to be on call unless we specifically say we're on vacation."

"When was the last time you went anywhere without your phone?"

Clay couldn't remember. Even now, not having it in his pocket was making him restless and itchy.

In the face of Clay's lack of response, Leigh said, "Exactly. The people who did this may know that you're aware of what's been done to you. If they get their hands on you again, they might never let go."

The thought made it hard to breathe. He tried to control the panic surging from deep inside, but he was already dealing with so much. When he spoke, his breathlessness gave away his fear. "Is that true, Payton?"

The older man nodded. "It is. But there are worse things than never being yourself again. They could make you hurt the people you love. They could make you hurt Mira."

No. That couldn't happen. "I'd find a way to fight it. I'd never do anything bad to her."

Leigh's hand fell to her side, and his skin felt cold without her touch.

Payton's eyes closed for a moment and he swallowed hard. "You wouldn't even know you were doing it. Trust me on this, Clay. The safest place for you is here with Leigh, where no one can reach you."

Clay nearly toppled to the floor under the weight of his defeat. He stumbled through the closest door and shut it, not caring where it led. All he knew was that he had to get away and think.

He was left standing in a bathroom, propping himself up against the sink so he wouldn't fall over.

Just a few minutes alone. That's all he needed to make sense of all of this and figure out what to do.

He slumped down onto the lid of the toilet. His whole body was shaking uncontrollably. A mixture of rage and despair slammed through his veins.

In the past few minutes, his world had been scrambled, leaving him swirling around, trying to find something solid to hold. Every thought he grasped was even more fucked-up than the last, making him wonder if he was completely sane. His mom hadn't exactly been the most stable woman on the planet. Maybe all of this was some kind of delusion—something he'd inherited from her, along with his creepy amber eyes.

And if he wasn't insane, the alternative was even worse. He was a puppet. Used. Just like he'd been when he was a kid. He'd promised himself it would never happen again—that no one would ever use him for any reason.

Here he was, a toy for the amusement of others, and he hadn't even known it.

Clay wasn't sure how long he sat there, letting his brain spin, trying to make sense of something where there was no sense to be had. His body settled, and the shaking eased enough that he felt like he could stand without puking or falling over.

What was waiting for him on the other side of that door was a fucked-up mess, but one he would face head-on, the way he always did. He wouldn't let anyone stop him from setting this right and finding the people responsible.

Clay wasn't the only one they'd hurt. Apparently, they'd hurt Leigh's brothers, too. That put her and Clay on the same side, somehow. It didn't mean he trusted her, but she might be the only person who had some clue of what he was going through. Doctor or not, he couldn't push that away. Not now, when he had nowhere else to go that wouldn't risk Mira's life.

He splashed water on his face and left the bathroom. Leigh was sitting near the door, coffee in hand, as if waiting for him to come out.

When she saw him, she straightened in her chair. "How are you feeling?"

"Pissed. Caged. Used."

She nodded, a flash of sadness dulling her eyes. "Garrett never tells me the truth when I ask him that. He always says he's fine, even though I know he's not."

"Is that your brother?"

"Yeah."

"Did they find who fucked with his head?"

"No."

"How does he manage? Is he hiding out in some posh vacation house, too?"

"No. He's in prison."

The thought of being locked up made Clay's core temp plummet. He'd drive off a cliff before he let someone put him behind bars. "What did these fuckers make your brother do? Did he hurt someone?"

She sniffed, staring in her coffee cup while tears glistened in her eyes. After a moment, she was back in control again and the tears were gone as if they'd never been. "I don't want to talk about it."

He was going to make her talk about it, but she didn't seem like the kind of woman he could bully. Better to get her to drop her guard and then pull the information out, nice and gentle.

Clay pretended that he didn't mind changing the subject. "Where's Payton?"

"He left to start tracking down answers. He said he'd text me when he had news. We're supposed to stay here until we hear from him."

The clock on the kitchen wall said it was nearly dawn. "You look tired. You should get some rest."

She lifted a dark red brow at that. "You really think I'm going to be that easy to trick? I go to sleep and you sneak out without me?"

"I wouldn't do that," he lied.

She went to the counter and dug in her purse. When she turned back around, a shiny pair of handcuffs was dangling from one finger. "Payton left them."

"Kinky."

"In your dreams. He also said you knew how to pick

the lock, so if I'm going to rest, it'll be with you and me locked up together so I'll feel it if you try to escape."

"So I am a prisoner. Just like your brother."

She flinched, and Clay instantly wanted to take back the callous comment.

"My primary goal is to keep you alive. If that means I have to sleep shackled to a dangerous man I barely know, then that's the way it is."

Clay moved closer, closing in on her and those dangling cuffs. "You really haven't thought this through, have you?"

"What's that supposed to mean?"

"All I have to do is knock you out and you'll never know I picked the lock until I'm long gone. It wouldn't even take much effort."

"That's why I've also hidden your car keys. And mine."

Clay patted his jeans, realizing that Payton must have taken the keys out when he stripped him. Bastard. "I'll walk."

"In this weather? You're not that stupid. We're in the middle of nowhere. It would take you a day just to get back to civilization where you could call for a ride."

"I can handle the cold."

"And where would you go? How exactly are you going to start hunting down whoever did this to you?"

That gave him pause. Normally, he'd start with his phone and try to trace the call that had triggered him, but what if something he heard or saw sent him back into one of those blackouts? "I'll ask Mira to collect all the calls and texts on my phone and see if any of them are from people I don't know."

"And you really think getting her involved is a good idea? Mira is sweet, and smarter than anyone I've ever met, but do you really want her mired in this? Do you really want to make her a possible target?"

The fact that hadn't even crossed his mind proved just how far off his game he was. His judgment was skewed, and he wasn't thinking straight. No way would he risk Mira. Not even if it meant it was the end of the road for him.

"I'm sorry, Clay. I know how hard this is—sitting around and waiting for someone else to do the work. But we have to trust Payton. If it weren't for him, both of my brothers would be dead instead of only one."

Clay wasn't sure how far his trust would extend, but until he had a better plan of how to attack his problem, there wasn't much sense in running into battle. Besides, Leigh looked all wilted and exhausted. She needed to rest and not toss and turn, wondering if he was going to try to sneak off.

"Fine. You have my word that I'll stay here for the rest of the night. Go get some sleep."

"Do I need the cuffs?"

"Not for sleeping. If you have something else in mind . . ."

She shook her head, smiling as she dropped the cuffs in her purse. "Nice try, Romeo."

A thrill raced through him as he realized that he'd been the one to make that smile happen. It shouldn't have mattered in the greater scheme of things. His life was a wreck; his job was at stake; he might have brought down all kinds of misery on the people he cared about. Still, that sweet, faint smile went a long way toward brightening his world.

"Get some sleep. I'll be a good boy."

"I'll take the bedroom at the end of the hall. Wake me if you need me."

Clay wouldn't. If there was one thing he'd learned, it was how to stand on his own. As soon as he figured out how to solve this current problem, he'd be back on his own two feet, not needing anything from anyone.

*   *   *

Grady assigned one of his men to follow each of the people Dr. Sage said might lead him to his target.

Acquire, but do not kill.

Those instructions made the job much harder, but also much more expensive.

One of his men followed Moneybags out into the countryside to an isolated home tucked away on a big chunk of acreage. His man reported back that he'd seen the target inside.

It had taken several hours for Grady to reach the location, but after a thorough scouting of the area, he decided that he liked it. There was no one around to hear gunfire or screams. There was only one person inside with the target—a woman of no consequence. He could kill her and stow her body somewhere only the coyotes would find. Problem solved.

Even the security system was a joke. It hadn't been updated in at least a year, and Grady was good with tech. It spoke to him, revealing its secrets in a way that made complete sense, unlike people.

Dawn would come soon, and with it all the inherent risks that daylight would bring. Mail delivery, newspaper service, meter readers—they all would come only with morning. Better to have the job done by then.

Grady hiked in to where his man was keeping watch, and settled down to wait for all the movement inside to die down. The couple inside was up late, but that only meant they'd sleep harder when they finally crashed.

It wouldn't be long now.

Chapter Six

Leigh was a fool to trust Clay.

She tossed in her bed, unable to sleep for fear that when she woke, he'd be gone.

She flipped back the covers and padded to the window for the tenth time in the past hour. Both cars were still there. She hadn't heard a door open or shut, but there was movement below on the ground. He was slinking around out there, sticking to the shadows, likely trying to figure out how to break a car window and hot-wire it without waking her.

A quick glance at the security system showed that it had been disarmed. Apparently, picking handcuff locks was not his only hobby.

Frustration scratched under her skin, and she barely held back an angry growl.

I can handle the cold.

Sure he could. He was all tough and manly. That didn't mean he was smart enough to remember he was also human. Without any fat to insulate him, he'd get cold easily, and the thought of him out there in the dark, shivering, was enough to drive her out into the cold herself.

Leigh eyed the loaded syringe sitting on the bedside

table. She could dose him again, ensuring he stayed put for at least another few hours. Then she'd be able to sleep in peace.

Of course, if she did that, he would almost certainly try to take off again at the first chance he got. What sane man would stick around a woman who kept drugging him against his will?

Leigh slipped on a robe she found hanging in the closet and tucked the syringe in the pocket, just in case. She left her room and hurried down the hall, which was open on one side—a minibalcony overlooking the living area below. Shadows of tree limbs blown about by the wind danced across the thick carpet. The moon was bright, giving her plenty of light to see.

Clay's door was open. She could hear him snoring quietly. As she neared, she saw his bulk lying on the bed.

If he was in bed, then who had she seen outside?

A flicker of motion in the living room below caught her attention. She turned and saw a shadow of a man slide over the floor. In one of his hands was the unmistakable silhouette of a long-barreled gun.

Fear stole her breath for a series of painful heartbeats. She heard blood roar in her ears as it flooded through her, carrying adrenaline to every sparking nerve ending. The urge to scream and run stampeded over her brain.

Finally, after what seemed like an hour, she was able to move enough to push Clay's door all the way open and slip inside.

He bolted upright in his bed. Any signs that he'd been asleep were impossible to detect. His eyes were bright and alert, his movement both powerful and fluid.

One look at her face and he was on his feet, heedless of his lack of clothing. Clad only in tight boxers, he seemed to glide across the space, and took her by the arms as if fearing she'd fall over.

"There's someone out there," she whispered, feeling the dry stickiness of her tongue across the roof of her mouth. "He has a gun."

The look of concern he'd been wearing changed swiftly to something darker and far more frightening. "Stay here."

He grabbed a handgun from his nightstand and slipped silently out of the bedroom, shutting the door behind him.

Leigh stood there in the room for a long moment, trying to make sense of what was happening. She'd known when she'd agreed to help Clay that there'd be danger, but she hadn't known that it would come from an armed gunman.

Clay heard the quiet click of the back door's lock opening. The alarm didn't go off, telling him that whoever was down there knew what he was doing.

Clay hurried down the steps and pressed his body flat against the wall on the other side of the doorway into the kitchen. The slight recess didn't hide him completely, but all the lights were off, and it was better than standing out in plain sight, providing a clear shot to whoever was out there.

The back door swung open. Clay could hear the wind howling outside and feel its chill wrap around his bare legs. A moment later, the wind quieted and the breeze stopped. The door was shut.

Eager energy flooded Clay's bloodstream, making his veins hum with the need for a fight. His body was primed to attack. His weapon was firmly in his grip, ready to be fired.

The man's footsteps were nearly silent as he crossed the kitchen, but Clay's whole system was running hot, heightening all of his senses. The ache of bruises and abused bones disappeared as if he'd never been hurt. There was no pain in this space—no fear—only anticipation and the thrill of impending battle.

The man's right foot came into view, showing the tip of a black combat boot.

Clay's muscles coiled, preparing to strike. He was willing to kill this man if it came to that, but he much preferred finding out who he was and why he was here. Disabling him was the smarter option.

Another step, and the intruder was within reach.

Clay charged, using fast, hard aggression to his advantage. He stayed low, slamming a shoulder into the man's stomach while pushing his weapon arm high. A rush of air came out as a gasp of pain—his reward for hitting the target.

He was acutely aware of Leigh's presence upstairs, and how unprotected she was. The enemy's gun was a problem. A single shot could too easily rip through the ceiling and find Leigh's soft flesh.

Even the thought of it stole some of Clay's stony calm, letting fear sink in along the edges where the thrill of a fight usually lived. That fear made his blood pump faster, giving him more strength. He took control of the man's arm, pointing it well away from the bedroom where Leigh was, and keeping it there.

The muzzle of Clay's gun was pressed against his opponent's ribs. He could feel the inflexibility of either bone or body armor. One option would leave him in pain. The other would leave him dead. Either way, if he pulled the trigger, it was going to be a really bad day for the fuckhead.

Only the need to question him kept Clay from firing his weapon. If his enemy's gun moved even one inch in Leigh's direction, the decision would be made. Easily.

Clay would find another way to get the information he wanted.

From the corner of his eye, he saw another man dart behind some kitchen cabinets, out of sight. A second later, the barrel of a gun appeared over the countertop, pointed right at Clay's head.

Some shivering kind of power slid over his mind, threatening to take control. He'd felt it before in Arizona, when he'd blacked out and woken up surrounded by men he'd killed. He still didn't remember pulling the trigger on any of them.

It's a kind of hypnosis . . .

Mind fuck was more like it.

Clay fought the compulsion to let go and give in, growling as he angled the man in front of him to act as a human shield.

There was a loud pop—similar to the sound of a suppressed round. The man in his grasp went limp, crumpling to the floor.

The weapon peeking over the counter now had only one target.

Clay stared at it and lifted his gun to fire as he dove for cover. Before he could discharge his weapon, a frantic buzzing filled his head. Something deep inside his skull snapped free, and then he felt . . . nothing. The entire world winked out.

Leigh couldn't let Clay deal with the threat of an armed gunman alone. He wasn't well enough to handle that kind of stress—not if he was suffering the way her brothers had. Their hold on reality had been tenuous at best. They had been distracted easily, breaking whenever the pressure of even little things became too much to bear. And this was no little thing.

There was no way Clay could do this alone.

Leigh rushed back to her room and dumped the contents of her suitcase onto the floor. The cushioned box holding her revolver tumbled out, along with her socks and underwear. Her keys were hidden under her mattress, and she shoved her hand under it, frantically searching for them.

Hard metallic edges met her fingertips. She fished the keys out and fumbled to unlock the box.

Downstairs, she heard a popping sound, kind of like a cap gun. She'd been to the range often enough to know it wasn't loud enough to be a gunshot, but it was definitely something.

She pulled the revolver out of its foam cradle and used the speedloader to load it.

Oddly, her hands were steady, even though the rest of her felt like it was going to shake apart.

Leigh hurried downstairs, keeping an eye out for armed strangers. The sounds coming from the kitchen were horrible, guttural things. Glass shattered against the floor. Deep male grunts of pain and rage punctuated the sound of bodies slamming into cabinets.

She slowly peeked around the corner and saw Clay with his hands wrapped around the neck of another man. A third man was crumpled on the floor, completely still.

Clay's opponent slammed his fist into Clay's ribs hard enough to make her wince. She knew the damage that had already been done there. If any of those ribs were cracked, a punch like that could easily break them.

She lifted her gun and barked out, "Stop!"

The stranger froze. So did Clay. He turned his head to look at her, but there was something terribly wrong with him. His amber eyes were glowing with feral hatred. His lips were pulled back in a snarl, baring his teeth. His whole body vibrated with chaotic tremors.

Leigh had seen this before. She knew what this was. The man facing her now was not Clay. Not even close.

Without looking away from her, Clay twisted the neck of the man, whose hands were lifted in surrender. The sickening sound of breaking bone filled the kitchen, stabbing at her ears.

A wave of nausea choked her as she processed what had just happened. Clay had broken the man's neck. The intruder had been ready to give up, and Clay hadn't cared.

He let the man fall to the floor and stalked toward her, his eyes on her gun. There was no mistaking that twisted expression of hatred. He was going to kill her, too.

Leigh set the gun on the floor and backed away. "It's me," she said, her voice so faint she wasn't sure he could hear her. "It's Leigh. You don't want to hurt me."

There was no flicker of recognition. He looked blank. Empty. Just like Hollis had the night he'd broken her arm—the night he'd killed himself.

That memory surged to the surface, threatening to drive her to her knees. So much pain and loss. A life full of promise thrown away—ended in the blink of an eye. Permanent and irrevocable.

"Clay," she said louder, trying to sound stern. "Stop right there. You know I'm not going to hurt you."

He didn't respond.

Leigh's back hit something hard, blocking her path. The wall. She was trapped.

She tried to dart out of the way before he could reach her, but he was too fast. He grabbed her arm and flung her to the floor. She scurried back on her elbows. The long hem of the robe kept tripping her up, preventing her from putting any distance between them.

"Clay!" she shouted, the sound of her voice loud and frantic over the heavy thud of her heart.

Payton had been wrong. Clay *was* going to hurt her. That vacant look in his eyes was proof that the man Payton trusted was nowhere to be had. Whoever was behind the wheel now was cold, methodical, and without feeling.

He stepped on the robe, pinning her in place. Then he reached down and jerked her back to her feet by her arms, tossing her back into the front door.

"Please. Don't do this," she begged.

No one was going to stop him. No one was going to save her.

And then she remembered the syringe in her pocket. She would save herself.

Clay had a painfully tight grip on her biceps and was slowly lifting her higher. The cold glass chilled her back. The wooden frame around the window scratched her skin, even through her robe and nightshirt. His grip was so hard that her fingers began to tingle from lack of blood.

If she was going to do this, it had to be fast — before she lost all feeling in her hands.

He didn't seem to notice her reaching in her robe pocket. His gaze was fixed on her, his eyes as empty as a freshly dug grave.

Clay grabbed her face, wrapping his fingers around her jaw. He began to push up, shoving her head hard against the door frame. Pain splintered along her skull. Panic closed her throat around a scream.

She uncapped the needle and jabbed it into his armpit — the only target she could reach. She shoved the plunger down hard.

He didn't even notice that she'd stabbed him. It was as if he hadn't felt the pain at all.

His eyelids fluttered. A momentary flicker of confusion clouded his eyes, and then they slid shut.

Clay collapsed onto the floor with a heavy thud. Leigh

landed on top of him, panting. Tears streamed down her face as she clumsily disentangled their limbs and hobbled away.

As much as she wanted to slump to the floor and sob with relief, she knew better than to give in to that urge. She was on her own—too far away from help to even bother calling for it. There were three men to deal with. And only one pair of handcuffs.

She left Clay where he lay and went to the closest man. He was breathing. His heartbeat was steady. A fringed dart was sticking out of the back of his neck— likely some kind of tranquilizer or poison.

A quick check of the second man proved true her suspicions that he was dead. Clay had killed him.

No time to dwell on the implications of that right now. She had too much to do.

Leigh gathered all the weapons and hid them in a drawer next to a wooden spoon and spatula. She found a roll of duct tape in another drawer and used it to secure the man she didn't know. Clay got the handcuffs, locked behind his back around the stair railing. She wrapped a nice thick layer of duct tape over the lock, preventing him from inserting anything into it.

Let him try to pick that.

Once she knew no one else was coming at her with the intent to kill, all her strength drained away. She sat down on the living room floor where she could see both of her prisoners. The dead man was out of sight, slumped against the kitchen cabinets. She was grateful she didn't have to look at him, too.

Her hands were shaking now. The rest of her was as well. Dizziness kept her on the floor while a chill curled around her and wouldn't let go. It was shock. She knew that, but knowing what it was called didn't make it any less unpleasant.

Clay's head was slumped forward at an uncomfortable-looking angle. His deep chest expanded evenly as he breathed. Seeing him asleep and relaxed like that, she could almost forget how he'd looked coming at her. Almost.

She was in way over her head, and there was only one person she could call.

Leigh forced herself to her feet and slogged up the stairs to where her purse and phone were. She dialed Payton, who answered so quickly, there was no way he'd been sleeping.

"We were attacked," she said. "Two men broke in. Clay killed one of them."

"Are you okay?"

The places where Clay had grabbed her arms and face hurt, and she felt brittle enough to shatter, but she was the only one left standing, which she guessed counted for something. "Yeah."

"Let me talk to Clay."

"Sorry. I had to knock him out again." She swallowed twice before she could get the words out. "He would have killed me, too, Payton."

"I want you to leave him there. I'll find a way to get back to him before he wakes up."

"No. I'm not going to abandon him. The one man left alive is also unconscious, with some kind of tranquilizer, I think. There's no way to know who will wake up first or what will happen when they do."

"Then restrain them."

"I already have."

"You can't stay. Whoever is behind this clearly knows where you are. You must leave."

"I'm not strong enough to move Clay, and I'm not leaving him here to be killed—not when I was the one to render him helpless."

She could hear the sound of a car engine revving in the background. "I'll be there soon to take care of everything. Then you can go home. I never should have involved you."

Leigh wanted to let him take over and make it all go away, but she couldn't bring herself to leave. "This is my one chance at finding a way to help Garrett. If that man in the kitchen knows anything, I want to find out what it is."

"Men who break into houses in the middle of the night are not usually inclined to give up information easily. And I know you don't have the stomach for torture."

A few years ago, he would have been right. "You have no idea how far I'll go to see Garrett free and well."

Payton was quiet for a minute. "Fine. Search the men and see what you can find. I'll head your way and be there in a few hours. Call me for any reason, and if you think you're in danger at all, I want you to leave."

"Of course I'm in danger. I knew I would be when you told me what was at stake."

"I never thought Clay would attack you. I'm so sorry, Leigh."

"Part of me expected it. After seeing how it was with Hollis and Garrett . . ."

"I'm still sorry."

"It's fine." What a huge lie that was. "Get here soon. I'm going to see what I can turn up."

"Be careful. They know where you are. More men may come."

"I know. I'll be armed."

And because she was no idiot, she filled another syringe and got it ready. There was no way she was sleeping any more tonight—not with those men in the house. It was best to just get dressed and do whatever she could to fix this as soon as possible.

With her clothes back on and her revolver sitting

within reach, she went to the men in the kitchen and went through their pockets. No ID. No money. They both had a phone, but there were no numbers or messages on them—as if they'd just been purchased.

Or maybe they had simply deleted the information. If so, then it might still be there, lurking where some computer goddess like Mira could find it.

Mira. Of course.

It was still before dawn, but this couldn't wait. Leigh knew how Mira felt about Clay and that she wouldn't hold too much of a grudge for being woken up at such a crazy hour.

Mira answered, her voice thick with fatigue. "Leigh?"

"Sorry to wake you, but it's important."

"I wasn't sleeping. What do you need?"

"You have access to Clay's phone records, right?"

"Sure. Why?"

"Is there some kind of GPS thing you can track?"

"Yeah."

"Can you look back and see where he's been recently?"

"What's this all about?"

"I need you to stop asking questions. I don't know how safe it is to talk on the phone."

Mira suddenly sounded more alert. "What is going on, Leigh?"

"I need a list of everywhere Clay has been. Can you do that?"

"How far back do you need me to go?"

"At least a few weeks. Longer if you can."

"Okay, but that's a lot of data. You're not going to be able to make sense out of it unless I pretty it up for you."

"Then do it."

"Is Clay okay? Can I talk to him?"

Leigh eyed Clay's slumped form. "He's sleeping, but fine." At least physically.

"I'll get you what you need. Where should I send it?"

"E-mail me."

"Are you sure everything is okay?"

Leigh desperately wanted to confide in Mira—to tell her how horrible it was to be sitting here with two men who might want to kill her and a third dead and growing cold on the floor. To not know if some other armed killers might be closing in on her right now. To not know if she'd be smart enough to find a way to save her brother.

She wanted to reach out for a bit of comfort from a woman she'd come to think of as a friend, but she didn't dare. If Mira knew how bad things were, not only would she worry, she might try to do something stupid like track Clay down.

If Clay could hurt Leigh, he could also hurt Mira.

"We're just trying to solve a puzzle. Really. Nothing to worry about."

"Which is why you're calling me this early in the morning. I'm not an idiot, you know."

"Of course not. You're brilliant and will save us with that wonderful mind of yours."

"That's me. The chick with the brain cape." Mira let out a frustrated sigh. "Call if you need anything else, okay?"

"That reminds me. If I were to erase all the messages on my phone, could you get them back?"

"Probably, unless it's really fried and nothing was backed up. Did your phone break?"

"Maybe. I'll let you know."

A skeptical tone entered Mira's voice. "I really wish you'd let me talk to Clay."

"You said he hasn't been sleeping well. We need to let him rest."

"Yeah. You're right. Have him call me as soon as he wakes up, okay?"

"I will," said Leigh, hoping her friend would forgive her for the lie. "Talk to you later."

Leigh collected both of the intruders' phones, removed the batteries, and stored them with her things so she could take them to Mira later. She'd packed everything and set it by the door in case she needed to leave fast. The keys to both cars were in her pocket, along with another king-sized dose of tranquilizer.

Now that her escape route was clear, she grabbed a chair from the kitchen and positioned it so she could see both the sleeping men and the exits. All that was left to do now was wait—for one of them to wake, for Payton to arrive, or for someone else to show up and try to kill them.

Whatever happened, she was as ready for it as she would ever be. Which wasn't saying much.

Chapter Seven

Clay fought to wake up. There was something important he needed to do—some threat he had to face. Someone needed him.

His mind was sluggish, moving too slowly for the frantic urgings pounding at the back of his brain. His head throbbed as if someone had taken a hammer to it. All he wanted to do was go back to sleep where the pain couldn't reach him, but there was a reason he couldn't do that—he just couldn't remember what it was.

As he surfaced on another wave of consciousness, he realized his hands were bound behind his back.

Rage sent a surge of adrenaline racing through him, giving him that last big push into wakefulness.

He tried to stand before his eyes were fully open, but something caught and held him back. He heard the jingle of metal and a scraping sound.

Handcuffs. He'd been cuffed to something.

"Easy," said a woman, her voice low and soothing but with more than a hint of fear. "You're safe."

Clay knew that voice but couldn't place it.

He pried his dry eyes open, fighting whatever was

weighing his lids down. As the initial burst of adrenaline wore off, sleep kept trying to suck him back in.

A cool hand touched his neck. He jerked away from it, unsure of its intent.

"Calm down, Clay," said the woman again. "I'm not going to hurt you."

His mouth was parched, making speech too much of a chore to bother with it. He needed to save his energy for combat, though he couldn't remember who he was supposed to fight.

Maybe the woman?

Finally, his heavy eyelids obeyed and he managed to peer through his lashes at her. Dark red hair, dark, concerned eyes.

Leigh. He recognized her. She was the one he needed to protect.

Details began trickling back. Men had come into the house. He'd fought one of them. The man had had a gun, and the way he fought screamed that he was a professional. A second man had aimed a weapon at Clay, and then . . . nothing.

"What happened?" he croaked out, his words grating the skin of his dry throat.

"Take a drink," she ordered in a no-nonsense tone that had Clay obeying without even thinking about it.

Cold water eased the dry burn and jolted him a bit more into wakefulness—enough for him to realize that she'd dodged his question.

Water dribbled down his chin. He reached to catch it, but the bite of handcuffs stopped him. "Uncuff me."

"I will in a minute. I just want to be sure." It was the fear in her voice that finally shoved away the remaining cobwebs of sleep.

Clay lifted his head and forced his eyelids open all the

way. The lights of the room stabbed him, dragging a hiss of pain from his chest. He blinked as tears flooded his eyes, washing some of the grit of sleep away.

Leigh was crouched in front of him, a stethoscope draped over her neck. She had a glass of water in one hand and a syringe in the other. Both hands were shaking, and she was so pale the little constellations of freckles on her cheeks were easy to see. So were the bruises along her jawline.

Something had happened to her—something that had terrified and hurt her. Only the certain knowledge that she was standing here, safe and alive, gave him room to breathe.

"You want to be sure of what?" he asked.

She hesitated for so long, he wasn't sure she was going to answer him. "You weren't yourself."

The terrible truth crashed down on Clay like a bucket of ice water as he pieced everything together. He was bound. She was afraid. She was bruised. He had a missing section of time.

"I hurt you, didn't I?"

She looked away, the truth plain in the way she couldn't meet his gaze. "I'm fine."

"That doesn't answer my question."

Leigh backed away, setting the water on a nearby end table. "Payton will be here soon. Everything is going to be fine."

A moan drifted in from the kitchen. Clay's body went on red alert, tensing for action. The cuffs jangled and held firm. "Who is that?"

"One of the men who broke in. I restrained him."

That wasn't good enough. If he got free, she was an easy target. She didn't even have her revolver on her—it sat several feet away, as if she'd have all the time in the world to reach it if she had the need.

"There were two intruders."

She gave him a shaky nod, swallowing hard enough that he could see the movement in her throat, below the darkening bruises along her jawline. "One of them is dead."

A flash of a memory hit him—his hands on a stranger's head, twisting. The muted snap of bones breaking beneath skin. The satisfaction of an enemy conquered.

Clay had done that. He'd killed the man. And if the other intruder got free, he'd do the same thing to Leigh. She wasn't trained to handle an opponent like him.

"Unlock the cuffs, Leigh."

She backed away, bumping into the couch. "I will as soon as Payton gets here."

If he hadn't already been able to see the truth of what he'd done in her eyes, he would have known it now. "I won't hurt you again. Whatever it takes, I'll hold it together long enough for you to get to your car and leave. I'm myself again. I swear it."

How long he'd be that way was another story, but for now, he was in complete control.

"I can't leave," she said. "If the man in the kitchen manages to get free, he could hurt you."

"Is there a chance he can get free, Leigh? Because if there is, you really need to let me go. He will kill you."

She shook her head. Her pretty red hair was a tangled mess, as if she'd tossed and turned in bed for hours. Dark circles haunted her brown eyes. She kept wiping her palms on her pants, alternating which hand held the syringe.

Clay craned his neck to follow her nervous gaze to the kitchen. A man clad in black and strips of silver duct tape lay on his side, struggling against his bonds. It wouldn't take much for him to get free. The fact that she'd used the cuffs on Clay told him which man she feared most.

That thought snapped something deep inside him

right in two, making him bleed. He'd done some pretty fucked-up things in his life, but he'd never before hurt a woman—at least not that he knew. Seeing the bruises he'd left on her soft skin made him want to rage and weep all at the same time. Whatever else happened, it would never make up for what he'd done. He could spend the rest of his life serving others and doing good, and it wouldn't even make a dent in his guilt.

Still, somehow, he had to get her to listen. Her life was at stake. "I know you're afraid, but this is way too dangerous. You need to knock him out."

"I can't drug him. I don't know what was in that dart. The drug interaction could be bad."

"I don't really give a shit about what happens to him. He broke in. He deserves whatever he gets."

"You don't understand. He may know something. What if he knows how to help you and Garrett?"

She intended to question him? "Hell no. That's way too dangerous. He'll say whatever he has to, to string you along just long enough for him to get free. You won't be able to trust a word he says, and then, just when you think he's given in, he'll break out of that tape and kill you dead."

"You don't know that's what will happen."

"You don't know it won't. Please, Leigh. Let me out of the cuffs."

She shook her head and bit her bottom lip. "I can't be sure what you'll do to him. And what you won't. I'm sorry, Clay, but I can't trust you."

Those simple words crushed him, grinding him further under the heel of what had been done to him. He wanted to scream at her, but she was right not to trust him. Any man who could leave marks on her and not even remember it could never be trusted.

Even so, he couldn't leave her to defend herself

against a threat she couldn't understand. She was a healer. She helped people. No way was she going to be able to see the kind of evil that man could do coming her way. Not until it was too late.

Clay went to work removing the tape covering the keyhole to the cuffs. Leigh knew he could pick the lock, and she was smart enough to protect herself from him by making the job harder. He only hoped that meant she was also smart enough to protect herself from the intruder lying on the kitchen floor.

"I'm going to question him," she told Clay, squaring her shoulders as if marching into battle.

"Wait until Payton gets here."

"No. I need answers. So do you."

Before he could think of a way to stop her, she left him cuffed to the wooden newel post and walked into the room with the enemy.

Everything inside of Clay rebelled at her putting herself in danger like that. He had to get free, and when he did, he had to convince her to get as far away from him as possible.

She knelt down next to the man. He could barely see them if he craned his neck forward. Her voice was gentle, coaxing. If that man in there had any kind of soul at all, the sound of her voice alone would have him spilling his guts in minutes.

The deep rumble of the man's response reached Clay's ears, but he couldn't understand the words. They seemed to carry on a conversation—her speaking, then him. Clay could hear no sign of distress, but the way the man was wiggling slightly meant that he was doing more than just talking.

The tape covering the lock was thick, and Clay had made it through only a few layers when he saw the man jerk as if yanking something free.

A thick jolt of panic speared Clay, stealing his breath for a moment. His fingers tingled, and he could do nothing to make them move faster to free himself.

"Leigh. Get away from him," he warned.

He saw a look of startled fear widen her eyes. She propelled herself backward, but it was too late. The man had freed his hands, and those hands were now batting away the syringe she held while taking her captive.

Clay had only seconds to act. He couldn't open the lock in time. The manacles were too tight for him to slip them off. Leigh had been careful in restraining him.

The scrape of metal on wood screeched in his ears as he pulled against the railing. Red flooded his vision as helpless rage took hold of him. He strained against the cuffs, feeling blood seep along his wrists.

The intruder tore away the tape holding his legs together, while easily fending off Leigh's inexperienced blows. She had no weapons. Her gun was left in the living room. Her syringe was lying on the floor somewhere. Even her fingernails were too short to be of much use.

Still, she fought him, kicking and punching with her free hand.

Leigh landed one good blow to his neck, stunning him for a few precious seconds. She tried to wrench her arm free, but his hold was too tight.

Clay roared in outrage and threw his weight against the newel post. The wood creaked and groaned but held firm.

She yelled again, only this time the sound was full of rage rather than fear. The intruder grunted in pain, and Clay strained his neck to see what had happened.

Leigh had freed herself and was backing up as fast as she could. Only she was headed farther into the kitchen.

"Don't let him corner you!" shouted Clay. "Come this way." Maybe if she got close enough, he could fend the man off with his feet—at least long enough for her to grab the gun.

Clay grabbed the newel post. His hands were slick with blood, but he managed to get a decent grip. With every ounce of strength left in his abused body, he pulled at the post. His ribs burned, and cuts along his skin re-opened under the strain.

He heard nails squawking. The post moved a fraction of an inch. But it wasn't enough. When he looked again to see what was going on, he saw that the intruder had control of Leigh's body. One thick arm was wrapped around her neck, and her hands were pinned behind her back.

The man's gaze met Clay's, then went straight to where Leigh had left her revolver lying.

"We don't need you alive," he heard the man tell Leigh. "Only him. I don't want to kill you, but I will if you don't settle the fuck down."

He was lying. He had every intention of killing her. Clay could see it in his eyes as he moved closer to the weapon.

Leigh had only seconds left to live if Clay didn't act.

Suddenly, that now familiar haze tried to cloud his head—the one that happened right before he woke up and found someone else dead. Just like earlier tonight. Just like in Arizona.

He couldn't give in to it. He couldn't lose himself right now. He'd hurt Leigh again, and if he did that, he knew it would kill him.

Clay fought the haze, gritting his teeth and putting every scrap of effort into pulling the newel post free.

The man was a few steps away now, moving slowly toward where he'd be within range of Clay's feet.

Blood dripped into his grip. He held the post low, tugging hard enough to hear the nails coming free. Pain burned along his arms and shoulders. His thighs shook as he used his legs for added leverage.

Leigh stared at him with a mix of hope and rage lighting her eyes.

Clay would not fail her. He would not let her die.

With a final hard shove of his whole body, the post ripped free and he stumbled forward. His wrists were still cuffed, but that wasn't going to stop him from fighting.

He barreled into their legs, sending both the man and Leigh tumbling to the ground. She was released and rolled aside, out of the way.

Clay gave the man no time to recover or regain his feet. He kicked at his head, only to have his blow diverted by the man's arms.

Leigh scrambled for the revolver and aimed it at the intruder's abdomen.

He saw the gun, went still, and raised his hands. Clay wasn't in the mood for more threats to her life, so he gave the man a hard kick to the head, knocking him out.

"Get these fucking cuffs off of me. Now."

Clay had been right. Leigh was not prepared for this kind of violence, despite that horrible, dark time she'd endured right before Hollis's death. She had no experience with hired gunmen—which that man had admitted to being—and no way to gauge the threat he had posed until it was too late.

What she did know was that Clay had torn himself apart working to save her. She wasn't about to make him do it a second time.

Using a kitchen knife, she cut the bloody tape covering the lock free and unlocked the cuffs. The skin along his wrists looked like it had been chewed up by a chainsaw.

Her stomach knotted into a queasy ball at the sight. Normally, seeing physical damage didn't faze her. But normally, she wasn't the cause of it, either.

Clay took the bloody handcuffs from her and rolled the man he'd fought onto his stomach. He paused in the act of latching the second cuff closed, then stopped, leaving it dangling open.

"What?" she asked, barely able to push the word out of her constricted throat.

"He's dead." His tone was flat and final, without any sense of satisfaction or grief. "We need to go."

"But Payton will be here soon."

"Fuck Payton. He must have led them here earlier."

"He wouldn't do that."

"Not on purpose. But someone knows where we are, and I'm sure as hell not going to sit around while we wait for reinforcements to show up. Let's go."

"Where are we going?"

He went to the kitchen and started opening drawers. He found the weapons she'd tucked away and set them on the counter. "Tranquilizer darts," he said as he saw the weapons the intruders had been using. Then he continued to search for something. "They didn't want us dead."

"That's good, right?"

"Probably not. If someone kills you, that's all the harm they can do. If they keep you alive . . . Well, let's just say that there are worse things than being dead." He pulled a clean towel from a drawer and ripped it in half. The cloth went around one wrist as he awkwardly bandaged his wounds.

"Let me do that. I have antiseptic and gauze in my bag."

"No," he barked, his voice hammer hard. Then more gently, "I don't want you anywhere near me—not after what happened. Just take your car and go. Don't tell me where. And don't go home, either. Find a hotel. Pay in cash. Go somewhere you've never been before."

His staccato orders were starting to scare her. He rattled them off as if he'd done this before. "You want me leave you to fend for yourself? You really have no idea what you're up against, do you?"

He paused in the act of knotting the torn towel. His amber eyes were bright with rage, his body vibrating with it. "And you do?"

"You forget I've been through this before with my brothers."

"And exactly how well did that work out, Leigh? One brother's dead, and the other is in prison."

She flinched, reeling back from the truth presented so bluntly.

Things had gone badly for Hollis and Garrett, but she knew more now. She knew what could happen, which made her better armed to prevent it from happening to Clay.

"I'm sorry," he said on a heavy sigh. "I didn't mean to hurt you."

"I'm tough. And you need me." Staring into his eyes, daring him to stop her, she took the strip of fabric he was trying to wrap around his wrist from his bloody fingers. The towel was a poor bandage—it wasn't sterile and it was going to stick to the wound—but if that was all he'd allow her to use, at least it would stop the bleeding.

"I won't be the asshole who makes your life a shittier place." His gaze lingered on her bruises, and something shifted in his expression, closing him off even more. "I've already done enough damage."

"And don't think I won't be more careful in the future. I'm not an idiot. But I also know I'm the best chance you've got at figuring out how to fix what's wrong with you."

"What makes you think that?"

"Because before he died, that man answered my questions. Well, he evaded them at first, but once he thought I had sodium thiopental in that syringe, he gave me information."

"Sodium what?"

"Sodium pentothal. Truth serum. I think the idea of me drugging him shook him up enough to slip and say something he wasn't planning to."

"What did he say?"

"If I tell you, then you won't have any reason to let me come along."

His mouth tightened and the muscles along his jaw bulged in frustration. "Why the hell would you want to put your life at risk again?"

"Because Garrett is worth the risk. If we can undo whatever was done to you and him, I can give him back his life. Don't underestimate the lengths to which I'll go to make that happen."

"Tell me what he said, Leigh." There was a warning in his tone—one she staunchly ignored.

She really needed to do a better job of patching him up. With all the blood smeared over his wrists, it was hard to tell exactly how much damage had been done. And the wounds needed to be cleaned, too. If he ditched her, he'd be out there on his own, most likely with some kind of infection to fight off. She would not let that happen, even if her brother's future wasn't at stake.

"No," she said. "Not until we're away from here, headed to wherever it is we're going."

He shook his head, and she heard a low growl emanating from his chest. "This is stupid. You're going to get hurt."

"What's stupid is leaving you alone with no one to stop you if you things go badly."

"Go badly? Is that what you call me killing two men

and putting my hands on you? I don't even remember doing it."

"I know. This isn't your fault any more than it would be your fault if you got sick or someone ran you over while you were walking on the sidewalk. This is something that was done to you, and like it or not, I'm the only person who knows the score."

Hollis's face popped into her thoughts. He'd always been so funny and easygoing. So laid back. When he'd snapped—when he'd hurt her—he had been someone else, someone dark and . . . empty. And when he was once again himself and realized what he'd done, the guilt had destroyed him.

Leigh tied the strips of towel and laid her hand on Clay's arm, trying to make some connection to him so he would lean on her, just a little. Instead, he removed her hand and took a step back. His expression closed up tight, leaving her guessing where she stood.

"I don't know how to stop it," he said. "I don't know what I'll do to you if you stick around."

"I'm willing to take that risk." Because while she'd never say the words and put the idea in his head, she knew what could happen if Clay was left alone. He could do what Hollis had done. He could end his own life.

Leigh was not going to let that happen.

"You and I are going to leave now. Together," she told him. "And once we're safely away, I'll tell you everything that man told me."

"I should just leave on my own. Fuck what he said."

"You do that, and there will be no one to stop you from hurting someone else. If you can't control yourself, then you can't guarantee you won't do something bad."

"And you can?"

"No, but I can knock your ass out if I see any signs that you've gone postal again."

"At serious risk to yourself."

"A risk I'm willing to take for Garrett."

Clay's mouth flattened, and a cold light filled his eyes. "So this is all about him. You're using me to help your brother."

She hesitated, wondering which answer would get him to cooperate. At first it had been all about Garrett, but she sympathized enough with Clay's situation that even if Garrett weren't involved, she would have seen this through. Clay was suffering, and it wasn't in her genetic makeup to walk away from that—not if she could help. And she knew she could. Someone had to.

"Yes," she finally said, hoping it would leave him his pride. After years of treating men, she knew how funny they could be about something so insubstantial. "I'm doing this for my brother."

Clay nodded and turned away. "Fine. Let's go."

Chapter Eight

Leigh was using him. Clay had almost believed that she was different. The fact that she wasn't stung more than he'd expected. At least he knew how to deal with users. Story of his life.

He led the way to her car, weapon in hand. If anyone else was lurking out here, waiting to strike, he was going to be ready.

She stowed her bags in the backseat and pulled out of the driveway, headlights off as he'd instructed. There wasn't a single flicker of movement or any signs that they were being watched. Nor did he have that itchy feeling at the back of his neck.

In the thinning predawn darkness covering the countryside, he saw no lights to indicate they were being followed.

"Where should I go?" she asked.

"North."

She glanced at him. "Can you be more specific?"

"We'll stop when I'm sure there's no one on our tail." And then he'd scour her car for bugs and tracking devices, which Mira loved to put in her friends' cars. "Can I use your phone?"

"Payton said you weren't supposed to talk to anyone."

"It's him I want to call."

She hesitated for a moment before pulling her phone from her waistband. Clay searched through her contacts until he found the right number and dialed.

"Is everything okay?" asked Payton when he answered.

"It sure as hell isn't. I left you a couple of presents lying on your floor."

"I heard."

"They were professionals."

"You're on Leigh's phone. Is she okay?"

Clay glanced at her, easily seeing the bruises he'd left on her jaw. His stomach heaved, and he had to swallow hard to keep from puking.

He still couldn't believe he'd done that to her. And he had no idea how he was going to stop himself from doing it again. "Not really. You never should have involved her."

"Where are you?"

"None of your damn business. You're the reason those goons found us."

"Impossible."

"It was your house we were in. Your car I drove there. You were the only one who knew where we were. Hell, they could have followed you when you came."

Payton let out a scalding curse—something Clay had never heard the man do before. "You're right. Whoever is behind this has connected me to you. You've got to find someplace safe."

"We're on it. I just wanted you to know you had a mess to clean up and that we're okay. And to let you know I'm disabling any tracking device I find. Chances are Mira put one somewhere in Leigh's car."

Clay saw her turn her head and give him a startled look.

"She does that to everyone she cares about," he explained to Leigh.

"Good idea," said Payton. "And don't forget about your tags."

Clay had been wearing them for so many years, they were practically a part of him. He reached under his shirt and fished out the dog tags, then tossed them out the window. "Don't let Mira worry about me, okay? She's really good at that, and I hate upsetting her."

"I'll do what I can to reassure her."

"We'll need to get rid of Leigh's phone, too."

"How will I reach you if I uncover any information?"

"You won't. I'll pick up a prepaid cell and call you when I can." *If* he could.

Payton was silent for so long that Clay thought he'd hung up. He was about ready to end the call when he heard the other man clear his throat. "I'm sorry about all of this, Clay. You should have never had to go through this."

"It's not your fault. But I will find whoever is at fault, and I will make sure they never do this to anyone else ever again."

Payton's voice was quiet and filled with regret. "Good hunting."

Clay hung up, pushing away all thoughts of Payton and focusing on the task at hand.

"How much cash do you have on you?" he asked.

"I don't know. Maybe two hundred."

He had another thousand on him—the emergency fund he always kept handy, zipped inside a secret pocket in his belt. It was enough for a few days—long enough for him to ditch Leigh and take care of business.

"You can't get rid of my phone yet," said Leigh. "Mira is going to be sending me some information."

"What information?"

"Both my brothers experienced lost chunks of time—they'd black out in one place and woke up in another. That happens to you, right?"

The memory of waking up covered in someone else's blood was still too fresh in his mind. "Yeah," was all he could shove out of his dry throat.

"If you can remember when those blackouts happened, then we might have a lead."

"I don't understand."

"I asked Mira to track your movements for the past few weeks—as far back as she could. If we know where you went when you weren't . . . yourself, then maybe we'll find out where the person doing this to you is."

"You think that whoever did this would be stupid enough to meet me in person when I'm like that?"

"If they think they're in control, what risk would there be?"

"It's worth a shot. I should have thought of it myself." That he hadn't thought of it told him just how clouded his mind was.

"Maybe you would have if someone wasn't screwing with your head. There's no telling what kind of measures they put in place to keep you under control."

"Measures?"

She squeezed the steering wheel and her shoulders tightened, creeping up toward her ears. "I've thought about this a lot since Garrett was sent away. I've done some research. Most of what I read was garbage at best, but in theory, with the right mind-altering drugs, it's possible that someone could have found a way to plant commands in your head."

"What kinds of commands?"

"If I was some evil genius bent on turning humans into puppets, I'd want to make sure that my efforts didn't go to waste."

"Meaning?"

"I'd want them to defend themselves when faced with a threat. I'd want them to answer only to me. I'd want them to have a kind of homing mechanism that would bring them back if they wandered off for too long."

Clay's blood jelled in his veins, making his whole body go cold. "They can't reach me now. If they did put something like that in my head, how long do you think I have before it goes off?"

She put her hand on his thigh, offering comfort where there was none to be had. He couldn't bring himself to push her away, even though he knew it was the right thing to do. That single point of contact, that fragile strand of support she offered, meant more to him than he ever thought possible.

"You leave the country for jobs all the time, right?" she asked.

"Yeah."

"How long are those assignments?"

"There's no set time frame. Usually I'm gone for a week or two."

"These people would probably know your habits. They'd know about your work. My guess is that you'd have at least that long."

"A few days to find these bastards and end them before I turn into some kind of mindless zombie wandering back into their clutches? Great."

"You don't know that. It's just a guess. We have no evidence. I'm sorry I even brought it up."

She started to pull her hand away, but he covered it with his, pressing her fingers against his thigh. He wasn't ready to let go of her touch yet. It gave him something else to think about—something that wasn't completely fucked-up and twisted.

"Don't be," he told her. "I'm glad one of us is thinking

clearly." The last thing he wanted was for her to withhold information because she thought he was too much of a pussy to face it. "What else did your research uncover?"

"Not much, really."

She was hiding something. He could hear it in her voice—feel it in the way her fingers twitched beneath his. "Spit it out, Leigh. I can take it."

She let out a sad sigh. "Whoever did this to you did it when you were a kid."

"You sound sure."

"I am. Either that, or they only do it to men."

"What makes you so sure that it has to be one of the two?"

"My parents were killed in an accident when we were kids. My brothers ended up in one foster home, me in another."

That simple confession given in such a clinical tone spoke volumes about Leigh. It spoke of tragedy and loss, of grief and loneliness. Not only had she lost her parents, but she'd also lost her brothers.

"How old were you?"

"I was six. Hollis was seven and Garrett was ten."

She was just a baby. At least Clay had had his mom around for a few more years. After that it was just him and the step-asshole.

"I got placed in a great home with a loving family. I still see them a lot. My brothers weren't so lucky. I think that whatever was done to them happened then."

"What makes you think that?"

"Because when I saw them a couple of years later, they were different. At the time, my foster parents said it was because they were growing up and their hormones were changing. It wasn't anything to worry about. But then when Garrett became a legal adult and adopted us, I knew they weren't the same carefree souls I'd known."

"They had to grow up fast. That doesn't prove much of anything."

"Except that both of them ended up like you. I didn't."

She had a point. "You think that the people who did this were your brothers' foster parents?"

"No, but I think that they let it happen—either with or without their knowledge."

A strange, distant memory appeared in Clay's head, fully formed. He was young. Colin, his asshole stepfather, was speaking to a man in the shadows on the front porch of their crappy, run-down house. The man handed Colin cash. Then Clay was suddenly in the man's car, driving away.

The memory lasted only a split second, but that was long enough to leave Clay shaking. He'd been afraid. Even as a kid he knew that the man in the car was bad news. But even more strange than the phantom memory was the feeling Clay had that he knew this man—he'd spent time with him. Shared meals, even.

He tried to remember what he looked like, but the details were fuzzy, as if someone had intentionally blurred them. The harder he tried to call the man into focus, the vaguer the memory became.

Clay's head started to throb. A slow, rolling nausea swept through him, leaving him sweating.

He let go of the memory and rolled down the window to stave off any stomach rebellion.

"Are you okay?" asked Leigh.

"Yeah. Sorry. Just a bad memory." He rolled the window up so she wouldn't get cold. "What if someone paid for us?"

"What? I don't follow."

"What if whoever did this paid your brothers' foster parents off—paid my stepdad—to do this to us?"

A chilling look of anger crossed her face, driving away

the normal softness he was used to seeing. "That would be in line with what I know about my brothers' foster parents."

"And definitely something my step-asshole would have done. He was all about making a quick buck—and not above using me to do so."

She shook her head, drawing attention to her wildly mussed hair. The crazy notion of sliding his fingers through it to work out the tangles took him by storm, and he had to fight the need to do just that.

"What if they're still doing this, Clay? There could be little kids out there right now being tortured by these monsters."

"I will stop them."

She glanced his way, but it was long enough for him to see the steely determination glinting in her brown eyes. "*We* will stop them. You try to ditch me, and I'll make what they did to you look like a sunny afternoon at Disneyland."

The seemingly sweet doctor had a thread of badass running through her. That was something Clay couldn't help but respect, and damn if it didn't turn him on. "I'm not making any promises, but right now, you're in as much danger as I am."

"More," she said, as if the word had accidentally popped out of her mouth.

"What's that supposed to mean?"

She shook her head, her lips clamped in silence.

"Leigh? If we're going to be a team, you can't keep secrets."

He wasn't sure she was going to speak. The road beneath them passed by in a hum of tires on pavement. Finally, she pulled her hand away from his thigh and donned an air of indifference he knew was a lie.

"That man I questioned? He didn't say much, but one thing he did mention was that they needed you alive."

"That doesn't surprise me."

"Me, neither, but what did surprise me—thanks to my naïveté—was that he admitted that he didn't care what happened to me. In fact, his exact quote was, 'No one's paying me to bring you back alive, sugar.'"

He would have killed her. If Clay hadn't managed to bust out that newel post, they wouldn't be having this conversation right now.

He'd almost lost her, which served only to highlight just how fragile she was.

Clay needed to abandon her at the first opportunity. She wasn't safe around him. She knew that better than anyone. Her bruises spoke louder than any words ever could.

He checked behind them for signs they were being followed and found none. They were still well away from the city, with only sparsely populated towns dotting the countryside. The highway was nearly empty. On the eastern horizon, the faintest glow of sunrise was starting to show.

"Pull over at this rest stop up ahead," he told her.

She didn't ask why; she simply did as he requested, pulling up under a light.

Clay got out of the car and retrieved his flashlight from his duffel bag. A thorough search of the vehicle revealed one of Mira's tracking devices, as well as something else he didn't recognize. It wasn't connected to any explosives he could see. But to be on the safe side, he waited until Leigh went into the bathroom before he tried to remove it. The little cinderblock structure was better protection from a bomb than standing around outside would be for her.

The device was held on to the underside of the car by a strong magnet. It consisted of a small circuit board and a thin antenna. No lights or sounds to indicate it was working.

Clay took it into the bathroom and mounted it to a plumbing fitting under the sink, out of sight. Mira's tracker went into the trash can, wadded up in a thick layer of paper towels. The trash was full and would probably be emptied soon, giving anyone who was watching the signal a false path to follow.

He hated tossing away Mira's hard work, but it was better than letting anyone follow them—including Mira. If she thought he needed her help, she'd do whatever it took to come rescue him. Even if it put her in danger's path.

Leigh was waiting for him with her hips propped against the car. She'd brushed the tangles from her hair, and now the silky red tresses whipped around her face in the wind. Her cheeks were pink from the cold, and she was huddled in, hugging herself like she was freezing.

His need to see her warm sped his steps.

"We're good to go," he told her.

"I can't believe I've been driving around all this time without knowing I was being tracked."

Clay shrugged as he got in the car. "Mira does that to everyone she likes. Take it as her way of looking out for you."

"It's a bit intrusive."

"You'll think that right up to the time when one of her gadgets saves your ass."

"That's what she said, too."

"You talked to her?"

Leigh nodded as she started the engine. "She called while you were in the bathroom. She compiled that list for us and sent it."

"Great. Now we need to print it off and then get rid of your phone."

She didn't argue about throwing away her expensive phone, which proved that she had at least some understanding of the danger they faced. Part of him wished she wasn't so smart, because at least that way she wouldn't have to be afraid. Still, he'd take her frightened and alive over oblivious and dead any day of the week.

"Does that mean you're not looking to leave me behind?" she asked.

"For now."

"I almost thought I'd come out of the bathroom to find the car hot-wired and you long gone."

"I considered it, but those tracking devices—or whatever that second thing was—lead right here. No way would I leave you alone for someone to find."

"That was considerate of you." He could practically hear her rolling her eyes as she spoke.

Clay ignored the sarcasm and opened the map he'd found tucked in her glove compartment while searching for trackers. "Looks like there's a decent-sized town up ahead about twenty miles. They'll probably have a library or print shop we can use."

He turned up the heat for her and scoured the map for a safe place to leave her—with or without the information the intruder had given her—somewhere Mira would find her but no one else would.

Once he got his hands on the list Mira had sent, he could retrace his steps and figure out where the hell he'd been going during those blackouts—especially the one the night before last.

Clay really wanted to know who he'd killed. And why.

Chapter Nine

Leigh could tell Clay was making plans to ditch her. She could see it in the way he refused to meet her gaze and his slight anxious fidgeting with the map. His body was so tense she could practically feel the vibration of his muscle fibers traveling through the air.

Rather than confront him about it and warn him she knew, she kept quiet, figuring out how to outsmart him. The only thing she could think to do was to make herself valuable enough that he didn't leave her the first chance he got.

She had to be a part of this. She couldn't trust that anyone else would want to find a way to save her brother as much as she did. If she failed this time, there might never be another chance, and despite what Clay thought, he wasn't able to do this on his own—not when he was always only one step away from turning into that empty, vacant husk of a man, willing to hurt whoever was in his path.

Leigh's jaw still ached from where he'd grabbed her, and the bruises were ugly, but none of that mattered. If that was the price she had to pay for Garrett's freedom, it was a small one.

Whatever it took, no matter how dangerous things got, she owed her brother for everything he'd given up for her. Finding a way to ingratiate herself with Clay was the least she could do. Greed, revenge, guilt, lust— whatever weakness she could find in Clay she would use to save Garrett. After all, he would do no less for her.

"Once we get rid of my phone and make sure no one can track us, I'll tell you what that man said to me."

He kept his gaze on the map. "You should tell me now."

"If I do that, you'll have no reason to keep me around."

He turned in his seat, his wide shoulders blocking out the glare of sunrise streaming in through his window. "You'll be safer without me around."

"I'm not going through this with you again. You're not getting rid of me. I'm the only one who can represent Garrett's interests, and that's exactly what I'm going to do."

"Does your brother have any idea what you're up to? Does he have even a clue about the kind of risk you're taking for him?"

"No, nor will he unless I decide he should know."

"He wouldn't want you to do this."

"How do you know? You've never even met him."

"Because any man who could create the kind of loyalty you're displaying right now would never be the kind of asshole who would willingly let his sister walk into danger."

Some kind of ache in his voice made her glance at him. His big body filled the space beside her, putting off strange vibes. It was like he was angry and intrigued all at the same time, and she didn't understand why he would be either. "You'd do the same thing for your brother or sister, wouldn't you?"

"Don't have any."

"Then Mira. You'd stick your neck out for her, right?"

"Absolutely."

"See? It's the same thing."

"No, it's not. You're a doctor. Your life is valuable."

"And yours isn't?"

He shrugged. "Don't get me wrong. I like living. But I'm damaged goods. I've hurt people."

"That doesn't make you less valuable."

"Tell that to the families of the corpses lying in Payton's living room."

"That was self-defense. They came after you."

Clay said nothing, offering her only stony silence.

She understood his guilt. He had killed those men, and there was nothing he could do to take that back. Chances were he'd killed others as well. By the time Hollis realized what was happening, at least three men had died by his hand. And then he'd killed a fourth—himself.

She wasn't going to let that happen to Clay. She wasn't leaving his side until he was free of these compulsions, or at least until he was locked up for his own safety, the way Garrett now was.

They pulled into town before businesses were open. After a fast-food breakfast, they found a place to print out the file Mira had sent. Clay wrote down Payton's number, as well as a couple of others, then made quick work of destroying her phone. The pieces went into three different trash bins on the street.

"Now what?" she asked, sticking right by his side, not letting him out of her sight.

He stopped by her car, opening the driver's door for her. "Now you hit the road. Find a bank here in town and get as much cash out as you can. Go somewhere you've never been before—somewhere you'd never normally go—pay only in cash, and don't leave until you run out of money. Call Payton before you come back to make sure it's safe."

"You still haven't accepted that I'm not leaving you alone."

"This isn't a joke, Leigh. We both know I'm too dangerous to be around."

"You're too dangerous to not have a keeper. At least I have the drugs to deal with you if you go off the deep end again. I'm the only one who can keep you from hurting someone."

His finger traced the bruises along her jaw so gently, it made her shiver. "And who's going to protect *you* from me?"

Greed, revenge, guilt, lust. Whatever it took.

Time to start looking for a weakness.

"I have information I'm willing to share, but only if you let me come along."

"Then I'll do it without your information."

So much for greed. "If I'm with you, we can find these bastards faster. And when we do, you can do to them what you want—just as soon as they tell us how to fix you and Garrett."

"I don't care how long it takes. And when I do find them, there's not a force on this earth that can stop me from making sure they never do it again. I don't need you for that. You'll only get in the way."

And there went revenge. Time to lay on some guilt. "You hurt me, Clay. I think that means you owe me."

He flinched, and his amber gaze slid to the ground. His shoulders drooped, and he seemed to fall in on himself, as if she'd taken something vital away from him.

Now she was the one feeling guilty.

"What do you want?" he grated out.

"To come with you. To bandage those cuts on your wrists. To make sure you find the people who did this.

And to make sure you don't hurt anyone else—at least not anyone who doesn't have it coming."

He looked past her, staring at the businesses behind her. Until now she hadn't realized how much she liked his direct gaze—how connected to him it had made her feel. She was floundering in this mess, unsure of herself and her ability to deal with it. Clay had been a source of stability for her, an anchor she could grab when she started to doubt herself. And now he was drifting away, out of reach.

She put her hand on his arm, feeling his muscles jump beneath the skin. "Don't push me away."

"It's for your own good. The fact that you won't be pushed means that anything that happens from here is your choice. This isn't a question of me exercising more control, Leigh. When it comes to this shit—whatever it was they did to me—I have none. I can't protect you. I won't even know I'm hurting you until it's too late."

She nodded, but he didn't see it. He wasn't looking at her. "I understand. I won't blame you. I'm a big girl, perfectly capable of taking responsibility for my own actions."

"Fine. Don't say I didn't warn you."

Payton's vacation home was a mess. Cleaning up the blood, broken glass, and bodies was going to take up precious time he wasn't sure he had. So far his leads had all hit dead ends. There was only one more left to pursue, and Payton worried what would happen to Clay once General Robert Norwood learned the truth.

Bob answered his phone, despite the early hour. "If this is bad news, it can wait."

"I'm afraid it can't," said Payton.

"Whatever. I wasn't sleeping anyway. What's wrong?"

Payton hesitated. Clay's life was in his hands. He had to be careful about how he did this. "First you need to know that I have the situation under control."

"Then why call me?"

"Because someone needs to know what's going on in the event that I'm wrong."

"About what?"

"Clay Marshall has been activated. Multiple times."

"What?" bellowed Bob. "How is that possible?"

"I'm working on finding who is behind it, but I wanted you to know about it. If I'm wrong and he turns on me, someone has to take him out."

"You let him live? Please tell me he's on his way to the facility—that you at least had the sense to lock him up."

"I know this man. He wouldn't survive that. At least not for long."

"So what? You let him roam around like a rabid animal? You know better than that. We've been through this before."

"He's not like the others." Bob didn't know Clay the way Payton did. He hadn't worked with him every day for a decade and watched him struggle to find some kind of life for himself. He hadn't seen Clay as a kid—neglected and scrawny, willing to do anything for even a scrap of affection. After what Payton and Bob had allowed to happen, they owed Clay more than a well-placed bullet or a life sentence in a secret, maximum-security holding facility.

"They're all like that. We made them like that. If you can't do this—if you're too close to the situation—then I will."

"No. Not yet."

"Where is he now? Is he anywhere near Sloane?"

Bob's daughter worked at the Edge alongside Clay.

Payton couldn't fault him for being concerned. "No. I've sent him away. He's with Garrett Vaughn's sister right now. She'll know how to deal with him."

Bob let out a prolonged sigh of fatigue and frustration. "Knowing how and being able to are two different things. If you get that woman killed, Vaughn will find out. He's not stable enough for that kind of news."

"I know. But Clay had to be watched, and I couldn't do it—not while I'm trying to track down who triggered him."

"It's got to be Norma. She's the only we haven't found."

"Maybe," said Payton, "but I'm not sure. This doesn't feel like her work."

"What's that supposed to mean?"

"You saw the report on Jake Staite. You saw what she'd done to him."

Jake and many other men had been tricked into thinking that they were recruited into a secret special forces division of the U.S. military. By the time people from the Edge had found him, he'd been drugged, brainwashed, and subjected to torture and experimentation. They'd managed to save Staite's life, but it wasn't much worth saving. He was being held in the same facility as Leigh's brother, kept isolated and sedated for his own safety.

Payton couldn't stand the thought of the same thing happening to Clay.

"Yeah, I saw it," said Bob. "Thanks for the nightmares, by the way."

"Then you know what Norma did. It's not like that with Clay. It's different. More . . . subtle, like it was one of the others."

"The researchers who aren't dead went legit. I checked, remember?"

"Maybe we missed someone. We thought Norma was

dead and we were wrong. Maybe we're wrong about one of the others."

"That's why you want to keep him alive," said Bob. "You want to use him as bait."

"If I have to, I will. I'm doing everything I can to track down the person responsible. If Clay is dead or locked up, then he can't lead me down the right path. Like it or not, we need him to be exactly where he is."

"Roaming free, able to hurt countless people?"

"Leigh won't let that happen."

"You'd better be right about this. I'm really close to something big—something that may help clean up what we did."

"What?" asked Payton, his voice betraying his eagerness. Any absolution he could find was more than welcome. If Bob had some to offer, Payton would grab it with both hands.

"Not yet. It's too soon. I need a couple more days. Just know that if Marshall goes off the deep end and makes a mess, it will ruin everything."

"I understand. I'll be in touch."

Payton hung up, considering his options. Bob was not the kind of man to exaggerate. He felt at least as much guilt over what they'd done in the ignorance of their youth as Payton did. If Bob thought there was some glimmer of hope that could make up for their past actions, then Payton had to respect that. He couldn't allow anything to destroy that fragile hope. Too many lives were at stake.

Which meant that if it came down to a choice between Clay and all the others, Clay was going to lose.

Mr. Grady had yet to report in to Richard, which meant that he was dead. Not that it was much of a surprise. Clay

Marshall was a man built to be a weapon. If the self-preservation programming had kicked in, Mr. Grady didn't stand a chance.

Or perhaps that was Richard's hubris talking.

Either way, none of the thugs had been able to find Marshall, so it was time to move on to another plan before he was locked away and out of reach the way Garrett Vaughn was. Richard remembered the names of only a few of his subjects, and most of them were now dead. Without the file he'd tasked Marshall to find months ago, Richard would never be able to prove that his methods were superior to Norma Stynger's. And if he couldn't prove that, then his funding would dry up by the end of the year.

Richard loathed doing what he now had to do, but he had run out of options. If Norma's lapdog could not be coerced, all of Richard's work—all of those decades of effort—would be wasted.

He dialed the number he hoped was still good and waited for an answer.

"Yes?" answered Adam Brink quietly.

"It's Dr. Sage. I need your help."

"I don't work for you. Find someone else." Adam's voice had deepened since Richard had last seen him, but the calm confidence that had been as much a part of Adam as his spine was still evident in his tone.

"There is no one else." Richard drew in a deep breath and uttered the phrase from memory. "Three rivers meet in the center of the lost pine forest."

"You can't trigger me like that. Dr. Stynger removed all of your controls."

Frustration raged through Richard. Norma had no right to toy with his work. None. And yet she thought that because they had once been friends and colleagues, she could do whatever she pleased. Bitch.

"She didn't remove all of them," said Richard. "I have information that you want—information Norma would never give you."

"I highly doubt you have anything of value to me."

"Perhaps you no longer care about what happened to Eli, then?"

Adam went silent, and the line took on a crackling chill that made Richard glad he wasn't in the same room with the man.

"What do you know?" asked Adam.

"Many things. Didn't Norma tell you?"

"She knows nothing more about Eli than I do."

"Are you sure? Do you really trust her so much to believe that she wouldn't withhold information in order to keep you in line, obeying her orders?"

"You're lying."

"I'm not. I know where your brother is."

"Where?"

"I'm not telling you. Unless you agree to do me this one little favor."

"Why should I believe you?"

"Why should you believe Norma?" countered Richard. If she was anything like she had been twenty-some years ago, she was still as ruthless and cutthroat as ever.

"What do you want?"

"Clay Marshall. Alive. I want you to bring him to me, unharmed."

"Why me?"

"Because the last man I sent is dead. He was supposed to be the best, but, then, he'd never met you, had he?"

"Flattery means nothing to me. Only answers. Give me something as a down payment or I hang up right now."

Adam wasn't bluffing. Richard could hear it in the

steely quality of his voice. "Fine. But only a tiny tidbit or you'll run off to find Eli when you should be helping me."

"Spit it out."

"Eli was adopted as a child. They changed his name."

"To what?"

"There's not a chance I'm telling you that. Not until you bring Clay to my labs. I assume you remember where."

"If you're lying to me, you'll regret it."

"What? You'll kill me?" asked Richard, amused.

"No. I'll give you to Dr. Stynger. She'll kill you. Eventually."

That threat was enough to make Richard reevaluate how he treated Adam going forward. The boy had become a man somewhere along the way, and given what Richard knew about him, toying with him was a bad idea.

"There is no need for threats. I'm telling you the truth about Eli. You'll see as soon as you bring Clay Marshall to me."

Adam's reply radiated complete confidence. "Send me whatever information you have on Marshall. You'll have him by the end of the week."

Chapter Ten

Clay drove for two hours before he felt like he was far enough away from Leigh's battered phone to be sure no one could find them. He stopped and bought a GPS, then pulled into a cheap roadside motel and paid in cash for a room.

The close quarters weren't lost on him, but chances were they weren't going to be sleeping here, anyway. Once they found a lead, he'd head out. They just needed a private place to stop long enough to dig up some bad memories. No sense in crashing Leigh's car if he went all batshit or something.

"I think I've figured out Mira's organization of the data," said Leigh. She sat on the end of the bed. The cheesy pink and blue geometric bedspread was so eighties it was a wonder her hair didn't get bigger by proximity alone. "If you can remember when you lost time, we should be able to start mapping out where you were. But not until after I patch you up."

"I'm fine." His wrists burned, but he'd been through worse.

"Don't be a baby. The last thing you need is to have those cuts get infected. Just man up and let me do this."

She set her medical bag on the counter by the sink and started digging through it.

"Do you insult all your patients?" he asked.

She paused in the act of setting out gauze and tape and looked at him in the mirror. "You're not my patient. I'm just helping out a friend in need."

"We're not friends, either."

"Then consider it a repayment for saving my life. You bled for me. It's only right that I help you stop bleeding."

"Fine. Whatever." As much as he hated subjecting himself to any medical procedures, she was right about infection. He couldn't afford any weakness right now.

He was just going to have to do as she'd asked. Man up. Ignore the queasy anxiety that plagued him every time he got near sterile gloves, tubes, and needles. The feeling was inconvenient as hell—a remnant from whatever had been done to him, no doubt. For all he knew, the assholes who'd fucked with his head had given him a hatred for doctors just to keep one of them from accidentally undoing all the hard work that had scrambled his brains.

Clay presented his bandaged wrists to her for inspection. She slowly removed the strips of towel, obviously working not to pull on the wound. Her gloved fingers fluttered over his skin, brushing but not really touching. He was torn between wanting her to leave him alone and wishing she'd take the gloves off so he could feel her skin on his again.

He watched her work, shoving the minor sting and burn of the cuts from his mind. Her movements were efficient. Her hands were steady. A look of deep concentration furrowed her brows. She held her bottom lip between her teeth, letting go of it now and then.

The crazy urge to lick away that little dent her teeth left consumed him, making him wonder just how she'd taste—how she'd sound if he gave in to the urge.

She leaned forward to reach for the scissors and gave Clay a nice view down the front of her blouse. Like a pervert, he couldn't help but stare. The dark shadow between her pale breasts sucked him in and didn't let go. As stacked as she was, she didn't show off the goods, but there was little she could do to completely hide them.

Her freckles became sparser and lighter the farther down they went. He wondered if she had them sprinkled across her belly and hips, too. And if he'd ever find out.

Not likely. As much as his body was on board with the whole discovery expedition, he had to remember who she was.

She wasn't some barfly looking for a romp. She was Mira's friend. She took care of the people he worked with. Hell, she was taking care of him right now—and as much as he hated doctors, he couldn't find the fire in his belly to hate her. At least not right now.

"There are a couple of places where you really tore the skin. They need to be glued or sutured."

"Glue. I won't be ripping that out if I get a bit rough."

She looked up at him, so close he could see the way her dark eyes dilated, eating up flecks of green and gold as her pupils expanded. "The goal is to avoid getting rough."

He shrugged. She was holding his arm, and the movement shifted her whole body slightly. It made him realize how vulnerable she was—how every little thing he did could so easily affect her. "Some things can't be helped. It's your job to get out of the way."

"Noted. Now, your job is to hold still while I do this, or we'll be literally stuck together."

The notion sounded nicer than it should have, which only proved how messed up he really was. The day he got involved with a doctor who was using him would be the day he was laid out on an autopsy table for scientific study.

Leigh finished the job and bandaged him up properly. "If you have any signs of infection—redness, fever—let me know."

She turned, and the strip of lights over the mirror lit the side of her face. Fingertip-shaped bruises lined her jaw. They were darker now than they'd been before. His stomach tightened at the thought of what he'd done and how it must have made her feel. She'd trusted him and he'd hurt her, scared her.

Clay reached out to angle her face so he could inspect them more closely, but she flinched away. It was an instinctive reaction—one based on what he'd done to her.

"Sorry," she said, and then she held still as if to prove she wasn't afraid of him.

Clay let his hands fall slowly, leaving them where she could see them. "You have no reason to be sorry. I'm the violent head case. Not you."

"I don't want you beating yourself up over it. That's not going to get us anywhere."

"Neither will ignoring it. I tried that for months— pretending that I wasn't losing time or waking up with injuries I couldn't explain. I promise it doesn't work. I'm facing this head-on, Leigh, and that means owning up to everything." Even though it made him sick. Better to be sick and careful than to hurt her again.

She still wouldn't look at him. "I'm going to clean up this mess and take a shower."

Her change of topic was painfully obvious, leaving him no choice but to respect it. She'd been through hell in the last few hours. He wasn't going to add to that by pushing her.

He couldn't make her accept that he was a threat any more than he could ask for her forgiveness. That was for men who knew they wouldn't hurt someone again. Clay could make no such promises.

Leigh cleaned her instruments and then took her suitcase into the bathroom, shutting the door behind her. The shower came on.

Clay stood there for a good minute, trying not to imagine her getting undressed. As mixed-up as his life was right now, the thought of Leigh naked was a much-needed distraction, but one he knew would lead him down the wrong path. She was caring and as sexy as hell, but that couldn't matter to him. For as long as he was a threat, he had to keep his distance. And as soon as he was no longer a threat, there would be no reason for them to be together.

Simple. Clear. Final.

Now all he had to do was get his dick to catch up to his brain.

He picked up the thick stack of paper and stared at the numbers without actually seeing them.

Clay dreaded what was going to happen next. He was going to have to slog through all those horrible mornings when he woke up not knowing how he'd made it into bed. The mornings when he cataloged bruises and cuts, wondering how he'd earned them. It was amazing how easily he'd been able to shove those days into a dark hole of denial and pretend they'd never happened. And now he had to dig them all out again.

Mira hadn't stopped working since Clay had called her, asking her to break into morgue databases. She'd known something was wrong—something big and bad and scary—but until now, she hadn't suspected it was this bad.

She stared at the screen, unable to believe what she saw.

After hours of collecting and organizing the list of

places Clay had been over the past two months and sending it to Leigh, Mira decided not to let that data go to waste. She located cameras near where he'd been and hacked into some of the servers that held security camera footage. Most of what she saw had been mundane stuff—shots of the back of his head or the side of his face. Images of him driving. One camera had captured him speaking to another man outside a restaurant. She never got a good shot of that man's face because the only camera that might have had the right angle was outside a bank. While she was confident she could crack the bank's security, she was also confident they'd find out eventually. Drawing attention to what she was doing was dangerous not only for her, but also for Clay.

Traffic cameras were easy, so she'd started with those, tracking his movements on a particular night about two weeks ago. Grainy images flashed as they were processed by facial recognition software until a hit on one paused the process.

There, staring almost directly at a camera, was Clay. He was close. The image was clearer than most. And what she saw scared her to death.

Clay's eyes were empty—hollowed out, as if what had made him *him* had been dumped out and replaced with sand. His jaw was slack, lacking the usual tension she'd come to associate with his intense personality. He didn't look like Clay at all. Instead, he looked more like the young men she'd seen filing out of her father's basement lab.

She'd been too young at the time to know what was wrong. All she knew was that it made her mom cry.

But now Mira knew more. She'd made it her life's mission to know more. All these years, she'd thought that Clay had been spared—that he hadn't fallen victim to her father. He was her hero. He was the one who'd saved her life when one of her father's subjects had cracked and nearly killed her.

Her father hadn't lifted a hand. He'd watched while Clay—only thirteen years old at the time—had charged in and beat the man off her. She'd still been sobbing when her father had retreated to his lab, furiously scribbling notes.

Now all of that made sense. It had been a test. Clay's test. Her father had done to Clay what he'd done to the others, carving out a part of him and turning it into something twisted and cold.

That was the look on Clay's face in the image staring at her. Empty, twisted, and cold.

Mira sat there for a long time, trying to figure out what to do. She burned with the need to confront her father, but it would only make things worse. He liked toying with her. He liked knowing that he held power over her. If she gave him even a hint of how much this upset her, he would use it against her. Against Clay, too.

Maybe there was a cure—a way to undo what had been done. She was only vaguely aware of the science her father had used to create his puppets. She'd avoided learning anything about it as a way of rebellion. Her father had wanted her to follow in his footsteps, but his path had been paved with pain and lifeless bodies. She refused to be like him.

Besides, as squeamish as she was, she was better off with electronics and the comforting predictability of logic. Medicine was too messy.

Unfortunately, that left her ill equipped to understand what had been done to Clay and the others. If she didn't understand it, then she couldn't find a way to fix it. If such a cure even existed.

But there was one thing she could do. She could find where her father stored his data and steal it from him. All she needed was a place to start hunting.

Clay was the key. If she tracked his movements long enough, eventually he'd lead her back to Dr. Richard Sage. And when he did, Mira was going to make sure that her father could never hurt anyone again.

Leigh stood under the hot spray of water, trying to gather her wits and find some sense of calm.

Clay shook her to her core. She wasn't sure exactly what it was about Clay that did it, but whatever it was, it was powerful and compelling. It left her trembling and struggling to find solid ground.

He hadn't so much as twitched an eye as she'd tended his cuts, as if there were no pain. She'd felt his gaze on her—seen in the mirror the way he stared at her. There was desire in his eyes, but she'd seen that from men before enough times that it didn't rattle her. What shook her was the fleeting insecurity lurking in his expression, as if he truly didn't know whether he was a good man.

Any man who would fight with his hands bound behind his back to save the woman who'd chained him couldn't be all bad.

But he was dangerous. She couldn't forget that for a minute. He was always only one instant away from turning on her. She couldn't trust him not to hurt her again. Doing so would be the worst kind of stupid.

She needed to help him find the truth fast, before she ended up doing something reckless—something she refused to name or allow to form in her mind. If she let even the vaguest hint of what she was feeling coalesce into actual thought, she knew she'd be doomed.

He was just a man who needed her help. A sick man. A way to save her brother. Nothing more. And he needed to stay that way.

The best thing for her to do now was to help him figure out where they needed to go to find whoever was behind this and force them to make it stop.

Simple.

With that decision made, she dressed and went to face him—with a fresh dose of tranquilizers prepared and ready to go in her pocket in case she needed them.

Clay sat on the bed with his back against the headboard. He had a small notepad propped against one knee, writing something. As soon as he saw her, he stopped, looking up at her.

His gaze swept over her, making her acutely aware of her dripping hair.

"Nice shower?" he asked.

"Better than I expected in a place like this, actually."

He hadn't looked away, and his scrutiny was beginning to make her nervous. "What? Haven't you ever seen a woman with wet hair before?"

A faint smile twitched at the left side of his mouth. "You're pink."

"The water was hot."

"It's just not what I expected. That's all."

She wasn't sure what he had expected, but all this talk about her appearance was uncomfortable. "Have you been able to remember dates?"

The smile that hadn't quite formed disappeared. "A few. Two nights ago for sure. Three weeks ago, but I can't remember which day."

Leigh sat on the edge of the bed, picked up the printed list, and flipped through until she found the approximate time he was questioning. "What do you remember?"

"I'd been working for three days straight with nothing but a few naps here and there. We were guarding a shipment in Los Angeles."

"What kind of shipment?"

"That's private client information. It doesn't matter, anyway."

"Then what?"

"I stumbled home, exhausted and ready to sleep for as long as I could. The next thing I remember was waking up when Mira called, saying I was late for work. The problem was, I wasn't scheduled to work again for two days."

"Could you have slept for two days straight?"

"No way. I never sleep that long. Plus I felt like I hadn't slept at all. I was just as exhausted as when I fell into bed."

There were symbols next to some of the GPS coordinates on the list. Mira's notes said that she'd marked the times he'd been at home or at the office.

Leigh went back three weeks and scanned the data. "It looks like you went home on Tuesday after being away for three days. You stayed at home for six hours, then left again around eleven on Tuesday night."

"Where did I go?"

"There are coordinates here, but I don't know where they are."

The mattress shifted, and then she felt his heat at her back as he looked over her shoulder. "I'm not sure. South of Dallas, but that's all I can tell without looking up the coordinates."

"We'll figure that out next. First we should look for patterns—places you went to multiple times, maybe."

"Check where I was two nights ago."

She slid her finger down the list of numbers until she reached the right spot. "See here. You were home; then you left for a few hours and came back again."

"It's not the same place as three weeks ago."

Leigh circled the coordinates. "Do you remember any other times?"

He moved away again, and her right side felt cold without him so close. She should have been grateful for the space, but when it came to Clay, she wasn't thinking clearly.

When he remained silent, she glanced up at him. He'd stripped off his flannel shirt and was inspecting his hands and arms.

"What are you doing?"

"Checking scars. I have a few I can't account for. I'm trying to remember when I got them." He ran his finger along a pink scar about an inch long along his biceps. "This one happened right after Mira's birthday. I missed her party. She thought I'd gone out and gotten drunk."

"You didn't tell her otherwise?"

"I didn't want to worry her. She frets enough about me as it is." Clay shrugged as if it didn't matter, but the sadness Leigh saw dulling his eyes told another story.

"I remember the party. It was a Friday night. She'd told me you were going to be there and that she wanted me to meet you."

He grunted as if amused. "She kept trying to get me to go see you, too. I think she was hoping to set us up. Pretty ridiculous, huh?"

"Yeah," she agreed, even as she wondered what it would have been like to meet him outside such bizarre circumstances. He wasn't her usual type—he was rougher around the edges and less refined than she usually liked—but he was a great-looking guy. And she could definitely see the appeal of having someone like him around after last night. Just the memory of that gunman's hands on her was enough to make her feel sick.

"I'm sorry," he said. "Mira had no idea about how fucked-up I was when she tried to set us up. She doesn't know what I'm capable of."

He'd thought she was thinking of him hurting her, not

the other man. Once again he was taking responsibility for something that was completely out of his control. "And we're never going to tell her. She's way too sweet to know what we're doing. Agreed?"

Clay nodded.

"Good." Leigh went over the data near the time of Mira's birthday party. "Look. They're the same as three weeks ago."

She handed the pages to him, pointing to where she'd circled the coordinates.

"They're not just close, but exactly the same. I think this is what we've been looking for."

Leigh scanned through the rest of the pages. "Those same coordinates show up multiple times. August seventh . . ."

He lifted his T-shirt and pointed to a pale scar that looked like a knife wound. "That's when I got this."

"August twenty-fourth."

"Cracked ribs."

"September ninth."

He shook his head. "I don't remember anything specific around that time. But more than once I've woken up to bruises."

"What do they have you doing that you get hurt so often?"

"Hell if I know. But I'm going to find out."

"Then there's something you should know," said Leigh. "That man told me that he'd been sent to find you so that you could finish a job."

"What job?" he asked.

"He didn't say. But whatever it is, I think that these coordinates might be the place where you'd do it."

Chapter Eleven

The coordinates were right in the middle of a hellhole near the Mexican border in a dimly lit bar teeming with low-life scum.

If Clay had known just how seedy the place would be, he would have dropped Leigh off miles away. Not that she would have stayed put.

"I can't go in there like this," she said, waving at her slacks and button-up blouse. "I'll stick out and draw too much attention. Give me a minute."

Clay studied the area, watching people go in and out of the bar while Leigh did whatever it was she felt she needed to do. When he looked at her again, she'd put on dark makeup around her eyes and unbuttoned her blouse a couple of buttons. A quick tousle of her hair and she looked like the rest of the women going in—ready for a party, and not the kind with paper hats and noisemakers.

He stared at her, soaking it in so he wouldn't be shocked once they got inside. Her eyes looked huge and haunted. No amount of makeup could cover up the fear he saw shining there. Her red hair was wild and mussed as if she'd just crawled out of some man's bed after a long night of rough sex. With those extra two buttons undone, her respectable blouse turned into fantasy wear, showing off the most glorious pair of tits he'd ever seen. Her lashes were long and thick, and her mouth was painted a glossy, lickable pink.

In that moment, he wanted to kiss her so badly he had to grab the steering wheel to keep from reaching for her. His whole body went into overdrive, his engines revving hard and fast. Desire vibrated through him, sizzling along his skin until the heat made him break out in a sweat.

"You ready?" he croaked, forcing his gaze away from what he couldn't have.

"As I'll ever be."

"You can't stay in the car, but I will take you somewhere safe and come back."

"No. Let's just do this. We have no phones. If anything happens, neither of us has a way of communicating with the other. We're safer together."

He questioned her logic. He was certainly safer with her around, but he couldn't say the opposite was true. But time was an issue, and she was a big girl, so he accepted her decision and got out of the car.

The crowd outside the doors parted as Clay walked through, staring at him as if they knew who he was. And were afraid to get in his way.

He used that to his advantage as he walked inside, taking on the demeanor of a man who expected crowds to part. Leigh trailed behind him, her bruises lending credibility to his act. Her fingers were fisted around the back of his jacket, the slight tug reassuring him that she was close enough that he could keep her safe—at least from everyone but himself.

A short man with bushy black hair and two missing teeth made a beeline for Clay as soon as he crossed the threshold. Clay's hand went to the small of his back, where his gun sat, and he stopped, allowing the man to approach.

"You're early," said the man, his greeting almost friendly.

Early for what? was the question.

"I was in the neighborhood," said Clay.

"And you brought company," he said, leering at Leigh's breasts.

"She's mine. And I don't share."

The man lifted his hands and smiled, showing off his missing teeth. "You have good taste. Come and have a drink. The next shipment isn't here yet."

"Shipment?" asked Leigh.

Clay could not let her get drawn into whatever mess awaited him here, so he turned on her and snarled, "This is business. Keep your mouth shut, woman."

Leigh flinched, and it wasn't an act. Genuine fear widened her eyes and made her cower. She let go of his jacket and took a step back.

It made him sick to scare her like that, but if she said the wrong thing in a place like this, it could be the last thing she did. Better to have her scared than passed around from one of these dirty assholes to another.

"Marshall has never brought a woman here before," the man said to Leigh. "You must be special."

She kept her eyes cast down, and the look was so alien on her, Clay wondered just how much he'd scared her. "Thank you . . ."

He sat at an empty booth. "Anton. Surely Marshall has told you of me."

Clay motioned for Leigh to slide in first, silently thanking her for getting the man's name. "I don't talk business with my women. Pretend she's not here."

"Of course," said Anton. He raised his hand to a waitress, who nodded and hurried to the bar. "The next shipment will be here in two nights. I found two this time. Same terms as always. Do you have the payment?"

"Yes."

Anton smiled and nodded. "Where shall we meet?"

"You pick this time."

"The warehouse?"

Clay shrugged as if he didn't care. "Suits me. What time? Sooner is better than later."

"You told me you couldn't accept delivery earlier than tomorrow—that you had a job to do that would keep you occupied."

That was the second person who'd mentioned this mystery job of his. Whatever it was, he needed to figure it out soon before he said something that got him in trouble. "My plans changed."

Anton squirmed in his seat as if worried Clay was coming across the booth for him. "Tomorrow night. Right after the bars close and the cops are busy elsewhere."

The waitress set three beers on the table and left. Clay gave Leigh's thigh a warning squeeze under the table. He picked his up as if to drink but didn't put it to his lips. "It will have to do."

Leigh picked up her glass and started to drink. He snatched it away from her and growled, "I want you sober for later. Not like last night."

A flash of anger brightened her eyes, but she hid it quickly, casting her gaze to the scarred table.

Anton grinned. "You two have plans. Shall we deal with the payment so you can go on your way?"

"It's in my car."

Anton laid some cash on the table and led the way out through the back. As they passed, people stared. Clay put his arm around Leigh, giving off the strongest territorial vibes he knew how. These people were afraid of him for some reason, and while he might never know what he'd done to deserve their fear, he wasn't above using it to Leigh's advantage. If they were afraid of him, they wouldn't touch anything that he'd claimed as his own. It was as primitive as it was effective.

The alley behind the bar reeked of vomit and piss. There were no lights, only the glow of the moon shining on puddles of who knew what to guide their way.

As soon as they were alone with Anton—out of earshot of the bar—Clay took Leigh's arm and urged her to hang back. Before Anton could guess Clay's intent, he grabbed the man by the shoulders and threw him against a brick wall, pressing a forearm against his throat.

Anton's eyes went wide and he held his hands up by his ears. "My friend, what is this?"

"We're not friends. And you're going to answer my questions."

"Of course. Whatever you want to know."

"Who do you work for?"

Anton's voice was quiet, as if he were talking to a wild animal. "The doctor, just as you do."

"What doctor? What's his name?"

"I don't know names. Only you do. You told me of him. You sought me out to acquire what he needed. What is this about?"

Clay ignored his question. "What's in the shipment?"

Anton frowned as if confused. "The same thing as always."

Clay increased the pressure against the man's throat just long enough to cut off his air and scare him. "Tell me."

"It's for the tests."

"What kind of tests?"

"I don't know. I would never pry into your business. You made it clear my questions were unwelcome."

Leigh stepped up next to Clay. "What exactly is being shipped?"

Anton hesitated, so Clay shoved him higher up the wall, telling him without words to answer her.

"Subjects," he squeaked out. "Children."

All the strength left Clay's body. Anton slid down the wall. Clay nearly toppled over in shock and disgust.

Children. He'd been helping some doctor gather children? Paying for them as if they were test tubes?

Anton tried to slip away, but Clay grabbed him by the back of his shirt and stopped him in his tracks. He flung the man around to face him and lifted him up to eye level. "You're going to take those kids back to wherever you found them. You're never going to touch another child again, or I will find you and kill you. Are we clear?"

Anton gave a shaky nod.

"Say anything to anyone about our meeting tonight, and I will find out."

"Yes. Of course. I won't say a thing. I swear."

Clay shoved the man away, glad to no longer be touching him. Anton scurried down the alley and out of sight.

"We should go," said Leigh.

Clay couldn't even look at her. Not after knowing what he'd done.

Kids. Someone had him collecting kids.

She tugged on his arm. He didn't dare move. If he took a step, he knew his knees would give out.

"You can't think about it now," she said. "That rat could be going for backup. He could bring more people here. We have to move. Now, Clay."

It was her order, given with such authority, that made Clay react. She was right. They needed to get out of here fast. He was in no shape to fight off a bunch of thugs. As it was, he was having trouble not puking his guts up, adding to the filth in the alley.

Clay focused on her, letting the sight of her dark eyes shove all the ugliness from his immediate thoughts. He managed to put one foot in front of the other all the way to the car, where she tucked him inside as if he were some kind of doddering old man.

He complied, not allowing himself to think. Just move. Breathe. Walk. Sit.

The car started and she drove away, hitting the nearest interstate. He didn't know where she was going. He didn't even care. If she drove off a bridge, he'd sit here calmly on the way down, accepting what came.

Clay couldn't wrap his head around what had just happened. It was one thing to kill men who were out to hurt him. It was another to hurt an innocent woman as he'd done to Leigh. But even in his craziest, most insane dreams, he'd never thought himself capable of hurting a child.

He let himself go numb inside, because the only other option was putting his gun to his head and pulling the trigger. It was what he deserved, but he didn't want to do that to Leigh—make her witness it and leave her to clean up the mess.

"You didn't do this," she whispered, miles later.

Clay didn't respond. There was no point. She was only trying to make him feel better, and there wasn't a thing she could say to accomplish that miracle.

"It was that doctor's fault. And I use the term loosely. No licensed physician would ever involve himself in human trafficking."

Silence filled the car. Clay didn't care.

Leigh's voice shook with such violence, it startled him. "We're going to find him—whoever is doing this—and stop him."

"I don't think I can," he said. His voice was strained, as if he'd been screaming.

"Of course you can. I can't do it without you."

"I gave up my right to keep breathing the moment I hurt a kid. You're on your own."

She pulled off the road into a vacant parking lot, parked the car, and turned to him. The heat in her tone blasted him. "You don't get to be that selfish."

He was so surprised by that comment, it shocked him out of his numb stupor. "What?"

"You heard me. You don't get to give up yet. You helped make this mess, and despite the fact that you didn't realize what you were doing, you may be the only one who can clean it up. You're thinking about killing yourself, and if you do that, who will help me?"

"You don't know what I'm thinking."

"I do. I've seen it before. I didn't catch the signs in time to save Hollis, but you can bet your ass I won't let the same thing happen to you—even if I have to lock you up in a cell next to my brother to make sure of it and go out on my own looking for a way to fix this."

Dark, violent rage seethed under his skin, making his tone sharp. "I won't let you lock me up."

"And I won't let you die. If I do, then everything you know dies with you. What will happen to the kids who may still be out there, hoping someone will save them?"

Oh God, no. He hadn't processed all of this enough yet to realize she was right. There probably were kids in danger right now, having who knew what done to them.

A memory bubbled up, as clear and vivid as if it had happened yesterday. He was little, strapped into a chair. A tube was hooked up to his arm, and his eyes were being held open with tape. Split-second images flashed across a screen, too fast for him to really see any of them. Whatever they were, they scared him. He couldn't move his head and look away. His eyes burned and tears streamed down his face.

Clay stumbled out of the car just in time to empty his stomach onto the ground. He knelt there on the cold asphalt, shaking. The wind cooled streaks of tears on his cheeks.

Leigh came up beside him and put her hand on his head. He didn't have the energy to push her away. And even if he did, nothing would change. He wasn't the man he'd thought he was. The things he'd done could never be forgiven.

But there was still one thing he could do. The need for justice burned hot in his gut. It strengthened his limbs and gave him the power he needed to get his ass up off the ground.

Leigh steadied him, her slender fingers clinging to his arm to keep him on his feet. Concern darkened her eyes and pinched her mouth, but she didn't avoid his gaze. She didn't cower in the face of his breakdown or shy away from the anger he could feel rolling out of him. She stood there, strong and solid, unflinching in her support, even though she knew he could snap at any minute.

If she could be this brave, then so could he. He'd face his demons and find whoever was responsible. And when he did, he'd make sure they didn't live long enough to ever hurt another child again.

Leigh was scared to death. She could feel Clay quivering on the brink of losing control. He'd fallen so fast after hearing the news about the kids, she wasn't sure she was going to be able to pull him back in time. He was spiraling down into that desolate void where Hollis had gone, and her desperation to grab him before he slipped away was still trembling through her.

Cold wind streaked through her hair, pulling away all warmth. Beneath her fingers, Clay was shivering. They needed to go somewhere quiet and figure out their next move. Standing out here like this wasn't safe. She still felt the need to put more miles between her and that horrible bar.

She went back to the car and grabbed a bottle of water for him. He rinsed out his mouth and seemed to be regaining his strength more by the second.

"We should go," she said, working to keep her voice gentle so she wasn't adding any more pressure on his already strained system.

He nodded. "I need to see that list again."

She wasn't sure if he was ready for more games of blackout concentration, but if it got him out of the cold, so be it. "It's in the car. Get in. I'll get it."

Leigh turned up the heat as he flipped through the pages.

"I want to go here," he said, pointing to a set of coordinates.

"Sure. Whatever you want. We'll go first thing tomorrow morning."

"No. Now, Leigh." His voice was steady, but his hands were still shaking.

She was exhausted from lack of sleep and being terrified way too often. She hadn't slept more than a few minutes since she'd met Clay, and while she had learned to function on little sleep in med school, her skills were rusty.

"Okay," she told him. "We'll head that way, but I can't keep going at this pace. I need sleep and food. So do you."

He grimaced as if the idea of eating turned his stomach. "I've had plenty of sleep, thanks to your knockout drugs. I'll drive."

"Look at your hands. Do you really think that's a good idea?"

Clay splayed his hands and watched them shake. He curled his fingers into tight fists, straining the healing cuts. "I'll be fine in a minute."

She doubted that, but rather than argue, she got back on the highway and headed toward Dallas. Near midnight, she was no longer able to keep going. Hunger and post-adrenaline letdown were sapping her strength and making her dangerous behind the wheel.

"I have to stop," she told Clay, who had not uttered a single word in more than an hour.

He shot her a look of frustration and disappointment but didn't argue.

She pulled into a restaurant that was open all night, hoping they would have something Clay could eat. The engine fell silent. She took off her seat belt and got out. He didn't move to open the door.

She leaned over to look at him sitting inside the car. "Are you coming in with me?"

"Not hungry."

"That may be, but now that Anton has seen my face, I don't exactly feel safe alone." She really doubted that anyone would find her here, much less do anything to her while she was in public. But it was as good an excuse as any to get him to come in. She didn't trust him not to run off alone if he thought he could get away with it.

A startled look crossed his face, as if he hadn't considered that. "You're right. Sorry."

He followed her inside. The place was mostly empty, with just one man sitting alone at a table, reading a book.

After seeing her seated, Clay went to the bathroom. She watched him go in, making sure he wasn't trying to slip back out to the car without her knowledge.

The waitress came to the table, and Leigh ordered

enough food for both of them, pretending it was all for her. Maybe if the food was in front of him, he'd eat it.

Clay came back out.

"I got you ginger ale. Hope that's okay."

He shrugged as if it didn't matter and drank.

Uncomfortable silence descended between them. She searched for a safe topic—one that would pull him out of this funk and get him to relax enough to eat. When nothing came to mind, she let out a sigh she hadn't meant to be so loud.

His gaze snapped to her face and then slipped down to her breasts.

Her shirt was still unbuttoned from the playacting she'd done earlier. A rush of embarrassment washed over her, and she moved to fix the slutty display. Before her fingers reached the first button, Clay's clenched jaw relaxed and his shoulders eased down from their tensed position. A hot look of pure male interest darkened his eyes as his pupils expanded. His whole body began to settle into the booth, the rigid tension melting away.

He picked up his glass and drank.

Leigh let her hands fall back to her lap. All those lovely little chemicals caused by arousal were being released in his brain, and while she hadn't intentionally chosen to turn him on, a good dose of lust was just what the doctor ordered.

Letting him stare should have made her feel dirty. It would have with another man. Instead, she found his apparent inability to look away thrilling. And after what she'd been through over the past few hours, she deserved to feel something other than fear and anger.

Enjoying the rush of feminine power, she leaned forward. His eyes tracked her movement, his lids lowering. A dark flush peeked out from under the collar of his T-shirt, and he shed his leather jacket.

Now it was her turn to stare as he propped his arms on the table. Muscles in his shoulders flexed and shifted, pulling his shirt tight.

It was just bone and tissue. It shouldn't have had the power to make her feel anything, but she'd run her hands over him and knew the texture and heat of his skin. And with him staring at her as if she might be a tasty treat, she found it impossible to look at him with anything resembling clinical detachment.

The waitress set the food down in front of Leigh, eyeing her warily. The slutty makeup, the display of cleavage, the mussed hair and bruises—it apparently wasn't something the waitress saw every day.

She looked at Clay. "Can I get you anything?"

He shook his head, his gaze still fixed on Leigh.

She dug into her food, keeping her attention away from Clay. His stare was too intense, his rapt attention too unnerving.

He followed her fork to her mouth, watched the bite of pancakes disappear. His throat moved as he swallowed. She gathered another bite and extended it across the table to him. "They're really good. Try some. I've got more than I can eat."

He sat still for a moment but then leaned forward and covered her hand with his, holding it steady. The heat of his hand was shocking. A faint tremor moved up her arm, but she couldn't tell if it was his or hers.

He opened his mouth and ate what she offered, letting his lips slide slowly over the tines of the fork.

She ate another bite, acutely aware that only a moment before his lips had been where hers were. Again he watched her, and this time he picked up his own fork and pulled a plate of eggs in front of him.

A shiver worked its way up her back, sinking in at the nape of her neck. A primitive sense of satisfaction filled her up, so raw and powerful she was shocked by the force of it. Something as simple as getting him to eat should not have given her so much pleasure, and yet she couldn't deny it, shining bright inside of her, making her glow.

Leigh stayed silent, worried that if she called attention to his actions, she'd ruin it somehow. Instead, they ate in silence. He offered her a bit of biscuit, which she ate from his fingertips.

Nothing so plain had ever tasted that good before.

She stopped when she was full, but Clay kept going, emptying the plates. When the last crumb was gone, he sat back and regarded her with a steady stare. "Thanks," he said simply.

"For what?"

"The food. The distraction." His gaze flickered to her breasts for a split second before returning to her eyes. "I'm better now. Solid."

"You were always solid. You just needed to remember it."

He let that pass by without comment. "You look tired. Let's find a place for you to sleep."

Part of her worried that if she slept she'd wake up to find him gone. The rest of her worried what would happen before she slept. Desire hummed through her, making her weak. His physical interest in her was obvious. The two of them together, alone, was a dangerous combination right now. If he looked at her with that hunger she'd seen earlier, she wasn't sure she'd be able to resist giving him what he wanted—only this time it would be more than food.

"Show me your hands," she said.

He frowned in question but held them out as she'd asked. They were rock steady.

She nodded. "I know you're anxious to go. You drive. I'll sleep in the car."

A hint of disappointment flashed over his expression before he hid it. She had no idea if he was disappointed because she didn't trust him or because he'd hoped to have the chance to seduce her.

"I promise you that I'll find you a real bed to sleep in soon. I just need to know what's at those coordinates. Once I do, we can figure out our next move."

He'd included her in his plans. That was a good sign—one that said he wasn't looking to get rid of her at the first opportunity.

Knowing the possible danger they faced, she wasn't sure if that made her feel better or much, much worse.

Chapter Twelve

Clay had a job to do. That's what both Anton and the intruder in the house had said. At first, he'd thought that buying the kids for the doctor was the job, but as he ran the conversation with Anton through his head again, he realized what Anton had said. Clay had rescheduled the shipment because he'd had a job to do, which implied that the shipment wasn't the job.

So what was it?

As the car flew through the miles, he racked his brain for some scrap of information that would tell him what it was he'd been told to do. Whoever was behind this—that doctor or someone else—was using him for a specific task. If he could find out what it was, then it might lead him back to them, allowing him to locate them and rid the planet of their diseased presence.

He tried not to think about what was happening to those kids, while alternately struggling to figure out where he'd taken them. Those thoughts were bleak and led him into a dark place where he couldn't function. He had to stay level and keep his wits about him. Floundering around, swamped by guilt and fear, wasn't going to save those kids.

There was no way to know how many there were. If he hadn't been so shocked by the news of what he'd done, he might have been smart enough to question Anton more thoroughly.

At least he was thinking clearly now. Food had done wonders for his sluggish brain and driven away some of the lethargy that had been dragging him down. From here on out, he had to stay sharp, and if that meant forcing himself to eat, then that's what he'd do.

Especially if Leigh gave him another peep show.

She'd done it on purpose. He realized that now. A professional woman who dressed herself modestly every day was not the kind of woman to forget that her tits were on display.

He'd been obvious in his leering—too brain-dead to have even a hint of subterfuge about him. She could have buttoned up at any time, and yet she hadn't. He'd stared and she'd let him, and that distraction had helped ease the kinks that had him all tied in knots, unable to function.

Of course it had also given him all kinds of fuel for future fantasies and left his cock twitching at the memory.

Leigh was curled up in the seat beside him, sleeping, his jacket rolled up to act as a pillow. He checked the locks on the doors again for the fiftieth time, making sure she wasn't going to tumble out headfirst.

As he reached the coordinates—a state park—he pulled into the camping area. This time of year there were only a few RVs and campers nearby. Keeping his distance from them so he wouldn't disturb anyone, he turned on a light to check the list of coordinates against the GPS. Unlike the bar near the border, his locations on the night he'd been doused in blood were more sporadic. Mira had tried to group together sections of time by location, but on that night, he'd never stayed in any one place for more than ten minutes. And while most of his time had been spent inside the park, there was no way to know which place was most important. It was a lot of ground to cover, and he didn't know how much time he had before the next horrible thing happened. He could flip out again or, if Leigh's guess was right about some sort of homing beacon in his brain, he could simply go back to whoever had done this, putting himself squarely under their control.

If they knew that he was no longer unaware of his actions, they might simply lock him up. Or even worse, they could turn him into the mindless puppet forever, taking away all signs of his free will.

Like fucking hell they would. There was too much at stake for him to mess this up. He needed to track down the bastards and end them before they got their hands on more kids. Period.

There were still a few more hours before daylight. He had a flashlight, and his night vision was pretty good. He could head out and start scouting, but he didn't want Leigh to wake up and find him gone. And he couldn't stand the thought of waking her. She'd been through too much since meeting him. The least he could do was let her rest.

The tick of a potential time bomb clicked away in his head, counting the seconds. With each one, his anxiety rose, making the muscles along the back of his skull knot. A dull throb started in his neck and crept over his head until it bored into his eyes.

Leigh shifted in her sleep, turning to face him. Her shirt was buttoned up again, hiding her breasts from his sight. He still remembered exactly what they looked like—smooth and pale, with her freckles disappearing near the edge of her bra. Even the memory was potent enough to make his cock swell inside his jeans.

Her hair was a mess again, tangled around her face in an almost wanton display that contrasted sharply with the innocence of sleep. The dark makeup she'd put on earlier was smudged around her eyes. The bruises that he'd given her were cast in shadows, but he could see them as clearly as if she were standing in sunlight.

He accepted the sickening punch to the gut seeing the damage caused, suffering through it as his due punishment. Without thinking, he reached up and slid his finger gently along the marks he'd left on her jaw, wishing he could take them back. The soft heat of her skin trickled into him, easing some of his tension by reminding him that she was alive and well. Not as good as she should have been had she stayed away from him, but at least she was safe for now.

She let out a soft, mewling sound of sleepy contentment—one that vibrated all the way to his core. It aroused him and consoled him all at the same time, curling around him like an embrace.

Clay forced his hand away from her before he accidentally woke her.

There were people around. It would be dawn soon. Leigh was as close to safe as she was going to get, and every second he spent with her was one more she was in danger.

He needed this to be over. Waiting around was not a luxury he could afford, no matter how sweet the view was. His smartest move was to set out and follow the path he'd taken the last time he was here. If he was lucky, he'd find some clue as to what he'd done that night and how to make sure he never did it again.

Clay scribbled a note so she'd know he hadn't abandoned her, and left it on the dashboard. His jacket had tumbled to the floorboard when she'd rolled over. He spread it out over her like a blanket, so she wouldn't freeze when he shut off the engine. As soon as he was sure she'd be warm enough, he grabbed a sweatshirt from his duffel bag to keep himself warm and collected the map and GPS. His loaded weapon went into the back of his waistband, ready to go if he needed it.

Clay slipped from the car and locked it up tight. A glance through the window confirmed that his actions hadn't woken her, proving just how exhausted she must be. His gaze lingered for a moment, his feet seemingly glued to the cold pavement. He didn't want to walk away from her, and if that wasn't proof of just how far off the deep end he'd gone, he didn't know what was.

With a force of will, he turned his back and walked away, heading toward the first set of coordinates.

Leigh sensed Clay's absence before she opened her eyes. The car felt empty without him, laced with a chill that had nothing to do with the temperature.

Faint morning sunlight streamed in through the windows. She blinked the sleep from her eyes as she took note of her surroundings. A few yards away, an elderly man descended from a RV and hurried off toward the campground showers.

Maybe that's where Clay had gone.

It was just after six in the morning, and despite the car's confines, she'd slept hard. Her neck was stiff, and one of her arms was numb from lying on it, but other than that, she felt human again.

A small piece of paper sat propped on the dashboard. She read Clay's note about scouting the area, and all signs of sleep vanished as a lance of fear plowed through her.

He'd gone out alone. She should have expected it. She should have taken those damn handcuffs with her and kept him chained to her.

As fear for him settled into frustration, she reminded herself that he was a grown man and more than capable of handling himself. So long as he didn't have another one of those freaky, vacant blackout sessions.

Leigh had no idea in which direction he'd gone, and she wasn't about to blindly stumble into the park after him. The best thing she could do was wait here, where he'd left her, and hope that he came back soon.

And when he did, she was going to have a long talk with him about the rules. No more running off alone. It was too dangerous.

She gathered a few things, grabbed the keys from the ignition, and headed for the bathrooms to clean up. She showered, changed, and did the best she could to cover her bruises with makeup. She hated the way Clay looked at them with guilt in his eyes. She hated the way it shoved a wedge of distance between them. She needed to keep him close, and constantly reminding him of actions he could not control was not the way to make that happen.

When she came out, she saw a shiny new Mustang sitting in the lot. The driver was idling in front of her back bumper, blocking her car in. He was busy talking on the phone, looking the other way, and hadn't noticed her yet.

Leigh's instincts perked up from their dormant state, whispering to her of danger.

She slipped back around the brick wall hiding the bathroom entrance and grabbed a mirror from her bag. Showing as little of her fingers as possible, she held the mirror at the edge of her hiding place and watched the man in the Mustang.

A minute later, another man slid out from under her car and hopped in the stranger's ride, and they drove off together.

Leigh went cold and stepped back into the steamy

bathroom, hoping it would rid her of this horrible chill of dread. There was no way she was going back to her car now. What if they'd planted a bomb? But she couldn't hide in here, either. Once Clay came back, he'd head straight for the car. There were no windows in the bathroom. She wouldn't be able to see him coming and warn him. And she couldn't stand out in the open. What if the Mustang came back?

Shaking and unsteady on her feet, she made a beeline for the RV where she'd seen the elderly man earlier. She knocked on the door, praying someone was inside.

A white-haired woman opened the door. She was dressed in a housecoat and had foam curlers in her hair.

"I'm sorry to bother you," said Leigh, "but I locked myself out of the car. My boyfriend went for a hike and has the keys. I hate to ask, but would you mind if I waited inside?"

A look of maternal sympathy shaped the woman's expression. "Poor thing. Of course. It's too cold to be out this early. Come on in. I'll make you something warm to drink."

Leigh stepped inside the cramped confines, noting the sweet little homey touches the woman had put up here and there. Pictures of what Leigh assumed were grandchildren dotted the little wall space available. Two bright yellow placemats sat on the fold-down table. On one of them was an open book of crossword puzzles.

"Have a seat there by the window. You should be able to see your boyfriend coming off the path."

Leigh sat. She made small talk with the woman and gratefully drank the weakest coffee on the planet. An hour passed and Clay hadn't yet appeared.

The sun rose higher and glinted off something in the distance, near the exit to the camping area. It was a shiny new Mustang, just past some bushes that had obscured it. Now that she noticed it, she saw two men sitting in the front seat.

They were waiting for Clay. She was sure of it, just as she was sure that as soon as he appeared on the trail, he'd be easily seen.

"Is that the only trail leading here?" asked Leigh.

The woman nodded, making her curlers bob. "It's the only trailhead, but it forks a little ways in. You're not thinking about going to look for your boyfriend, are you?"

"It's warming up. I'm sure he'll be back soon. I've already taken up enough of your time."

"It's no bother. Really."

Leigh glanced at the Mustang again and tried to hide the wave of anxiety sweeping through her. "Thanks so much for your hospitality. It was lovely meeting you."

Before the woman could keep her any longer, Leigh rushed out into the cold and headed for the trailhead. She tried not to look like she was hurrying—tried to make her steps measured and methodical, rather than frantic. Her dressy flats were not meant for this kind of ground. Their slick bottoms kept slipping on the mulch covering the path.

She could practically feel those men watching her. The urge to turn around and look was nearly overpowering, but she had no way of knowing if they were looking for her, too. If they knew her face, they might recognize her. As it was, all she'd let them see was the back of her head. She'd come out of an RV, not her car. Hopefully, that was enough to throw them off.

If not, she was screwed, because her revolver was trapped in the trunk.

The land dipped down. Ahead of her, she could see signs marking two distinct paths. She hadn't been able to see those signs from the trailhead, so she took the chance of looking behind her. Sure enough, she'd gone downhill so far that the parking area was no longer visible. No one was behind her.

Leigh didn't dare take one of the forks. Fifty-fifty odds were not good enough for her. Instead, she headed off the path into the surrounding brush and found a place to hide from strangers while she waited for Clay.

Chapter Thirteen

Clay found nothing. He visited every area he'd been to before and hadn't seen a single sign of blood or combat. That didn't mean he hadn't missed a bullet hole in a tree or something. There simply wasn't time to scour every trunk and branch along the two-mile-long path.

He needed to get back to Leigh. Every minute he was away from her piled up on top of him—a huge weight of anxiety growing heavier by the second.

She'd almost certainly be up by now, and even though he'd left a note that she shouldn't come after him, there was no guarantee she'd listen.

Clay hurried back up the hill toward the parking area. Cold air burned his lungs as he pushed himself harder. He'd been neglecting his body too much lately—not eating or sleeping enough—and that was more than evident in his lack of stamina. If he was going to have any hope of keeping Leigh safe, he was going to have to get his act together. Her life could depend on his strength, and right now, she wasn't in good hands.

That was going to change.

He'd just spotted the sign pointing to the parking area when he heard something in the brush to his left. His hand curled around the butt of his weapon, but he didn't pull it out. There were too many people around who would be scared by the sight of his gun. And these days, he looked a little wild around the edges, like he might crack at any minute. The last thing he needed was to have the cops come rushing out here to find the deranged gunman slinking through the park.

"Clay. It's me."

He heard Leigh's voice a second before he saw her pop up from behind a screen of brush. Her skin was ghostly pale, and fear hung around her eyes.

His hand left his weapon, and he rushed toward her. "What's wrong? What are you doing out here?"

"I came to warn you."

"About what?"

She teetered as she stepped over a fallen log. Clay grabbed her arm to steady her, and she fell against his chest with an audible sigh of relief. "I didn't know what else to do but come out and try to stop you."

Her arms reached around him, hugging him. The soft press of her breasts against his ribs drove all other thoughts from his head for a moment. He was shocked by the contact, knocked off-kilter so hard, his head spun trying to figure out what to do.

He wrapped his arms around her body, being careful not to get carried away. Her hug was one of relief. Nothing more. He couldn't let himself get too swept away by something so innocent and simple, no matter how good it felt or how hard it was now to concentrate.

"There are two men in the parking lot. I saw one of them come out from under my car. I don't know what he did, but it can't be good."

That news got Clay's head back into the game. He pulled her away by the arms so he wouldn't be distracted by the dizzying rush of having her curves plastered against him.

A slight wince tightened the skin around her eyes, and she pulled her shoulders up as if trying to avoid his grip.

Clay immediately loosened his hold. "Did they see you?"

"I don't think so. I was in the bathroom. I used a mirror to watch them from the other side of a wall."

Smart. "I'll deal with this. Stay here and hide again. I'll come back for you as soon as I take care of the threat."

"You can't. The men are still there, sitting in their car by the exit. I think they're waiting for you. They'll see you as soon as you walk up the hill."

There was only one way out of the camping area, and that was assuming the car was safe to use—which it wasn't.

"I'll cut through the trees and come out near their car. Exactly where was it?"

"It looked like they'd pulled off the road where it turns into the parking area. They're in a new black Mustang."

"And there were two of them?"

"Yes."

"Did you see any weapons?"

She shook her head. Little bits of dried leaves clung to her hair. He pulled them out, careful not to tug on the red strands.

"I don't want you to go," said Leigh. "What if something happens and you go . . . empty again?"

She'd nearly said *crazy* but stopped herself at the last moment. He could hear it in the pause between words and the subtle change in her mouth's shape. If he hadn't been watching her pink lips so closely, he might not have seen it at all. At least his raging hormones were good for something.

"I'll be fine," he said.

"You don't know that. You *can't* know that."

"All the more reason for you to wait here, out of harm's way. If I do snap, I don't want you around."

"What about the nice old couple in the RV? Will you go after them? Will you hurt someone else? If I'm with you, at least I can stop you."

"But at what risk to yourself?"

"At least I know the risks. Those other people will have no clue until it's too late."

He wasn't going to let her come with him. Not this time. The bruises she wore were a stark reminder of what could happen. No amount of makeup could hide that. "Stay here. If I'm not back in an hour, then call Payton."

Clay heard a noise behind him and spun around to face it. There, a few yards away, slinking through the brush, was a man in a black jacket.

Clay gave Leigh a solid push toward her hiding place. "Hide."

He didn't know if she obeyed or not, but he had no attention to spare right now. Another movement on his left caught his eye, and he knew there were at least two of them.

A buzzing haze hovered over him, threatening to steal his control. He fought it off, shoving it away, but not nearly far enough. He could feel the threat hanging there, just out of reach.

"I see you," he said as he moved away from Leigh, drawing their attention to him. "I will shoot." His weapon was up and ready, but he had yet to pick his target.

"Don't shoot," said the closer man. "We're not here to hurt you." His voice was familiar, tickling Clay's memory with a name he couldn't quite recall.

The man stepped out of the trees, his hands held high. He had a crooked nose and a deeply receding hairline that made his forehead look like a fleshy horseshoe.

"Tell your friends to come out where I can see them."

"Come on out, Buddy. Don't make Marshall shoot me."

Buddy. The name pulled at Clay's memory, tugging on a thread. He felt a brief flicker of companionship for the man but could not for the life of him recall who he was.

Buddy did as Horseshoe Head said. Clay waved the tip of his gun. "Get over there."

Buddy complied, keeping his hands in sight.

"What do you want?" asked Clay.

"Doc put a price on your head. We figured we'd come out and see if you can beat his offer. If so, we'll let you go."

Whoever this doctor was—assuming it was the same man who had Clay collecting children—there was no way Clay was walking back into his grasp. Still, their use of his last name, the same way Anton had done, made him wonder if he hadn't had dealings with them during one of his blackouts.

"What's he offering?" asked Clay, more to give Leigh time to get away than because he cared.

"Fifty grand."

"And you think I have that kind of cash on me?"

Horseshoe Head shrugged. "Guy like you's gotta have some hidey-holes with cash stashed here and there."

A guy like him? Apparently, these men knew him better than he knew them.

The sway of branches in the brush showed the path of Leigh's progress. She was staying low and out of sight. All he had to do was keep these assholes chatting for a bit longer and she'd be home free.

"How did you find me?" he asked.

"Doc said you might be here. Said he sent you on a job here a couple of nights ago—thought you might come back to clean up after it."

"What job?" Clay asked before he could stop himself. As much as he craved information, he couldn't let these men know that he wasn't this Marshall guy they thought they knew. That could be dangerous. If they were willing to deal with Marshall, then that's who Clay would be for as long as it took Leigh to get out of here.

Horseshoe Head frowned in confusion. "How the hell should I know?"

Buddy had been watching him closely. "He doesn't remember."

"You're one of them?" asked Horseshoe Head. He was starting to look worried, like he was suddenly standing with the wrong man.

The movement in the brush stopped. Leigh wasn't nearly far enough away yet. She wasn't even out of range of stray bullets.

Clay struggled for a way to alleviate these men's suspicions. "I don't know what the fuck you're talking about. Are we making a deal here or not?"

"Depends," said Horseshoe Head. "You got the cash?"

"Yes," lied Clay.

"Good. We'll just keep the woman here with us until you can get it and bring it back."

Like hell. The last thing he'd let these assholes do was touch Leigh. He didn't even like it that they knew she existed.

The sway of brush started again, and she was moving much faster. He winced inwardly, hoping she wouldn't draw any attention to herself. As long as he kept their focus on him, he had to believe she'd be safe.

Clay shrugged as if he didn't care. "I don't even know her last name. We're not exactly close enough for me to ask her to play hostage."

He didn't come out and say that she wasn't enough to

guarantee his cooperation. It was better to let them reach that conclusion on their own.

"I told you he was with a woman," said Buddy. "High heels in the backseat weren't big enough for Marshall here."

"I owe you twenty," said Horseshoe Head to Buddy. Then he looked at Clay. "Forget the woman. We'll all take a trip together."

"I don't think so," said Clay, lifting his weapon and training it on Horseshoe Head. "I'm the one with the gun. What's to keep me from shooting both of you?"

"No way you can hit both of us before we take you out." His voice was calm, laced with the certainty of a man who had nothing to prove. "And then there's the noise. One of those old fogies up top is bound to have their hearing aid in. The cops will shut the park down and you'll have no way out."

"Neither will you," said Clay.

"Doc will take care of us. You've gone rogue, so I doubt you can say the same thing." He opened his jacket, revealing his holstered weapon. "But I'm willing to chance it if you are."

The buzzing haze slid over his mind like a swarm of bees. His whole body vibrated with the urge to give in and let go.

With a snarl of rage, Clay fought back the compulsion. He would not lose control. He would not put Leigh in that kind of danger again.

Her path had circled around when he wasn't looking, and now the brush near Buddy was rustling in that all-too-familiar way. She was so close that he didn't dare fire on the man for fear of hitting her.

Clay wanted to scream at her to run. He had no idea what she thought she was doing sneaking up on an armed man like that. As the brush swayed slightly, her intent became all too clear. She was headed right into trouble.

He had to do something—take these men down or find a way to get them out of here. The only option he could think of was the one he had wanted most to avoid.

"Fine," he said, lowering his weapon. "Fifty thousand is no problem. Let's just go and get this over with. I have things to do."

Horseshoe Head gave him a good-natured grin. "That's the spirit. No reason for bloodshed among friends. Everyone gets what he wants."

"Except the doc," said Buddy.

Leigh had somehow managed to get close enough to Horseshoe Head that Clay could see her face through the dead weeds. Determination shaped her mouth, but her skin was pale with fear.

"Yeah, well, he's got it coming after that thing he had Marshall do last month."

Clay had no idea what the man was talking about, but he didn't dare ask any more questions. "We should go." And get away from Leigh as fast as possible.

Horseshoe Head waved his hand, indicating that Clay should go first. In that same moment, Leigh lunged out from her concealed position and hit Horseshoe Head in the back.

He pulled his weapon and swung around to face her. His spin went too far, and he started to tilt sideways. Leigh jumped back as he crashed into the brush. A syringe was sticking out of his ass.

Buddy drew steel and aimed for Leigh. Clay didn't think—he simply charged.

The buzzing in his head became a roar. As milliseconds passed and he flew through the air, he felt his control slipping away. Leigh had used her drugs on the other man. She had none left to stop Clay from hurting her again.

He couldn't give in to the noise and the pressure growing inside his skull. Not now, when she was so close.

Clay hit Buddy hard, taking him down. The gun flew away in a metallic spiral. Clay didn't see the fist coming toward his head, but he felt the jarring impact against his jaw. He'd been in enough fights to know better than to slow down and catalog the damage. Instead, he shot back with his own attack, going for a hard strike to the other man's throat.

Buddy rolled away, holding his neck. His face turned red and his mouth gaped open as he struggled to suck in air. Clay didn't wait for him to pass out. He slammed his elbow into the man's temple, rendering him unconscious. Chances were his throat was crushed and he wouldn't ever wake up, but after pointing a weapon at Leigh, it was exactly what he deserved.

Leigh scrambled from the brush and raced to where Clay stood. She was shaking hard, and so pale he could count every one of her freckles. Fear and horror haunted her dark eyes. Her hands fluttered over his face as if making sure she wasn't seeing things.

"Are you okay?"

Clay gave a tight nod. Adrenaline and rage were still riding him hard, making him want to lash out and crush something with his bare hands. The buzzing roar in his head was quieting more with every breath, but it wasn't gone yet. He had to fight it every step of the way, and until it was gone, he didn't trust himself.

He took a long step back, moving out of her reach. "Stay here," he barked. Then he went to each man, patting down their pockets. He found car keys, which he flung into the brush. The cash he pocketed. Their wallets, complete with their IDs, went into Clay's pocket for disposal elsewhere.

Leigh bent over Buddy, feeling for a pulse. "He's dead."

Clay said nothing. He simply grabbed Buddy by the arms and started dragging him into the woods.

She followed him. "What are you doing?"

"Someone could walk by at any minute. I'm not leaving their bodies out in the open."

"What about him?" she asked, pointing to Horseshoe Head. His ID had listed his name as Lew Argel, but the chances of that being his real name were slim.

Clay considered killing him—something he never would have done a few days ago. But a lot had happened in those few days, and Lew had seen Leigh. With Clay. If Lew was walking around, breathing, he was a threat to her.

"We could question him," she said. "He'll wake up in a few hours."

"And just how am I going to get him to the car without someone seeing him? We're sure as hell not going to hang out here for the next group of thugs to arrive. Whoever this doctor is, he apparently knows where I've been and that I'm retracing my steps. Staying here is too dangerous."

Leigh bit her lip in indecision. "I've got some stimulants in my bag. I could wake him. It's a risk, but seeing as how I've already assaulted him—"

"You're not touching that car—not until we know what they did to it."

"Okay. I'll stay with him. You go back and check out the car."

Clay wanted information. He wanted to know what Lew had meant when he'd talked about that thing the doctor had Clay do last month. Maybe knowing that would lead him back to the asshole pulling the strings.

And maybe it wouldn't.

The longer they were here, the greater the risk. Without a guarantee of information, the reward wasn't worth it. If it had been just Clay, he would have done it in a heartbeat, but Leigh was here, too. He had to remember that, even if it meant giving up a chance at information he desperately wanted.

Besides, he could tell she didn't want to do it. Guilt plagued her expression, and her posture had closed in, making her look smaller. He didn't want to be the jerk who pushed her to do illegal, unethical things simply because of something he wanted.

He'd find another way—one that didn't force Leigh to do bad things. She'd already done enough of those for him.

Including risk her life to knock Lew out. Clay shoved the memory from his immediate thoughts. He couldn't function with that kind of fear and fury churning through him. He had to concentrate on the job at hand and get both men out of sight of the trail before someone stumbled by.

Later, he promised himself, he'd let her know just how he felt about what she'd done. Later, he'd tell her how reckless she'd been, and how if she ever took that kind of risk again, he was going to tie her to a hotel bed somewhere and leave her there for the maids to find. By then he'd be long gone.

Of course, once the image of her splayed on a bed was in his head, it took on a life of its own.

Leigh was fucking with his concentration. Maybe she didn't mean to, but she was rattling him all the same. Cold and methodical. That's what he needed to be right now, but instead, his blood was running hot, his mind churning with fear that had the power to weaken him and make him hesitate.

The only thing he could think to do was pretend she wasn't there, so that's what he did. He slung Lew's limp body over his shoulder and hiked out into the woods.

Chapter Fourteen

Leigh was not a child. She was not an idiot. She'd done what needed to be done, and if Clay was too angry to see that, then screw him.

She tromped back to her car, being careful to keep an eye out for more strange cars. The lot was as she'd left it, with a couple of RVs and the shiny black Mustang parked near the exit.

Her belongings were still in the bathroom where she'd left them. She found a long stick and used a hair tie to attach her compact mirror to it. She wasn't sure what they'd done to her car, but that man hadn't been under there long enough to do much.

There were no puddles of fuel, coolant, or brake fluid. As she used the mirror to scan the undercarriage, she saw no obvious wires or hoses cut. What she did find was a cell phone duct taped in a shallow recess. There was nothing connected to it—no wires or bricks of plastic explosives.

Leigh scooted under the car far enough to see it better. The ground beneath her was frigid, and a rock was digging into her back. As gently as she could, she peeled back one side of the tape. The phone flopped down, dangling from the remaining tape.

There was definitely nothing else holding it on to her car, so she eased the tape free and shimmied out with the phone in her hand.

It was on. The GPS had been activated. Her guess was that they were planning to use it to track her car's location.

A quick scroll through text messages and calls revealed a fight with a girlfriend and a bet on some football game. There was voice mail, but without the password, Leigh couldn't listen to it. But maybe Mira, in all her technical glory, could.

Leigh removed the battery and slipped the phone into her suitcase. She'd ship it, along with the other two phones she'd collected, to Mira as soon as she could.

Clay came into view, and she could tell by his walk that he was furious. His steps carried none of his usual grace, and his chin was down as if he were getting set to charge. Before he could start screaming and draw attention to them, she got into the car and started it up. She'd just adjusted the seat so she could reach the pedals when he got in beside her.

"Before you throw a fit, I want you to know that I checked the car. They'd taped a phone to it. My guess is that they wanted to use the GPS to track us."

"I see," he said, his tone frighteningly calm. "You just crawled under there and checked it out."

"I used a mirror on a stick. I was careful."

"Like you were when you stabbed that man in the ass? Was that the kind of careful you were, Leigh?"

He had no right to be mad at her. "I did what I had to do to make sure you didn't get killed. Both of those men had guns. They would have shot you. I've seen gunshot wounds. I know what they can do to a body." And she couldn't tolerate the thought of seeing that kind of damage done to Clay. The mere idea made her stomach curl in with nausea.

"I had it under control."

Now it was her turn to be mad. Anger burned under her skin, heating it until she could feel the flush sweep over her. When she spoke, her voice was hot as well, aiming her boiling frustration right at him. "Like hell you did. You haven't been in control of yourself for weeks. Maybe longer. If you don't believe that, then you're fooling yourself and it's going to get both of us killed."

She put the car in gear and hit the road, too furious to sit still in the parking lot.

"You're free to walk away whenever you like. Now is good," he said.

"No. I do that and Garrett is doomed to stay in that prison forever. You're my best shot at seeing him free, so like it or not, you're stuck with me."

"You're just like the others, aren't you? Willing to use anyone at any time so long as you get your way."

"This isn't some petulant whim," she snapped, gripping the wheel tighter. "I already lost one brother, and I'm not going to let you force me to lose another."

"So instead, you're going to make him lose you, is that it?"

The speedometer hit eighty, and she eased up the pressure on the accelerator. "I'm the best chance he has, which means you're the best chance he has. If that means using you, then consider yourself used."

Clay fell silent. She didn't know where she was going, and she was too angry about his questioning her ability to ask. The miles flew by as she headed back toward Dallas. At the first major town, they stopped and she shipped the phones overnight to Mira. When she got back in the car, he was watching her with expectation. He squinted and shielded his eyes from the sun.

She said nothing in a petty effort to get back at him. Let him wonder what she was doing. Served him right.

"You're not going to tell me what that was about, are you?" he asked.

"Why should I? You've made it clear you don't want my help."

He closed his eyes and leaned his head back against the seat. His voice came out flat and defeated. "What I want and what I need are two different things."

"What's that supposed to mean?"

"It means that I need you, as much as I hate the idea. You're the only thing standing between me and a strait-jacket."

He still hadn't looked at her. His eyes were closed, and his hand covered them as if the light hurt. Now that she looked at him closely, she could see brackets of pain etched around his mouth and a fine tremor in his fingers.

"Did you get hurt back there?"

"It's just a headache."

"I have aspirin in my purse."

"No, I'll puke those up. This one's bad."

"You say that like you've been through this before."

"I have. It happens sometimes, after the blackouts."

"But you didn't black out. Did you?"

"No, but it was close."

She pondered that, wondering about the implications. "Do you remember what made you feel like you were going to . . . you know."

"Go batshit crazy?" he asked, not lifting his head. "Yeah. I saw that fucker pull a gun on you. I almost lost it right there."

"You were afraid?"

"Understatement of the decade."

"Do you think that it's fear that makes you lose it?"

He let out a long sigh laced with pain. "I don't know, Leigh. And don't take this the wrong way, but right now, it's all I can do to keep from puking all over your car. I'm not up for any complicated puzzles."

Garrett and Hollis had headaches like this, too. None of the meds they'd tried had worked. All that helped was a cool, dark, quiet room.

Leigh found a small motel and got a room out of sight of the street. She got him inside, pulled the curtains. It was too dangerous to leave the door open, so she turned on the AC unit so that it poured cold air into the stuffy room. Clay put his gun on the bedside table and collapsed face-first onto the bed.

"I could give you something for the headache," she told him.

"I'll be fine in a few minutes, and I can't afford to be slowed by drugs right now."

She accepted his decision and pulled his boots and socks from his feet. She doused a washcloth in cold water and draped it over the back of his neck to help with the nausea.

He didn't fight her, which told her louder than words just how much he was suffering.

Leigh felt helpless, and she was no good at that. She had to do something, to fix the problem. She couldn't just sit around and watch him hurt.

His whole body was tense, which probably wasn't helping matters. Minute vibrations ran through his forearms, tightening muscles and tendons.

Leigh stroked his arm, hoping her light touch would soothe him in some small way.

He groaned into the pillow, giving her wordless permission to keep touching.

The hair along his arm was soft. His skin was hot beneath her fingertips. She increased the pressure slowly until she was kneading away the tension from the bandages at his wrist to his elbow. The sleeve of his sweatshirt was pushed up, its bulky fabric barring her path. Her fingers inched under the fabric but couldn't go far.

Clay sat up enough to pull both shirts off over his head, stripping himself to the waist.

Leigh's breath caught in her throat. It wasn't his action that surprised her as much as it was the trust he'd offered. He hated doctors. He knew she had the power to disable him and that she'd already done so twice. It would be nothing for her to do so again.

The temptation to go against his wishes and give him something for the pain was nearly a compulsion. She hated his suffering. But if she drugged him, she'd snap that fragile thread of trust he'd extended to her, likely forever. So rather than following her need to ease his pain, Leigh followed her instincts and simply accepted his silent invitation to touch him.

The wide expanse of his back should not have been as intriguing as it was. She'd seen plenty of naked men before, but never had they made her feel this kind of quivering weakness. As cold as the room was, he seemed to radiate heat. The aging AC unit hummed beneath the window, as loud as her frantic pulse beating in her ears.

Leigh stroked his back, petting him. She was careful of the colorful bruises along his ribs, barely grazing over them. The tightly corded muscles flanking his spine began to loosen after a few minutes. His breathing deepened and evened into that of sleep.

She could have stopped touching him. She probably should have stopped touching him. But she liked the feel of his skin beneath her hand too much. The subtle dips and contours of his back and the changes in the temperature of his skin intrigued her. She couldn't remember the last time she'd been with a man like this. Maybe she never had. It wasn't wholly sexual, but it wasn't completely innocent, either. At least not if the tingling heat sliding through her was any indication.

Leigh was no longer chilly, even with the arctic air blowing from the vents. A melting warmth spread through her limbs and curled in her belly. The feeling was as intoxicating as it was inconvenient. Desire had been absent from her life for a long time. She'd been focused solely on finding help for Garrett, with little time for a social life. And the few dates she'd been on hadn't evoked even a fraction of the languid need she felt now.

Not that she would act on it. Wanting something and taking it were two distinct and separate things, and she refused to do anything that might jeopardize Garrett's freedom. Or Clay's. If they failed to find the person behind his blackouts, she knew that Clay would end up locked in a cell next to her brother's.

That hard fact cooled her libido and sent blood racing to her brain, where it belonged.

The best thing for Clay now was sleep. And it was best for her, too. Knowing he was no longer suffering eased something inside her, allowing her to relax fractionally.

Leigh forced herself to leave his side and got off the bed. There wasn't a whole lot she could do, so she grabbed the thick stack of pages of data Mira had compiled and sat down at the little round table by the window. She cracked the curtains open to let in enough light to read and started scanning the numbers.

A few hours later, she started noticing a pattern. The tiny notepad by the phone became filled with coordinates and dates as she made connections from one week to the next. She was so excited by her discovery that she briefly considered waking Clay to tell him. Even as she discarded the idea, her gaze strayed from the pages to where he lay sleeping on the bed. Only he wasn't sleeping anymore. He was watching her.

"How do you feel?" she asked.

"Better."

He was on his side, his arm curled under the pillow. The sight of his bare chest captured her attention. She'd seen it before but was still mesmerized by how beautifully he was built. Lean muscles shifted along his ribs and abdomen as he sat up, making her fingers itch with the need to touch him again.

She cast her gaze back to the paper in front of her, seeing none of the numbers she knew were there. His image still blazed in her mind, so bright it cast a shadow over everything else.

"You're cold," he said.

She had been a moment ago, but not any longer. Her internal thermostat had kicked in, heating her from the inside out. "I'm okay."

He got off the bed and reached past her to turn off the AC unit. She felt his warmth, smelled his skin, as he drew close. His was a familiar scent now—one that had the power to excite her in ways no other man's ever had. She knew he was dangerous, but she'd also seen the gentler side of him. The wounded side.

It called to her on a deep level—one she hated admitting she had. She was too smart to want a broken man in her life, and yet the idea of turning him away left her dissatisfied and empty.

Maybe she was the one who was broken.

Leigh could feel him hovering nearby. He hadn't moved away. She could see his bare feet in her peripheral vision and had to steel herself against the need to let her gaze wander up his legs.

Her hair shifted, and it took her a second to realize that he'd touched it. She froze, unsure of what she felt. The strands tugged against her scalp again, and his fingertips brushed across the nape of her neck.

Her hair was probably a wreck. It always was when she didn't keep it tied back and under control.

Self-conscious of her appearance, she glanced up at him. Rather than finding an amused grin at how ridiculous she looked, what greeted her was an expression of sheer enjoyment.

"I wondered what that would feel like," he said.

"What?" she squeaked out between too-rapid breaths.

"Running my fingers through your hair."

While she watched, he did it again, only this time his fingers glided along her scalp, setting off nerve endings no brush had ever managed to spark.

The urge to close her eyes and moan in pleasure nearly choked her, but she was able to utter a lame apology. "It tangles easily. Sorry."

"Don't be. It gives me an excuse to touch it." He said it like he'd thought of touching it before—like he was thinking about doing so again.

Leigh was confused by the shift from his earlier anger and pain to this quieter side. "What's gotten into you?"

"When the headache goes away, it's like . . . flying."

Concern flickered through the rational side of her mind, while the rest of her put the focus squarely on the gentle, repetitive tug on her scalp.

She stood up. With no room for the chair to move in the cramped space, she was forced to step forward, which put her only inches from his body.

He didn't step back. If anything, he swayed forward slightly and pulled in a deep breath.

Leigh risked a glance at his face. His jaw was tight, but it wasn't the same tension that had been riding him before. This was different. It was hotter and more fluid, somehow. Before his suffering had been obvious, but now that was gone, leaving behind a thrumming kind of pressure that had nothing to do with pain.

His hands slipped from her hair to her shoulders and stayed there. His gaze dipped down to her breasts, the amber in his eyes darkened to a rich bronze. He licked his lips, and his fingertips tightened slightly over her shoulders.

Watching his tongue move over his mouth felt like striking a match. Something small but fierce flared to life inside her, lighting up all the spaces that had gone for too long without heat. One small breeze would make it go out, and she didn't want that.

She was going to kiss him. She didn't know if he wanted it or not, but the compulsion to feel his lips against hers was too much for her to fight. Once she knew what it was like, her curiosity would be satisfied, and she'd be able to concentrate again.

Leigh went up on tiptoe and pressed a small, chaste kiss against the corner of his mouth. His whole body went still for a moment. He stared down at her and his jaw bulged as if he was holding himself back.

"Do that again." His tone was hard, making his words either a demand or a dare.

Leigh didn't care which. She pressed her hands against his bare chest to steady herself and kissed him again. Only this time, there was nothing chaste about it. She flicked her tongue across his lower lip, lingering as she tasted him.

Clay shuddered. His hands moved over her—one going up to cup the back of her head and the other sliding down to press against the small of her back.

Contained strength was evident in his hold. His arms didn't move, but his fingers curled against her, drawing her fractionally closer. Restraint vibrated through him, like electricity through high-tension wires. He surrounded her with hard heat. Only his mouth was soft.

He made no move to kiss her back. She would have

thought it was because he wasn't interested, but the thick bulge of his erection pressing against her abdomen proved otherwise.

"Why won't you kiss me?" she asked.

"Because if I do, I'm afraid I'll scare you away."

She didn't know what he meant by that—she didn't scare easily—but she desperately wanted to find out. He'd offered her a wickedly delightful challenge, and she was more than up for it.

Leigh smiled as she rose on tiptoe again. "Do you want me to stop?"

His voice was a rough whisper. "God no."

She needed no further encouragement.

Her lips met his, and she toyed with him, nibbling at the edges of his mouth. She tasted him again, sliding the tip of her tongue along the seam where his lips were pressed closed.

She needed him to open for her so she could get what she wanted. She wasn't entirely sure what that was, but she could feel the prize dangling there, just out of reach.

Leigh sucked on his bottom lip, pressing her teeth against the soft skin just hard enough for him to feel them.

He changed in an instant, as if a switch had been flipped. His restraint evaporated and his hold tightened, jerking her against him from chest to thigh. Heat poured off him. His mouth opened, and his tongue plunged past her lips as if staking a claim.

A moan of surrender rose from deep in his chest, vibrating her nipples so that they tightened almost painfully. Desire spun through her in a dizzying rush. She clung to his hard shoulders and tried to find enough oxygen to stay upright.

Clay's mouth moved over hers as if he'd been starved all his life and her kiss was the only thing that could feed him. His hands slid through her hair as he held her head, refusing to let her withdraw.

He kissed the way he fought—taking complete control over the situation and bending it to his will, with hard, fast force. Not that she was complaining. Toying with him had been fun, but this . . . this was overwhelming pleasure, potent desire. It consumed her and left her panting for more. She gave in to the rush, letting it wash over her as he worked his magic, making her go soft inside even as he drew her tighter.

His hands slid between them, working at her buttons. She was all for it. The idea of rubbing her bare breasts against his hot chest compelled her to help him speed up the process of getting naked.

Her hands were shaking too hard to be of much use, and after what seemed like forever, he finally gave up and jerked her shirt open, popping the last few buttons free. One clicked against the table. She didn't care where it had fallen, not when Clay was looking down at her now with lust darkening his skin.

She still had her bra on. It wasn't anything fancy, and yet the way he was looking at her now made it feel like the sexiest lingerie ever stitched together.

He slid one finger along her skin, just above the lacy edge of the cups. His breath came out heavy and hot, expanding his chest until the sight blocked out all else.

Leigh smoothed her hands over his pecs, feeling the racing of his heart beneath. Clay's fingers slid down her torso and came to rest on the button of her slacks. He tilted her head up, a silent question in his amber eyes. She nodded and was rewarded with a slight tug as the button worked free. Her zipper hissed down, barely audible over their rapid breathing.

Clay turned her around until her back was pressed against his chest. He moved her hair aside and kissed the skin just below her ear. She shivered in response, her whole body lighting up with the need for more of his mouth.

He held her in place with one arm looped around her, just below her breasts. She wanted to scream at him to finish stripping her bare, but the words were stolen as his teeth scraped along her throat.

Raw, sizzling sensation soared through her, making her knees sag. Clay held her up and forced her higher with swirling licks of his tongue and sharp little bites.

The collar of her shirt scraped across the nape of her neck, slipping down to bare her shoulders. He kissed every inch of her skin as it was exposed, until she was shaking from the constant barrage of pleasure.

His hand grazed her belly, moving lower until the very tips of his fingers were poised over her mound, above her panties. Another inch lower and he'd be able to feel what he'd done to her—how wet he made her.

Her hips bucked forward. She wasn't sure if she'd done it on purpose or if her instincts were driving her now. Whatever the case, his middle finger fluttered across her swollen clitoris, setting her whole world on fire.

She let out a whimpering howl of need, ashamed by the noise even as she reveled in his reaction to it. His erection jerked against the small of her back, hard and insistent.

Leigh wanted him. This was no longer a game of challenge. Nor was it something to prove to him that she wasn't going to be scared away. His kisses and touches had pushed her past all of that, into a realm where need and desire ruled all else.

His finger moved in a slow circle over her clit. The fabric of her panties irritated her. She needed his skin on her skin so badly she could think of nothing else. She grabbed his hand and shoved it inside her panties, showing him what she wanted.

His growl of approval was overridden by her own sharp gasp of pleasure. He parted her labia, sliding easily along the slick folds.

His touch was better than she could have imagined. His fingers were burning hot and slightly rough, creating a delicious friction that became the center of her universe. He cupped her breast, and she couldn't find enough coherent speech to tell him to take her bra off. And she certainly couldn't do it herself—not when she was trembling like this, strung tight and clinging to his hard thighs in an effort to stay upright.

Clay's fingers stroked her with expert skill, dipping and sliding until she was hovering on the verge of orgasm. She tried to hold it off. She didn't want him to know the kind of power he had over her body. It was an unfair advantage—one he would doubtlessly use against her if he thought it was for her own good. If he came with her, then the playing field would be even. Her advantage would equal his.

She tried to turn around so she could get his jeans off. All she needed was a moment to gather herself and ease back down off the cliff. But Clay didn't let her have it. He held her in place, his arms tight vices around her hips and ribs.

"I want this," he told her, his breath sliding along her throat where his lips and teeth kept working their stinging little miracles.

His fingers sped their wicked pace, and he lightly pinched her nipple through the lacy layers of her bra. Searing sensation shot through her, connecting his teeth and fingers with pulsing arcs of electricity. Leigh gasped and arched, no longer able to stop herself from falling. She tumbled headlong into the first wave of her climax, crashing hard.

Her body convulsed in his grip, completely out of control. She heard the mewling sounds of pleasure she made but could not stop them from pouring from her mouth. Clay didn't pull back—instead he pushed her higher, forcing her to feel every throbbing second of her release, drawing it out as long as possible.

When the last wave lapped over her skin, all her strength fled. She let herself go, trusting Clay to hold her up.

He swept her into his arms and laid her back on the bed. The look on his face was one of pure male conquest. At any other time, it would have irritated her, but right now, with her body still humming from what he'd done, she felt he deserved to be wearing that look. It suited him, and with any luck at all, she'd get to see him look at her like that again very soon.

Clay's gaze fixed on her mouth, then slipped down to her breasts. That expression of hunger made her want to jerk the bra from her body so she could watch him as she bared herself completely.

He drew circles over her skin, slipping just below the lacy edge.

Leigh pulled her shirt off and reached behind her to unhook her bra. Before she'd finished the job, she saw him go utterly still. His expression of lust disappeared, leaving behind a layer of disgust.

She went cold instantly, wondering what it was he'd seen in her that had put him off so completely. She followed his gaze, wondering if she'd developed some giant hairy mole or something. Instead, she saw the dark bruises circling her arms—the ones he'd left on her the night they'd met.

Clay stumbled back from the bed as if it had spouted spiders. "I did that to you, didn't I?"

"I'm fine." She tried to make her voice reassuring, but she was still thrumming with the languid effects of her orgasm, with little blood left in her brain to make things come out right.

He closed his eyes, anguish tightening his features. Gone was the flush of lust that she loved to see, and in its place was the cold chill of self-loathing.

Clay grabbed his sweatshirt and shoes from where they'd been tossed earlier and made a beeline for the door. "I'm sorry," he said, his back to her as he fumbled with the locks and staggered out into the cold.

Chapter Fifteen

Clay hadn't been this foolish since he was a teenager with more dick than brains. How the hell could he have let things with her go that far? If not for those unexpected bruises, he would have slept with her—after having hurt her just a couple of days ago. That concept was so fucked-up, he couldn't even begin to wrap his head around it.

The cold air outside the room slapped him in the face, helping him shed some of the heat she'd generated in him. He had no idea where he was going, but once he had his feet and chest covered, he started walking, putting some distance between him and Leigh.

She'd been so responsive, so hot in his arms, that he was sure she'd set him on fire. All he'd been able to think about was getting his cock in her and making her give him that sweet cry of surrender as she came again.

As long as he lived, he'd never forget that sound. He'd never forget the liquid heat of her spilling over his fingers, or the way she arched into him, silently begging for more. Even now, as disgusted as he was with himself, thoughts of her still had the power to leave him iron hard and throbbing.

Her scent clung to him, rising to meet his nose with every breath. A hint of arousal was mixed in with the lighter scent of her skin, mingling together in a way he was sure was designed to drive him mad. The short trip to the edge of sanity was at least one he could enjoy, unlike the darker, more dangerous path he was on now.

Clay tucked his head down, put the hood of his sweatshirt up, and headed down the street, away from the cluster of restaurants nearby. He didn't dare go inside where it was warm or speak to anyone, but he couldn't go back to that room, either. Not yet. Not until his head was clear and screwed on straight. And sure as hell not before she was dressed again, covered from head to toe.

Just the memory of her breasts barely restrained by that bra was enough to leave him breathless. It was good that he'd stopped things before they'd gone any further, but he violently regretted not having taken the opportunity to see her naked breasts. Then again, if she had been bare, he wasn't sure he would have found the strength to walk away. He'd be balls-deep inside her right now, blissing out, all for the low, low cost of the dwindling scrap of self-respect he still had.

Maybe it would have been worth it.

A cold front had moved through, whipping up the wind and sinking into his shirt to suck away the heat Leigh had generated. He sped his pace, but it did nothing to stave off the shivers racking him.

He heard a car engine right behind him, keeping pace with his speedy walk. He didn't need to glance over his shoulder to know it was Leigh. She was too caring to leave him walking out in the cold for long.

"Get in," she called through the open window.

No way. Not yet. He wasn't ready to be that close to her, trapped in the car, where her scent could tease him right back into stupidity. "I need to clear my head."

"It's too cold."

"I'm fine."

"You're shivering. Just get in."

He moved toward the car and she pulled to a stop. Rather than getting in, he bent down to the window. Beneath her jacket, he could see broken threads sprouting from her blouse where a button had once been.

Another wave of guilt hit him. He'd treated her too roughly, tearing her clothes like some kind of barbarian.

"I need some time alone, Leigh. I'll come back to the room in a little while. I promise."

Her lips flattened with frustrated indecision. "I didn't mean to hurt you."

"You didn't. And I really can't talk about this right now. Just let it go, okay? Please?"

She nodded, and he hated the look of desolation that haunted her dark eyes. "At least take your jacket."

It was lying on the front seat. He reached in and grabbed it, more to make her feel better than anything. The cold kept his thoughts focused on something other than the heat that had built between them.

"Don't be too long," she said.

"I won't," he promised.

"If you're not back in an hour, I'm coming to look for you."

She drove off. Clay checked his watch. He really didn't want her to worry about him, and she was too soft not to. Maybe it was her profession that made her so caring— though the doctors he'd known had been so cold and cynical they wouldn't know what caring looked like if they sat on it. Whatever the case, she wasn't like them. She was risking her life for him, and while maybe her motivations were focused around her brother, Clay still had to own up to the fact that he was also benefiting from her selflessness.

His knee-jerk reaction was to push her away—to drive her off so far she'd never come back. But his fear was that she'd continue to pursue those responsible for his blackouts on her own. She had the list of coordinates. She had the car. There was nothing stopping her from taking off and doing this without him. He'd heard what those thugs in the park had said about a price on his head and this doctor asshole sending people to find him in the places he'd been before. The thought of her walking into a trap set by one of them scared the shit out of him.

Clay turned on his heel and headed right back for the motel. By the time he got there, he'd run through at least a dozen nightmares where Leigh was gone and tossing herself into danger. When he shoved his way through the door to find her sitting on the bed, he nearly sagged with relief.

She looked up from where she was sewing a button on her shirt. Her hair was damp around the edges, her face scrubbed clean. She wore modest cotton pajamas with little blue puppies on them. They were faded and baggy, but he could clearly see the outline of her nipples scrunched tight against the fabric.

"I bought some sandwiches," she said, throwing him a neutral lifeline. No heavy questions, no deep conversation. Just food.

"Thanks," he said, meaning more than just for the food.

She nodded and went back to her button, ignoring him as if he'd vanished.

Clay couldn't tell whether she was mad or offering him the space he'd so desperately asked for. The need to figure out which drove him toward her.

"Have you eaten?" he asked.

She shook her head. "I waited for you."

He washed his hands, ridding them of her scent, and dug into the bag, willing to accept whatever she offered. If she wanted him to eat, he'd eat. If she wanted him to bark like a dog, he would have done that, too. Anything to break this awkwardness between them.

Until now he hadn't realized just how much he'd begun to enjoy her presence. She was easy to be around—at least when he wasn't struggling to control himself. She wasn't like so many women, throwing his mistakes in his face so that he had no choice but to choke on them.

Clay set out the food. "Which do you want?"

"I like them all. You pick."

He grabbed one of the turkey sandwiches and scooted it to the far side of the table. She watched him, accepting his silent invitation to come and sit with him.

Leigh said nothing as she ate, and Clay did his best not to stare at her mouth. He finished off one sandwich and eyed a second.

"Go ahead. You're still hungry. I got what I wanted."

The way she said it, with lingering softness, made him wonder if she was talking about the food or something else.

He'd made it through half of the last sandwich before he could no longer take the silence. "I'm sorry."

She wrapped her lips around her straw and drank. "About what? Kissing me and making me come or leaving like you hated it?"

"Both, I guess. If I hadn't kissed you, there would have been no need to leave. And I didn't hate it. Not one second." If he thought it was safe for her, he'd do it again in a heartbeat and count himself lucky.

"You didn't have to leave. At least not on my behalf." Her gaze met his, and he could see now that she was angry. She was holding it back, hiding it, but he could see it flickering there in her eyes.

"We both know that what we did was a bad idea. We're working together. That has to come first."

"Meaning there can be no second? I don't know about you, but I'm fully capable of multitasking."

He just bet she was, and the images that presented were enough to make his mouth go dry with lust.

Clay took a swig of soda. "But I'm not. My brain is all fucked-up. I'm struggling to stay sane here, and I can't fight these compulsions I keep feeling *and* my desire to sleep with you."

"All the more reason not to fight it. Your desire, I mean."

"I could hurt you again." And that was his true shame. "Seeing those bruises on your arms . . . it reminded me of just how out of control I really am. I don't know what's going to set me off. If I went all batshit while I was with you like that, I'd never forgive myself."

"Do you really think that sleeping with me will trigger that side of you? Does that make any sense at all?"

"Maybe not, but it's not worth the risk of hurting you again."

She let out a humorless laugh. "Then you've never felt the way you made me feel. Pleasure like that is worth a hell of a lot of risk."

Her praise went to his head and then straight to his cock. It swelled, making its desires known with painful effectiveness. "We should drop this line of conversation. I like you too much to take risks with you. Please, just leave it at that."

She didn't nod or make any sign that she agreed, but she pushed a notepad toward him, sliding it across the little table. "I saw a pattern in the coordinates. I think I know where we should go next."

He flipped through the pages, taking note of how much work she'd done while he'd slept. "I'm not sure how safe it is to go anywhere at this point. You heard what those men said. This doctor guy is hunting for me, sending people where he thinks I might go."

"So we just sit around here? I don't see how that's going to help."

"It won't." Clay expelled a long sigh that did nothing to relieve his tension.

"Wherever this place is, you went there a lot. In fact, you went there almost as often as you went home or to work. See?" She held out the stack of pages and flipped through them. "Everywhere there is an X is when you went here."

There were a hell of a lot of Xs.

"I think we should check it out," she said.

"We could be walking into a trap."

"At least this time we'll know what to expect. That makes it about as safe as it can be."

"I don't like it."

"I know, but there's no way to know how much time you have. If that doctor put something in your head to make you go back to him, then we have to do this now."

"Do you really think that's possible?"

Leigh shrugged, and he tried not to watch her breasts jiggle under her shirt. The stupid little blue puppies should have been a huge turnoff, but all he could think about was how he wished he could be one of them right now, nuzzling up against her chest.

"At this point anything is possible. I'm keeping a dose of tranquilizer handy in case you start to wander off. That's part of the reason I was so freaked-out earlier. I was afraid you weren't yourself."

"I'm sorry I scared you."

"Forget it. Water under the bridge. We need to move forward. Garrett needs me to move forward. So do those kids."

Clay had tried not to think about them. Knowing they were out there ate at him in a way he wasn't sure he was strong enough to take. He'd shoved his worry deep, burying it as far down as he could. Her mentioning them made helpless fury rise to the surface, forcing him to start the process of shoving his rage and fear down all over again. "Okay, then. We'll go here next."

"It's not far. It's a storage facility pretty close to your house."

"We should go in after dark."

She held up her hands. "This is your area of expertise. You plan and I'll follow along. Right after you let me change your bandages."

"They're fine. I'll just—"

"Nope," she said, cutting him off. "This is my area of expertise, and you're going to shut up and let me keep you healthy."

She was going to put her hands on him again and make him crazy, and there wasn't a single excuse he could think of to make her back off. Best just to have it over and done so he could shove his head into planning their next move—one that involved as little touching as possible.

Adam stood in Clay Marshall's living room, searching for something that would lead to him.

The place was Spartan, coated in dust, as if no one had bothered to really clean for months. A trio of empty beer bottles littered a scarred coffee table. The couch was worn, with sad, flat cushions dented in the shape of a big man. A pillow and blanket sat rumpled at one end of the couch, as if someone had slept here.

An obvious bachelor pad; there were no decorations or softer touches—just dingy white walls and mismatched furniture. The flat-screen TV was new and too big for the room, sitting on the hearth, blocking the fireplace. Power cords stretched across the dated shag carpet to reach what few electrical outlets there were.

This was not a home, but a place where one could sleep and eat in solitude. One of the bedrooms was empty. The other had only a bed, a dresser, and one nightstand. There were few dishes in the cabinets, and those looked like something picked up from a variety of garage sales ten years ago.

Clay Marshall didn't live here; he merely subsisted.

Adam had researched him and knew the man had enough money to live much better than he did, which begged the question of why he lived like this. It was almost as if he were punishing himself.

Not that Adam cared. Marshall was simply a tool to use—one that would pry from Dr. Sage the name of the brother Adam had lost. Now all he needed was another tool that would dig up Marshall from wherever he was hiding.

Adam had almost given up on finding one here when he saw what he was looking for. There, mounted next to the door, was a framed photo that had been kept in pristine condition. No dust or cobwebs, it hung perfectly straight, right where Marshall would see it every time he left the house. The position indicated that it wasn't here for guests, but for the man himself to see.

Adam pulled the frame from the wall and pulled the photo out. On the back was scribbled, *Mira and me on her twenty-third birthday.*

The couple on the front was smiling. Marshall's arm was around this pretty young woman. She leaned into him, complete trust evident in her pose, and for some reason, it made Adam wish that anyone trusted him half as much as Mira trusted Marshall.

There was something familiar about her.

Her canted eyes. He'd seen eyes that exact shade of green before—bright, with a starburst of vibrant gold radiating out from the center. A familiar, keen intelligence glittered in her eyes, only he didn't remember ever feeling as drawn in by them as he was now.

Data shifted in Adam's mind, changing shape as he went through images and names of people he knew, searching for where he'd seen Mira.

And then it hit him. He hadn't seen her before. He'd seen her father, years ago. They had the same eyes.

This photo was of Mira Sage, daughter to Dr. Richard Sage—the man who'd sent him to find Marshall.

Adam wondered how Dr. Sage was going to feel when Adam used his daughter as a tool. Perhaps the same way Adam felt about the good doctor using Eli as one.

Sometimes karma did work.

Chapter Sixteen

The coordinates led Clay and Leigh to a storage facility that had seen better days. The asphalt was cracked, with dead weeds poking out around the edges. A rolling gate barred their path, but the ground had settled, making the latch not quite close.

"Are you sure you don't want to wait in the car?" asked Clay.

"I'm sure."

"I'm getting set to do something illegal."

She gave him a pointed look, trying to stifle the guilt her admission caused. "I've committed assault on at least one person a day since meeting you. A little breaking and entering doesn't seem like such a big deal."

"Assault?"

"Giving drugs to people without their consent? Yeah. Big no-no. If anyone reports me, I'll lose my medical license."

"You don't sound too worried."

Oh, she was worried, all right, but her decision was made years ago, the first time Payton came to her with a gunshot wound he didn't want her to report. He'd offered to pay her brother's enormous legal fees in exchange for her silence. She'd accepted. Patyon's expensive lawyer took over the case and proved Hollis's death had been a suicide. Garrett had been acquitted of murdering his brother. The price—going against her principles—had been worth the reward.

Not that Garrett's life was much better now than it would have been if he'd been convicted of murder. He was still locked up in a secret facility, cut off from the world, and refused to come out until they found a cure for what had been done to him. Which she would find. She had to believe that.

Leigh couldn't look Clay in the eye. "If it means help- ing my brother, then it's worth it. After all, he was the one who put me through med school to begin with. Seems fair somehow."

"You're a good sister. I'm sure Garrett appreciates what you do for him." Clay covered her hand with his, sending a barrage of delicious shivers marching up her arm. She was sure he hadn't intended to offer anything but comfort, but her rebellious hormones could only re- member how those fingers had made her feel a few hours ago.

"Actually, he wishes I'd quit trying to help him. He says he's a lost cause." She forced herself to look at Clay, hoping he hadn't interpreted her statement wrong—that she could ever believe for one second that giving up was the right thing to do. "He's not, you know. I believe that."

Clay nodded and pulled his hand away. "Then it's best if we get in there and see what we can find. I just pray to God it's not a pile of dead bodies I hid in there."

That thought was enough to chill any lingering heat from his contact. She kept forgetting what Clay was like when he checked out and left his body—when that other man took over and turned him cold and hollow.

He moved the car to the parking lot of a neighboring

grocery store and they walked over to the storage facility. The gate opened with a slight push, and once they
slipped in, he shut it behind them, using a chunk of rock
left for that purpose to hold it closed.

"I haven't seen anyone on our tail, but keep your eyes
open," he said.

"There's a camera mounted on the side of the office."

"It's probably not monitored. My guess is it's there as
a deterrent more than for active surveillance. That model
is too old for Web-based monitoring, and there's no one
inside."

The office building was mostly dark, with just one
light left burning over the front desk. There were no
signs of movement inside, or any that she could see out
here.

"Do you know which unit we're looking for?"

"Nope. But if I was wanting to do secret stuff, I'd pick
one near the back, away from prying eyes."

He moved purposefully, checking behind him every
few steps to make sure she was still there and that no one
was following them. His vigilance scared her more than
a little, but so far he hadn't shown any signs of tension or
fear. He was clearly in his element now, slinking around
in the dark with possible danger lurking around every
corner.

Leigh, on the other hand, didn't like the jarring bursts
of adrenaline at all. They made her jumpy and queasy.
She had no idea how Clay could stand it.

He came to a sudden stop and went still.

She looked around, sure someone had jumped out,
but saw nothing. "Clay?"

His posture changed, and all that relaxed smoothness
seemed to spill out of him. His spine went rigid and he
reached into his pocket. As he stared down at the keys,
unmoving, Leigh started to worry.

She slid in front of him and shone her flashlight so its glow splashed onto his face. "Clay? What's going on?"

"I know where we're going." He sounded shocked and sickened at the same time.

"Where?"

"This way."

He led the way down the rest of the row into the deep shadows at the end. The security light here was broken. Not just burned out, but shattered, as if someone had bashed it out—or shot it.

He singled out a key and slid it into the heavy-duty padlock on one of the units. It went in easily, turning without effort.

"Stand back," he said and waited until she did as he asked before he hefted the overhead door up along its track.

Lights came on automatically. Clay aimed his weapon, moving it as he sought out a target.

"There's no one here," she said. "The lights must be motion activated or something."

A desk sat in the back corner of the unit, complete with a single chair. One section of wall was covered with corkboard. Clinging to it were dozens of photos and sticky notes. A bunch of boxes were stacked across one half of the opening, forming a sort of wall.

Clay stepped inside, caution dripping from him. He looked overhead and low to the ground as if searching for traps. His flashlight beam gleamed off a thin wire near the floor. "Trip wire. Stay out there."

He didn't need to tell her twice. She kept an eye down the row of storage units, making sure no one had found them.

Going only so far as the threshold, she watched as he crouched behind the boxes with his pocketknife in hand.

"What are you doing?"

"Disconnecting the trigger device from the explosives. Move out to the other end of the row—just to be safe."

Leigh took a terrified step back, nearly stumbling over her own feet. If she hadn't ditched the slick, dressy shoes and bought a pair of nice, grippy tennis shoes earlier, she would have fallen. "Explosives? Are you kidding me?"

"No, but I built this device."

He built it? Theoretically, she knew he was a badass, but she figured he was more like a bodyguard than some kind of demolitions expert. "What the hell is it you do at your job?" she asked.

"Little of this. Little of that. I'll be done in a second. After you move away."

The last thing she wanted to do was distract him, so she did what he asked and hurried several yards away. As the seconds ticked by, the muscles in the back of her neck started to clench with worry.

He was in there, risking his life like it was no big deal—like his life was of little value. That was how Hollis had acted, too, right before he'd killed himself.

"All done," he called out.

Leigh ran back, anxious to see him alive and well with her own eyes.

He stood up, pocketing his knife. "Come in and get out of the wind."

She wasn't sure she wanted to go in there, but standing out here in the open, backlit like she was, wasn't the safest option, either.

Leigh took a deep breath and stepped inside. Clay reached high and slid the door down behind her. He shoved the padlock through a metal plate on the inside of the door—one she was fairly sure wasn't a standard feature on these units—and bolted them inside.

As she became aware that she was locked up with a man who was not always so nice, an uneven attack of anxiety hit her.

He watched her, and the subtle frown of acceptance told her that he'd read her thoughts.

His voice was low and soft, as if speaking to a wild animal. "I'm not trying to trap you in here with me, Leigh. I don't want anyone to see the light and start nosing around. Say the word and you can leave anytime you want." He held out the keys to her.

She took them, mute. They jangled in her grasp, giving away how unsettling this whole situation was to her. Not only was being in here nerve-racking, but being anywhere in a small, enclosed space with Clay had the power to steal her breath away. It made her all too aware of his size and power. While part of her was still clamoring with fear, the rest of her was perking up to attention, watching for an opportunity to get them right back to where they'd been earlier, with his hands drawing the kind of pleasure from her she'd never forget.

That she could even think of sex right now proved she was crazy.

"I'm okay. Just jumpy."

"You've got those drugs with you, right?"

She patted her jacket pocket and nodded.

"Good. One wrong look from me, and you use them. I won't hold it against you later, okay?"

For some reason, that made her feel better. While she wouldn't have done anything differently, there was still a small part of her that felt guilty for drugging him. His acceptance made that guilt lighten. She'd been carrying around so much lately that until now she hadn't realized just how much her failure to help Garrett had been weighing on her.

Clay went to the wall of photos and notes. The light

from the desk shone over them, leaving dark shadows lingering behind the curled edges. "This is my handwriting, but I have no idea who these people in the photos are."

Leigh unpinned one from the wall. It was a photo of a white man in his thirties. He was looking to his left, and the angle of the shot was high, as if it had been taken from a rooftop or window. "He doesn't look like he's posing. I doubt he even knew his picture had been taken."

She turned it over. All that was on the back was a date—one she remembered as being a day when Clay had lost time.

"Did you write this?" she asked, showing him the back.

"Yeah. I did. Not that I remember." He moved away and went to the desk and started rifling through the drawers.

The notes were cryptic, most listing single words that meant nothing to her. *Zebra, cantaloupe, mountain.* "Any idea what the words are all about?"

"None. But I found a camera. Step back and let me take a photo before we start taking stuff down. The position may be important."

"We should call Payton." The prepaid cell she'd bought earlier, when she'd stopped for shoes and jeans, was tucked in her pocket.

Clay nodded. "Yeah. Maybe he'll know what all of this means."

Leigh made the call while he took the SD card out of the camera and slipped it into his wallet. He started opening boxes just as Payton answered.

"Yes?"

"It's Leigh. We think we found something. Can you meet us?"

"Where are you?"

"At a self-storage facility right near Clay's place. There are a bunch of photos and notes here, as well as several boxes full of who knows what."

Clay waved to get her attention. "Ask him if he's ever heard of something called RC101886. It's written all over the notepad on the desk."

Leigh repeated the question.

Payton's voice went cold and hard. "Tell Clay to stop whatever he's doing. Now. Don't touch anything."

"What? Why?"

"Don't ask questions, just do it. I'll be there as soon as I can." Then he hung up.

Leigh looked at the phone in shock. "Payton says to stop touching stuff. He sounded pretty freaked-out."

"Yeah, well, he's not the only one. I've never seen any of this stuff before, and yet it's all so fucking familiar." He pressed the palms of his hands against his eyes. "I swear I'm going crazy, Leigh. I keep seeing little flashes of things, like I'm peering through someone else's eyes."

She went to him and pulled his hands down, forcing him to look at her. "You are not going crazy. I won't let you. Those flashes are good—that means we're on the right track. All you need to do is hold it together a bit longer. We'll find whoever did this to you and we'll make them undo it."

"What if it can't be undone?"

His words spoken aloud sparked the secret fear inside of her, making it flare to life. "I refuse to believe that. We will fix this, Clay. You need to trust me on that."

"I want to, but—" He stopped short, cutting off what he'd been about to say.

"What?" she asked.

Clay put a finger to her mouth, reached over, and turned the light over the desk off. The small room was plunged into darkness.

She felt his breath at her ear as he whispered, "I heard something."

A bolt of terror ripped through her at the sudden dark. She fumbled in her pocket for the phone and hit a button to make the screen light up. The underside of Clay's face was bathed in blue light. His jaw was bulging in anger, but his touch on her mouth and his hand on her shoulder were gentle.

Through the metal door, Leigh could hear muffled voices. "This is the place . . . thought I saw light."

A second, deeper voice replied, "You're imagining things. No one's here."

"He'll come. We find the locker first and wait."

Clay pulled her toward the wall of boxes. The screen on the phone went dark, and she pushed another button to light it up.

This time the beep sounded incredibly loud, echoing off the concrete walls.

Clay leaned close to her ear—so close she could feel his lips brush the outer rim. "Turn it off. If they hear that . . ."

He didn't need to finish his sentence for her to fill in the blanks. She cradled the phone inside her jacket and muted it.

Footsteps grew nearer outside. The door of a nearby unit squeaked as they pulled it open.

Clay took her by the shoulders and pulled her down to a crouch next to him. His weapon was in one hand; the other he used to cradle her neck, under her hair. His thumb moved in soothing strokes along her throat.

Their door rattled.

"Locked," said one of the men, right on the other side of the overhead door.

"Then cut it," said the second man, as if the first one was a complete idiot.

"There's no lock to cut, jackass."

"Skip to the next one. It's probably broken."

"We need to find his stash before he shows up."

The voices became more muffled as they walked away.

"Stash?" whispered Leigh.

The light on her phone went out again. She could no longer see Clay, but she could feel him nearby—feel the heat coming off his body and the slight vibration of tension in his hand. The scent of his leather jacket and the warm body beneath wrapped around her. Her fear began to fade the farther away the voices got.

"I have no idea," said Clay. "Maybe they're looking for weapons."

"Are there weapons here?"

"Could be some in those boxes. I haven't opened all of them."

Another door rattled as the men outside lifted it.

"What do we do?" she asked.

"We can't move until they're gone. They'll hear us if they're not close enough to see us. And there's a good chance they'll have a buddy guarding the way out to let them know if I show up. Or try to leave."

"So we're stuck?"

"Yeah. Get comfortable. This could take a while."

Clay could hardly think straight with Leigh sitting so close to him in the dark. He could smell her shampoo and the sweeter, more subtle scent of her skin. Fear radiated out of her. He kept trying to soothe her with gentle touches, but all that did was draw him tighter.

In the dark like this, there was nothing to distract him from the sound of her rapid breathing or the trembling of her body beneath his hand.

He tried to run through options for escape, recalling

the possible ways in and out of this place. But he came up empty.

If he thought he could open the door enough to slip out and take these men on, he'd do it in a heartbeat, but it would make too much noise, and there was no way he was risking Leigh's safety by drawing any attention to their hiding spot.

"Payton's on his way," whispered Leigh. "He's going to be walking into an ambush."

"Give me the phone."

She did. He sent a warning text, telling Payton to stay the hell away. His hand brushed hers as he handed her the phone. It was shaking harder than the rest of her, and cold to the touch.

Without thinking about the consequences, Clay slid her hand inside his jacket, under his shirt. Her frigid fingers were a shocking jolt against his stomach, but he'd suffer through that a million times over if it meant he could do something to make this fucked-up situation easier on her.

The light on the phone went dark again, and she sucked in a startled breath. Her fingers clenched against his skin, and his traitorous body took the movement to heart. In the matter of a few seconds, he was hard and aching, despite the danger perched just outside.

His dick really did have a mind of its own—a deranged, one-track mind.

"It's going to be fine," he promised. "Eventually they'll get bored or the sun will come up and scare them away. We just have to hold out for a few hours at most."

"I wish we could turn on the light." Even as quiet as her voice was, he could hear a tremor running through it.

"If there's even a small crack under the door or a hole in the metal, they could see the light. Our best bet is to stay quiet and in the dark."

From down the row of storage units came a heavy clang, like something had hit one of the metal doors.

Leigh jumped and her fingers dug into his skin. "What's that?"

"Probably a piece of broken lock flying around. Nothing to worry about." He hoped.

Her fingers relaxed against his abdomen again. "This reminds me of when I had to sit around, waiting for the verdict in Garrett's trial. I'm so tense I feel like I'm going to shatter."

He stroked her hair, enjoying the cool slide of the strands between his fingers. He knew that touching her like this was playing with fire, but he couldn't help himself. His need to soothe her combined with the giddy thrill he got every time his hands were on her was enough to make him lose his mind. He didn't care about consequences, which wasn't like him at all.

"What trial?" he asked in an effort to get her mind off their current situation.

"The police thought he'd killed Hollis. He hadn't, but we weren't sure the jury was going to see it that way."

"But they did," he guessed.

"They did. But it took three days of deliberation, and I don't think I ate or slept the whole time. Payton pulled some strings and got the trial expedited. If not for him, I might still be waiting for the trial, wondering if Garrett was going to be convicted for something I know he didn't do."

Clay wanted to ask her how she knew, but it seemed less important than the other detail she'd revealed. "Payton helped? Did he know your brother?"

"No. At least he said he didn't. He was doing it as a favor for me."

"Favor?"

"Repayment for services rendered. I've patched up

more than a few gunshot wounds for people connected to Payton—at his request."

"You mean you patched them up and didn't report them."

"Right. Another black mark on my career. After this is over, you'll have more knowledge to bring me down than any other man alive."

Clay grabbed his flashlight from his jacket and up-ended it on the concrete floor before turning it on. Enough light spilled out that he could see her face. And that she could see his. Their bodies blocked the light from reaching the doorway, reducing the risk of the minuscule light being seen. It was still a slight risk, but this was important. He tipped her chin up until he was looking in her eyes. He needed her to know that what he said was true. "I would never do that to you. When this is over, I'll never breathe a word to anyone. I swear it."

Her hand slid around to his back as she leaned forward, hugging him. "Thank you. If I lost my license, I don't think Payton would need me anymore. And if he doesn't need me, then I have nothing to offer him in exchange for visits to see Garrett."

"Wait. What? Why do you need Payton to see your brother?"

"He's being held in a secret location. I don't even know where it is. I have to drug myself unconscious in the car before he'll take me there. I don't even know what state it's in."

Anger seethed just under the surface of Clay's skin. How dare Payton do that to her?

"That fucking bastard," said Clay, too loudly. Leigh covered his mouth, and the soft touch of her fingers helped mute some of the searing fury pounding through him.

"No. He's not. He saved Garrett. He's still saving him

every day—protecting him from what he's capable of. Without Payton, both of my brothers would be dead. For that I owe him everything."

"Bullshit." Payton was using her, but she was too emotionally invested to see it. Clay wasn't.

Or maybe he was and his feelings for Leigh were getting in the way. In either case, Clay was no longer sure that he could trust Payton. The man had some kind of agenda of his own—one that involved Leigh's brother.

A memory hit him, filling his mind as if it had suddenly been illuminated by the flash of a camera. He sat in a room with two other boys. They were young. So was he. His scrawny legs stuck out from under a hospital gown, covered in small scrapes and bruises.

The two boys were afraid. They were looking to him for support, but he had none to offer. This place scared the crap out of him, even though he knew better than to let it show.

A man in a white coat walked in. Clay couldn't see his face—as if someone had blurred it out. But whoever he was, Clay knew he was bad news.

As the door shut, he saw another man standing in the hallway. His face was familiar, but Clay couldn't quite place it.

He had hidden a fork under his thigh. His fingers were wrapped around it, waiting for the man to get close enough to strike.

The other two boys raced around his bed, hiding behind him for protection.

The man in the coat had a syringe in his hand. The outlines of more were visible in the pocket of his coat.

Terror bubbled up, and Clay found a way to convert it to rage. He propelled himself from the bed, shoving the fork into the man's groin.

The memory disappeared, and already, Clay could

feel it dissipating, like a dream. Only fear and the familiar face of the man in the hall lingered.

"Are you okay?" asked Leigh.

"Yeah," he said, though he wasn't sure how true that
was. He was sweating and sick to his stomach.

That hadn't been a dream. It had happened—he'd
somehow blocked it out. Or maybe someone had
blocked it for him. That would certainly explain the
blurred face if whoever had done it didn't want to be
recognized.

Then what about the man in the hall? Clay was sure
he knew him.

Leigh watched him with concern. Her bottom lip
quivered slightly before she bit it and stilled the movement. He could barely see her in this light. She was more
shades of gray than color, with deep shadows painting
her skin.

The need to see her naked by this light struck him out
of the blue. With all the shit floating around in his head,
with thugs lurking outside, the fact that he could even go
there proved how screwed his brain really was.

At least thinking about her luscious body all naked
and laid out for him, draped in heavy shadows, was a
pleasant thought. Unlike all the others he was battling.

The phone buzzed and lit up. Leigh grabbed it and
checked the screen. "It's Payton. He's outside and says
it's safe to come out."

And suddenly, just like that, Clay knew who had been
standing in the hall, watching some doctor do God knew
what to Clay and two other little boys. He was much
younger in that memory, but Clay was certain of the
man's identity.

It was Payton.

Chapter Seventeen

Leigh felt the shift in Clay well before the lights came on for her to see it. Tension vibrated out of him, along with a hard, rigid chill. He moved away from her to unlock the door, and by the time it had lifted, his gun was in his hand.

Payton stood outside, breathing hard. His tie was slightly crooked, and his hair was no longer perfect. Lying at his feet was the crumpled form of a man. Another was sprawled a few feet away.

Leigh rushed forward to check on them, but before she could cross the threshold, Clay grabbed her arm and pulled her to a halt.

"I just want to see if they're alive," she explained. "They won't hurt me."

"It's not them I'm worried about."

"Clay?" said Payton, concern making his tone heavy. "What's going on?"

"That's what I'd like to know," said Clay.

Payton's hands came up toward his shoulders. "I took them both down. You're safe now. But we really need to go before anyone else arrives."

"How did you take them down?" demanded Clay.

Payton shrugged. "I've been training with Bella. She's taught me some things."

"Bullshit. You're not the man I thought you were."

"I have no clue what you mean, but we really should go."

"Not until I get the truth." Clay stepped toward Payton with lethal intent in his every step. "You knew about what they did to me, didn't you? You were there. I remember."

A flicker of fear crossed Payton's features, ruining his usual composure. "I don't know what you think you remember, but that's completely understandable. You're dealing with a lot right now. Let's go somewhere safe and talk about it."

"We're not going anywhere with you."

Leigh was confused by what was going on between the two men. Something had happened, but she couldn't figure out what. "Clay? What's all this about?"

"Payton was there when they fucked with my head. I was a kid, scared out of my mind, and he stood there, watching as someone drugged me and two other boys."

"You've got it all wrong," said Payton. "You're confused. Please, just come with me and we'll talk about it."

Raw fury fell from Clay's tongue. "I don't trust you."

Leigh put her hand on Clay's shoulder, hoping to calm him down. "This could be a trick your mind is playing on you."

He shrugged her hand away and growled, "It was no trick."

"Think about it. How better to alienate you and cut you off from any help you might find than to make you distrust your friends?"

"I don't distrust them all. Just him. He was there, Leigh."

She opened her mouth to try to talk some sense into

him when Payton beat her to it. "Clay is right. I was there. I have no excuse for what I did, but I'm on your side now. I swear it."

Clay let out a low growl. Leigh's body went cold as the implications of what Payton had just said sank in.

Her voice was faint and barely audible over the howling wind. "You were there? You let this happen? To my brothers?"

"I did. And I'll tell you everything, but not here. It's not safe."

"How can you stand there so calm, knowing what you did?" asked Leigh.

"Because he's just that cold. Any man who would let that happen to a kid is a sociopath."

"No. I'm not. I regret what I did, and I've spent years trying to make things right. I'll never be able to make up for what I did, but I can at least help lessen the pain of those whose lives we ruined."

"We?" snapped Clay.

Payton shook his head. Sadness and regret fell off him, making the air around him seem colder. "There were many of us. We thought we were doing the right thing. We were wrong. If you want to know any more than that, then you need to follow me."

Clay let out a scoffing laugh. "Fuck that."

Leigh stared at Payton. She needed the truth. She needed to know how to fix this so that Garrett could have a life. "I'll go with him."

Clay whirled around to face her. His amber eyes were wide with disbelief and scorn. "You believe him?"

"I believe he knows something. I need to know what that is. For Garrett's sake."

"You're not leaving with him."

"I'll do what I think is right. It's up to you to come along or not."

Payton's gaze slid past them, into the storage unit. "We'll need to take this all with us."

"Why? So you can destroy the evidence?" demanded Clay.

Payton marched closer and didn't stop until the barrel of Clay's gun was shoved under his chin. Anger poured off Clay, but Payton was calm and accepting. "Pull the trigger if you want. It's no less than I deserve, and God knows I'm tired. But know that if you do, everything I know dies with me. I'm probably the only person on the planet who knows all the connections and can piece the puzzle together and help you find who's doing this to you now. If you want your life back, I'm your only shot."

Clay stared at Payton for a long minute. Leigh really didn't know if he was going to fire. She'd never seen him this angry—even when he wasn't himself, he hadn't been running this hot, shaking with rage.

"One slip," whispered Clay, "and I won't give a shit what you know. Understand?"

Payton nodded as much as the barrel of the gun would allow. "I would expect no less of you. You are as we created you to be."

Clay shoved away from Payton. "Go get your car and drive it down here."

Payton turned and left.

Leigh stood there, feeling the cold wind sink through her clothes. Everything she'd thought she'd known had suddenly shifted, leaving her wobbly and off-balance.

Clay stowed his weapon and cupped her face. His hands were strikingly hot against her skin. "Do not let your guard down around him. I know he's helped you, but you can't let that sway you now. He's not a good man."

"I know. I'll be careful."

"You stay with me, okay? Please don't go wandering off with him. It would—" His words cut off in a strangled sound of frustrated rage. When he spoke again, his voice was calmer. "I can't stand the thought of you being with him. Promise me you won't trust him."

"I promise. If he was involved in what happened to my brothers, then he's the enemy, even if we are forced to work with him."

"For now. We'll see where this goes. Until then, stick by my side."

Leigh nodded and let her head fall to his shoulder. He hugged her tight for a moment before pushing her away just as Payton's car slid down the row.

"Come with me."

She followed Clay inside and watched him shove a few things from the desk into his pocket. She couldn't see what they were, but she didn't dare ask what he was hiding now that Payton was within earshot. Instead, she acted as though she hadn't seen anything, grabbed a cardboard box, and carried it to Payton's trunk.

They loaded up everything in less than five minutes, emptying the storage unit of everything but the furniture and lighting.

"I have a safe place we can go," said Payton.

"Safe?" asked Clay as if it were a joke.

"I'm not going to hurt you. Neither of you. I understand your lack of faith, but—"

"But nothing," said Clay. "We're taking your car and all the boxes. You can take ours."

"Will you at least follow me home?"

"To your house? Not a chance."

"I have a safe room. No one will be able to find you there or hear anything we say. Right now the only thing we have on our side is knowledge. If the others find out what we know, we'll never be able to find them."

"The others?"

Payton clamped his lips together and shook his head.

"No. Not unless you come home with me. It's the only place I'm sure is safe."

Clay looked at Leigh as if seeking her opinion. She didn't know what to say. She was floundering here, still trying to catch up with the news that Payton was behind what had been done to Clay and her brothers.

"Do you have a better idea?" she asked.

"Not if we're going to get answers out of him."

"Then we should go. I've seen you fight. Payton's no match for you if things go badly."

Clay glared at Payton. "Fine. Lead the way."

When Payton had said he had a safe room, Clay had not pictured the sprawling, labyrinthine mass of tunnels and rooms beneath his estate. Behind several layers of security, including a secret entrance hidden by a false wall, there was no way anyone was going to find them.

"How many people have died down here?" he asked Payton.

He pushed a cart loaded with the boxes and items from the storage locker. "Two. Both of them deserved it, if you must know."

The heavy steel vault door shut behind Leigh, locking with a resounding clang of metal on metal.

"Are we prisoners?" asked Leigh.

"Not so long as I have this gun pointed at his spine," said Clay.

Payton glanced behind him. "Of course not. I won't hold you here against your will. Has the part where I told you that I'm trying to make up for past wrongs not quite settled in yet?"

"Some things can't be forgiven," said Clay, remembering the way he'd hurt Leigh, and those kids he'd collected for the doctor.

For a moment, that gave him pause. He liked to think he was a decent guy. He tried hard not to be a dick, and yet he'd done horrible things that he felt the burning need to set right. Maybe that was how Payton felt, too. It didn't mean he was going to trust the man or feel pity for his mistakes, but at least it helped ease some of the bulging rage running under Clay's skin.

Payton unlocked a room and shoved the cart inside. It was an open area, with twelve-foot-high ceilings and thick, plush carpet. One corner contained a couple of couches and a TV; another was a full kitchen on a much smaller scale than the one upstairs. In the third corner was a large table and chairs, and in the last was a workout area, complete with a variety of equipment.

"The kitchen is fully stocked. So is the bar. Avoid any live TV, but there are several hundred movies you can watch. Sleeping quarters are down the hall to your right. Use whatever you like."

"We won't be here that long," said Clay.

Payton stared pointedly at the cart overflowing with boxes. "You have no idea what we're dealing with here. It could take weeks to sort through all of this information. Identifying the people in the photos on that wall alone will be days of effort."

"What's the point?" asked Clay. "How the hell is a scrapbooking fest going to help us find out who did this to me? I don't know any of the people in those photos."

"No, but I do. Once we figure out who everyone is and which of them are still alive, then we may see a connection. Those photos could narrow down the choices to help us find the person pulling your strings."

Clay looked at the boxes, dreading what was in them.

"You said not to touch any of them," said Leigh. "You completely freaked, like they'd be filled with live grenades or something."

"I was worried you'd discover my involvement. Now that you know, there's nothing for me to hide, is there?"

"You were there," Clay practically shouted. "You know who did this. Just give me a fucking name and point me in the right direction. I'll kill the asshole and be free by sunrise."

"I'm afraid it's not that simple. Even if killing one person could free you—which it can't—there were dozens of us involved. I've tried to track everyone's movements, but I learned a few months ago that I made a mistake. At least one person I thought was dead is alive, which means that there could be others, too."

"Dozens?" breathed Leigh as she sank into a nearby chair. "There were dozens of people willing to hurt kids? And they got away with it? How does that happen?"

"It was a different time then. The fear of a world war ran rampant. We were trying to protect our way of life—trying to protect our country."

"By ruining its children? And the Ass for Brains Award goes to . . ."

"I'm serious, Clay. There was no excuse for what we did, but there was a reason. And like it or not, apparently not everyone who worked on this project has abandoned the cause. These boxes could hold information on not only who is behind this, but also what they're doing now."

A hot burst of fury detonated in Clay's gut. "That's why the doctor wanted me to bring him more kids. He's doing to them what he did to me."

"He?" asked Payton, as if that shocked him.

"That's what the guy who was providing the stolen kids implied."

"Did he mention a name? Stynger, perhaps?"

"No. No names."

Payton went to the kitchen and poured himself a drink. He sloshed it back and poured another. "I thought for sure that she was behind this. After what she'd done to Razor's friend . . ."

"Whoa. Razor is involved in this, too?"

"You mean Razor, as in Roxanne Haught?" asked Leigh.

Payton nodded. "It's a long story, but the short version is that a friend of Razor's got recruited into what he thought was a special ops group. It wasn't. He ended up being subjected to all kinds of drugs and mental and physical conditioning. It changed him. It made him stronger, faster, and completely violent."

Leigh perked up. "We should talk to him and see if he knows anything. Maybe he met this doctor or heard something. Where is he?"

Payton's eyes filled with guilt as he stared at his glass. "He lives in a cell next to Garrett's. I'm sorry, but seeing him is far too dangerous to risk."

"Then let Garrett talk to him. Or you do it. We can't sit around without pursuing every possible lead. Garrett is counting on me."

"We can't allow contact between the men. There's no way to know what could happen."

"Exactly how many people do you have locked up, Payton?"

"Too many. That's all I will say."

"I don't mind taking the risk," said Leigh. "My brother is worth it."

Payton shook his head. "I've already made my share of bad decisions. I know you want to help, but the answer is no. I never should have let you see Garrett. I should have let you think he was dead. It would have been kinder."

She covered her face with her hands, but not so fast that Clay couldn't see the look of desolation that scrunched her features.

Seeing her in pain made something dark and predatory rise in him. He went to her side and crouched in front of her. He put his hands on her knees, startling her. She jerked and her lips parted on a silent gasp. She'd gone pale, which caused the bruises along her jaw to stand out, reminding him of what was at stake.

Her gaze met his. She covered his hands with hers and gave him a silent, pleading look.

She needed him, and while she may not have said the words, he could see in her eyes how much she was counting on him to see her through this.

Her need made him stronger. It sealed up all the tiny cracks in his weary resolve and filled him with purpose.

He stood and turned toward Payton. "My patience is officially gone. You're going to tell us everything so we can fix the mess you made. Sit the fuck down and start at the beginning."

Payton nodded slowly. He grabbed the bottle of whiskey and two extra glasses before sitting down at the table. He filled the glasses and slid them to two empty seats. "You're going to need this. There's no happy ending with this story."

Clay squeezed Leigh's knee gently. "You don't have to do this. You can get some rest if you want. I'll make sure we get the truth."

"No, I need to be here. If there's anything I can do . . ."

There probably wasn't, but if the thought gave her some hope to cling to, then Clay was all for it.

He took Leigh's wrist and led her to the table. The feel of her skin soothed him, and the steady beat of her pulse reminded him that she was alive and safe. He was going to do everything in his power to make sure she stayed that way.

He sat between her and Payton and set his weapon on the table as a not-so-subtle reminder for the man to tell the truth.

Payton ignored the gun and stared into his drink. "We were trying to save the world—or at least our way of life." He let out a laugh, but Clay heard no humor in it. "Most of us were young, with no children of our own. I think they recruited people like us on purpose, because we hadn't yet learned the true value of a child. They were simply lumps of clay for us to shape into what we desired—people we thought we were offering some grand opportunity."

"Which was?"

"There were different focuses. Some of the experiments were designed to increase intelligence. Others to make people more physically capable. Strength, speed, stamina. Some wanted to go further, but those ideas were tossed out as too dangerous. At the time, we thought these were all great things that we were going to hand out like shiny little gifts." He emptied his glass and refilled it. "That's not the way it turned out. Things didn't go as easily as we'd hoped. Some of the researchers grew desperate, worried that their funding would run out and they'd fail. They cut corners. Took risks. Not all of us knew what had happened until the gears had already been in motion for too long to stop them."

"What kind of risks?"

He shook his head. "I still don't know all the details of what was done. Most of the data was destroyed before I could find it. I wasn't one of the brains—I was simply the guy who knew which buttons to push to get people to do what I wanted."

"You were the guy who acquired the children," guessed Clay.

"One of them."

Leigh's fingers tightened around Clay's. "Did you give them my brothers?"

"No. That was someone else. But Clay, what you're going through now is all because of me. I saw you playing with Mira when you were little. She'd invited you home because you'd scared away a bully who'd been hounding her. You had a black eye and she had a serious case of hero worship. Her dad and I were friends, and I happened to be at his house that day. You were so skinny, your clothes too small and dirty. It was obvious you were neglected. Getting your stepfather to loan you to me was easy." Shame made his voice crack.

"Did he know?" Clay had to shove the words out. "Did he know what you were going to do?"

Payton shook his head. "That was part of the deal. No questions asked."

"I can't believe a parent would agree to such a thing," said Leigh.

"Most wouldn't. Enough did for us to continue the research."

"So what exactly was done to me?"

"I don't know. After you left my sight, I wasn't told anything. I have my ideas. I've seen patterns over the years—things that men like you, Hollis, and Garrett have in common. But there were records. If we find them, then you'll know for sure. I believe that whoever is activating you now has access to those records."

"And you have no idea who it is?"

"All I have are guesses. I've kept tabs on everyone from back then, and as far as I know, all but one of them is working on legitimate research."

"And that one?"

"Is a woman. I've been looking for her for months with no leads. She's well funded and stays hidden. And she doesn't use children. She prefers fully grown men."

"Then it couldn't be her," said Leigh.

"I haven't ruled her out, but we need to be sure."

"It's not a woman," said Clay. As the words left his mouth, he knew they were true.

"What makes you say that?"

"I have no idea, but I'm certain. I can almost hear his voice in my head, whispering." But the harder he tried to isolate the voice, the more his head began to throb. Finally, the pain was too much and he let go of the thread, letting it snap back out of reach.

Leigh put her hand on his in an obvious show of comfort.

Payton saw the gesture and his eyes narrowed for a fraction of a second. Clay couldn't tell if it was anger, regret, or suspicion he'd seen flash against the other man's features, but it was definitely something.

"So you think that if we look through all of this stuff that the person or people responsible will become known?" Clay asked.

"I sincerely hope so."

"And then what?" asked Leigh. "Even if we know who is doing this, we still have to find a way to undo it, right? That's what you meant when you said that killing them won't solve the problem."

"I'm not even sure there is a way to undo it, but taking this doctor alive is our best chance at fixing those who are suffering."

"That's going to make the job much harder," said Clay.

"I know. But I have some ideas that might draw them out of hiding."

"Like what?"

Payton glanced at the boxes they'd collected. "That code you mentioned—RC101886—refers to a specific file. My guess is that either the doctor has the file or is looking for it."

Bells chimed in Clay's head as puzzle pieces clicked together. "I was tasked to do some kind of job. Do you think finding this file would be it?"

Payton nodded his head. "It's possible. Let me do some checking first. I have contacts who may have information we can use."

"Enough with the cryptic bullshit. Just tell us what the damn file is."

Payton shoved to his feet. His expression was hard, with a clear warning that he wasn't going to bend. "No. Not yet. Not until I'm sure. If I guess, it could get you killed. I won't risk your lives like that."

"I don't understand," said Leigh. "How are we supposed to help if we don't know what you do?"

"Just go through those boxes. Spread out the photos for me to look at. I'll reach out to my contacts and come back in a few hours with answers."

Clay stood. "We want answers now."

"I know, but trust me when I tell you that if I give them to you now, you'll wish I hadn't." Payton's gaze flicked to Leigh and back. A look of warning was in his eyes.

Either he was trying to tell Clay that it was Leigh whom Payton was trying to protect, or he was blowing a hell of a lot of smoke. Clay wasn't willing to take the risk with her life. He didn't want to trust Payton, but they didn't have a whole lot of people around who had any clue what was going on. As it was, Payton was their only option.

"Do not lock us down here. Understood?"

"I'll give you the codes to get out. But please, don't leave. Not until I'm sure it's safe. It will take me several hours to do what needs to be done."

"We're not making you any promises," said Leigh. "You don't have the right to ask for them. Just go and do what you need to do. The sooner I never have to see you again, the better."

Payton straightened his tie and smoothed his hair, regret hanging heavily on his shoulders. "I understand."

Chapter Eighteen

Payton hadn't thought his guilt could be any worse, but seeing the betrayal on the faces of Clay and Leigh had driven home just how evil his actions had truly been.

He'd been deluding himself, thinking he could make up for what he'd done, but he'd been wrong. There was no way to forgiveness for him. All he could hope for was that their hatred would not keep them from letting him help.

He needed to help. He needed to do what he could to repair the damage. And this was his chance. All he had to do was set the right trap and see who walked in.

Payton called Bob Norwood, purposefully using a line with limited security. He knew people listened to his calls, and sometimes that worked to his advantage, which was why he kept this line.

"What now?" answered Bob.

"Do you remember that time in Argentina?" said Payton, purposefully slurring his words.

"You're drunk."

"It was spring, and we met those two busty girls in the market. They were sisters." He let a leer enter his voice as if he remembered the day fondly.

Bob fell silent as the meaning of Payton's words sank in. There were no girls from the market. They'd been in Argentina for a completely different reason—to trap one of the techs working with the Threshold Project. Word had spread that he was looking to make a quick buck by selling secrets to the highest bidder. Payton and Bob had been ordered to set up the lab tech, making him think that there was a buyer interested in the data. They'd let the whole conversation be overheard, which drew several potential buyers out of the woodwork as well. In one day, they'd taken down four bad guys. That had been one of the good days.

"I remember," said Bob. "Are you sitting around, reminiscing with a bottle tonight?"

"It's been a hard day. I found some of the old files. They brought back too many memories."

Bob took the bait, working with Payton as he had years ago. "Which files?"

"The RC series."

"Where did you find them?"

"We got a tip from some old associates. That led us to raid a storage locker today. Found the disks sitting in a box."

"Were you able to break the encryption?"

"Not yet. I don't trust e-mail, so I'm taking it to one of our facilities tomorrow morning. The eggheads will be able to crack it; then it will go in the vault with the others."

"At least you won't have to ever worry about hunting it down again. Once it goes in that vault, it will never see the light of day."

"Thank God for that. I'm getting too old for this, Bob. I need to be done."

Bob sighed. "You're also too old to be getting shit-faced. Go to bed. Sleep it off."

"Maybe I'll dream about the sisters tonight."

"Yeah," said Bob. "Good luck with that."

Payton hung up, feeling the rush of victory shoot through him. A second later, his secure line rang.

"What the hell, Payton?" demanded Bob.

"Sorry to spring it on you like that, but I knew you'd catch on."

"A warning would have been nice."

"But not nearly as much fun."

"So what's this all about?"

"It's not Stynger."

"How do you know?"

"Clay is certain. I need to know who is behind this. The only thing I could turn up was that they either have a specific RC series file or need it."

"So you're trying to draw them out with news that some files have resurfaced."

"If they already have what they need, they won't want us to know what they know. If they don't have what they need, then they'll want it. Seemed logical to me."

Bob sighed. "I was sure it was Stynger."

"Any sign of her on your end?"

"No. I have to play by the rules. At least for now."

"What does that mean?"

"It means I might have an early Christmas present for you. We'll see."

"I could sure as hell use some good news."

"Me, too. I don't like having my baby girl so close to this stuff without backup."

"Sloane is fine, and Lucas would take a bullet for her before he'd let anything happen."

"I keep hoping she'll get pregnant and decide to quit."

Payton grunted. "Don't hold your breath. Sloane is too much like you to sit quietly at home—baby or not."

"We've got to stop it, Payton. We have to shut Stynger and anyone else down for good and make it all go away."

"I'm doing my best. I wish I could say it was working."

"Maybe your plan tonight will do some good."

"We did get intel from a storage locker tonight. That could lead to something as well."

"What kind of intel?"

"I don't know yet. I was afraid to look too closely while Clay was watching. He already mistrusts me."

"Why?"

"Because he knows the truth—what was done to him was my fault."

"Not just yours."

"Yeah, well, I'm the closest target."

Bob grunted. "Tell me about what you found. Maybe I can help sort it out."

"It was a place Clay used during the times he was triggered—a kind of secret office. There were weapons, ammo, tactical gear, paperwork, and photos. My guess is they were some of his targets. Clay's head is in a bad place, and I didn't want to shake him up, but chances are those people are all dead by his hand." That was probably where the blood on Clay had come from—a night out playing assassin.

"And you don't think he'll remember that?"

"Eventually, maybe. For now I think it's best if he doesn't."

"I agree. Heaven knows I wish I could forget."

"Me, too, Bob. Me, too."

If Leigh felt shaken by what Payton had told them, she could only imagine how Clay must feel.

He hadn't said a word since he'd come back into the room after testing to make sure they could get out of

their underground hiding place if they wanted to. His
face had been grim, and he'd headed right for the boxes
stacked on the cart, as if something inside them would
solve their problems.

Leigh lifted one of the lids and saw that the box was
full of ammunition. She went to the next and found several gun cases stacked inside. The next held several
spools of some kind of wire and what she thought might
be bricks of explosives.

"What the hell were you planning to do with all of
this?" she asked before she could think better of it.

He didn't respond. When she looked up, she saw him
staring into a box. His jaw was clenched, and his fingers
had tightened into fists, crushing the cardboard edges.

She went to his side to see what upset him. Sitting on
the top of one of the opened boxes was a photo of two
young Hispanic children, no older than seven or eight.
One boy, one girl. Both were sad and dirty, with tears
leaving clean streaks on their faces.

Leigh picked the photo up and turned it over. There
was writing on the back, but it wasn't the same bold,
printed letters as the rest of the notes she'd seen. This
writing was smaller, with all the letters crammed tightly
together.

"It's instructions for pickup," said Clay, sounding like
he'd just taken a punch to the gut. "These are the two
kids that asshole Anton sold to me."

He stumbled to a chair and collapsed into it.

Leigh yearned to go to him and offer some kind of
comfort, but she couldn't think of a single thing to say.
He'd had a hand in abducting two children, and there
was nothing a few paltry words could do to fix that. All
she could think to do was move his focus from guilt to
something more constructive. If she let him languish in
this dark place, the guilt would eat him alive, just as it

had Hollis. It was guilt that had stolen her brother's life, and she would not let that happen to Clay.

"We'll find them," she said. "We'll find them and take them home."

"I don't know where to look. I can't remember a fucking thing." He hit his head with the heel of his hand.

Leigh grabbed his wrists and pulled them down. The bandages reminded her to be careful of his wounds.

She stepped forward, shoving her way between his knees. She put his hands on her hips and covered them with her own to keep them there. "You don't have to remember for us to find them. Somewhere in these boxes may be a clue or a name—something that will lead us to the next step. Stop beating yourself up over this and concentrate on finding the doctor."

His fingers clenched against the curve of her hip. "I can't ignore the fact that I was the one who did all of this."

Leigh tipped his head back so he'd look at her. "You have to. You have to pretend these things were done by someone else. Because the man who took those kids was not the man you are right now. You were used. You're not responsible."

"I am. Intellectually I get it that I didn't know what I was doing, but that doesn't change that I was the one who did these things." He nodded toward the photos spread over the table. "I probably killed these people, and I don't even know why. I may never know why."

Leigh picked up the closest photo—one of a man with graying hair and a bulging belly. "Would you kill him if I asked you to?"

"No. Not unless there was a good reason."

"If I wanted a child, would you steal one for me?"

"Fuck no!"

"See? Not you. The man who did these things is not you."

Clay closed his eyes and leaned forward until his face was hidden against her abdomen. His arms slipped around her in a hug so tight she could feel the strain of his guilt vibrating through him. "I think maybe it would be best if I let Payton put me in that place where your brother is."

Leigh stroked his back, hoping it would ease him at least a little. His shirt was pulled tight over his muscles. "You can go there if you want. I won't stop you, but how is that going to help find the doctor? How is it going to help find the kids?"

"It won't. But it might keep me from hurting someone else." He pulled away and headed into the kitchen, a heavy sigh falling from his lips. She missed the warmth and strength of his embrace immediately but didn't dare admit to herself how needy that made her. Right now she had to stay strong for both of them.

"You've got me for that."

He went through cabinets until he found some coffee and put some on to brew. "And in exchange, I help you help Garrett? Somehow I don't think he would approve of our arrangement. Especially when there's no guarantee I can do any good."

Clay was slipping away. She could feel him withdrawing as if he'd accepted he could never fix what he'd done and was simply willing to prevent further damage. Lock himself away. Throw out the key.

A man like him would never survive that kind of life. He might not know it now, but Leigh had seen the helpless rage her brother had suffered. He hated being unable to do anything for himself. He hated depending on Leigh for filtered news of the outside world. He was allowed no Internet access, phone, or any other means of communication.

Clay would rot in a place like that. He'd be left alone

with nothing to think about but his guilt, straining to remember something that might help. Garrett hadn't killed anyone that they knew of. He hadn't helped abduct children. The things he'd done paled in comparison to what Clay had done. Locking him up with that burden would torture him until he found a way to make it stop. Permanently.

She hadn't seen the signs in Hollis in time to stop him. If they put Clay away, she wouldn't be able to watch him. She wouldn't be able to protect him.

Leigh needed to keep him safe. As long as he was still fighting, looking for answers, she had hope for Garrett. If Clay gave up . . .

A shuddering darkness squeezed the breath from her lungs at the thought of losing Garrett. He was barely holding on. If not for her visits, she didn't know if he would have lasted this long.

"Are you okay?" asked Clay.

She plastered a fake smile on her face. "Fine. I think I'll lay everything out as it was hanging on the wall in that storage unit. Where's the camera you used to photograph it?"

He reached into his wallet. "Here's the data. The camera is on the cart."

She headed toward it, hearing his footsteps growing nearer. His fingers wrapped around her arms so gently her bruises didn't hurt. It didn't matter that he exerted no pressure. One touch from him was enough to bring her whole world to a rocking halt.

Clay stepped forward until her back was so close to his chest that she could feel his heat radiating into her. His hands slid around her waist, reminding her all too keenly of the last time she'd been pressed against him like this.

Her body remembered, too, and the pleasure he could

give. A fine quivering warmth started in her chest and spread down into her belly. Her nipples beaded inside her bra, and her breasts began to ache. He'd barely touched them, and she couldn't convince her traitorous hormones that there was no reason he should.

There was nothing more between them than this situation, and yet everything inside her screamed for more.

She cleared her throat, and her voice came out breathless and faint. "What are you doing?"

His mouth moved over her hair. "I can't seem to stop touching you. I'm sorry."

Leigh tilted her head back to his shoulder, unable to stop herself. "Don't be. Your touch is the only thing that seems to drive all the bad stuff away."

"Leigh."

She felt his chest contract with a heavy breath and wasn't sure whether it was exasperation or relief. She turned around to see which, but all she saw was desire. It darkened his skin and made his pupils flare wide, despite the bright lighting in the room. His lips were parted slightly, and his breathing was fast and heavy.

When she was caught inside his embrace like this, the rest of the world seemed to fade away. She knew troubles lurked just past his skin, but for now they seemed far away, unable to hurt her.

She wanted him to kiss her but refused to make the first move. He'd cut things off last time, and she wasn't about to set herself up for another round of rejection.

"I want you," he whispered.

Her heart did a backflip in her chest. A rush of excitement poured into her veins, heating her skin until she was sure she'd combust.

"But?" she asked, waiting for him to deliver the killing blow. He wanted her but he was too dangerous. He wanted her but they had to work together. He wanted her but he knew he wasn't going to live to see Christmas.

"But we have work to do. People depending on us. I can't be that selfish—not after everything I've done."

It took her a minute to work moisture back into her mouth so she could speak. Desire laid over her like a soft, warm blanket, muting everything else around it. There was no sense of urgency in this space, only a need to let go and give in. "Work. Of course."

She gathered up the jagged pieces of her self-control and took a long step back. Now that he was no longer touching her, now that his scent was not filling her head, she could think straight.

Her body vibrated with restless energy and sexual frustration. If she kept staring at him, seeing her own needs reflected in his eyes, she was going to do something reckless. Instead, she turned her back and made a beeline for the coffee he'd made.

The liquid sloshed inside the mug and burned her lip. The pain gave her the final push back into something resembling a responsible adult.

Leigh went about the task of re-creating the wall of photos and notes from the images stored in the camera while Clay emptied out the rest of the boxes. Nearly an hour later, he broke the silence spanning between them.

His voice was filled with disappointment. "I thought there'd be more here than this—some kind of clue or something obvious, rather than a bunch of seemingly unconnected nonsense."

"Let me see what you have." She went to the table where he was working to find an array of notes spread out in front of him. Like the others, the sticky notes contained only one or two words—none of which made any sense.

"What the hell does a giraffe have to do with anything?"

"No clue."

"It could be a code name for something or someone."

"Even if it is, how does that help?"

She shook her head, feeling her ponytail flopping across her back. "What about that one?" She pointed to a note that read, *Wed. 3 Wilson's Cliffs.*

"Does that make more sense than the rest?"

"Wilson's Cliffs is a club. Exclusive, members-only kind of place."

"You think this is a meet of some kind?"

"Or your next target."

"Great. So I can go there and see if anyone trips my batshit trigger and sends me into berserk-o land again." Clay ran his hands over his hair in frustration, making a mess of it.

The urge to slide her fingers in and straighten that mess stole over her, but she shoved her hands in her pockets instead. Touching him was only going to make her all hot and needy again. It wouldn't do a thing to help them figure out the puzzle.

"Do you think that's what would happen?" she asked.

"I don't know. Maybe. Maybe not. There's no way to know for sure."

"There are no Wednesday the thirds floating around on the calendar, so that has to be a time. Or maybe a hole on the golf course."

Clay shoved away from the table. "I give up. This is all a tangled mess of bullshit that makes no sense. I need to be out there looking for this doctor asshole, not stuck in here, waiting for the man who brought all this down on my head to do something he's not willing to tell us."

"Like it or not, we need Payton."

"You do. He's the only link to your brother."

"And the only link to you if you get thrown in that facility. Without Payton, I'd never see you again. I don't know about you, but that idea bothers the hell out of me. So for now, we play nice and stay here like he asked. I'm sure he'll be back soon."

A long sigh of surrender fell from his lips. "Fine. Whatever. I'm going to grab a shower and clear my head."

"You should try to eat. Maybe get some sleep."

"Yeah," he said, though his voice was empty of everything but frustration and weariness.

He went down the hall toward where Payton had told them there were sleeping quarters. She ached to follow him and find a way to ease his tension, but there wasn't much she could do. And if she followed him, she wasn't sure how she'd be able to keep her hands to herself.

The only time she'd truly relaxed since meeting him was when he'd held her in his arms and stroked her until she fell apart. As delicious as that idea was, she couldn't stand a repeat performance of him storming off, furious and guilt ridden because of the bruises he'd left on her. He hadn't been in control then. It hadn't been him who had hurt her. That charge was squarely on the shoulders of whoever was pulling his strings.

Hollis had never believed that she'd forgiven him for breaking her arm. He couldn't accept that he wasn't responsible for his actions during that time.

He'd died thinking that she blamed him. He'd simply wandered away that night after they'd had dinner and watched TV, and put a gun to his head. She hadn't seen it coming. She hadn't even considered that he'd hurt himself.

Maybe she had a blind spot for such things. Maybe Clay was down the hall right now, thinking about eliminating the possibility that he could ever be used to do bad things again.

He'd seemed so disheartened when he'd left, like he'd

given up. Leigh couldn't let that happen. She needed to keep him focused and fighting. It was her job to make sure that he didn't do anything stupid.

A sudden surge of anxiety grabbed her with cold, clammy hands. She couldn't lose Clay. She'd already lost too much. Her world was an empty, threadbare place she was barely holding together. If something happened to Clay . . .

Nothing was going to happen. She wouldn't let it happen.

Leigh squared her shoulders, preparing for the fight she knew was to come, grabbed her medical bag from the cart, and headed out into the hall in search of Clay's room. She was keeping him alive, even if she had to drug him unconscious to make it happen.

Chapter Nineteen

Clay saw the shadow of footsteps flicker beneath his door before he heard the light knock.

Leigh. She was here, and his body lit up like the Fourth of July with her sudden nearness. A giddy, boyish thrill raced through him, only to be pounded flat by reality. If she was here at his door, then something had to be wrong. Maybe she'd found something else in the jumbled mess of photos and notes.

He crossed the small room, registering the feeling of thick, soft carpet under his bare feet without allowing himself to enjoy it. Everything about this space was luxurious but not ostentatious. The towel around his waist was ridiculously soft. The hot water had gone on for miles. Low lighting, hidden beneath wooden trim, spilled a golden glow on the pale walls. A subtle shimmer of something metallic ran through the wallpaper. A matching sheen glistened in the dark bedding, like strands of silver.

Clay wasn't used to fancy furnishings, but this place didn't make him feel like the proverbial bull. There were no frills or knickknacks to destroy. The furniture was solid and sturdy. It was as if Payton had the place designed to put men at ease. Then again, if this was some kind of bomb shelter or a safe haven to wait out the zombie apocalypse, he wouldn't really want a bunch of men trapped down here, raging at one another.

Clay paused with his hand on the door. He'd just stepped from the shower and wore only a towel. He hadn't bothered to cover himself, hoping that his lack of clothing would embarrass her enough to drive her away.

Droplets of water cooled on his back, but the moment he cracked open the door and saw her standing there, all he felt was heat.

She was so damn pretty. He couldn't get over it. Every time he thought he'd gotten used to her curves, the heat in those dark eyes, or the shape of her kissable mouth, he was proven wrong. Her hair was messy, with wild strands of it curling at her temples. His hand tightened on the doorknob in an effort to keep from reaching to touch.

Shadows of fatigue hung below her eyes. The constellations of freckles on her cheeks appeared darker against her pale skin. The bruises he'd left on her jaw had faded slightly but were still there as a reminder of what he'd done. He wanted to kiss them away and beg for forgiveness he knew he'd never deserve.

Her presence hit him like a physical blow, driving the oxygen from his lungs. He stood there like a jackass, mute and still.

Leigh's voice wavered with uncertainty. "I came to rebandage your wrists."

His brain had gone to a whole slew of places, imagining why she was here at his door. He'd already imagined her raging at him for the things he'd done, for failing to find a way to save her brother. He'd also imagined her all sultry and sweet, coaxing him to take what she once had offered. Or fiery and demanding, ordering him to make her come again.

He had not considered her showing up in the role of physician, completely practical and reasonable.

As his fantasies faded in the face of reality, he stepped back, allowing her inside.

Her scent slid around him as she entered the small space. It seemed darker than before, but even more mouthwatering. The urge to snuggle close and breathe her in struck hard and fast, leaving him shaking.

His gaze slipped down to her breasts against his will. The buttons on her blouse gaped slightly as she pulled in a deep breath. All he could think about was the sound of those buttons flying off as he'd ripped her shirt open, followed by the little gasp of excitement she'd given him after.

She looked him over from head to toe, pausing at the bulge he felt growing under his towel. A flush of embarrassment heated his face, but there was nothing he could do about his cock. It refused to lie silent and obedient, despite Clay's constant reminders that it wasn't getting anywhere near her.

Leigh pushed the door shut. The quiet click of the lock being engaged sounded as loud as a grenade going off in the room. And it rocked him just as hard.

He stood frozen on the thick carpet, refusing to move. He didn't even breathe.

She set her medical bag on the bed and stepped in front of him, only inches away. Her fingers touched his arm, sending an electric jolt through him. She lifted one wrist for inspection, then the other.

Clay let her do as she pleased, knowing that if he did more than stand there, the only action his body would want to make would end with her on the bed beneath him.

His cock wedged against the towel, threatening to pull it loose. Leigh inched closer until he could feel the soft give of her belly pressing against the tip of his erection.

Sensation so intense it was like raw, living need poured through him. His skin grew too tight as every muscle in his body tensed against the urge to reach for her.

She said nothing, simply stared into his eyes. Some kind of internal debate was waging within her. He could see her indecision in the way she held her bottom lip in her teeth, see her desire in the expansion of her pupils as she continued to stare.

He wanted to tell her to leave—that he wasn't sure how much longer her could keep himself from touching her—but rampant lust fused his throat shut, trapping him in silence.

Leigh pressed her hands flat against his chest. This was it. She was going to push him away and free him from riding the painful edge of possibility.

Instead, she closed her eyes as if soaking in the feel of him. Her lips parted. The little dent left by her teeth teased him, daring him to lick it away.

Clay held fast, refusing to do anything more than stay exactly where he was. No matter what she did to him, so long as he didn't move toward her, he'd stay in control. If he didn't touch her, he couldn't hurt her again.

She tilted her head forward and placed a soft kiss at the base of his throat, like a sweet little gift.

His heart kicked hard enough that he was sure she could feel it beating against her mouth. Then her tongue swept out, dipping into the hollow of his throat, and he was no longer sure of anything.

"Leigh." Her name, a single word of warning, was all he could squeeze out.

She ignored him, letting her mouth trail up his neck and over his jaw. When she could reach no higher without his cooperation, she gripped his head and pulled it down to her mouth.

Her kiss wasn't gentle. It was a demand. An order for him to obey. And like the puppet he was, he bowed to her whim and kissed her back.

His body ignited, his resolve going up in a fiery wash of flames. Gone was every sliver of concern and indecision. She'd burned them all away, leaving him room to simply feel.

The towel around his hips fell to the floor. Leigh slithered down his body in a trail of warm skin and hot, wet kisses. She took his cock into her hands and peered up at him from beneath reddish lashes. As her fingers slid over him, her eyes dared him to try to walk away now.

Not in this lifetime.

Leigh had won. She'd conquered him completely, and surrendering to her was going to be the sweetest failure of his life.

Her lips grazed over him, teasing him to the point of madness. He tried to stand there and take it like a man, but he wasn't that strong. He had to touch her.

His fingers slid into her hair, close to the scalp. He could feel the heat of her excitement radiating out from her skin. And then she opened her mouth over him, and all he felt was wet, hot pleasure.

Clay reveled in it, throwing his head back in abandon. There were no dark thoughts for him here, in this place of shivering warmth. She cast some kind of spell over him, driving away everything but the slick glide of her mouth and the fiery sweep of her tongue.

His fingers curled against her scalp, tangling in her hair. He didn't try to control her movements—she knew exactly what to do to send him screaming to the edge.

He hadn't come in weeks. Maybe months. He couldn't remember. What he did know was that he was barely holding back now, skating so close to the line that he was no longer sure where it was.

Clay tightened his hold in her hair, easing her head back. She looked up at him in question, her lips swollen, dark, and wet. A flush of arousal covered her cheeks and spread down her neck to disappear beneath her blouse.

"I want to see you," he choked out, his voice strangled by lust.

She smiled, but it was more than a curving of her lips. It was a sultry invitation—an offer of feminine delights.

Leigh rose to her feet and stepped back out of his reach. Her fingers went to the top button and popped it free. Then it went to the next and the next.

He stood there and watched, his cock thrusting out, red and shiny from her mouth. With each open button, his erection jerked toward her with embarrassing eagerness.

When the last button was undone and her blouse was hanging open, with only shadowy hints of what lay beneath visible to him, she paused.

"You're not running from me this time." It wasn't a question. Like everything else she'd done since walking into the room, it was a demand—a statement of fact.

Clay swallowed and nodded. Any words he spoke would be blubbering gibberish laced with humiliating need.

Leigh stripped the shirt from her torso, displaying her breasts. The lacy bra lifted them up like an offering, distracting him from the dark marks ringing her biceps.

He thought he was going to have to try not to look at them, but then she reached behind her, unlatching her bra and letting it fall to the floor.

Clay no longer had any reason to look elsewhere. Better even than his fleeting fantasies, her breasts took his breath away. Full and round, with large pink nipples drawn tight. His mouth watered for a taste. His hands itched with the need to touch.

As he watched, she cupped herself, catching her nipples between her fingers and pinching slightly. Clay stared in rapt attention, learning how she liked to be touched even as he clamped down on the sudden urge to come.

She toed out of her shoes and slipped off her jeans. The lacy pink panties stayed on—an unspoken barrier of "Do Not Pass." He accepted it, too overjoyed by what she was offering to let it rob him of this high.

Her waist was smaller than he'd imagined. Or maybe it was the womanly flare of her hips and the sweet swell of her belly that created the illusion. Whatever the case, he was enthralled by her shape, imagining all of the ways he could fit her tight against him.

Leigh caught and held his gaze as she moved toward him again, coming close enough to touch. And then she kept coming, until her hot, soft skin was plastered against his.

Clay shuddered and gave up fighting for control. She was too much temptation—too potent to resist. His self-control was a tattered shambles, and there wasn't enough of it left for him to hold back.

He wrapped his arms around her, sliding his hands over the smooth heat of her back. She offered him a shiver of her own and closed her eyes as if enjoying the feel of his hands on her.

Until this very moment, he wasn't sure she would. Sure, he'd made her come before, but they'd both lost their heads a little back in that motel room. She'd had time to think since then, to decide what she wanted. And didn't want. He was certain he'd fallen into the latter category until this very moment.

He kissed her mouth, giving in to the need to taste her

again. With her sweet tits pressed against his chest, he wanted to kiss her all over, but there was something about her mouth that kept drawing him back for more. She made soft little noises of approval and excitement, kissing him back like she was dying for it. The fact that she would let a man like him get this close went to his head, making him puff up with pride. She was all smooth intellect and control, while he was a raging berserker determined not to drive her away.

Clay forced himself to be gentle when what he wanted to do was toss her to the bed and rip away that last lacy barrier standing between them. If she was half as slick and ready as she'd been yesterday, he'd have no trouble sliding his cock inside her, over and over, until they were both too weak from coming to move.

While that was the best idea he'd ever had, he couldn't guarantee things would go that way. The panties were still on. He wasn't going to push her. And yet the longer he kissed her, the more impossible it became to think that he'd never get to feel all of her naked and gliding against him, from head to toe.

Clay felt her legs tremble. His own weren't too steady, either, so he wrapped his arm around her ass and lifted her up enough to get her to the bed.

She sprawled back onto the coverlet, her skin gleaming and flushed. Her breasts swayed, and Clay knew he'd reached the end of his control. He went on all fours, crawling over her until he reached her waist. The scent of arousal hung around her, an intoxicating perfume that drove him mad with the need to feel her come against his fingers again. He didn't dare touch her there. Not now. Not yet. But soon, he promised himself. Soon, he would feel her hot and slick in his hand, quivering and screaming as she came.

That thought spurred him on. He kissed the indentation of her waist, moving up her ribs, one by one. Each delicate bone got his attention, with nibbling kisses and gentle sweeps of his tongue. His path moved between her breasts. A deep red flush spread down her chest, and it thrilled him to know that he'd been the one to put it there.

She wanted him—at least she wanted what he was doing to her now. The agonizingly slow progression was killing him, making his cock slick with the need for more, but he refused to rush her. A woman like Leigh was meant to be savored, and that was exactly what he was going to do.

She tried to grab his head and drag it up for another kiss, but Clay had given her enough control. It was his turn to take what he wanted.

He fought her hold and lifted her breast to his mouth, swiping his tongue over the puckered tip. Leigh arched off the bed and hissed in pleasure, digging her fingernails into his scalp. The sweet sting of pain glided down his spine and tightened his balls.

He barely held back his orgasm. She was too much to take—too intense and potent for him to keep at arm's length. She crawled into him, warming him from the inside out, driving away the filth and terror of reality. He wanted to chain her to him and never let go. Never before had anyone made him feel like his life was a place of hope rather than bleak and endless desolation.

Clay was so shaken by that thought that he went still. This kind of thing was too heavy for him. Too serious. All he wanted was to get back to where he'd been a second ago with her soft noises of pleasure filling his ears and her writhing dance of abandon making him crazy.

She must have sensed his weird shift in mood. Her hands lifted his head until she could look into his eyes.

He didn't want that. He didn't want her to see what

she did to him—laying him open and stripped of his defenses.

But rather than gloat at her victory, all he saw was concern. She pulled up enough to kiss the tip of his nose. "Where did you go?"

"Nowhere good."

Leigh smiled, washing away the slimy remnants of his stupid thoughts. "Want to talk about it?"

"Fuck no. I don't want to talk at all."

Her smile went dark and hungry. "Good."

She reached over and opened her medical bag. Out came a ribbon of condoms. Whatever thoughts he'd had liquefied and leaked out of his brain. He hadn't even been thinking about rubbers, though he sure as hell would have once he'd gotten to the point of no return. He didn't have even one condom with him. Her pulling those out was more than a rescue; it was an offering.

Clay may not have been completely sane, but he wasn't crazy enough to turn down a chance to get inside her.

She wiggled beneath him. A second later, those pink panties went flying across the room.

He had to look. He'd never had a woman as beautiful as her naked, and he'd be damned if he let the opportunity pass him by.

With one scorching kiss that was part warning, part apology, Clay moved down her body, forcing her thighs wide to make room for his shoulders.

She was even prettier than he could have guessed. Damp red ringlets, the same shade as her eyebrows, shielded wet, pink flesh. Her clit was swollen and begging for his tongue.

He didn't even try to resist. There was no point in wasting effort when he was going to need every bit of his strength to please her. Instead, he gave in and feasted on her, letting her taste go to his head. Her hips bucked and sharp little cries of pleasure echoed in the room. As her breathing sped, so did he. Everything he did seemed to shove her higher, until she coiled tight and clutched his head. Even her breathing went silent, only to be let out as a high cry of completion.

Clay kept her flying for as long as he could. When the last little tremor shook through her, he raised his head.

Leigh lay sprawled in total bliss, panting. Her skin was flushed and glowing with a sheen of sweat. Her heart beat so hard, he could see it jiggle her breast. As much as he wanted to sit back and give her a minute to recover, it wasn't going to happen. He was too wired— too close to the brink of completely losing control to risk it. His only choices were to get up and leave or roll on a condom and take what her careless sprawl offered so beautifully. And he wasn't a strong enough man to leave her—not now when she was all laid out like an offering.

Clay found enough functioning brain cells to fumble a condom onto his cock, and then he covered her, praying she wouldn't shove him away now that she'd found release.

Her arm was over her eyes, but as the tip of his erection pressed against her slick heat, she looked at him.

He froze, poised at the brink of ecstasy.

Her lips parted and her tongue darted out to wet them. He couldn't stop himself from kissing her again, sipping the sweetness of her mouth.

She moaned and her legs wrapped around him, pulling him closer. The tip of his cock was bathed in her heat. She hugged him tight, testing the limits of his control as he rocked slightly deeper.

He wanted to shove himself all the way in and let go. Only the fragile softness of her body, all curvy and hot under him, reminded him to be gentle. Sweat cooled on his back. His arms shook as he held his weight above her. With each kiss he gained another inch, another tugging glide of fist-tight pressure.

Her mouth left his, her breaths coming out as hot caresses against his jaw. She bit at his neck, straining beneath him to lift herself and find just the right angle to send her flying again. Instinctively, Clay knew what to do. He shifted his hips, finding that spot his fingers had found earlier—the one that made her scream and fall apart in his arms.

She gripped his arms tight and flung her head back. Her hair made a wild mess against the dark covers. A choked sob rose from her lips as her pussy clenched around him.

Clay couldn't hold back the flood any longer. As she hit her peak, he gave in and let himself go. Stinging pleasure streaked along his skin and coalesced at the base of his spine. Jolts of sensation pulsed along his cock as she fluttered around him. His orgasm went on for hours, days. It robbed him of breath and rocked him all the way to his foundation.

Finally, when the last trembling pressure eased, he was able to breathe again. Oxygen filled his starved lungs, perfumed with the scent of their heated skin.

He collapsed atop her, struggling to get his elbows under him so he wouldn't crush her. Her breasts cushioned his weight; her hair cradled his cheek. He felt like he'd been scraped clean—like all the bad shit was gone. It was a ridiculous thing to feel, but he couldn't seem to make it go away.

He was still inside her, but his cock was still too hard for the condom to have a prayer of leaking. He could stay another minute, just like this, cradled by her softness.

Sappy. That's what he was. One good fuck and he'd turned into some kind of soppy love song, some hormonally brain-dead kid.

But damn, it felt good.

Finally, he rolled away but didn't go far. He tucked himself right up against her like the needy bastard he was.

She turned onto her side, staring at him. Her orgasms shone in her eyes, making them sparkle with witchy secrets. He didn't know how she did it, but she'd somehow taken away a weight he'd been carrying around. His burdens felt lighter—like he had a prayer of shouldering them to the end.

Her slender finger traced his face. He was so fucking glad he'd shaved and not left beard burn on her delicate skin.

She petted his shoulder and chest, stroking him with slow, gentle sweeps. He closed his eyes and groaned, flopping onto his back so she could do as she pleased.

Her hands moved lower, and he knew that if they went any farther south, she'd see just how much of a horndog he was. Despite his world-rocking orgasm, he still wanted more.

Part of him wondered if he could ever get enough of her to sate him.

She found his cock, still stiff, hard, and twitching in an effort to get closer to her.

A sexy little growl of feminine approval filled the silence, and he risked peeking at her face to see what that sound looked like.

Heaven—that's what she looked like—or at least as close to it as he was ever going to get. Flushed skin, mussed hair, dark, hungry eyes, and pink, swollen lips. It all melded together in perfection so potent he almost had to glance away. He didn't. He soaked it in and reveled in it, wondering how he was ever going to get through another day without getting to see her face.

"I'm going to go get us some food," she said, promise glittering in her eyes. "And when I get back, it's my turn to be on top."

Chapter Twenty

Mira was only halfway to work when she nearly dozed off and crashed her car. Rather than kill herself, she pulled over at the closest coffee shop and headed inside for enough caffeine to make it safely to work. There, she could sleep in one of the on-call rooms if she needed to, but at least she'd be around if anyone heard anything from Clay.

Anxiety had taken its toll on her. Lack of sleep had done even more damage. She felt sluggish and fuzzy and continually on the brink of tears.

Clay was out there, suffering, and she hadn't been able to help nearly enough.

She took her coffee from the counter and turned to leave, running right into a man behind her. Searing coffee sloshed over the side of the cup, splashing against her hand and his shirt and tie. Pain made her drop the cup, which sloshed even more of her drink on his shiny leather shoes.

She gasped in horror at what her clumsiness had done. "I'msosorry!" Her words ran together in a near sob.

He pulled his steaming shirt away from his skin and

looked down at her. Way down. He was taller than any man she'd ever been this close to before, and her dulled wits were too shocked at his appearance to realize she needed to step back.

There was no sign of pain or anger on his face. In fact, he looked completely calm. His pale gaze slid over her face and down her body, crinkling slightly with concern. "It's okay. Are you burned?"

She realized then that she was cradling her hand. It did sting, but she'd gotten only a few drops on her—he was wearing most of it.

"I'm fine."

"Hold this, would you?" He thrust his own paper cup at her—which she took—and he turned around, exiting through the front door.

Mira stood there, her mouth hanging open for a second before her sluggish brain caught up to reality.

She'd hurt him. Maybe seriously. And he'd left before she could really apologize for what she'd done.

She hurried out after him, offering the woman behind the counter a brief word of apology for the mess. The cold air hit her in the face, cooling the wet burn on her finger. He was at his car, the trunk open. Faint morning sunshine filtered through the heavy layer of clouds. Traffic streamed by on the road in front of the coffee shop. A constant line of cars moved through the drive-through.

"I really am sorry," she said as she neared him. "I'm such a klutz."

He glanced over his shoulder, giving her a smile that showed a bit of his dazzling white teeth. "It was my fault. I shouldn't have been standing so close behind you—not before you had coffee."

Now that her brain was catching up with events, she realized how handsome he was. Sharply defined cheekbones, dark brown hair smoothed neatly in place, inky black eyebrows over pale gray eyes the same color as the clouds overhead.

"Close?"

He shrugged, and his smile turned self-deprecating. "I liked your perfume."

Before she could tell him she wasn't wearing any, he pulled his tie off and started unbuttoning his shirt.

"I ruined your clothes," she said as she realized why he was undressing.

"It's okay. I'm on my way out of town on business and have a change in my suitcase. No harm done." He stripped his wet shirt off, baring his chest.

An angry red patch of skin glowed across his abdomen, spreading from just below his pecs down almost to his waistband.

She reached for him, aghast at the damage she'd caused, and then thought better of touching a stranger. "I'm so sorry."

"It's really not a big deal. You saved me from that tie." He leaned forward to unzip his suitcase, and a whole series of lean muscles along his abdomen clenched.

"Tie?" It was all she could think to say in the face of so much raw male beauty. She'd seen plenty of well-built men in various states of dress in the locker rooms at the Edge, but never once had one of their bodies rendered her stupid.

He nodded, politely ignoring her painfully awkward question. "A gift from Mom. Now I can tell her that a beautiful young woman ruined it, and she won't ever again ask me why I don't wear it."

"Ruined?" Mira groaned, and then she finally processed the rest of what he'd said.

Beautiful? *He* thought *she* was beautiful? A man built like a god with a face to match thought frumpy ol' her was beautiful?

"It's no big deal. I can probably save the shirt."

"At least let me pay to have them cleaned."

He slipped a clean shirt on and started to button it up, saving her from staring. "No need. Really."

"I insist."

He stopped dressing and turned to face her. There was something in his eyes she'd never seen in a man before—at least not one who was looking at her. That look was filled with heat and blatant interest. It was the kind of look that people like Bella and Razor got from men.

"Do you really want to make it up to me?" he asked.

She nodded, unable to speak.

"Then take me to dinner."

That shocked her tongue back into place. "Dinner? I can't."

The heat in his gaze died down, replaced with disappointment. "Husband?"

"No."

"A boyfriend, then?"

"No."

"A girlfriend?"

"No."

"Then why can't you?" He asked the question like it was completely reasonable for her to go out with a complete stranger.

"My life is a mess right now, and I—"

He held up his hands, stopping her words from babbling out and embarrassing her further. "Say no more. I didn't mean to push."

"You weren't pushing."

His gaze slipped to her mouth for a split second before coming back to her eyes. "Then have dinner with me."

"I don't even know your name."

"Adam." He held out his hand to shake hers, waiting for her to touch him.

Mira wasn't sure she could take it. She already felt like she was on overload, struggling to keep up with even the simplest of conversations with this man. And yet she felt like she owed him something for what she'd done. Refusing to shake his hand would have been adding insult to injury. Literally.

She slid her palm against his. He closed his long fingers around her hand, engulfing hers. His skin was slightly rough, and warm despite the frosty air. His finger inched along the inside of her wrist, his grip overflowing hers. For the briefest second, she thought that he'd stroked her on purpose, but the contact was too short for her to be sure she hadn't imagined it.

"Okay," she whispered, feeling a crazy thrill rush through her.

"Okay what?" he asked as he tucked in his fresh shirt. She watched his fingers dip below his waistband, jealous of their journey.

The thought of touching him, of feeling his skin beneath her fingertips, pulled all the moisture from her mouth.

She pried her tongue from the roof of her mouth before she could speak. "I'll buy you dinner. I owe you that much."

He smiled and plucked a business card from his briefcase. "You don't owe me anything, but I'm too eager to see you again not to take you up on your offer."

Eager to see her? No one was ever eager to see her, especially not hot, hunky men who were as smooth as Adam was.

"I should say no," she told him.

"And crush my tender feelings? You wouldn't do that, would you, . . . ?"

"Mira."

His smile widened at the sound of her name, and he slipped his business card into the side pocket of her purse, giving her no option to reject it.

"I'm only gone for the day, Mira. You pick the place and I'll be there. Tonight at eight?"

Tonight seemed too soon and yet not nearly soon enough.

Shocking herself, she nodded her agreement as he took his coffee from her hand. His fingers brushed hers, and suddenly her burn no longer hurt. All she could feel was the hot tingles left behind in the wake of his touch.

Adam was . . . shaken. He'd planned to ingratiate himself with Mira and lure her off someplace private tonight, using whatever means necessary.

He hadn't planned on reacting to her on such a primitive level.

She didn't have the flawless perfection of models and movie stars, but there was something compelling about her that pulled him in and didn't let go. She was genuine, without façade or artifice, with a kind of innocence about her that intrigued him.

Adam had never met anyone so open. Even though he'd planned their meeting, he hadn't expected her to follow him to his car, trailing after him with a string of apologies on her sweet lips.

He could have easily overpowered her right then and there, shoving her into his trunk. The task would be done and he'd be on his way. But for some reason, he couldn't bring himself to brutalize her in that way. Innocence like hers was rare and precious. He didn't want to completely crush her.

Perhaps that was inevitable. A man like him could not

operate under the guise of mercy. He had to be ruthless and give Dr. Sage what he wanted so that Adam could locate his brother. If Eli was like the rest, he was suffering. Adam refused to let his brother go through that alone.

Even if it meant crushing Mira's fragile innocence.

Tonight he would meet her. He would drug her. He would take her to Sage and be done with his task. Whatever happened to her after that was none of his concern. Eli was all he could allow himself to care about. If Mira was a casualty of finding his brother, he was going to have to find a way to accept that and move on. Somehow.

Chapter Twenty-one

Leigh had to get some air. Clay filled up the room and then some. She loved that about him even as she struggled to find enough oxygen to think clearly.

Thinking was not something Clay had allowed her much time to do. She'd tried to keep control of the situation, but he'd stormed in, all eager and willing to please. She had no defenses against that kind of thing.

If he'd been a jerk or pushed her, she could have stopped. Her body would still be clamoring for more, but at least she would have left the room with all of the pieces of herself intact. As it was, Leigh was scared to death that she'd left something vital behind, that she'd bared some essential part of herself and given it to him without realizing what she'd done. And there was no getting it back.

But whatever she'd let go, it didn't feel like a loss. She felt stronger, more capable. She could keep moving forward, doing whatever needed to be done.

After she got her fill of him.

A little part of her mind laughed at that thought. There was no getting enough of a man like Clay. All she could hope for was to get as much as she could before they parted ways.

So that's what she was going to do. She was going to gorge herself on the hunky, naked man in that bedroom until he begged for mercy.

With his discarded towel wrapped around her, she grabbed some snacks and headed back into the lion's den.

Clay watched her, his amber eyes sparkling with intimate knowledge of a shared secret. The sheet was pulled to his waist, leaving bare the lean expanse of his chest and abdomen. Not even the bruises riding his ribs could diminish his raw beauty.

Beneath the wrinkled edge of the sheet, she could see the unmistakable tent his arousal caused.

"Don't you ever get enough?" she teased.

"We've barely gotten started."

She set the tray of food on the bed and crawled in beside him. "Eat."

His grin was filled with delicious intent. "I like it when you get all bossy."

She glanced pointedly at his erection. "Apparently. Now eat." She put a chunk of apple to his lips to keep him from saying anything else that would scatter her wits further.

He accepted her tribute in manly fashion, taking the bite from her hand as he sprawled out with his hands stacked behind his head. Lean muscles flexed, distracting Leigh from the bite she was about to take. She still couldn't believe that she'd had sex with him. He was much more untamed and unapologetically male than the men she usually dated.

With him lying here like this, relaxed and smiling, she could almost imagine what it would be like for them outside all of the terror and drama. That was a fantasy, of course, but one that made her ache for beautiful, ethereal things she dared not let solidify in her mind.

This brief respite from danger was just that. It couldn't last long. And while she wanted nothing more than to spend the day in bed with him, time was ticking away—time she wasn't sure Clay had.

Leigh waited until he'd eaten his fill before bringing up harsh reality. "We should probably get back to work."

His smile faded, and the glittering light of promise in his eyes was snuffed dead. He let out a long sigh. "So much for you being on top, huh?"

She tried for a negligent shrug, but her body was too stiff and jerky to pull it off. "We'll save that for later."

"No guarantee there will be a later, Leigh. At least not for me."

"That's what I'm fighting for. There's nothing I want more than to see you and Garrett both free men, able to go to sleep, knowing exactly where you'll be all night long."

A deep sadness etched grooves around his mouth. "You and I both know that once this is over, things between us will be different."

Different, yes, but she couldn't go there now. The future was too full of minefields. She didn't dare go there if she could avoid it. "That's a worry for another day. Today is already chock-full."

He scrubbed his face with his hands, and she couldn't help but remember just how those fingers could make her feel—how his palms had been slightly rough as they'd slid over her, finding all the secret little hollows of pleasure she hadn't known were there.

"So what do we do next?" he asked. "Payton thinks we should stay here. I can't make heads or tails of those notes I wrote. That note about a possible Wednesday meeting isn't for hours—assuming it's even this week. Where does that leave us?"

Leigh clutched the sheet a bit tighter around her

breasts. The air in here was much colder now that Clay wasn't heating her from the inside out. "What do we know?"

"That I'm fucked in the head."

"Details. That's what we need. For instance, you know that you were sent to do some kind of job."

"Yeah, stealing those kids, finding some files, or something else entirely. That gets us jackshit, Leigh."

"No, it means that this doctor still needs you. It means that whatever horrible thing he wanted you to do is not yet done. It also means that he might send someone else to do it."

"How do we stop me or anyone else from doing a job when we don't even know what it is?"

She bit her lip, wondering about the intelligence of even bringing this up. Still, since she'd shared her body with him, it seemed silly not to share her idea as well. "You do know what the job is. You just don't remember."

"How does that help?"

"If we restrain you and then find a way to wake up that other side of you, then we can—"

He sat up, making the muscles in his abdomen clench hard. "Not only no, but *fuck* no. I'm not going to intentionally go all psycho and risk your life."

"I can always sedate you if things get out of hand."

"*If* things get out of hand? I've killed people. Just talking about this means things *are* out of hand."

"Do you have any better ideas?"

"Yeah, sending you to the farthest reaches of China, halfway around the world, where no one can find you until this is all over."

"You know that won't help."

"Maybe not, but it will sure as hell make me feel better." He shook his head. "I can't even believe that you would consider something so stupid."

"It could work."

"No, it couldn't. Even if you could find some cage strong enough to hold me, it's not like I can turn it on and off like a switch."

"Something has been triggering those episodes—besides whatever verbal cues they used—like when those armed men attacked us in Payton's house."

Clay went still. His eyes became distant. All the color bleached from his skin and he swallowed hard.

"You know what did it, don't you?" she asked.

He nodded. "Yeah, but there's no way I'm telling you, so just forget it."

"You said yourself that we could find a cage strong enough to hold you."

"No, I said *if*. That's a long way from accepting your idea as a valid choice."

"It could work."

"Bullshit. Even if everything else lines up, what makes you think that my psycho side would tell you anything?"

He had a point. "Fine. Maybe it was a stupid idea."

"Not stupid, but way too dangerous."

She took his hand in hers because she couldn't stand to not be touching him. His fingers tightened on hers, and his thumb slid over her skin.

"Out of curiosity, what is the trigger?"

"I'm not telling you that."

"Why not? Don't you think it's in my best interests to know what not to do?"

His mouth went flat, and then he stared into her eyes. There was something desperate lurking in the amber depths. Gone were all hints of lust, and in their place was something she couldn't name. All she knew was that it scared her—like a silent warning of impending danger.

"I'm sorry, Leigh. I want to trust you that much, but I just don't."

His statement, so flatly given after what they'd shared, left her feeling cold and empty. She wanted to be the kind of person who could understand his reasoning and forgive his lack of trust in her, but she just couldn't. She'd dropped everything to come help him. She'd risked her life for him, and yet it still wasn't enough to gain his trust.

The bleak truth hit her in the gut, snuffing out all the little flickering flames of hope that had begun to glow inside of her. If Clay didn't trust her now, he never would. And if he never trusted her, then they'd never have anything more than they did now.

That wasn't enough for her. Not anymore. Not even close.

She had to back away fast. Close her heart up tight before he could wiggle in any further. She couldn't stop caring about him, but she had to find a way to put a wall between them—separate what she needed to do to save her brother from the way she felt.

So that's what she'd do. No more sex; no more emotion. She would be all about the job until it was done. And then she'd never see Clay again. It was the only way to save herself from heartbreak.

Chapter Twenty-two

Payton heard Leigh's and Clay's voices behind the door. He knew he wouldn't have much time alone, so he hurried to the piles of paper and photos spread across the dining table. There was evidence here that had to be destroyed before it could get out. The lives of innocents were at stake.

As he gathered up the notes containing code words for different operations he'd executed years ago, one of the photos caught his eye. He stared at it, unable to believe what he saw.

Dr. Norma Stynger sat on a bench at a park. Her garish red lipstick was like a slash of blood across her mouth. She was as skinny as a praying mantis, clad in a designer suit that barely hid the sharp angles of her bones. She was older now than he remembered but not diminished by the passing of years. Age had given her a ruthless edge, but her pale green eyes were the same—shining with greed for knowledge and the power that came with it.

Sitting next to her on the bench was a man Payton had not seen in months: Dr. Richard Sage. He looked livid. His fingers were splayed toward her, as if he was trying to hold himself back from strangling her. Spittle flew from his lips, the tiny drops highlighted by a ray of sunshine. Whoever had taken this photo was high above them, perhaps atop a nearby building.

The date stamped in the corner was recent—only three weeks old.

Payton sank into a chair, his legs suddenly giving out. He'd known for months that Stynger was still alive, but seeing her still hit him hard, reminding him of his carelessness and all the lives it had ruined.

Poor Jake Staite was still a rabid mess of rage and frustration. They had to keep him sedated most of the time, for his own safety, and for the safety of those Stynger had ordered him to kill.

Jake's torment had been caused by Stynger, but if Payton had done his job years ago and made sure she'd gone up in flames in that building where he'd trapped her, none of this would have ever happened. Jake would be alive and well, serving his country, not locked up in a concrete room, sleeping his prime years away.

Seeing Stynger with Richard Sage was not a good sign. Payton couldn't tell from this photo, but the anger displayed and the public meeting place left only a few possible options: Sage knew what Stynger was up to and was pissed, Sage thought he knew and was pissed, or Sage had no clue and was pissed.

The last option seemed unlikely. Sage had thought she was dead like all of the rest of them had. Maybe he was angry that she hadn't come to him sooner to tell him she was alive.

None of that really mattered, anyway. The real thing that mattered was that the two of them had met. They'd worked side by side on the Threshold Project years ago. Both had intimate knowledge of the research. If the two of them were meeting, it had to be about that. There was no catching up on old times for these two. They'd always hated each other.

Sage had sworn he'd gone legit. Both Payton and Bob had kept tabs on him over the years.

Maybe they hadn't been looking closely enough. If Sage was back in the game, then he was going to have to be stopped.

Payton headed upstairs to where he could get cell phone reception. He dialed Sage's work number and asked the woman who answered to let him speak to him.

A couple of minutes later, Richard Sage came on the line. "What do you want?"

"I'd like to see you," said Payton.

"What makes you think I'd set foot in the same room with you?"

"I have information that I think you should know."

"Then tell me now. My time is too valuable to waste on you."

Time to test the waters. "Norma Stynger is alive."

"She is?" said Sage a little too quickly. There was no hesitation, no shock in his tone.

At least now Payton knew that Sage was still willing to lie to him. "She is. I believe she will approach you."

"About what?"

"The old research. I think she may want to recruit you."

Sage's voice became a jealous hiss. "Her work was always inferior to mine. If she did try to recruit me, it would be because of my success."

Ah. That explained the anger Payton had seen in the photo.

"I know you met with her," said Payton. "My only question is what she wanted from you."

Silence filled the line for a moment. "How do you know?"

"I know everything, Richard. Eventually. So answer my question."

"The bitch did approach me."

"And?"

"I was shocked that she was alive after all these years."

"What did she want?"

"The same thing she always wanted—to steal my work and put her name on it."

"Did you give her your research?"

"You know I couldn't. You destroyed it all. Remember?"

Payton had—or at least he thought he had. He'd also thought he'd killed Stynger, so he wasn't taking anything for granted.

"And even if you hadn't, the only thing I'd give that cheating bitch is a hard shove off a tall building."

"Did she tell you anything else?" asked Payton. "Anything that could help me find her?"

"She said she got funding for her work and that she's making great strides."

"Funding from whom?"

"She didn't say. After she gloated about it, I wasn't inclined to ask. Especially considering that her funding was always better than mine. She gets all the best equipment and I have to scrounge for everything I need."

Sage's slip of the tongue spoke volumes. "You mean everything you needed? Past tense?"

"Of course that's what I meant," said Sage, but the breathless quality of his words told Payton everything he needed to now.

Sage may have been legit before, but he wasn't now—or if he was, it was simply a cover for his real work.

"That's good," said Payton. "Because if you were dabbling with your old research, I'd be obliged to hunt you down and kill you."

"The way you did Stynger?" asked Sage. "You don't scare me, Payton. Besides, I gave up on the Threshold Project years ago. It brought me nothing but ulcers."

That was a lie, too, but one Payton let slide. He had the answers he needed.

If Sage hadn't been working on the old research before, he definitely was now. There was no way he'd be able to resist competing with Stynger. Their professional rivalry ran too deep.

"I suggest you watch your back," warned Payton.

"And I suggest you keep your nose out of my business. Don't bother calling me again. I'm disconnecting this number. If I find out you've been snooping around at my workplace again, you're not going to like what happens. Neither is Mira."

Sage hung up, leaving that ominous statement hanging in Payton's ear. An oily film of panic coated his throat, making it hard to breathe. He'd been so caught up in what was going on with Clay, he hadn't stopped to consider the danger Mira faced.

Sage knew that Payton cared about her. Sage wasn't above using his daughter to get what he wanted. History had proven that with crystal clarity.

Mira had an urgent package from Leigh waiting in her mailbox when she finally made it in to work. Thoughts of her meeting with Adam had filled her head, giving her a much-needed break from worrying about Clay. Until she read the note that Leigh had included with the phones, asking for help. Leigh wasn't sure what Mira should look for but asked her to be thorough.

With Clay on the line, there was no way she'd be anything less.

At least Mira knew he was still alive. That counted for

a lot. What little sleep she'd had had been filled with horrid dreams of zombie Clay coming at her, guns blazing. His eyes had been empty, and he hadn't even flinched as he'd pulled the trigger over and over.

Even now, in the light of day, those nightmares had the power to make her hands shake.

She wished that she was with him now, making sure he was being careful and staying safe. She loved him like a brother, but she knew how boneheaded he could be. He didn't like to be pushed around, and Leigh wasn't exactly a doormat. As much as Mira had wanted to see the two of them together, she'd hoped it would be under better circumstances.

But it wasn't, and all she could do to help was figure out if there was any useful information on these phones.

She powered up the first one. There was no password protection on the device. She read through e-mail and text messages, finding little of interest. There could be more incriminating messages he'd erased, but she wouldn't know that until she checked for deleted entries.

The contact list was vague—mostly first names or initials. As she scrolled through the listings, an entry caught her eye: Dr. S. It was next to a number she knew all too well.

The phone slipped from Mira's hands and landed on the floor. Plastic pieces spun away and the battery flew under her desk.

She left them lying there and grabbed her own phone from her belt. Her hands were shaking with panic as she pulled up the list of phone numbers she'd blocked—all various numbers for her father.

Just to be sure, she picked up the pieces of the battered phone and shoved them back together. Holding both phones side by side, she compared the numbers.

She hadn't imagined it. The numbers were the same. The number was for her father's office.

Sick with dread, she checked the other two phones. Both contained listings for that number as well.

Whoever owned these phones, her father had sent them after Clay. The question was, why?

Richard Sage had always been a possessive man. He stamped his claim on people as if they were things. Apparently, Clay had been stamped, and Mira's father wanted him back.

She didn't know what to do. Her father had always thought of her as his possession. He'd kept close tabs on her for years, despite her moving from place to place in an effort to avoid him. She'd even found bugs in her apartment once, three years ago.

That thought stopped her cold. She hadn't swept her place in weeks. She was hypervigilant about using her security system—one she'd designed herself. If anyone got close to her place, it recorded their image and sent it to her phone. The only person who knew the codes to get in was Clay.

Who looked just like those empty men who were victims of her father's experiments.

Panic gripped her with sharp claws, squeezing the air from her lungs. She doubled over in her chair, shoving her head down between her knees. Flickering black spots bloomed in her vision as her brain struggled to find enough oxygen to work. Slowly, the dizziness faded, leaving behind a greasy, queasy kind of fear.

Clay had been in her office, too. She let him in all the time. What if her father was watching her right now?

She felt his eyes on her, making her skin crawl. The urge to locate and destroy any possible bugs pounded through her, but she didn't dare act rashly. Instead, she picked up her phone and rushed to the ladies' room. Surely Clay hadn't been in here.

She picked the stall in the farthest corner and locked the door. Her head hit the cold stainless steel, sucking away some of the sickening heat rising out of her. The faint rattle of the lock jarred her, making her realize just how hard she was shaking.

Mira had thought her father was out of her life. She'd thought she could simply ignore his existence and move on. She'd been wrong.

Now that Clay was involved, so was she. It was her fault that her father even knew Clay existed. If not for his brave defense of her on the playground and her grateful invitation for him to come home and play with her, her father never would have met him.

At least some small part of what had happened to Clay rested on her shoulders. She had to find a way to make it right. But how?

Her choices were limited. She could either charge in and confront her father directly, or she could take a more subtle approach and try to destroy him from the inside of his computer networks out.

She was definitely better at the latter. The former scared her to death but was the faster alternative. And there was no way to know how much time Clay had before something really bad happened.

A lot of the men touched by her father had killed themselves. She remembered him ranting about it on the phone when he hadn't known she could hear him.

That couldn't happen to Clay. She wouldn't let it happen. Even if that meant she went to see her father and killed him herself. He deserved to die. She wouldn't miss him. She would only miss the kind of man he should have been.

With no other good ideas springing to mind, Mira got into her car and headed for the gun she kept locked in a safe at home. As soon as she had it, she'd find him at work and make sure he never hurt anyone else ever again.

Chapter Twenty-three

Leigh kept her head down, poring over the maze of photos and notes, which made even less sense than it had last night. She'd barely spoken ten words to Clay since she'd left his room to clean up in private and gather her wits.

Keeping her distance from him was harder than she'd thought it would be. She kept having to squelch the urge to reach for him or say something inane, just to break the awkward silence.

Every few minutes, she felt him look at her. As soon as the weight of his gaze was gone, she'd sneak a peek at him, soaking up the sight of his broad shoulders and those hands that could make her feel things she'd thought impossible.

She couldn't help feeling cheated somehow. Clay's ability to trust had been stripped from him—stolen. It wasn't fair, but there wasn't a damn thing she could do to fix him. It was best if she held herself at a distance, emotionally, refusing to be drawn in any further than she already had been.

Garrett needed her to focus, not stare like some lovesick schoolgirl.

She didn't love Clay. Nor was she planning to. Falling for a man so inaccessible would be stupid, and Leigh was no idiot.

Clay's head jerked up as if he'd heard something. He jumped from his chair and took off at a sprint, leaving her sitting at the table.

She wasn't sure what had gotten into him, but it was her job to make sure he didn't lose control and hurt anyone—no matter how little he trusted her. The way he'd run out of here made her fear that something had just gone wrong. Maybe he'd hit his time limit and had gone running back to the doctor who'd done this to him.

The ever-present syringe of sedative was tucked into her pocket, ready to go if needed. She followed after him, hearing only his heavy footsteps pounding up the stairs at the end of the long hallway.

The massive vault door had been left open as Clay had demanded. As she moved past it, up the stairs, she could hear Clay's deep voice followed by that of a woman. She moved faster, slipping around the corner just in time to see Clay engulfing Mira in a hard hug.

A fist of jealousy punched Leigh hard, stopping her dead in her tracks. She knew they were friends, and she wasn't some possessive harpy who staked a claim to every man she slept with. And she'd already decided to push Clay away. Still, she couldn't quiet the sickening sense of loss she felt watching the two of them connect on such a deep level.

That closeness was something she'd never have with him, and for that, a small part of her wept.

Clay pulled away, holding Mira's face in his hands. His expression was one of sheer relief. "I'm so glad you're okay."

Mira grabbed his hands and held on tight. "I'm the

one who should be worried about you. Not the other way around."

He smiled and pulled her to him for another hug. "I hate not being around to look out for you."

"And I hate to break this up," said Payton from the opposite doorway, "but it's not safe for Mira to be here." He looked freshly cleaned and shaved, in a pristine suit and tie.

Mira turned toward him. "I had to come, Payton. I couldn't trust this to a phone call."

"Trust what?" asked Clay, his body going tense.

Until now, Leigh hadn't realized just how relaxed he'd been since sleeping with her, but now that the tension was back, it was painfully obvious.

Mira stepped away from him, looking at the floor. Guilt haunted her eyes. "It's my dad, Clay. He's the one who did this to you."

"What?" asked Clay, his voice a whisper of thinly controlled violence.

She shook her head, making sudden tears spill down her cheeks. "It's true. I found his phone number on all three of the phones Leigh sent me. He hired them to come after you. *You*, my best friend." Betrayal made her words bitter shards of sound. "I just went to his work, and the place was abandoned. Everything was gone."

"You went to confront him?" asked Payton, clearly horrified by the idea.

"I had a gun," she said, as if that made it better.

Clay took her by the shoulders, looking like he was barely keeping himself from shaking her. "What the fuck were you thinking, Mira?"

"I was thinking that I was going to make him undo it. He's killing you. Making you sick. I'm not going to sit by and watch it happen."

Payton swept in, all cool and calm in the midst of too

much fiery emotion. He took Mira by the hand and pulled her away from Clay to sit on the couch. He knelt down in front of her, his voice gentle. "Tell me exactly where you went and what you saw."

"I went to the labs where he was working last year—where I thought he was still working. I haven't spoken to him in months. The building was locked, so I looked in the windows and saw . . . nothing. No people, no furniture, no equipment. The place had been cleaned out. All that was left were compression marks in the carpet."

Payton got a strange look on his face that Leigh didn't understand. He hadn't been surprised when Mira told them that her father was to blame, but he had been surprised to hear that the labs were empty.

"What does that mean?" asked Leigh, trying to make sense of all this.

Payton lifted his head toward Leigh. His expression was hard and cold. "It means we need to find him."

Mira shook her head. "I tried locating him with his cell, but I couldn't. It's like his phone doesn't exist. He didn't answer when I called, and all I got was a beep. I didn't leave a message. I was too furious. The landline is a disconnected number. So is his home number."

Clay stalked toward Mira. "Where is the gun?"

"In my purse."

He took her purse from her shoulder and removed the gun. He checked it with a few smooth, efficient movements and shoved it in the back of his waistband, next to his own weapon.

"What are you doing?" she asked.

"Keeping you from getting killed. There is no fucking way you're going after your own father with a loaded weapon."

"Someone has to make him stop hurting you."

"I'll do it myself."

"No, you won't," said Payton. "A few words from him and you won't even remember you wanted to kill him. I'm the one who needs to go."

"You?" demanded Clay, incredulous. "What the hell are you going to do?"

"Question him. Get the information we need."

"How?" asked Leigh.

Payton's head came up. The look on his face startled Leigh enough that she took a step back. The man standing before them wasn't the suave, metrosexual bachelor she thought she knew. He was darker, frightening in his intensity. "Any way I can."

"I'm going with you," said Mira. "He's been watching me. Listening to me. I found bugs in my house. That's not something I can just let slide."

"You found—" Clay's words cut off as if he'd choked on them. Rage darkened his face and made his jaw bulge.

"What did you do with them?" asked Payton.

"Nothing. I just grabbed my gun and ran. I didn't want him to know that I knew—it was like letting him win, somehow."

"Good. We can work with that," said Payton.

"What does that mean?" asked Clay.

"It means that Mira needs to go on as if she believes she's not being watched. And the two of you," said Payton, pointing at Clay and Leigh, "need to stay here and keep your heads down."

Leigh shook her head. "But we were going to—"

Clay cut her off, talking over her. "Fine, but don't be long. I'm not sitting around here forever." He grabbed her wrist, giving her a slight squeeze.

She looked up at him, searching for meaning in his silent signal. All she saw was hard determination and furious contempt. Still, she trusted him enough to stay quiet, even if that trust wasn't reciprocal.

"I'll leave now," said Payton. "It may take me a few hours to locate him if he's not at home. I'll call you as soon as I learn anything useful." He offered Mira a hand up off the couch. "You should leave now, too. If your car is also bugged, you could be drawing your father or his people here right now."

"What do I do?" asked Mira.

"Pretend everything is fine. Act normal. Go back to work."

"I think my office is bugged, too."

"Then go shopping or see a movie—just don't go anywhere alone. It may not be safe."

Mira slung her purse over her shoulder. She sniffed back her tears, casting one last shame-filled look at Clay. "I'm sorry. About everything. If you'd never met me, if I'd never brought you home that day, my father wouldn't have even known you existed."

Clay's voice turned gentle. "This isn't your fault, runt. Don't ever think I blame you for even one second, okay?"

Mira nodded and shuffled out. Payton saw her to the door and returned a second later. His face was grim. "Stay here. I'll be back as soon as I can."

Clay said nothing. Leigh watched him, sure he was hiding something. The moment she heard the sound of Payton's engine starting, she said, "Why did you cut me off a minute ago?"

"Because I didn't want him to know where we were going."

"Why?"

"I don't trust him. It's only an hour before the appointed time on that note I left. Get your stuff. You and I are taking a little trip, and if Payton is the liar I think he is, we won't be coming back."

*   *   *

Leigh pulled into the parking area outside Wilson's Cliffs Country Club. Clay scanned the area, searching for signs of why he'd written himself a note to come here.

The place was lavish, shining with money and prestige. The lawn was winter brown but still managed to appear lush. In the center of a wide circle drive was a ten-foot fountain with a curved stone bench around its perimeter.

"This is the right place," said Leigh. "Guess we'll see if it's the right time, too."

"We'll sit here and watch for a minute. I still have no idea what I'm here to see or do."

"Whatever you want."

Leigh was treating Clay differently now. She was colder, more distant—all business. There had been a time when he would have welcomed that, but that time had passed. He liked the fiery side of her—the woman who came apart in his arms and made him feel like there was still a piece of his life that wasn't all blood, confusion, and chaos.

Seeing Mira again—feeling terrified to be so close to her—had been a stark reminder of just how dangerous he was to be around and how Leigh was risking her life to help him. Yeah, she was doing it for her brother's sake, but that didn't mean that he couldn't appreciate what she was doing for him as well.

Leigh was making sure that the people he cared about—people like Mira—didn't get hurt by him. The only problem was that now Clay cared about Leigh, too.

If he could have sent her away, he would have. He didn't like putting her at risk. But he wasn't that stupid. Like it or not, he needed her.

A man walked outside, huddled in a dressy wool coat. He flipped up the collar and looked around with glaring nervousness.

"What about Captain Obvious over there?" asked Leigh. "Does he look familiar?"

"I can't tell. It's too far away. I don't suppose you have any binoculars in your car, do you?"

She reached behind her and pulled the camera from the backseat. "How about a zoom lens?"

Smart. Clay zoomed in on the man and snapped a few photos. He brought them up on the display and enlarged them, but there was nothing about the man that rang any bells. "Guess I need to go out there."

"What? You can't do that. You don't even know why you're here. What if you're supposed to observe a meeting of some kind and not let them see you? What if you're just here to take photos?"

More likely he was here to kill someone, but he didn't want to admit that aloud. "And what if I'm supposed to be the one doing the meeting? This man could have information we need. Besides, it's ten past three. He won't wait out in the cold all day."

"I don't like it."

Neither did Clay, but that was the story of his life these days. "I'll be careful. If I get in trouble, drive away."

She stared into his eyes for a moment, and he swore he saw a flicker of the woman he'd been naked with a few hours ago—all heat and fire—only now it was anger he saw rather than desire. "You really don't know me at all, do you?"

He wanted to. He wanted to spend more time with her and learn what made her tick. He wanted to take her somewhere fun, hear her laugh. But mostly, he wanted her to live through having known him, and for that reason, he ignored her question and stepped out into the cold.

Clay was normally good at shifting gears from personal life to work, but this time he kept missing his mark, making his brain grind and smoke in an effort to fall into place.

Leigh was back in the car, likely stung by his dismissal. He didn't like thinking he'd hurt her in any way, but at least this time the damage hadn't left a mark. It was the best he could offer, given the circumstances. If she was pissed at him, maybe she would leave if the shit hit the fan.

As he neared the man by the fountain, he could feel Leigh's gaze on his back. He kept his eyes cast down, pretending he wasn't looking, in case he wasn't supposed to be here. If the man didn't speak to him, he'd pass by and head into the lobby.

The distance between them closed. He saw the man's feet shift, take a few steps, then come to a halt.

"You're late," he said.

Clay put on his best poker face and looked up. "You waited."

"Yeah, well, my boss isn't the kind of man who likes excuses. He wants this done."

Clay wanted to ask who his boss was, but if he was already supposed to know, it would blow his cover. "Then let's get it done."

The man pulled something from his coat pocket and handed it to Clay. It was a plastic room key for a swanky hotel in downtown Dallas.

"Room two-fourteen. Information on your target will arrive there at midnight. Finish the job by dawn and we'll make it worth your effort."

That sounded a hell of a lot like he was asking Clay to kill someone. "Why the rush?"

"Why do you care?" snapped the man. "All you need to know is that you do the job and we'll get you the files you want. End of transaction."

Files? That's what this was about. Finally some answers, though not nearly as many as he would have liked.

The urge to ask about the files nearly choked Clay. He tried not to let his curiosity show on his face. "How do you want it done?"

"Quickly. And we don't want anyone asking questions. Make it look like an accident."

"No problem."

"There'd better not be," said the man. "Fail us and you won't get another chance at that data. Your employer isn't exactly the most forgiving man. If you don't bring him what he wants, I doubt you'll enjoy what happens next."

Clay gave the man a long, hard stare. "I said no problem. You worry about your end, because if I do this and you don't give me those files, you're going to find out just how unforgiving *I* can be."

The man's mouth flattened in anger, but he looked away first. Clay had scared him.

Good. If he was going to play the part of a hired assassin, he needed to sell it. And Mr. Fancy Pants here was clearly buying.

He turned around and walked casually back into the building. Clay waited until he was out of sight before going back to Leigh.

"Drive," he said as he got in.

She did. "What happened?"

"I think I was just hired to kill a man."

"You . . . what?"

A queasy sense of dread fell over him, chilling him. "Makes a hell of a lot of sense, don't you think? I have all these blackouts and wake up with blood on my hands. I wasn't out line dancing."

"Who did he ask you to kill?"

"No idea. I have a room key for a hotel. I'm supposed to be there tonight for instructions."

Leigh's hands were tight around the wheel, her knuckles white with strain. "What are we going to do?"

"The man said he'd give me files. I'm not going to kill anyone to get them, but if I can find a way to stage someone's death and get that information, I think that's our best bet."

"How are you going to manage that?"

"Fake blood. Maybe a dose of that drug of yours." He glanced at her to see how she took that idea.

Not well. Her shoulders inched up toward her ears and she went pale, swallowing hard. "It's one thing to drug someone who's trying to hurt me. It's another to do so to some random person on the street. Without knowing their medical history, it's dangerous."

"This person is clearly already in danger. If I don't pretend to kill them, then whoever that guy I met was, he'll just send someone else who will do the job right. This way we can at least warn the target to get the hell out of town or go to the police."

"He'd tell them about you. You could be arrested."

"I'll wear a mask. We need that information."

"We don't even know what it is."

"No, but we know that Mira's dad wants it, and that he's willing to send me out to kill someone to get it."

"Are you sure this is his doing?"

"The man I met mentioned my employer. I assume he's talking about Richard Sage, since I have no memory of any of this. He's sure as hell not talking about Bella—my real boss."

Leigh pulled over into a parking lot at a strip mall, well away from the shops. Her hand trembled as she put the car in park. She didn't look at him, and for some reason that bothered the piss out of Clay. He needed to know what she was feeling, what she was thinking. He didn't like standing on the far side of the wall she'd put around herself. It made him lonely and furious all at the same time.

She let out a long, slow breath and nodded, as if trying to convince herself of something. "Okay. We'll do this your way. I'll give you what you need to incapacitate a full-grown man if that's what it takes to help Garrett."

"I can't promise that the files will help him, Leigh."

"I know. It's a chance I'm going to have to take, no matter how much I loathe the idea."

She was crossing a line in her mind. He could see her regret for her decision in the way she couldn't lift her eyes above her lap.

Clay couldn't ask her to do this. She was right. This was way different from defending herself. "I'll find another way. I'm good with my hands. I should be able to overpower him and knock him out."

She turned toward him then, all cold logic, with no hint of the emotion he'd seen a moment ago. He hated it that she could freeze up on him like that.

"Should be? What if you're not?" she asked. "What if he fights back and you lose it again? Then you'll really kill him."

She had a valid point. It only pissed him off more, making him feel edgy and out of control.

"We'll wait and see who it is. If it's some old lady, that's one thing. If it's a man in his prime, that's another. I may have to play it by ear, but I can plan for different scenarios."

"So what do we do now?"

"We'll hit a store for some stuff to make fake blood, and I'll need a mask. Once everything's ready, we wait."

"In that hotel room?" She didn't sound as if she liked the idea any better than he did.

"Hell no. We'll get a different room. I'm going to need some time to prepare and plan, and I don't want to do that out in the open. Besides, you look like you could use some sleep."

She snorted as if the mere thought was ridiculous. "Yeah, right. That'll happen.

He'd done this to her. He'd ripped her from her life and shoved her into a nightmare. He hadn't meant to do it. Hell, he hadn't even asked her to do it. But that didn't change the fact that she was here because of him—exhausted, afraid, and compromising her principles.

He hoped to God that whatever was in those files was worth it, because if it wasn't, he'd just inadvertently destroyed a life he would have gladly died to save.

Chapter Twenty-four

*A**ct normal.*

Mira could do that. She had a lifetime of practice doing that. First when she'd learned that her father was involved in something shady. Later when she learned the details of what he'd done. And recently when she'd had to cover for Clay at work, making up lies for why he wasn't there.

Tonight was going to be much easier. All she had to do was have dinner with a gorgeous man who had the power to make her shake with excitement just thinking about him.

She sat in the car she'd borrowed from work, waiting outside the restaurant she'd chosen for Adam to arrive. The whole day had been a string of tension and fear, knowing that her father could have been watching her, tracking her wherever she went.

She'd showered and changed in the locker rooms at the Edge, hoping that he hadn't gone so far as to bug the bathrooms. At the last minute, she hadn't been able to climb into her own car. She just couldn't take another minute of wondering whose eyes were on her. It was too creepy and unsettling.

Instead, she grabbed a set of keys and checked out a company car. At least this way she could have an evening out—a few hours to relax—before going back home to her fishbowl.

The restaurant Mira had picked for her date with Adam was one she'd never been to before. She didn't want anyone using her habits against her.

It was an Italian place that seemed fairly innocuous. It wasn't attached to a hotel. There were no veiled messages or awkward pressure. Just two people out to share a meal. No big deal. Normal people did this all the time.

Act normal.

Of course, had she done that, she would have stayed at work until ten and gone home to a bowl of cereal and a cheesy sci-fi movie. She would not be out on the town, on an actual date with—

There he was, getting out of a sleek black sedan. His long stride echoed confidence with each step. He didn't look around or wonder if she'd show the way Mira had wondered about him. He moved like a man who knew she'd be here. No worries, no questions.

A shiver of excitement wriggled along her skin, dragging away a pile of tension she was more than ready to part with.

She got out of the car, anxious to speak to him again. Giddy, like a teenage girl, she hurried to the front door. The glass swept open, and there he was, holding the door for her to enter.

He'd seen her rush. She hadn't been playing it cool the way women were supposed to do. The fact that he had to have seen her scurry made a blush heat her cheeks.

He smiled at her—a warm, genuine smile she felt all the way to the pinched toes she'd shoved into high heels. The added height hadn't made much of a difference. He was still a head taller than her and most everyone else around.

"I'm glad you came," he said, his quiet voice sliding inside her like a favorite tune.

"You knew I would. You can't fool me."

The place wasn't busy on a Wednesday night. The hostess seated them immediately.

That's when Mira realized her mistake. This wasn't some family restaurant with bright lighting and kids squirming in their seats. This place was dimly lit. Romantic. The booth backs were high. Curtains hung from the ceiling, gathered back at the end of each seat to give the illusion that each table was its own private room. A very small, very cozy room.

The hostess showed them to their table. Adam stood, waiting for her to sit.

Mira slid over the leather cushion, acutely aware of how dark it was here. The only real source of light was a few candles floating among rose petals in a crystal bowl of water at the center of the table.

Adam sat. The hostess left. He ignored the menu in front of him and stared at her with a knowing little smile tilting his mouth. "Nice place."

Her blush grew hotter, and she ducked her head in an effort to hide it. "I, uh, didn't realize it would be so ... dark. I've never been here before."

"I'm your first, then. Good to know."

She was so not touching that comment. Instead, she stared at the menu as if the secrets to cold fusion and frictionless surfaces were printed there. The words swam together in an unintelligible pile of letters.

The waitress came. Adam ordered some wine for them. She didn't care what kind, so long as it would give her something to do with her hands.

"You're nervous," said Adam.

"Sorry. It's been a rough day." Which, while true, had nothing to do with the shivering tremors racking her fingers. That was all Adam's doing—him and memories of that hard body and the way his thumb felt as it slid across her wrist.

Mira rubbed at the spot, willing the memory to fade.

Adam reached across the table and took her hand, turning her palm up for his inspection. His long fingers glided over her hand in a soothing gesture. Concern creased the skin between his dark brows. "Tell me what happened today."

She couldn't breathe. Not when he was touching her. She wasn't normally so bowled over by a guy, but Adam was not just any guy. He was so confident and suave. So incredibly handsome. Even now he was holding her hand as if he'd been touching her for years, as if he knew just how she liked to be touched. The perfect pressure, all the right spots. The gentle little massage he gave the muscles at the base of her thumb was pure pleasure. It made her wonder how his hands would feel on the rest of her body.

Which made her struggle to breathe.

The waitress came to take their order. She still had no clue what was on the menu. She wasn't even sure if it was written in English.

"She's not ready," he told the woman without taking his eyes off of Mira. "Soon."

And just like that, Mira was thinking of more than just a plate of pasta and sauce. Adam's low words, his direct gaze—it was all a devastating plot to make her look like a complete idiot, melted into a wriggling mass of needy hormones.

When she spoke, she sounded like a breathless twit. "I need my hand to read the menu."

He grudgingly let go, but the smile he gave her was pure sin. "I'm always rushing things," he said. "But sometimes it's nice to eat dessert first, don't you think?"

Think? Not a chance. Not while he was around. Her IQ had dropped a hundred points just being in the same room with him.

It was completely unfair. She'd never been this instantly drawn to a man, and he was going to think she was a drooling idiot before their salads arrived.

Mira gathered her formidable will and focused on the menu. She found something she liked and pointed to it when the waitress came back.

She clutched her glass of wine in both hands and drank, hoping to dial down her tension meter, just a bit.

"What do you do?" asked Adam. He sat back against the seat, his long arm sprawled across the top of the cushion. His shirtsleeves were turned up just enough that she could see his thick wrists and a peek of forearms layered with muscles.

She cleared her throat. "I'm a professional nerd."

A black eyebrow shot up at that news. "Nerd?"

"I do tech stuff. Keep the networks at my office running. Tinker with gadgets. That kind of thing. What do you do?" Until now, she hadn't realized that his business card hadn't listed his title—only his contact information.

"I acquire rare objects for people."

"Like art or something?"

"Sometimes," he hedged. "What does your company do?"

"Private security, mostly."

He grinned at that. "Ah. You're a kick-ass mercenary, are you?"

"Hardly. I'm tech support. I do work with a bunch of kick-ass mercenaries, though. They keep trying to toughen me up. So far, it hasn't exactly stuck."

He leaned forward, a glint of wickedly delightful intent in his eyes. "I'm glad they failed. I like you the way you are, all feminine and soft."

No one had ever called her that before. Girly? Yes, but in the sense that she wasn't tough, sucked with weapons, and was terrified of spiders. Soft? Absolutely. Bella was always hinting that she should hit the gym—that she was too soft and one of these days it was going to get her hurt. But no one—ever—had said those things the way Adam had, as if they were good. As if he found those things attractive. As if he found *her* attractive.

The waitress saved her by delivering their food. Mira stared at it, so off-balance, she wasn't sure what she was supposed to do with it.

He ate, watching her with those pale gray eyes. Hunger was evident in his expression, but she had no idea if it was for the food or something else. If she hadn't known better, she would have thought he was trying to seduce her.

He *was* seducing her. She just wasn't sure if he was *trying* or not. A man like Adam was walking seduction. Women probably fell at his feet, begging for his attention.

Mira managed a few bites, washing the food down with sips of wine. She hadn't eaten all day, and the lack of sleep was beginning to wear on her. Fatigue made her eyelids heavy, and she set the wine aside for fear that she wouldn't be able to make it safely home.

They spoke of random things while they ate. Adam's choice of topics put her at ease, while his every move thrilled her to her core. She was an odd combination of relaxed and excited by the time they finished eating.

The waitress left the check. Mira reached for it, but Adam was faster.

She held out her hand. "Tonight is my treat. I owe you for the ruined clothes, remember?"

He shook his head, tucking some bills into the black leather folder. "I told you that you owe me nothing. But if you agree to have dinner with me again, I'll let you pay next time."

He wanted to go out with her again? After she'd sat there, alternately mute and stammering, floundering to sound like the intelligent grown-up she was? "Uh, okay."

Adam checked his watch. "I have to go now. Early day tomorrow. May I walk you to your car?"

She wanted him to do more than that. She wanted him to run those hands all over her frumpy self. If he'd asked, she would have gone home with him, even though she'd met him only that morning. *That's* how stupid he rendered her.

"Sure," she said.

He checked his watch as they left. His hand was at the small of her back, sending a flurry of excitement marching up and down her spine.

Her heel slipped out from under her, making her stumble. Adam caught her against his side before she could fall.

He checked his watch again.

A wave of dizziness slammed into her from out of nowhere. She grabbed his arm to keep from tumbling to the pavement. He took her weight and kept her moving forward at a brisk pace.

"It's okay. We're almost there," he said, his voice soothing.

She wasn't sure what he meant. She couldn't drive like this. In fact, she wasn't even sure she was going to make it another three steps.

Mira stopped in her tracks, unable to stay upright. A moment later, Adam swept her up into his arms and cradled her against his chest. "It wasn't supposed to happen this fast. I should have been more careful."

"What?" she asked, confusion swamping her. All she could do was cling to his neck in the hopes that it would make the world stop spinning. She wanted to enjoy this ride and breathe in his heady scent, but her head was too twisty to hold it upright.

"Shhh, Mira. Everything is going to be okay. I just need you to come with me for a little while."

Adam tucked her into a seat and buckled the belt. There was something wrong, but she couldn't figure out what it was.

He appeared next to her and started the car. "Just lie back and relax. I'm not going to hurt you."

And that's when Mira figured it out, just as the haze crowded her mind, sending her spiraling down in a wild spin of grogginess and fear.

Adam had drugged her. He was taking her somewhere. And the fact that he'd said he wasn't going to hurt her meant that she was probably never going to wake up again.

Chapter Twenty-five

By nine, Clay had finished doing everything he could to be ready for pulling off his pretend hit. He didn't dare move in too soon for fear of walking into some kind of trap. He had to be careful. Dr. Sage was still looking for him. He might even know where Clay was supposed to go.

Clay wasn't going to give the doctor or anyone else a chance to find him. Staying hidden until the last minute was his best bet.

So now all that was left was the grueling wait—that time before an operation that crawled by, inching past in a series of torturous moments filled with impatience, anxiety, and second-guessing.

Leigh hadn't said a word to him since they'd walked into the cheap little pay-by-the-hour motel room. She was as cold and standoffish as she'd been all night, keeping to her side of the room. She'd barely looked at him. Instead, she went through her medical supplies and gave him what he needed without a word.

Her silence grated on his already raw nerves, stretching his patience thin. "Why won't you talk to me?"

She didn't look at him. "It doesn't seem like there's

much to talk about. You've already made your plans. I've already given you the drugs you need. What more do you want from me?"

He wanted her warmth. He wanted her to look at him with something other than frigid logic, shoving a cold, icy wall between them that he couldn't seem to crack. He wanted her to touch him, so he could feel the heat of her fingertips sliding into his skin. But mostly, he wanted to hold her so that he could convince himself that everything was going to be okay.

Clay stood up and crossed the room to where she sat on the bed. The yellowish lighting glinted off her fiery hair, making it glow. "I want you to tell me why you're mad."

She looked up at him, frowning. "I'm not mad, Clay."

"Then why the ice maiden routine?"

"Is that what you think this is?"

"I don't know what else to call it. You've hardly spoken to me since we had sex. Is this some kind of buyer's remorse kicking in?"

Her pupils flared at the mention of sex. Her lips parted slightly, and her tongue slipped out to wet them. She looked away as if the gaudy design on the bedspread was the most intriguing thing on the planet. "I don't regret sleeping with you. But I also know that you and I don't have any kind of a future together. You won't ever trust me the way I want. I don't blame you for it, but it seemed logical that I stop letting myself get closer to you. Nothing will ever come of it."

That pissed him off, sending his whole body into a chaotic fury. The power of it washed over him, leaving him shaking and speechless. He tried to hide his immediate, visceral reaction to her casual dismissal, but he shouldn't have bothered. She wasn't looking at him.

After several moments of struggling to get himself

back under control, Clay managed to shove away enough of his anger to speak. "So because we're not going to grow old together, you just close yourself off?"

She looked at him, finally, and he saw the faintest flicker of emotion in her gaze. "I'm not closed off. But I'll be damned if I let myself fall for you."

"Who's asking you to?"

"You are. Every time you touch me. Every time you look into my eyes. You make me forget the way things really are between us."

"And just exactly how is that?"

"I'm using you to help my brother. You're using me to help you not kill any innocents. It's a partnership—a symbiosis—and that's all it needs to be."

That wasn't enough for Clay. It made him a selfish bastard, but he wanted more. He wanted to know that she was right here with him, feeling lost and confused, excited and so turned on she could barely think straight. That was rare—at least for him—and he wasn't willing to let go of it for fear of what might happen tomorrow. He needed it too much, because, truth be known, he wasn't sure how many tomorrows he'd have. If they didn't find a way to fix him, his choices were prison or death.

Clay knew which he'd choose.

His time with Leigh was precious. She was precious. He wasn't willing to take either of those for granted.

He covered her hand with his, willing her to open up to him again—to share her sweetness with him, her warmth. "You mean more to me than that."

She closed her eyes as if his words hurt, but she didn't pull away. "Don't say that. We were better off when we were merely tolerating each other."

"No, we weren't. I liked thinking that you cared about me. It made me stronger, braver."

Finally, she looked at him. Her expression was bleak and heartbreaking. "I already lost Hollis. If we fail to find some kind of cure, I'm going to lose Garrett. And you. The more I care about you, the harder that will be."

"So we won't fail."

"Just like that, huh? You simply speak the words aloud and make it so?" She shook her head, and several strands of dark red hair slipped over her shoulder. "You know as well as I do that it doesn't work like that."

"You've lost your faith. It happens. I'm the guy who's going to help you find it again. Once we have those files—"

"What?" she demanded. "We don't even know what they are. For all we know they're grocery lists for the rich and famous."

"You know better than that. This is important. I can feel it."

She sighed and her eyes closed in defeat. "I hope you're right."

Clay knew he shouldn't touch her anymore, but he had to offer her some kind of comfort. He couldn't stand knowing that she suffered without at least trying to do something to ease her.

He cradled her sweet face in his hands, silently begging her to look at him again, rather than avoiding his gaze or staring straight through him. Her skin was so warm and soft. Her bruises were fading, reassuring him that one day she'd no longer have to see what he'd done to her whenever she looked in a mirror.

He brushed his thumbs across her cheeks, fighting the urge to feel the supple texture of her lips against his fingertips. Her heart pounded in her temple. The cluster of freckles on her right cheek seemed dark against her too-pale skin.

"Look at me," he whispered. So far she hadn't pulled

away, but he could feel her trembling on the edge of indecision, ready to fly away at any moment.

Finally, her eyes opened. They were so dark and full of compassion. Pain lingered there, too. And fear.

If he could, he would have washed it away, but he wasn't that kind of man. He was a mess, completely incapable of fixing anyone else's problems, much less his own. But for her, he had to try.

"By tomorrow morning, you and I will know what's in those files. It may be a cure. It may lead us to one. Or it may be nothing. But whatever the case, I won't stop looking. As long as it takes, I'm going to hunt Sage down and make him tell us how to fix your brother. I swear it."

Her gaze held his. "You almost make me believe in miracles."

"It's not a miracle," he told her. "It's simply a matter of being willing to do whatever it takes."

"And are you?"

"I am. For you. For your brother. And myself. We all need this. I'm going to make it happen." And if he did, maybe—just maybe—he'd find a way to give her what she needed so she wouldn't push him away again. Maybe he'd earn the right to find some small place in her life. Because the idea of not being near her scared him more than being locked up in some dank cell.

"Okay," she said. "I believe you. I trust you." She wasn't looking past him now, and the force of her dark stare was almost too intense to handle. It laid him bare and stripped him of his defenses. He didn't know what it was about Leigh that made him feel this way, but when he was with her, he felt fragile and invincible all at the same time. She could tear him apart with one frigid word or build him up with a single hot glance.

It was her heat he wanted now. He needed it—needed to feel alive and powerful and . . .

Clay didn't dare finish that thought. It was too heavy. Too selfish. Asking more from her than she was willing to give was unthinkable.

So rather than think, he moved. He lowered his mouth to hers, closing the distance slowly enough to give her time to turn aside. If she denied him, he knew it would tear something vital from his chest, but it was a risk he had to take.

Clay needed her. It was as simple and scary as that.

His lips met hers in a kiss so light he questioned whether he imagined it. He forced his eyes open, searching for some kind of sign he should back away.

Her hands slid up his arms and clutched his shoulders. A soft moan lifted from her mouth, and with it came the sound of surrender.

In a heartbeat, she became fierce, digging her short fingernails into his skin. A thrill of excitement raced through him, making him go hard so fast it hurt. Her mouth ate at his; her tongue slipped inside to taste and make demands. Clay met every thrust and glide with one of his own, giving her whatever she wanted.

Leigh shoved him down onto the bed and straddled him. He pulled his weapon out and set it within reach on the bedside table.

The expression on her face was feral, like a warrior goddess on the hunt. Clay was more than happy to be her prey, if that's what she wanted. Right now, he was willing to give her anything.

Her hand went to his belt. The leather slipped free of the buckle.

"This is just sex," she said, as if it were a warning. "It doesn't mean anything."

She was wrong. It meant a lot. But Clay wasn't about to correct her, not when she was about to open the doors of heaven and let him in.

*   *   *

The heinous lie fell from Leigh's tongue like acid. It burned all the way up her throat, making her feel hollowed out as it passed. Before she could confess the truth, she leaned down and kissed Clay. With his lips to occupy hers, speaking became impossible.

Her body had been humming with a low thrum of desire for hours. She'd tuned it out, focusing instead on everything else. But now it was everything else she wanted to block out. The growing heat that consumed her was much nicer than reality. The feel of Clay's mouth moving against hers had the power to wash all the dark worries away, leaving her shivering with a vibrant glow.

Leigh got his belt open and slid her hand inside to grip his erection. She wasn't gentle, but his deep groan of approval told her that he didn't mind. He arched up off the bed, lifting her body along for the ride. His hands were at her blouse, popping open the buttons.

She didn't dare stop kissing him. She knew if she did, the spell would be broken and thoughts would start creeping in. Dark, sad, lonely thoughts that would crush her if they got the chance.

Rather than let them win, she focused all her energy on Clay. His jeans went down just far enough for her to get her mouth around his cock. She sucked on him, working her own jeans down her legs. He gripped the bedspread and hissed out his pleasure. His hips bucked slightly, as if he couldn't hold them still.

She shoved his shirt up, baring his abs to her questing hands. He was hot and hard everywhere she touched. His scent filled her head, making her a little crazy. She needed him inside her. Now.

It took only seconds to straddle his body and slide down on his cock. The intense stretch shocked her but didn't make her slow down. The compulsion to feel him fill her up was more than she could fight. She was already fighting too many things—too many emotions—to battle lust as well.

The slick glide of flesh on flesh drove her wild. She rocked against him, taking inch after inch of him until she could take no more. He hit a sweet spot deep inside her that had her careening toward orgasm with embarrassing speed.

His hands pulled her bra down to cup her breasts. His gaze was fixed on his big hands against her pale skin, watching with both awe and desire tightening his features. As his fingers squeezed her nipples slightly, she felt a shock wave rock through her, all the way to her womb.

Leigh went still except for the fine tremors running through her. She fought the urge to come, wanting to make this last—hold the dark at bay for a while longer.

On the other side of release lay scary things. Here, trapped inside passion, were only consuming pleasure and wicked anticipation. And she was going to take as much as she could stand.

She lifted her hips and slid back down. Their moans melded together, heating the air between them even more.

As she started to move again, Clay grabbed her hips and pinned her in place. His eyes were wide with startled realization. "Condom."

He wasn't wearing one. She'd rushed him, leaving herself no time to even remember the need.

Shock rattled her, and a forbidden little thrill raced through her veins. She'd never done this before—not even by accident. She knew better. She had always been careful, almost paranoid. Clay had made her forget all of that.

Leigh started to pull away so they could remedy the oversight, but his grip tightened. His voice came out, nearly a growl. "Hold still."

He was close. She could see the strain to hold back in the way his abs clenched, the way his shoulders tightened.

Leigh held still. "I'm not on birth control," she said, more because she thought he should know. Oddly, she wasn't as freaked-out by the idea of what could happen as she should have been. Which only proved how close to the edge of sanity she'd gone.

His cock jerked inside of her, hitting a deep, secret place that made her whole body shiver with pleasure. She was panting and breathless but found enough air to warn him. "If you don't let me move away soon, I'm going to come."

He groaned.

One second she was filled with hot, hard flesh, the next she was lying on her back, empty and cold. Clay was at her medical bag, pawing through it with frantic speed. She heard the crinkle of plastic. Saw his arm move as he smoothed the condom over himself. And then he was back, shoving her thighs wide and driving back into her with enough force to make her expel a heavy breath.

Leigh grabbed him around the neck to hold him close. She buried her face against his throat, offering him hot, openmouthed kisses as he moved. One stroke, two ... that was all it took to send her spinning out of control. As her orgasm bore down on her, Clay kept moving, shoving her higher, drawing it out until she didn't think she could take any more.

The edges of her vision faded. Little black spots bloomed in her eyes. Finally, she was able to drag in enough breath to make them go away.

But Clay gave her no rest. He didn't slow or fade. He was like a machine, working to push her right back up to those shimmering heights again before making her fall.

Her voice began to grow hoarse, and only then did

she realize how vocal she'd been. She tried to apologize for likely screaming his ear off, but there wasn't enough air for her to form coherent words. Already she felt herself coiling again for another fiery explosion.

Clay gave her one more hard push, and she was lost. The world faded into a glistening haze of pleasure. She floated in it, feeling as if she were made of light and air — as if nothing could ever touch her.

Except Clay. She could feel his hands, hear his rough groan of completion vibrating against her breasts. He shook with the force of it, his erection throbbing and thick as it pulsed hard inside her.

For one brief, insane moment, she wished she could have felt what that would have been like without any barriers.

She was still blissed out, limp and more sated than she'd ever been, when he pulled away from her. She didn't have the strength to open her eyes and see where he'd gone. A moment later, he lifted her up and set her on the other side of the bed, between cool sheets.

His hot body wedged against hers. He pressed soft little kisses over her temple while his hand smoothed along her ribs and stomach, petting her.

"Sleep now," he whispered. "I'll be back soon."

Exhaustion was pulling at her, but she had enough sense left to force her eyes open. "You can't go alone."

"They could be watching. They can't know you're involved. I promise I'll be quick and careful."

Fear for him hit her, but it was muted by the haze of afterglow surrounding her. "You won't have any way to contact me if things go badly."

His gaze caressed her face. He offered her a small smile that belied the worry in his amber eyes. "I'll be back by two. If I'm not, then go to the police. Don't trust Payton."

There was no way she was sleeping now. Her buzz was gone, leaving her feeling chilled to the bone with worry. "I'm not sitting around here, wondering if you're alive or dead. If I have to, I'll hide in the trunk so no one will see me. But I am coming along."

His shoulders dropped on a sigh. "I don't want to fight with you."

"Then don't. I'm going with you, Clay. You may need me."

"I'm sure I will," he said, and the way he said it, with a flash of sadness, made her think that he was talking about something else.

He got off the bed, giving her a great view of his fine ass as he looked over his shoulder. "Get dressed. I don't want to be late."

Clay felt electronic eyes on him everywhere he went. He had on a baseball hat, its bill pulled down over his eyes, but there were cameras all over this place.

He tried to focus on the job—on getting in and out of room two-fourteen as fast as possible—but Leigh had rocked his foundation, leaving him feeling off-balance. Her sexual aggression drove him crazy, giving him no choice but to go along for the ride. Feeling her clinging heat against his bare skin had been more than he could stand. And when she'd looked down at him and told him so calmly that she wasn't on birth control—as if she was okay with whatever he decided—he'd nearly lost it.

He refused to trust her, and yet she had shown him the kind of trust most men never received. It was both humbling and devastating, changing the shape of things he'd always believed were true.

In that moment, he would have done anything for her. And that scared the shit out of him.

He'd been scared a lot since meeting her. Scared for her. Scared of her. A woman like her had the right to demand only the best, and Clay was nowhere close. It made him wonder what it was she saw in him—what kept her at his side.

Maybe it was nothing more than her need to save her brother, but she could have done just as much good from the safety of that motel room. Instead, she was hiding in the car, lying under a blanket in the backseat. It was a crappy hiding place, but he'd known that if he'd tried to leave her in that motel, she would have found a way to follow him that would have proven even more dangerous.

Better to just give in and accept that when it came to helping her brother, she had no self-preservation instincts.

Clay tried to shove all that out of his mind as he took the stairs to the second floor. He kept his head down, looking around only enough to find the room he sought.

He drew his weapon, slid the card key in the door, and eased inside, ready for anything. All that greeted him was an empty room. He locked the door. A thorough check of the space showed him no sign of instructions.

The clock turned over to midnight. A manila envelope slid under the door. Clay raced to peer through the peephole, but there was no one outside. He opened the door to check the hall but again saw no one. He was in the middle of a long hall. The only way someone could have disappeared so quickly was if they had a room nearby.

The hair on the back of his neck lifted. Too many people were after him, and he had no idea which of them might be able to simply tell him to bark like a dog and he'd do it.

Rather than risk turning back into that man who

would hurt Leigh, he grabbed the envelope and ran for the nearest exit. The cold air hit him in the face, but he didn't slow down until he slid in behind the wheel.

"Stay down," he said, trying not to move his lips in case anyone was watching.

"Are you okay?" asked Leigh from the backseat.

Clay pulled out and headed for the interstate. "Yeah. Just not taking any chances."

A few minutes later, when he was sure no one was following him, he pulled over and parked outside a pancake house that was open all night.

"You can get up now."

Leigh crawled over the seat to get in front. Clay picked up the envelope and slit it open. In it were a few pages stapled together. The first was blank. The second listed simple instructions: Eliminate target immediately.

Make it look like an accident. That's what the man he'd met by the fountain had said.

Clay flipped to the last page, which consisted of a single photocopied picture in black-and-white—a photo of his target, the man he was supposed to kill tonight.

It was Payton Bainbridge.

Chapter Twenty-six

Mira woke up in a hospital room, too dizzy and confused to figure out how she'd gotten there. An IV bag hung to her left, but her clothes were still on. If she'd had some kind of accident, wouldn't she have been in a gown?

She pushed her head up, hoping that would make it stop spinning.

Adam sat in a chair at the foot of the bed, watching her.

Everything that had happened slammed back into her with enough force to steal her breath away. She'd met him for dinner. He'd nearly charmed her pants off. Then she got so tired.

"You drugged me," she croaked at him.

He stood, the movement a masterpiece of smooth power. "I had no choice, and for that, I apologize."

She backed away from him as much as the bed and her sloppy head would allow. "Why am I not raped or dead? Why drug me for no reason?"

"I assure you there was a reason."

As her mind began to clear, she noticed the smaller details. The room had no TV, no phone. There was a camera mounted in one corner of the ceiling. The window on the adjacent wall did not overlook a parking lot or even a hallway bustling with medical staff. Instead, it showed a lab of some kind, filled with white-coated workers. She recognized a couple of the people, though she couldn't remember any names.

Anxiety began to creep in. "What is this place?"

"You're agitated. Please, just lie back down."

Adam took a step forward, but she pointed her finger at him. "Stay away from me. I don't know who you really are, but if you come any closer, I'll scream."

He stopped halfway to the bed. "This is your father's facility."

"My father?"

Sirens and warning bells went off in her head. Full-blown panic was only seconds away. She had to get out of here. Now.

Mira yanked the IV from her vein, ignoring the blood that welled up. She flung her legs off the side of the bed and tried to stand.

Her legs wouldn't support her weight. She started to crumple to the ground. Adam was at her side faster than she could blink. He pinned her against his body, mocking her for every naughty little fantasy she'd had about him.

She couldn't believe how easily he'd fooled her. Handsome, charming, flirtatious. That's all it took for her to turn stupid and forget that it was suspicious that a man like him would want to have anything to do with the queen of the nerds.

Mira tried to free herself from his grip, but he was too strong and she was too dizzy. He controlled her flailing hands easily, pressing his thumb against her vein to stop the bleeding.

"Let me go," she growled at him.

"As soon as you stop bleeding. You're in no shape to

be on your feet for another hour at least. The fluids were meant to help flush out your system."

"If I have to crawl to get out of here, I will."

At that moment, Mira's father, Dr. Richard Sage, walked through the door. He stared at her with the same expression of supreme disappointment that he always wore. Only this time, there was something else in his face—a kind of smug excitement, as if he'd won some contest she couldn't understand.

Suddenly, Adam seemed the lesser of two evils.

Without effort or permission, Adam lifted her back onto the bed with one arm. He kept his thumb on her wound and shifted slightly so that he was between her and her father.

If Richard noticed, he gave no indication that Mira could see. Then again, she wasn't exactly at the top of her game.

"What do you want?" she demanded. "Why am I here?"

"Because Adam is a genius. He saw the obvious solution to my problem. If I hadn't been so busy lately, perhaps I'd have seen it myself."

"I don't give a shit about your fucking problems," said Mira, knowing he'd hate the vulgar language.

His mouth turned down in a frown of distaste. "Really, Mira. What would your mother say if she could hear you now?"

"She'd tell me to kick you in the balls, you heartless asshat."

Richard looked at Adam with apology in his tone. "You should not have had to put up with her behavior. It's truly shameful."

Adam's body vibrated with a silent growl. "She is certainly nothing like her father."

"Your job here is done," said Richard. He pulled an envelope from his pocket. "Your payment, as promised."

Adam went still. She couldn't even feel the pulse of his thumb against her skin, as if his heart had stopped beating for a second.

He stared at the white envelope as if it held the secret to the universe, but he didn't move to reach for it. Instead, he slowly lifted his thumb to see if she'd stopped bleeding. She had, and only when he saw that did he reach out.

The envelope went inside his shirt, like he needed to hold it close to his heart.

"You may leave now," said Richard.

Adam squared his shoulders and seemed to grow even taller. "I think I'll stay. See how this plays out."

"It's none of your concern."

"Call it curiosity, then."

"I would have thought you'd be anxious to scamper off for your family reunion."

"It's waited decades. It can wait a few more hours."

Mira had no idea what was going on, but she used the opportunity to look around for some kind of weapon. The only thing she could find was a plastic pitcher of water next to an empty cup. It wasn't much, but it was all she had to work with.

Pretending she was going to pour herself a drink, she picked it up. At the last second, she flung the ice water at Adam's head and darted for the door.

Her father grabbed at the back of her shirt, slowing her for a split second. The fabric popped from his grip, and she was free.

She ran down the hall, her stocking-clad feet slipping precariously on the slick tile floor. Panic pounded through her veins. Her blood pressure skyrocketed. She felt blood drip from her hand.

This building was bigger than she'd thought. She had no idea which way to go. Finally, her head cleared enough for her to start looking for exit signs.

She hit a stairwell door, and the only way to go was up. She'd made it all the way to the landing before a team of security guards stopped her cold.

They shoved her against the wall, grabbed her arms, and pinned them roughly behind her. Her shoulders burned, and a terrified gasp of pain erupted from her lips.

The two guards holding her face-first against the wall seemed to evaporate in a series of short, deep grunts. She turned around to see where they'd gone and saw Adam standing over their bodies, his hands fisted as if ready to throw another punch. He was soaked from his hair down, dripping with the water she'd doused him with.

He took her by the arm, and his touch was so careful compared to that of the other two men that she was too shocked for a second to fight. But then that shock dissipated and she tried to wrench her arm from his hold.

"Let me go," she screamed at him.

He moved faster than she could see, and somehow she was plastered against his body, with her hands trapped between them. Her feet barely touched the floor. Her blood smeared over his pristine white shirt, blooming out in a watery mix of orangey pink.

It struck her that this was the second shirt of his she'd ruined.

"If you try to fight your way out of here, one of those guards may decide to shoot you down. I won't let that happen."

"Then why bring me here to begin with?"

"I needed something your father had. It wasn't supposed to be personal." He set her down and started walking again.

She tried to drag her feet, but he kept going, and she simply slipped over the tile, moving along with him. "When someone drugs and abducts me, I'd say it's pretty fucking personal."

He stopped and looked down at her. His pale gray eyes were bright with fury. "I don't want this any more than you do. Believe me."

She snorted at him. "Yeah, that'll happen."

Mira's father rounded the corner with two burly guards flanking him. "Put her in room twelve."

"Not until she stops bleeding," said Adam.

"It's a tiny hole. She's not going to bleed to death."

Adam said nothing, merely stared back. The two guards behind her father paled. Richard's mouth tightened in frustration. "Fine. Cover the pinhole if you must, but then leave. You're only causing trouble."

"I'll leave when she does."

"That was not our deal," said Richard, his tone one of quiet warning.

"Consider me bonus security, then."

Richard shook his head and waved a hand in irritation. "Bring her along. I have a first aid kit in my office. We'll deal with the mess she made, and then she can make that call."

"What call?" asked Mira, feeling a whole new layer of panic settle over her.

Her father said nothing as he turned and started walking away. His guards waited expectantly for her to follow.

Adam propelled her forward, leaned down close to her ear, and whispered, "Do as he says and I will get you out of here alive."

Clay sat in stunned silence as he stared at the photo of Payton. "What the hell?"

"They want you to kill Payton? Why?"

"I have no idea, but it sure puts a new spin on things."

"In what way?"

"Sage is using me to get these files. The price for the files is Payton's head. If the people involved in all of this mind-control bullshit want him dead, then he's working against them in some way."

"He knows what happened. He was involved. He said he was trying to set things right. Maybe they want him dead to keep him from going to the authorities."

Clay shook his head, trying to jostle his brain enough to shake things into place. "There has to be something I'm missing that would help all of this make sense. Maybe something in those photos?"

"We can go through them again. Maybe the man you talked to is in one of them, and now that we know what he looks like, we'll recognize him."

"I don't know how that will help, but it's worth a shot."

"We could always go with our original plan," said Leigh. "Find Payton. Ask him nicely to pose for some gruesome fake death shots."

Clay shook his head. "It won't work."

"Why not?"

"I thought all they'd ask for was photographic proof of a kill. Since there was nothing in the instructions about that, then they're going to be waiting for news reports or some other form of independent confirmation. I can't fake that."

"Payton has powerful friends. Maybe he can."

"Or maybe he'll refuse and we'll never get our hands on those files."

"We have to trust him," said Leigh. "I know that's not your strong suit, but he's the only ally we've got right now. If he is involved in all of this, then he'll want those files as much as we do."

"For some nefarious purpose, no doubt."

"You don't know that. So far he's kept you safe."

"By risking your life."

"No, by giving me a chance to help Garrett. If this works out, I'll never be able to repay him."

Clay rubbed his eyes, feeling the beginnings of a headache form just out of reach. "I'm out of better ideas. I guess we call him."

Leigh turned the phone on and held it out to Clay. The last thing he wanted to do was talk to the man who was at least partially responsible for fucking him over, but he didn't see any other options.

"We need to meet," said Clay as soon as Payton answered.

"You left. I found no sign of Dr. Sage, so I came home to tell you. I've been trying to reach you for hours."

"The phone was off so no one could find us. Especially you."

"I see." Disappointment hung on the words.

"Listen, Payton. I don't trust you. I'll never trust you again. But I also don't want to see you dead, which is exactly where things are headed. Something big has come up. We need to meet."

"Name the place. I'll leave immediately."

They made plans to meet in the alley behind an aging strip mall that had been slowly abandoned over the years. No one had bothered with upkeep, leaving plenty of shadows where lightbulbs had blown out. The back wall had been tagged with graffiti until it was a colorful mural of gang signs and adolescent boredom.

Payton pulled in, killing his headlights as he made the turn.

Leigh grabbed Clay's hand. It had been the first time she'd touched him since they'd left the motel. Until now, he hadn't realized just how cold he'd grown without the contact of her skin on his.

"Let me go talk to him," she said. "You're too angry with him."

"Like hell. I don't trust him, so I'm sure as hell not going to sit here while you go out there. Who knows what he'll do?"

"He won't do anything. He needs us."

As they argued, Payton had come closer. Clay felt the back of his neck tighten. He pulled his weapon and held it on his lap.

"See?" said Leigh, nodding at the gun. "You're too angry."

"This isn't angry. This is careful."

Payton passed his window and pulled on the handle of the back door. Clay unlocked it and turned in his seat so that he wouldn't have his back to the man.

"What happened?" asked Payton.

Rather than respond, Clay tossed the stapled trio of pages at him. Payton glanced through them, flipped to his photo. Rather than surprise, all Clay could see in the man's face was anger.

"If I kill you, they'll give me some files—which is apparently what Sage has tasked me to find, at least in part."

"Any idea what's in the files?" asked Payton.

"None. You?"

"Could be anything, but if Sage is after the information, it's either incriminating or something he needs to continue his research."

"Could it be a cure?" asked Leigh.

Payton's mouth tightened. "Perhaps." He looked right into Clay's eyes. "Are you going to kill me?"

"No," said Leigh as if the mere thought disgusted her.

Clay said. "I haven't decided yet."

Payton merely nodded, leaning back in the seat, relaxed,

as if they weren't discussing his murder. "If I were you, I'd have already pulled the trigger."

"No one is killing anyone," said Leigh. "We'll find another way."

The prepaid cell rang, vibrating in the cup holder where Clay had set it earlier. Leigh jumped.

"I should have turned it off." He reached for the phone to do so, but Leigh took it from him.

"You can't answer that. We don't know who it is."

"I wasn't going to answer it."

She looked at the screen, frowning. "It's Mira."

"Maybe she can help us track down the people who want Payton dead."

Leigh pressed the TALK button. "Hi, Mira."

Clay watched as her eyes grew wide and she started to shake. Her knuckles went white as she gripped the phone harder. When she spoke, her voice quivered with horror. "Mira?"

"What is it?" asked Clay, barely resisting the urge to rip the phone away from her.

Leigh ignored him and went quiet. "I understand. Two hours. We won't be late. Just don't hurt her. Please." She jerked and stared at the phone as if it might grow fangs. "They have Mira. If we don't get those files in two hours, they're going to hurt her."

A huge surge of fury ripped through Clay, shredding him as it went.

Payton shoved his way out of the backseat and pulled Clay's door open. He eyed the weapon in Clay's lap. "Do it now. Call the news stations and report the body. Whoever sent the kill order will know I'm dead within the hour. That will give you time to get the files and get to Mira."

Clay didn't want to kill Payton, but with Mira at stake, there was no question about whether he'd do it.

He got out of the car to kill the man who had been more like a father to him than anyone else alive. At least now he knew where Payton's loyalties lay. He might have been a heartless bastard who ruined lives, but if he was willing to give his up to save Mira, then as far as Clay was concerned, Payton was a fucking hero.

Clay lifted his weapon and aimed at Payton's head.

Chapter Twenty-seven

Clay wasn't joking. He really was going to kill Payton.
It took Leigh a moment to muddle through her shock over hearing Mira's frightened voice, followed by the rough orders of a man willing to hurt her. But as soon as she started thinking clearly again, she realized that she was about to witness a murder.

She flung herself out of the car and stepped right in front of Clay's gun.

He jerked the barrel up, rage twisting his mouth. "Get out of the way, Leigh. This has to happen."

"No. It doesn't. The two of you can't jump straight to murder without even taking five minutes to think of other options."

"I don't need five minutes," said Payton. "I've been dealing with danger for most of my life. I've already run through the options. So has Clay. This is the only thing that makes sense. At least this way my death will mean something."

"He's right, Leigh. If you don't want to see what's going to happen, then close your eyes."

"No. I've spent my life healing people. I'm not going to stand by while a good man dies."

"I'm not a good man."

Leigh turned to Payton, searching for some way to talk sense into him. "We have two hours before they'll call back with instructions on where to meet to make the exchange. We have time to find the people who have the files and take them."

"How?" asked Clay. "They said they'd get the files to me as soon as they'd confirmed the kill. I have no way of contacting them. How are we going to find them?"

"Do we even know why they want you dead?" she asked Payton. "Think. Whoever is doing this must be really mad at you."

"There's a long list of people who want me dead. It doesn't exactly narrow things down."

Apparently, there was a lot about Payton that she didn't know. But now was not the time for a history lesson. "Start at the top. Who do you think has both the motive to kill you and the means to find those files and hire Clay to do the job?"

"If I knew what was in the files, I could start somewhere, but unless whoever was on the phone told you, I'm afraid I can't think of anyone specific."

Clay's voice came from right behind her, low but insistent. "Out of the way, Leigh. You're wasting time we don't have."

Leigh ignored him. "The man at the fountain was mid-thirties, dark hair, brown eyes, expensive clothes."

"That could be one of a hundred people I know," said Payton. "Without seeing his face . . ."

A shard of hope lanced through her. "Wait. We got his photo."

"That's right," said Clay. "We did."

He went to the car and got the camera. He handed it to Payton, who scrolled through the photos.

"I know this man. I know who he works for."

"Who?" demanded Clay.

Payton shook his head, anger rolling off him in furious waves. "No. I've got this. Go wait for me in the parking lot at the Edge. I'll be there in less than an hour with those files. While you're there, stock up on ammunition. We may need it."

Payton could not remember a time in his life when he'd been more furious. Senator Gregory Kerrington II had a lot of explaining to do. Too bad Payton was in no mood to hear it.

He pounded on the senator's door until lights in the house started to come on. When one of his staff opened the door, Payton shoved his way in, ignoring the outraged protests of the young man.

Greg came down the stairs, his wife on his heels. As soon as he saw Payton, he stalled on the steps. "Go back to bed. I'll deal with this."

Both Mrs. Kerrington and the curious staff disappeared, leaving Payton alone with the man who'd ordered his death.

"We'll talk in my office," said Greg. "Unless you mean to gun me down right here."

The senator had aged since Payton had seen him last. His hair was thinner, and under that excellent dye job, probably a lot grayer, too. He hadn't kept himself in shape, and out of his perfectly tailored suits, it was obvious that his age hung on him in heavy folds. His publicity shots no longer matched his current appearance, especially the genial twinkle that had doubtlessly been Photoshopped in his eyes.

"Office," was all Payton could choke out. The second the doors shut, he exploded. "You could have at least had the decency to kill me yourself."

Greg's face showed not a hint of remorse. "I'm too old for that and you know it."

"Why?"

"You know too much. Both you and Bob."

"So you're planning to have him killed, too?"

"No one can get to him. You ... you were an easier target."

"That still doesn't answer why. I've known too much for years and this is the first time you've come gunning for me. Hell, I'm the one busting my ass in an effort to make up for what all of us did. You're too worried about reelection to bother helping the people we damaged."

"I didn't damage anyone. I merely did what I was told. If you understood that, you wouldn't be such a threat."

"So that's what you tell yourself so you can sleep at night. Must be nice and cozy all wrapped up in your denial like that."

Greg's face reddened with anger. "Why are you here?"

"I should kill you. Heaven knows you deserve it."

"You'd never make it off the property."

"Which is one of the two reasons you're still breathing."

"And the other is?"

"The files. I want them. Now."

"What files?" asked Greg, doing a decent job of pretending ignorance.

"The ones you offered to hand out in exchange for my murder. Give them to me."

"I don't know what you're talking about."

"Your aide. I saw him make a deal with Clay. My life for the files, which means you have them. Give them to me."

Greg laughed. "I don't think so. They're far too valuable to let go. Besides, word is that you have your own files to transport."

"The only way you'd know that is if you'd tapped into my phone lines."

Greg shrugged. "Seemed like a good idea to keep tabs on you. Based on what I heard, I was right."

Payton's patience was at an end. He grabbed Greg by the lapels of his robe and slammed him into the bookcase. "The files, Greg. The life of a woman I care about is on the line. Don't make me beat the information out of you."

"You don't have the balls to assault me."

Payton tightened his fist and slammed it into the man's nose, breaking it. Blood gushed down his chin and he sputtered in shock.

Payton pulled his fist back. "Care to go another round? I'm sure your plastic surgeon could use the money."

Tears streamed down Greg's face, mixing with the blood. He pointed to his left. "There. In the safe."

Payton shoved him in that direction. "Open it."

Greg did. Payton emptied it out, leaving behind cash, passports, and jewelry. Anything else that even remotely resembled a file was coming with him.

"What's in here?" Payton asked.

Greg hesitated for only a moment before shoving out the answer. "Locations of old sites. Lists of participants and last known addresses. All of the RC codes."

Bingo. "All of them?"

"All that I know of. But they won't do you any good."

"Why not?"

"They're encrypted. None of my associates could break it."

"Now, why would you want to have access to those files, Greg?" asked Payton, already knowing the answer. "Were you looking for some people to do your dirty work—people you could control without any question of loyalty?"

Greg's lips pressed together, as if holding in the truth. Which only confirmed it.

"Is there anything else you have that is even remotely related to the Threshold Project?" asked Payton.

Greg shook his head. Anger burned in his eyes, but he was too much of a coward to do anything about it. That didn't mean that there wouldn't be more hits ordered on Payton's life, however.

He gave Greg a good shove, pushing him into his desk hard enough to make his pens rattle. "If I so much as think someone is following me — by your orders or not — I'm coming back to take you out in your sleep, understood?"

"You wouldn't dare."

"If you really believe that, then I guess you have nothing to lose. Good luck with that."

Payton left, burdened by the knowledge that there was at least one more man he was going to have to kill before he died.

"He'll show," said Leigh. "He cares about Mira as much as you do."

Clay scanned the entrance to the underground lot at the Edge, searching for headlights. "I doubt that."

"He was willing to die for her. That has to prove something."

"Maybe," Clay grudgingly admitted. "Maybe he's just that good of an actor and knew all along he'd find a way out. I don't trust myself to know the difference anymore."

Leigh covered his hand with hers, and he wasn't sure if he should push it away so he could concentrate or beg her to touch him more so he could find a moment of blissful distraction.

Mira's life was in danger. Because of him. It had to be his fault. If he'd managed to get those files before now, she'd be at home, snuggled safely in bed, or watching one of those stupid B movies she loved so much.

Clay had taken her for granted. He'd always assumed that she'd be there—that she was the one permanent fixture in his life. She was the only family he had, and now he realized just how much that meant.

"We will get her back, safe and sound," said Leigh, telling him exactly what he needed to hear so he could pull in his next breath.

If it weren't for Leigh, Clay would probably not be breathing at all. It made him wonder how he was going to keep going once they went their separate ways.

The thought left him feeling too empty and desolate to consider. He was already dealing with too much shit to add any more, so he shoved those bleak thoughts aside and willed Payton to hurry the hell up.

A minute later, Payton pulled in, just as he'd promised. Until Clay saw his face, he wasn't sure the man would actually show. Only his willingness to end his life had allowed Clay the room to let him go.

Payton got out of his car. There was blood on his shirt and a promise of retribution in his pale eyes. "Any word from Mira?"

Leigh glanced at the phone. "No. We have another few minutes before they're supposed to call."

Payton had a stack of folders and envelopes in his hands. "I'm going to make copies of everything. I'll be back in five."

"Copies?" asked Leigh.

"No, it's a good idea. Whatever information is in there, we're going to want to know what it is."

Payton nodded and headed into the building. "I'll hurry."

A few minutes later, the phone rang. Leigh jumped, fumbling to answer it. She was silent, listening. A male voice was barely audible, the words completely muffled.

Clay held a notepad and pen ready for her to use if she needed it. She wrote down a string of numbers that Clay recognized as coordinates.

"I want to talk to Mira. We need to know she's okay."

He heard nothing coming through the plastic; then there was a lighter, fainter voice. Mira's.

Relief fell over Clay but lasted for only a second. The sound of her voice changed pitch, moving into a choking sob.

"We're coming, Mira," said Leigh. "Just hang on."

The man's voice came back. Leigh's expression changed to one of pure, undiluted hatred. "He'll never go for that."

More deep words, only this time they were harder, louder—choppy with anger.

"Fine," grated Leigh from between clenched teeth. "But if you give her so much as a hangnail, I'll—" She looked at the phone, then at Clay. "He hung up." Her chin quivered and she started breathing fast with panic.

"What's wrong, Leigh. What did he say?"

She closed her eyes and pulled in a deep breath. When she let it out again, she seemed more in control. "He said to be there in ninety minutes. After that, he's going to start cutting off her fingers—one for every minute we are late."

Nausea hit Clay like a fist in the gut. "Oh God. Mira."

"We need to go. Now."

Payton came out carrying a briefcase, two rifle cases, and a duffel bag. Clay laid on the horn to get him to hurry. Payton had barely lifted his foot from the pavement when Clay took off, leaving a layer of rubber behind.

Leigh had to raise her voice to be heard over the engine. "He said I have to go alone."

"Like hell," said Clay. "I'm going. I won't risk you, too."

"You can't," said Payton. "Sage will trigger you, and you won't even remember or care who Mira is. I'll go."

"He said it had to be me. If anyone else goes in, Dr. Sage said he'd kill her."

"His own daughter?" asked Clay, outraged.

"It doesn't surprise me," said Payton. "He already murdered his wife."

The engine roared as Clay hit the highway. "I'm going to kill that fucker. He doesn't deserve to live."

Payton leaned forward so they could hear him. "You won't be able to do a thing to him. Sage was the man who put those controls in your head. He also made sure that there was a fail-safe in place that would keep you from hurting him. Sage may be a dick, but he's not a fool."

"I'm the one who has to go. You two need to accept it. Besides, if she is hurt, who better to be there for her than a doctor?"

Payton pulled something from his duffel bag. "We'll equip you with an earpiece. We'll be able to communicate with you, but we won't be able to see anything. You need to remember that."

"Will you be able to hear me?"

"Yes. And those around you."

"They'll know I've got to be wearing some kind of device. What's to stop them from using that to trigger Clay?"

"He won't be monitoring comms. I will."

"Fuck," spat Clay, furious at the whole situation. He needed to act—to do something to help—not sit by useless and impotent while his best friend's life was at risk.

Payton ignored the outburst and went on. "I'll help

you in any way I can. If you get into trouble and need us to come in, say the word 'noodle' and we'll storm the place. We won't be far."

"Noodle," repeated Leigh. "Got it."

"Here's some body armor. Put it on now and we'll get the comms working on the way, too." Payton shoved the vest into the front seat. "How are you with firearms?"

"I know which end to point at the bad guys. I've been to the range a few times. That's about it."

"That's okay. I picked up a gun with an extended magazine. You've got a lot of bullets, so just keep firing until you hit what you need to hit."

"I really hope it doesn't come to that," said Leigh, sounding like the idea made her queasy.

Clay put his hand on her thigh, giving her a reassuring squeeze. "You're going to do fine."

"I hope so. For Mira's sake as well as mine."

Leigh was in way over her head. She'd lied to both men, and now she was seeing just how much danger that lie had created.

Not that there was any choice.

Dr. Sage had said that they could send only one person in for Mira, but he hadn't said it had to be her. She'd said that to cut through any argument the men would have.

Clay couldn't go because they could control him. If he walked in there, she and Payton would have one more bad guy to take down.

Payton couldn't go because there was no way Clay would ever trust him to do so. As little as he may have trusted Leigh, he trusted Payton even less. He would have found some way to go along to keep an eye on Payton, and they'd be right back to facing an additional bad guy.

And while Leigh had briefly considered that being a woman, she might be in less danger—that a man would be less likely to hurt her—she now knew the flaw in that logic.

Dr. Sage had killed his own wife. He'd threatened to kill his daughter. He'd have no trouble ending Leigh's life.

But even knowing what she did now, she still believed that this was the only way to keep Clay out of the hands of the enemy. She was going to have to suck it up and pretend she was completely capable of an armed rescue.

They made it to the coordinates with five minutes to spare. They were in farm country, with no sign of anyone nearby. It was pitch-black, with only the distant glow of Dallas miles away.

"There's no one here," said Clay. "Where the hell are they?"

A text came through. "Apparently, they can see us. They want me to get out and start walking west."

Clay let out a low growl of frustration. "I don't like this."

"We don't have much choice," said Payton. "Just remember what I told you, and you'll be fine."

Leigh nodded and stepped out into the cold. Wind sucked her body heat away, despite the body armor. She'd broken out into a nervous sweat, and now that cooling sweat was going to ensure that she suffered.

Clay hurried around the car and took her by the shoulders. "Don't take any chances. If you see anything you don't like, just say the word and we'll come get you."

"I'll be fine," she told him, hoping that it wasn't a lie. "You'll see."

Clay kissed her. It was too fast for her to sink in and really enjoy—just a brief skimming of his lips filled with a barely restrained desperation she'd never felt from him before. "Stay safe."

Before she could think twice or beg for a reprieve, Leigh turned and started walking.

She'd made it maybe a quarter of a mile when a black SUV approached. It skidded to a stop. The door opened. There were three men inside. All big, all serious, all armed.

The one holding the door open said, "Get in."

Leigh did.

Chapter Twenty-eight

"This is insane," said Clay. He fought the urge to drive after her, knowing that if he did that now, it was going to get all of them killed.

"You need to stay steady." Payton pulled from the trunk one of the rifle cases he'd taken from the Edge's armory. "Leigh needs us to be her backup. And so far, there's nothing coming through her earpiece to indicate she's in trouble. Let this play out."

Clay wasn't sure how steady he could be, knowing Mira and Leigh were both in danger like this. His hands were shaking, and a furious ripple of anxiety kept pulsing through him. "I want to hear what's going on."

"No," said Payton, his tone hard and final. "They'll assume you're listening. The risk of your being triggered is too high. You know that."

Clay scrubbed his hands over his face. "Yeah, I fucking know. It doesn't make it any easier."

"Stay busy. Stay calm. This will all be over soon."

The headlights of the SUV bounced over the road, weaving toward an old farmstead. Clay grabbed a pair of binoculars and watched as three armed assholes shoved Leigh into a run-down barn. His view from the ridge where he stood was clear. He didn't even bother to find cover. They already knew he and Payton were here.

"No windows," said Clay. "That's going to make it impossible to pick any of them off once they're inside."

"Sage is no fool. He knows we're armed. He picked this place on purpose."

"He knew we wouldn't go firing indiscriminately with Mira and Leigh inside."

"Like I said, he's no fool."

"I should sneak up there—get a little closer."

Payton stalked toward him, wearing a look Clay had never seen on the older man before. It was hard, cold, with more than a hint of badass. "Get behind that rifle and keep your eyes open. If things go bad, I'm going to need you ready to fire. There are a lot more of them than there are of us, so you need to man up and keep your head in the game, understand?"

Payton was right. Clay was scattered—his worries for the women sending his thoughts all over the place. This wasn't like him. He was usually calm and cool under fire.

Then again, usually the lives of the women he loved weren't at stake.

Panic flickered around the edges of his consciousness as that thought simply sprang to life, fully formed. He didn't dare look at it or even acknowledge that he'd had it. Not here. Not now. Instead, he shoved it away and put his eye to the scope.

"I see two men outside," said Clay. "One of them is watching us."

Payton lay down on the cold ground and eased behind the second rifle, settling in as if he'd just slipped into a favorite bathrobe. "Let him watch. We're playing by their rules. At least for now."

"And as much as I hate their rules, we're going to do whatever we have to to keep Mira and Leigh alive. I know you have it out for Sage, but all I care about is the women."

"Agreed."

But when he got them home and reassured himself they were both safe and whole, he was going to come gunning for Sage and deliver the payback that he had coming his way, even if that meant Clay had to stab out his own eardrums. That man was never going to threaten his loved ones again. Ever.

Leigh stepped into the dimly lit barn. Apparently, she wasn't fast enough for the man behind her, because he gave her a good shove, making her stumble forward.

The paint left on the wood had mostly peeled off. What had once been a concrete floor was now more the consistency of gravel. Large pitted areas had lifted up and crumbled away. In the center was an oil stain the size of a child's wading pool. Stalls lined one side of the barn, and on the other were stacks of moldering hay bales. A couple of folding tables and chairs had been set up, along with an array of electronic equipment. On the screen of one laptop, Leigh could see the colorful blobs indicating the heat signatures of two people.

"They can see you," she whispered, hoping that her voice was loud enough to carry to the matching earpiece Payton wore.

They'd taken her gun away, and the syringe of tranquilizers she'd kept on hand, but either hadn't noticed the earpiece or pretended they hadn't.

She scanned the room, counting men. She wanted to convey whatever information she could to Payton in the hopes that it would help if things turned ugly. "Which one of the six of you is Dr. Sage?" she asked. "And where is Mira?"

A muffled sound of fear rose from one of the stalls—
a woman's voice.

Leigh moved in that direction on pure instinct. "It's
okay, Mira. I've got what they want. We're going to walk
out of here in just a minute."

The stall door creaked open, revealing a man in his
sixties, with a stooped posture and round glasses. He was
mostly bald, with wispy bits of white hair over his ears.

Her first thought was that Dr. Sage didn't look like a
deranged mad scientist. Her second thought was that the
gun he held against his daughter's side proved how
wrong appearances could be.

"Open the briefcase," he ordered.

Leigh didn't hesitate. She set it on the chunky floor
and showed him what was inside. Paper, USB drives. She
didn't spare the stuff more than a glance. It had no meaning compared with Mira's life.

"Let her go. You have what you want."

"Not until I'm sure that it's authentic." He nodded to
one of the armed men. "Check the drives."

A man took the briefcase and slipped one of the
drives in. The dark screen flared to life. He frowned.
"There's data here, but it's encrypted."

"You have what you want," said Leigh. "Let Mira go
now."

A shadow shifted behind Mira, forming the shape of
a man. He'd been hiding in the darkness near the hay
bales, so still that she hadn't seen him until now. He was
tall, lean. He looked angry, but his gaze was fixed on that
gun at Mira's side, as if he could move it through sheer
will alone. "I'll take the women outside and drop them
off a few miles away."

"No," said Dr. Sage. "If the data is encrypted, then we
need Mira to decrypt it."

Leigh barely kept herself from screeching at him.

Instead, her voice came out as a harsh, guttural thing. "That wasn't part of the deal."

"It is now."

Mira stared at the computer screen, knowing that she couldn't let her father see this information. He'd done bad things, but she'd hoped that all of that was the in past.

She knew better now.

The information contained in these files was dangerous. It had the power to destroy lives, and Mira was not going to help him do that. Not anymore. She'd been an unwilling participant in her father's experiments for years. He'd used her—changed her.

But she was no longer her father's puppet. It didn't matter what it took; she was not letting him get this information. Ever.

Before she could think better about her decision, she deleted all the data on the drive and replaced it with a repeating string of text listing the URL for a foul-mouthed blogger who liked to rant about the color of paint used in men's bathrooms across the Midwest. Once that was done, the old data overwritten multiple times, she re-encrypted the information with a simple substitution cipher, making it look like it had before—a bunch of gibberish.

"I'm sorry, but I can't do it," said Mira. "This encryption is beyond my ability. You'll have to find someone else."

Her father turned toward her, looking at her as he had for years, with disgust and thinly veiled hostility hovering in his eyes. She hated that looking at his eyes was almost the same as looking into a mirror. She hated knowing she had that connection to him—that the two of them shared anything in common. But mostly she hated that part of his success was at least partially her fault.

"Of course you can do it," said her father. "You're just not trying."

He grabbed Leigh by the hair. She yelped in pain and leaned sideways, trying to relieve the pressure on her scalp. He dragged her to where Mira was sitting at the computer and pressed the barrel of his gun against Leigh's temple. "Perhaps you should try harder."

Hot, sickening terror set in the pit of Mira's stomach, burning like a live coal. There was no question as to whether her father would kill Leigh. She knew he would.

Mira tried not to show her fear. Her father would feed on it, and it would make him stronger, bolder.

She shrugged as if she didn't care what happened to her friend, even though her nerves rattled so hard they threatened to tear her apart. The damage was already done, and she couldn't undo it. Not with the number of times she'd rewritten over the data. There was no getting it back, which had been her exact intent when she'd made the decision. "There's nothing I can do if the data is corrupted."

"If the data is corrupted, then they failed to bring me what I needed, and you've forfeited a life."

Bravado was not Mira's strength, but she shoved her chin up and pretended like she was some tough chick like Bella. "Then kill me now, because there's not a fucking thing I can do about corrupted data."

"It's not you I'll kill first. I'll kill your friend. Slowly." He moved the gun to Leigh's arm.

That stopped Mira cold. Sweat broke out along her spine.

Leigh quivered in his grasp, but Mira couldn't tell if it was fear or anger. "You fire one shot, and the men I brought with me will swarm in here and take you down."

Richard looked unconcerned. "I hardly think they'd risk you womenfolk in the cross fire. Besides . . ." He leaned close to Leigh's ear and whispered something Mira couldn't hear.

Leigh went white and looked like she might throw up. "That won't work. He wasn't listening," she said, though she didn't sound certain.

Richard smoothed her hair behind her ear and plucked out the comm unit she'd been wearing. "Then I guess you won't be needing this anymore." He crushed it under his heel.

The expression of horror on Leigh's face told Mira everything she needed to know. That had been their lifeline, and now it was gone.

Adam stepped out of the shadows behind her, moving silently. He hadn't been far away since they'd left the lab. Everywhere she went, she could feel his eyes on her, watching her. His gaze had been steady and intense, filled with some hidden meaning she couldn't translate. "Perhaps one of the other drives will work," he suggested, his voice smooth and calm.

Mira stared at him in shock, realizing instantly what he was doing. He'd been standing behind her. He could have easily seen the screen—and that she'd been able to open the file for one brief moment.

She'd been so intent on deleting the information that she hadn't had the presence of mind to consider that there was more left for her to destroy. "He's right. I should see if any of the other drives are salvageable."

Mira went through the drives, one by one, deleting data as fast as she could. Adam's shoulders blocked Richard's view of her screen, so even if he had looked her way, he wouldn't have been able to see anything.

"If you make Mira nervous," said Adam, "it's only going to take her longer to do what you want. Why don't you let the woman have a seat and stop waving the gun around?"

"I know my own daughter," said Richard. "She never does anything without the proper motivation."

Mira ground her back teeth together in an effort to keep her mouth shut. Anything she said would only make it that much worse for Leigh.

Adam kept talking, his voice so calm and reasonable, it helped soothe some of the nervous chaos rioting in Mira's stomach.

She had to do something to prevent her father from getting any of this data, while still giving him enough to let them go. After several tense, brain-racking minutes, she knew what she had to do. It was so simple, so symmetrical, she wondered why she hadn't thought of it before.

"I need to connect to the network at the Edge," she told her father. "I've been working on some new encryption algorithms that might help."

"No outside connections," said her father. "I won't have you contacting anyone."

Adam shifted his body just enough that he came a few inches closer to her. "She already has men outside who can contact whomever they like. No one is going to move in while you have these women at gunpoint. If you want the data, then you need to let Mira access her tools. You hold all the cards here, Sage. Let her do her job and we'll be long gone before reinforcements arrive. The longer you take, the more men will pile up outside."

Richard looked at one of his men. "Take two men and make sure no one is sneaking up on us." Then he turned to Mira, a warning of violence in his gaze. "You have ten minutes to get me what I want, or I start motivating you."

Chapter Twenty-nine

Mira was in big trouble. Leigh was in even more. She knew she was expendable, unlike Mira. It was going to be Leigh who took the first bullet.

She'd stitched up enough gunshot wounds to cringe at the thought of what Dr. Sage's gun would do to her arm—her right arm.

The question was, was he bluffing or did he mean it?

Based on the way Mira's fingers were flying over the keyboard with frenetic haste, Leigh guessed that her time was running out.

She had waited too long to say that her legs felt like noodles—uttering the code word that would have Clay and Payton charging in here like the cavalry. Now the chance was gone and she was on her own. And all she could think to do was to give these men what they wanted.

The tall guy was right. If gunfire broke out, there was a really good chance that she or Mira would be caught in it. At least the way things were now, no one was shooting.

Mira's fingers stopped, sending the room into silence. "There. I think that's it."

Dr. Sage shoved Leigh toward the closest goon, who caught her with a less-than-gentle grip.

Sage went to his daughter's side. His eyes scanned the screen, and a slow smile spread over his face. "This is it. You did it."

"Good. Leigh and I will be leaving now."

Mira got up off the stool, but Dr. Sage grabbed her arm. "You still have three more drives to go through."

"Do it yourself. I installed the program on your machine. It will decrypt any files using the same or a similar code."

Dr. Sage stared at Mira for a long minute, studying her face. She started to squirm, twisting her fingers together in a childlike gesture of guilt.

The tall man grabbed her hands. "I'll take them back to the road and drop them off. It's a half-mile hike to where their backup is parked. That will give you time to clear out."

"No," said Dr. Sage. "One of my men will do it."

The tall man went completely still for the space of three heartbeats. Then his expression changed, going dark and feral. "We had a deal."

"What do you care?" snapped Dr. Sage. "You got what you wanted from me. I don't even know why you're still here."

"To see the job through to the end."

"Adam, I think you'll be happier if you don't see what happens next." Sage looked to where the tall man's fingers were wrapped around Mira's. "It seems like you've developed some kind of attachment."

Leigh's whole body went cold as the reality of the situation set in. Sage had never planned to let them go. Now that he had what he wanted, he was going to kill them both.

She struggled to keep her breathing steady and not hyperventilate, but with bleak terror rampaging through her veins, her body was an alien place completely out of her control.

"I won't let you kill her," said Adam. There was some quality to his voice that made the primitive parts of her brain shove out the command to flee. Only the crushing grip of the goon holding her arms kept her feet planted.

"It's none of your concern," said Sage. "Leave now. Your presence is no longer needed or desired. I want no witnesses."

This was where Leigh was going to die, in this run-down, dingy barn—and there wasn't a thing she could think to do to stop it from happening. Sage was going to kill both Leigh and Mira, and very likely take out Clay and Payton.

No witnesses.

Gunshots rang out in the distance.

Clay saw Payton's face and knew things had just gone to hell. "What happened?"

"Comms went dead. Stay here," ordered Payton. "I'm going in."

"Not alone, you're not." He wasn't sitting on his ass out here, watching everything happen. Not when Leigh and Mira were in there in need of help.

"You're a liability. Sage already said the trigger phrase once. He knows you're here. He'll turn you on us inside of ten seconds."

"Not if I can't hear him."

Clay grabbed Leigh's medical bag and pulled her stethoscope from it. He shoved the earpieces in, held the flat pad next to his weapon, and fired.

Pain blasted his eardrums. A wave of dizziness spun over him, and loud ringing set up shop inside his skull. He doubled over, unable to tell where the ground was until he crashed into it.

Payton's face appeared in his line of sight. His mouth

was moving—his face contorted with rage. Clay heard nothing but a loud, constant ring.

He shoved Payton aside and hopped behind the wheel. "Cover me," he shouted, hoping it was loud enough for Payton to hear.

He sped over the uneven ground, going airborne at times and leaving deep ruts furrowed in the ground when he landed. Leigh's car was never going to be the same again, but he'd gratefully buy her a new one if they all made it out of this alive.

Bullets sparked off the hood. Two men stood outside the barn, firing at him. One of them went down, thanks to Payton. The other one ducked for cover, popping up only to take more shots every few seconds. One of his bullets hit the windshield, making it burst into a thousand cracks. Clay kept driving.

In the rearview mirror, Clay saw flashes from the muzzle of Payton's rifle. He could feel the shots vibrating in his chest, but none of the sound penetrated through the ringing in his ears.

This was as close as he was going to get without getting shot, so he skidded into a spin, letting the car slide into some low brush. It acted as a screen, giving him enough concealment to climb out of the car unscathed.

His head was still spinning some, and his balance was off. He kept a firm grip on the car door to give himself a reference point and something to keep him steady.

There were more men out here than they'd originally thought. Apparently some of them had been keeping out of sight. But they were here in force now, decked out in body armor and as much firepower as a small army.

Light from inside the barn spilled out over them, giving Clay several visible targets. Inside the barn he could see Leigh struggling against one of the men. Mira's body was mostly blocked by a tall man, but Clay could see her as well—pale, shaking, and afraid.

The odds were bad. There were at least eight of them. All Clay had going for him was the cover of darkness and the certain knowledge that there wasn't a single one of them who was going to stop him from saving the women he loved.

A man appeared out of the brush, only ten feet away. The barrel of his gun zeroed in on Clay.

The buzzing haze of rage that always came to him right before he blacked out hit him as hard as a charging bull. He could feel it pulsing at the edges of his control, urging him to let go, give in, stop fighting. He tried to stave it off, but the need to fight pounded at him. It clawed at his mind, ripping away what little sanity he had left.

A boiling scream rose from his chest. He could feel the power of it vibrating within his lungs, but he could hear nothing. He rose from his crouch behind the car, weapon raised, and began firing.

As soon as shots were fired, the situation in the barn changed fast.

Leigh found herself lying on the floor, unsure how she'd landed there. A burly guard raced by. Maybe he'd knocked her over. She wasn't sure.

She rolled away from the stampede of feet, watching as Dr. Sage aimed his gun at his daughter. His gaze was fixed on the doorway where Clay stood, his chest heaving, blood smearing his cheek.

The look on Clay's face was horrifyingly familiar. The hollow stare he wore, the feral snarl, the careless disregard for the danger he faced—all of that told her he'd been triggered.

This was no longer the man she loved.

"Stop right there," ordered Dr. Sage.

Clay kept walking. He didn't even slow.

Across the room, Adam glided toward the doctor, putting himself squarely in front of the gun pointed at Mira.

"Clay?" said Mira, uncertainty making her voice waver.

Leigh pushed to her feet. "That's not Clay."

Two burly men in body armor stood in front of Dr. Sage, guarding him with their bodies.

Dr. Sage glanced to where his gun was aimed, seeing Adam standing there. "Out of the way, Adam. He won't care if I kill you. Mira, on the other hand . . . well, she was always a useful lever when it came to Clay."

"I'm afraid I can't do that," said Adam. "I promised Mira I'd get her out of here alive."

"Stupid move," said Dr. Sage. He fired.

Adam flinched in pain. A bright red starburst began to spread out over his white dress shirt. Behind him, Mira let out a shocked breath and went down hard. She was bleeding. The single bullet had gone through Adam, into Mira.

Clay charged. Dr. Sage swiveled his gun around toward Clay.

Leigh screamed an incoherent warning, but the sound was drowned out by gunfire. Clay's body jerked as bullets hit his chest, but he kept on moving, firing shot after shot.

There was nothing she could do for him, but Mira was bleeding. So was Adam.

She made the only choice she could. Even though it ripped her heart out to abandon Clay, he was too dangerous to approach. Instead, she crouched and ran toward Mira. If Clay had been himself, that's what he would have told her to do. It was part of the reason she loved him.

Blood pooled beneath Mira, seeping from a wound below her left breast. Her eyes were open and wide with shock. Her hand clutched the wound to stop the bleeding, but it was bad. Blood seeped out from between her fingers.

Leigh shoved Mira's hands aside and applied pressure to the wound. "You're going to be fine." She hoped it wasn't a lie.

Leigh looked up to gauge the danger.

Both men in front of Dr. Sage had fallen. A fine mist of blood covered Dr. Sage's face and shirt. Clay advanced on him, weapon raised. The barrel of the gun shook in his hand.

"You can't do it," said Sage. "I made sure of that."

Clay made a noise somewhere between fury and pain. It vibrated the cold air in the room, sinking into Leigh to steal away her warmth.

To her left, Adam began to move. He pushed himself up on one arm and lifted his weapon.

"Don't you dare hurt Clay," growled Mira. Her voice lacked volume. Leigh wasn't even sure that Adam had heard her.

Clay came to a full stop. His face was contorted with fury, and he struggled as if trying to break through an invisible wall.

Dr. Sage grinned, smug satisfaction wrinkling his face. "You were always so easy to train, like a puppy desperate for a few scraps of food or affection."

"Cover your ears," shouted Leigh.

Clay didn't respond—not even a flicker of recognition lit his eyes.

The tranquilizer was here in the barn somewhere. It

was the only thing she could think of that would stop Clay without killing him.

She scanned the room, looking for the man who'd taken it from her.

Mira tried to sit up. More blood welled from between Leigh's fingers. "Hold still. You'll bleed out if you try to move."

Adam's eye twitched, and he pushed to his feet. "I don't think he can hear."

Dr. Sage's grin faltered. His hand started to shake, along with the gun in his grip.

He was going to shoot Clay. The tendons in his wrist were shifting as his finger tightened on the trigger. And there was nothing Clay could do to stop him.

One of the guards who had been killed lay only three feet away. Leigh pressed Mira's hands hard against the wound, telling her silently to keep up the pressure.

Leigh lunged for the weapon and fired before anyone else could stop her. Her shot ripped a hole in Dr. Sage's side, sending him screaming to the floor. An eerie stillness fell over him. He didn't so much as twitch.

She'd killed him, and she couldn't muster even a flicker of guilt for ending his life.

Clay turned and saw her holding the weapon. His eyes were empty. He had no idea who she was.

A gun went off. Clay spun around, blood flying from his arm.

Adam slumped back down, panting. The gun in his hand clattered against the crumbled concrete. His shirt was soaked with blood. His skin was pale.

Clay's arm hung uselessly at his side, but that didn't stop him from advancing. Fury burned deep groves around his mouth as he charged the closest person — Mira.

His intent was clear. Leigh had seen that look before, right before he'd killed. If she didn't do something, he was going to murder Mira, and there was no way he'd ever forgive himself for that. If he hurt Mira, he was as good as dead.

Leigh couldn't lose him. She loved him. She couldn't let him destroy himself like this, and there was not a single doubt in her mind that hurting Mira would kill him.

"Clay," whispered Mira, pain ringing in her voice. "Please don't do this. It's me. You know me."

Clay continued to advance, an empty husk of the man he once was. He was only a few feet away from Mira now. Blood dripped from his arm, leaving a trail on the broken concrete.

Leigh had no drugs and no way of stopping him except with the gun.

Tears made her vision wobble. She blinked them away as she lifted the weapon. He was wearing a bulletproof vest. None of the shots he'd taken to his torso had slowed him down much.

Normally, anatomical data flowed through her easily as she cataloged things that could go wrong with the human body. But now, as she went through the list of ways to disable without killing, the knowledge turned her stomach.

This wasn't just any man. It wasn't just any body. This was Clay.

Only it wasn't. She had to remember that.

Leigh steadied her aim and fired. Clay's leg crumpled beneath him, making him stumble. His gaze turned to her, twisted with violent intent. He pushed himself to one leg and began to hobble toward her.

She fired again, hitting his other leg. Clay fell face-first onto the giant oil stain. His head bounced off the concrete. He didn't move. Leigh's voice rose in a scream of grief and denial as she raced to his side.

Her fingers met the hot skin of his neck, and there, fast and hard, she felt the beat of his heart.

He was alive but bleeding badly. And there was no way to know how much damage she'd done to him.

Payton appeared in the doorway. "I'll get your med kit from the car."

After that, things blurred together in a haze of post-adrenaline letdown and a frantic rush to stop all the bleeding. By the time Leigh had finished seeing to Clay, Mira, Adam, and two of the guards who'd survived, the dead had been airlifted out along with the wounded. Clay had been one of the first to be flown away.

She sat back, peeling off her bloody gloves as two men in black carried off the last wounded guard. Payton stood over her, offering her a bottle of water.

"Where are the police?" she asked, suddenly realizing how odd it was that there had been no lights or sirens.

"They're not coming. I've taken care of everything. All you need to do is keep quiet. None of this ever happened." There was something in his expression that scared her—some kind of warning she knew better than to ignore.

"Where is Clay? I want to be there when he wakes up."

Payton's mouth flattened into a hard line of refusal. "I'm afraid that's not possible. We've taken him somewhere safe."

Exhaustion loomed over her, threatening to crush her, but she found the strength to push to her feet. "You *will* let me see him."

Payton shook his head. "I'm sorry. That's out of the question. Once he's stable, he'll be going to the facility where Garrett is housed."

Locked away. Stolen from her.

"Like hell. I did everything you asked. I want to see them both."

"It will only hurt you more. You need to let them both go."

Discard them, as if they didn't matter? Not in this lifetime. She loved them. She would not stop until she found a way to free them. "If you don't let me see them, then I'm going straight to the press with everything I know."

Payton rocked back in genuine shock. "You wouldn't."

"Try me. You can't steal the men I love from me and not expect me to react."

"I could have you locked up. You've broken the law. Many times over."

"Then who would you get to patch up all those gunshot wounds you don't want reported?"

Payton sighed. "I'm not trying to hurt you. I'm trying to protect you."

"I'm a big girl. I'll protect myself."

He shook his head in regret. "If he survives, I'll let you see him. After you've had time to think. This isn't the life you want, Leigh. Not even close."

Chapter Thirty

Leigh had to wait three weeks to see Clay. Payton insisted that he needed time to recover from his injuries and for his hearing to return.

Leigh used the wait to her benefit. She spent the time with Mira while she recovered, gathering every bit of information she could. When the date to see Clay finally came, she was more than ready.

Part of her had hoped that the feelings she'd had for him would fade with time and distance, but instead, they'd grown more powerful, blooming into something she could no longer deny. She loved him, and because of that, she was willing to do whatever it took to save him. No matter the risk.

Payton took her to the facility as usual, insisting she be drugged unconscious for the transport. She woke up inside a car, parked inside a huge hangar that led to a series of secure doorways underground.

Payton took her bag from her and dumped its contents on a stainless-steel table. Keys, wallet, makeup bag, condoms, and a syringe fell out.

He lifted a brow in question.

"I plan to have sex with him," she said, as if daring Payton to tell her to abstain.

"And the drugs?"

She shrugged. "Self-defense, in case things get out of hand. I'm assuming you'll afford us some privacy, which also means I need to deal with any problems that arise myself."

"He's been in control since arriving here—ever since he found out that you and Mira were safe and that we found those children in Sage's lab and took them home."

It had taken Leigh two days to work through the almost debilitating relief she'd felt knowing that Dr. Sage's work had been shut down and that the children he'd been holding there were now back with their families. Until now, she wasn't sure that Clay had been given the same information.

"Good, then I shouldn't need to drug him," she said, trying to sound more confident than she really was.

Payton hesitated in indecision. He took the condoms and syringe and shoved them back into her purse. Everything else stayed on the table. "You're making a mistake getting involved with him like this."

"I love him," she said, uttering the words aloud for the first time. It felt good to say them, while at the same time it scared her to death.

"I'm sorry," was Payton's response.

He turned and led her to a solid metal door. A camera was trained on the entrance, and an armed man stood at attention, wearing the same black uniform as the people who'd come to the barn via helicopter two weeks earlier. He didn't spare her a single glance.

"You have an hour," said Payton. "Make the most of it. This is the last time you'll ever see him again. I won't be a part of you torturing yourself over and over."

Leigh steadied her nerves, dried her sweaty hands on her skirt, and went to see the man she loved.

Clay was dreaming. He had to be.

Leigh appeared in his doorway, her body bathed in light. Her red hair fell in soft waves over her shoulders. She was safe and whole, and so beautiful, it made his chest ache with longing for things he could never have.

The door shut behind her with a metallic clang, casting them both back into the dim light of his prison cell.

He'd been here only three weeks, but it had felt like three years. No one would tell him anything about what had happened that night in the barn. The last thing he remembered was the barrel of a gun pointed at him, and then ... nothing. He'd woken up in a hospital, a cast on one leg and several bullet holes ripped through him.

Payton had told him that Leigh and Mira were alive and safe, but that was all the detail Clay had received. He'd been left to imagine the rest, wondering what had happened. And who he might have hurt.

They hadn't let him have crutches—only a hollow, lightweight cane—which made him wonder just how much damage he'd done.

Clay had no way of knowing if he'd hurt Leigh again, and the worry was eating him alive. He'd hardly slept or eaten since he'd gotten here, but all that weakness went away as he stared at her.

He didn't dare move. He stayed planted where he stood—next to his bed, where he'd jumped up as the door had opened. If he took so much as one step, he'd want to pull her to him and never let go.

For all he knew, she was here to scream at him for hurting her again.

She took one hesitant step and then another. The next thing he knew, she charged him, flinging herself at him.

The feel of her body against his was like heaven. Her soft curves and feminine strength melded into him, filling a dangerous void that had been growing for days.

Clay tipped her face up for a kiss, unable to stop himself from indulging in her mouth. Maybe he was taking advantage of her pity for his imprisonment, but right now, he couldn't bring himself to care. She was too sweet to resist, opening to him with an eagerness that left him aching and breathless.

Leigh pulled away, color high in her cheeks. "I'm so sorry I had to hurt you."

"Hurt me?"

"They didn't tell you?"

He shook his head.

Her dark eyes closed in regret. "I shot you. Twice. I didn't want to, but Mira was there, bleeding. She couldn't get away." She let out a long, shaky breath. "It seems that all your mistrust of me was valid."

He tipped her chin up so she'd look him in the eye. "You stopped me from hurting Mira. I'd never hold that against you. You shooting me proves just how wrong I was not to trust you."

"That is insane logic."

He shrugged. "If the shoe fits . . ."

"You're not crazy. I'm going to get you out of here."

"You can't, Leigh. No one can. This is where I need to be. As much as I hate it, we both know that this is the only way to keep me from doing more damage."

"No. I refuse to believe that. There's another way, but there's no time to explain," she whispered. "We need to hurry."

"Hurry? What are you talking about?"

She pulled her purse from her shoulder and unzipped

it. "We only have an hour alone, and I don't know how long this will take."

Clay covered her hands. "Slow down. I don't know what's going on. What are you doing?"

She went still and her mouth trembled. "Mira and I think we found a way to help you. I don't know for sure if it will work, but she said you'd want us to try."

"Try what?"

"Payton knows your trigger phrase. He heard it through my earpiece when Dr. Sage said it. I can't trust him not to use it on you."

The idea of Payton using him wasn't a new one. It burned like acid, but Clay knew that if he dwelt on it, suspicion would eat him alive. He was stuck here and needed to learn to accept that.

"You need to worry less about me and more about yourself."

"How can I when you're locked in here? We both know this place will kill you. And Garrett. This is our best shot at freeing you."

"How?"

"I'm going to try to . . . reset you—replace your trigger phrase so that no one else can ever use it against you."

Clay wanted to hope, but he didn't dare. False hope in a place like this was a death sentence. "I don't want to waste even a second of our time together. I just want to be with you, hold you—for however long we have."

He wanted to tell her that he loved her, but that wouldn't be fair to her. He didn't want to give her any reason to sit around and wait for him to get out of this place. Chances were he never would. Leigh needed to move on with her life.

He needed her to be happy.

She squared her shoulders, aligning them with stubborn intent. "Payton wouldn't let Mira come here. And she's still a little weak. I'm sorry, but you're stuck with me."

"There's no one I'd rather see than you, Leigh. Including Mira." It was as close to a confession of love as he would let himself get.

"I know you don't trust me, but I need you to let me do this. I promise I've taken every precaution possible. Mira checked my plan to make sure I didn't miss anything. You trust her, don't you?"

Clay cupped her face in his hands, holding her so that she had no choice but to look into his eyes. "I trust you more than anyone else on the planet. I know that's not saying much, but it's true. I should have told you everything before. I should have told you that every time I see a gun pointed at me, I lose it. Maybe if I'd told you that before, I could have saved you a whole pile of pain."

Tears pooled in her eyes. "That means a lot, Clay. You have no idea how much. I only hope you feel the same way after today."

Her tone set off warning sirens in his head. "What does that mean?"

She stepped back and pulled a syringe from her purse. He expected her to come at him with it, but instead, she jabbed it into her arm and shoved the plunger.

A sick sense of panic flooded him. "What are you doing?" he demanded.

Her eyes had gone a bit glassy, and her head seemed loose on her neck. His wounded body was still slow and clumsy, but he managed to grab her arms to keep her from falling.

She looked up at him with apology shining in her gaze. "I saw seven blue trout swimming in the river today."

Something in Clay snapped. He felt himself slipping

away in a buzzing haze. Part of him went to sleep, but the rest of him was wide awake and waiting for instructions.

Clay stood in front of Leigh, staring blankly at her. There was no emotion on his face—no rage or fear, just simple acceptance.

His trigger phrase had made him a blank slate—a puppet for her use.

Leigh struggled to stay awake. She'd gone through a test run of this before but hadn't taken into account just how much the lingering effects of the sedative Payton insisted on would slow her down.

"Those words I just said will never again affect you. Instead, you have a new trigger phrase, which I will give you in a minute. Do you understand?"

Clay nodded.

"Also, from now on, when you see a gun aimed at you, it will no longer bother you—not like it did before. You are in control of your own actions. You decide what to do and when. No one else can ever make you do anything you don't want to do. You are in complete control."

A wave of sleepiness crashed into her. She had to hurry before she could no longer speak.

"I'm going to whisper some words in your ear now. No other words can ever bring you to this state. Do you understand?"

Again, he nodded.

Leigh went up on her tiptoes and started whispering random words. She kept her voice too low to be overheard by any microphones that might be in the room. She didn't know if anyone was listening, but she refused to give anyone a weapon to use against him.

After five minutes of stringing together nonsensical words and medical terms most people had never heard of, she started to slip into sleep. Unconsciousness was only seconds away, and she had to finish this.

"That's it," she told him. "No other words will ever work. You're free now. You can wake up."

She felt him come to attention in a split second, catching her as she collapsed.

Adam wasn't usually sentimental, but in this case, he made an exception. The blood- and water-stained envelope that Sage had given him crinkled now that it was dry. He should have burned it now that he'd committed the information to memory, but he found he couldn't part with this tangible link to his brother.

He pulled the single sheet of paper from it and smoothed it over his thigh. The name Sage had written there was smeared and watery but still completely legible.

Eli was alive and well, living under a name given to him by his adoptive parents. Sage had supplied the new name, along with an address and Eli's place of employment: the Edge.

It truly was a small world.

Now all Adam had to do was approach his brother—find a way to slip into his life and see whether Eli held any memories of their brief time together. The fact that getting closer to Eli also meant getting closer to Mira sent a wild thrill sliding through him.

He wanted to see her again, not that the feeling would be mutual.

No—sweet, innocent Mira would not soon forgive him for tricking her, drugging her, abducting her, and shooting a man she loved. The one searing look of contempt she'd shot him before being airlifted to safety was enough to tell him to keep his distance.

If Eli had been working anywhere else, perhaps Adam would have had the self-control to stay away. But wherever Eli went, Adam would follow. Mira was just going to have to find a way to deal.

Adam folded the paper up and tucked it away for safekeeping. Then he picked up the phone and made the call that would put him in arm's reach of Eli.

And Mira.

Chapter Thirty-one

It was his love that woke her.

Leigh opened her eyes, recognizing the bright light of her own bedroom and the feel of Clay's hands on her skin. He stroked her face and hair, and in every gentle sweep of his hand, she could feel his love for her.

He smiled down at her, his amber eyes bright with hope. "There you are. I was starting to worry you'd never wake up."

"How long was I asleep?"

"Most of a day. Mira said that was to be expected — that I didn't need to freak out."

"Mira?"

"Payton talked to her on the phone. She told him what you did. It worked," he whispered, as if saying the words too loud would ruin everything.

Leigh blinked up at him, confusion muddling her thoughts. "What worked?"

"Your plan. Mira told Payton everything when he found out what you'd done. She told him how she'd found some of Sage's research in those files we copied, and how to reset the trigger phrases, along with the names and last known addresses for the people that

Sage had mind-fucked. That's what he'd been looking for—more people like me he could use. Apparently, he'd lost the data somewhere along the way and wasn't able to remember the names of the kids he'd screwed up."

Details began to filter back to her, coalescing slowly into something that made sense. "I went to see you. I . . ."

"You injected yourself with that anesthetic—the one Mira said screws with your short-term memory."

"It must have worked, because I don't remember a thing."

"That was dangerous," said Clay.

"I didn't have a choice. Mira said her dad's research indicated that there had to be a control phrase—that not having one could leave some kind of bizarre void that could cause problems—but I knew that if anyone had that phrase, you'd still be at risk. The only way I could think to protect you was to make myself forget."

"So no one could torture it out of you," he guessed.

She nodded. "After all we've been through in the past few weeks, I had considered the possibility. This is some pretty messed-up stuff we're dealing with."

His expression darkened with a promise of violence. "There are others out there like me. Payton asked me to help track them down."

"So you're not going back to prison? That means our plan worked."

He gave a darkly amused grunt. "It worked, all right. Payton tested me. He tried to trigger me with the phrase Sage had used—the one Sage whispered in your ear when you went into that barn. Payton also pointed a shitload of weapons at me—even fired a couple so close I could feel the heat of the bullets. None of it gave me that buzzing kind of haze that told me I was about to go dark-side."

"So . . . you're free?" she asked, daring to hope.

He gave her a slow nod. "I'm myself again. No one controls me. And the fact that I know I won't be going around hurting people means that maybe there can be some forgiveness for me."

"Of course you can be forgiven. I knew that wasn't you—not the real you."

"I guess I needed to know it, too."

He needed to forgive himself and let go of the guilt. Leigh understood that and was going to be by his side, encouraging him the whole way. Whatever it took. She would be his example. Her sole focus would be seeing Clay and Garrett well again.

"I want to go back and help Garrett," she told him. "If it worked on you . . ."

"Mira told me she found his trigger phrase and is keeping it safe—not even Payton knows she has it. Payton said that as soon as you're recovered, you can go back and see if your solution works on your brother, too."

"It will," she said, feeling the hope of certainty spreading out through her on silver wings.

"But you're not going anywhere right away," he said. "Whatever shit you pumped yourself full of can't be good for you. You need to rest and recuperate for a few days."

He was right. The dangers of drugging herself again so soon were too high, and she knew Garrett well enough to know he'd want her to wait another day or two. She didn't trust anyone else enough to do the job right—except Clay, and he'd already been through enough.

No, saving her brother from his nightmare was going to be her job alone. And her joy. He'd spend Christmas this year as a free man.

"I suppose I can wait a little while," she said.

Clay gave her a wicked smile. "I have a few ideas on how to make the time pass quickly."

Her body heated in instant response, growing soft and languid at just the thought of what he'd do. Even bandaged and wearing a cast, Clay had more power over her than any other man she'd known. It was an unfair advantage, but one she reveled in.

"Does this mean you're going to stick around for a while?" She'd meant the question to be light and teasing, but it came out different, quivering with insecurity and hope.

All signs of humor faded from his face. He moved over her, holding his body above hers on the bed. His gaze slid over her cheeks and mouth, coming to rest on her eyes. "I plan on finding a way to fit into your life, Leigh—wherever you'll have me. I'm not too proud to admit that I need you. Through this whole mess, you've been my rock, giving me something to hold on to so I didn't go over the edge. I can't let go of you yet."

"I don't want you to let go." Not ever.

She didn't say the last part for fear she'd scare him away. What they had was so new and fragile, she hardly dared to breathe too hard.

"That's good. I worried that after everything—all the danger and bullets . . . after my complete lack of trust in you—that I'd blown my one chance to be with the woman I love."

"Love?"

His eyes crinkled at the corners with a smile. "Yeah. And damn if it doesn't feel good to say it. I love you, Leigh."

He kissed her, cutting off whatever response she might have made. His mouth ignited feelings in her that she'd never thought to feel for any man. It was more than merely physical—though heaven knew it was that, too—it ran deeper, all the way to her soul.

She sensed his kiss had been timed as a sort of

rescue—a way to keep her from feeling pressured to say anything back. But it was one rescue she didn't need.

Leigh pulled her mouth from his. "I love you, too."

His whole demeanor changed. She saw a flash of insecurity evaporate, and in its place was something hot and beautiful. He seemed to grow bigger, stronger, as if her words had the power to change him.

Maybe they did. She certainly felt different knowing that he loved her. She felt safe for the first time in years. Whatever problems came their way, they no longer had the power to scare her. She was free to live her life on her own terms. And the life she wanted was with Clay.

Payton met General Robert Norwood at a private airstrip outside of town on Christmas Eve. It was cold and dark, but both of those things worked in their favor. Bob had been insistent that no one know about their meeting, and when Bob insisted, Payton listened.

"It's good news," said Bob as he huddled against the wind. His chopper had taken off. The car picking him up to take him to see his daughter would doubtlessly be here soon.

"I could use some of that."

"Based on recent events, and pulling in every favor I've ever earned, I was able to get approval for this." He handed Payton a folder.

Payton scanned the documents, barely able to believe what he'd read. "You're hiring the Edge?"

Bob nodded. "It's all off the books—something I've been working on for months—but we finally have everything we need to find the people we hurt and try to make it right. All we lack is manpower."

"You can't send your own men?"

"Not for this. I'll retain some oversight."

"Meaning?"

"One man. He'll go to work for Bella, but he'll report back to me. I'll let you know who I choose within the week."

Payton tried not to get his hopes up too high. "I don't know if Bella will go for it or not."

"Then don't tell her. Just hire him. I don't care what it takes. You have no idea what this cost me. Don't fuck it up."

"No, of course not. I'll do what I must. Any chance we have to fix things is worth whatever I have to do."

"Good, because there's one more thing—a string I couldn't find a way to cut."

"What?"

"You're not going to like it any more than I do, but it's nonnegotiable."

"Just spit it out."

"You have to hire Adam Brink, too."

Payton had thought it was cold outside until the chill inside his body made the wind feel positively tropical. "Absolutely not. He can't be trusted."

"I never said you had to trust him. But you do have to hire him."

"Why?"

Bob looked away, scanning the horizon. "Because he scares powerful people. They want him watched. He came asking for this to happen, so it's going to happen, and while it does, you're going to keep your eyes fixed on him. Got it?"

"I'll do what I can," said Payton.

"This is going to be our only shot at making things right. After this, my gun is empty. I've done everything I can."

The way he said it made Payton wonder exactly what this miracle had cost Bob. For years they'd worked, scrambling for whatever resources they could manage to find. This opportunity opened up doors neither of them had had keys to before.

It gave them the power to find the people they'd hurt and take down those who were still doing the hurting.

Dr. Sage survived his wounds. No one but Payton and a handful of others knew that. Nor did they need to know. Sage had spilled his guts about his research and the names of those he'd had killed, in case Clay ever needed to know for the sake of closure. But the really useful information had come from Sage's brief encounters with Norma Stynger. Apparently she was the one with all the power. Sage was dangerous, but by comparison, he was a stinging ant. Stynger was a rabid velociraptor. They had to find some way to take her down, and this could be their only chance.

"Thanks, Bob. I'll do everything I can to make your sacrifice worth the cost. I swear it."

"I know you will. That's why I was willing to take the risk. You've kept my baby girl safe for years. I owe you at least the chance to make up for what we did."

There would be no forgiveness for men like Payton and Bob, but at least now they had an opportunity for repentance. And revenge.

Read on for an excerpt from
Shannon K. Butcher's next Sentinel Wars novel,

Falling Blind

Coming from Signet in April 2013

There was not enough brain bleach in the world to scrub away the things Rory Rainey had seen. Her visions were getting worse, and if she didn't find the person who could make them stop, she was going to go batshit crazy.

As frequently as the mental images were slamming into her lately, that inevitable insanity wasn't far away.

Rory kept her head down and her gaze firmly on the sidewalk in front of her. While her eyes saw only dirt and concrete dimly lit by streetlights, her mind saw much, much more. A riot of TV shows and video screens blazed in her head, one image superimposed upon the next until it was all merely a blobby glow of color and light. Nearby someone was staring down at a newborn baby. Someone else was reading a book, but there was too much visual chaos in Rory's head to make out the words. Brief glimpses of the same nearby sections of street fired in her mind, repeating over and over as the few people still out at that late hour drove by. As she moved down the street, she got close enough to a couple having sex in one of the surrounding buildings to catch what they were seeing. The man was all fleshy and sweating, his face red with effort. The harnesses and implements twisting the woman into a vaguely pretzel-like shape made Rory speed her pace until that sight faded.

Ugh. Not enough brain bleach in the world.

She was in a bad part of town that had been hit hard by the recession. The streets were lined with abandoned storefronts and condemned buildings. It was late and cold, and there was little foot traffic as she made her way to the homeless shelter she often visited. She didn't need the shelter—she had her own home. Nana's home. But that shelter was one of the places where she'd noticed that the visions receded.

Little, fleeting moments of peace had come to her there. What she saw was *real* and hers alone, making it quiet and oh, so precious. At first she'd thought she was getting better, that the space between mental barrages was getting longer. But then she left the shelter and the visions were there, waiting for her.

Her fumbling, painful experiments had led her to believe that someone inside that shelter was blocking her curse. If she could only figure out who they were and make them teach her how they did it, she'd be free.

But her potential savior had left, and Rory had never been able to track the person down. Once in a while her visions would fade and she'd know she was close, but she'd never figured out who was to thank for that reprieve.

A flash of hot pink hair and chain-clad leather burst into her mind, making her stumble in shock. Rory's hair was hot pink, and while she wasn't the only one who had the artificial feature, chances were slim that there was another woman with her hair and jacket nearby.

Someone was watching her.

Rory tried to sort through the jumbled images to focus on who was behind her, but there were so many flashes, and most of them were so bright, that she could hardly see the ground in front of her feet. There were too many people still awake in the city, too many sights slamming into her for her to latch onto a single one for very long.

And just because someone looked at her was no reason to wig out. Lots of people looked at her. That was one of the side effects of having hair louder than a freight train.

Still, her instincts were screaming at her, and she'd learned the hard way that she should trust them. As she continued walking, the hair on the back of her neck rose in warning. Being out at night was dangerous. There were monsters everywhere, and for reasons she refused to think about, they wanted her.

Rory increased her pace, anxiety driving her forward. She cut through an alley to get off the street and shorten her walk. The shelter wasn't far now, and while the remodeling wasn't finished, the doors were open and they were letting people inside to escape the cold.

Bright pink consumed her vision, blocking out the wet pavement at her feet.

That was her hair—her back—and whoever was watching her had followed her down the alley. Definitely not some random pedestrian.

Well, hell. Now she had to do something. No way could she just keep walking, playing the role of prey. She'd never been much of an actress.

Rory stopped dead in her tracks, gripped the gun in her purse, squared her shoulders in a way that shouted she was not some fragile victim, and turned to face whoever was following her. She really didn't want to have to shoot someone, but after what Matt had done to her, she had learned to be more proactively defensive in her thinking. Two days and nights spent in a flooded basement filled with tentacled demons that lived on human flesh and blood had a way of curing a girl's poor decision-making habits.

Anxiety tightened her grip, but she kept her breathing even, struggling to see the alley looming in front of her over the splashy colors and lights in her head. She saw no one, only a slight flicker of motion she couldn't even trust to be real.

"I saw you," she yelled into the night, her breath misting in the cold air.

Another fleeting glimpse of pink came to her, again showing her the back of her own head.

There was no way someone could have slipped past her. Even with her crazy visions, she wasn't that blind—at least not yet. If the visions got any worse . . .

She wouldn't think about that now. She had to stay positive, and convinced that there was a cure for her faulty wiring.

A low hiss rattled out from behind her.

Fear streaked along her veins, and she whirled around to face the threat, gun raised and level.

A demon stood there, black and shiny, easily blending into the wet pavement. Larger than a big dog, its forelegs were too long for its heavily muscled body, pushing it nearly upright. There wasn't a single hair on the creature, but something thick and oily seeped from its skin, leaving smears behind its every step. Its face was disturbingly human, with eyes that glowed a bright, sickly green.

Rory took a step back, unable to control the impulse to flee. The demon's pointed ears twitched as if it heard something, and a second later, in the midst of flashing sights that were not her own, she saw the back of her head again. Only this time it was much, much closer.

There was still someone behind her. Or some*thing*.

She steadied her gun and aimed at the demon in front of her while she spared a quick glance over her shoulder. Sure enough, the demon's bigger, uglier twin was right behind her, its bright eyes flaring with hunger.

Rory knew better than to hesitate. This was a kill-or-be-eaten kind of situation if ever there was one—something she was way too familiar with these days.

Stupid demons fucking up the city. Someone needed to get rid of them, and while she really wished that someone was anyone but her, there was no one else around.

She fired her weapon three times at the closest demon. Chips of brick flew as bullets hit a building. One of her shots sucked less than the other two, hitting the demon in the shoulder. It roared in fury and cowered, twisting its head at an awkward angle so it could lick its wound. From behind her, she heard the other demon charge, its claws scraping across the asphalt. She turned and pitched her body to one side, working to find a clear shot through the flashes and sparkles filling her head.

She landed hard enough to rattle her teeth but managed to stay on her feet. Before she could even steady the weapon, the demon was flying through the air again, claws extended and yellow teeth bared.

The beast really needed a good dentist. That random thought slid through her as she moved on instinct, leaping out of the way. Her shoulder slammed hard against a brick wall, no doubt adding to the bruises she naturally accumulated thanks to her shitty vision.

It was only when she tried to move again that she realized she'd hit more than her shoulder. Pain gripped her knee, scraping along her nerves and digging into her spine. Her leg refused to bend. She looked down and saw a small section of shiny nail protruding from under the side of her kneecap. Attached to that nail was a length of discarded two-by-four from a pile of construction refuse. The board was more than six feet long, and there was no way she could drag it along with her. But if she pulled the nail out, she'd bleed faster.

Rory knew the folly of that plan much too well. If she bled, these two demons would become the opening act to dozens more.

One of the demon's eyes flared as it smelled her blood and charged.

She was used to fear. She'd lived with it for years and had been intimate with it for a couple of horrible nights. That time had taught her how to function despite the terror screaming through her, but that didn't mean she didn't feel it. Her poor ribs were taking a beating as her heart thundered against them. The clammy chill of sweat coated her skin, making the gun harder to hold. But holding it was important, so that's what she did.

She raised the weapon and fired, sending the greasy beast skidding back on the wet pavement.

That wouldn't keep it away for long. There were only a few more bullets in her gun. She had no choice but to free herself and hope she could sprint fast enough and reach the shelter before the rest of the demons nearby smelled her blood and came running. Because they definitely would.

She pulled in a deep breath and jerked the nail from her knee. The bent metal was coated in her blood, and she could feel wetness cooling her jeans.

Both demons were slinking toward her now, their forelegs awkwardly bent at their sides, their muzzles low to the ground as they weaved their way closer. One lifted its head and howled, letting out an eerie, mournful sound.

From somewhere that she guessed was a few blocks away, an answering howl rose. And a little more distant, another. Then another.

Sometimes she hated being right.

Those howls were the dinner bells, and Rory was the main course.

Like hell.

She aimed for the head of the bigger demon and fired. Her shot was true, and a chunk of oily skin and bone erupted from the thing's head. It staggered and took a clumsy nosedive into the street, its legs twitching. Its twin bent down and licked the wound, though whether it was helping or hurting the wounded beast, she had no idea. Nor did she give a fuck.

She hadn't killed it—not if it was like most of the creatures she'd seen. All she'd done was buy some time and increase her odds of surviving, if only from zero percent to one percent. One ravenous demon was more than enough to kill her just as dead as two could.

Someone in an apartment nearby looked into a nearly empty refrigerator, and whatever magic curse haunted her decided that she really needed to see a bowl of fuzzy green stuff right now instead of the demons trying to kill her.

Frustration raged inside her, but she tamped it down. She had to stay calm and focus on what was real and in front of her. The angrier she got, the more chaotic her visions would become—the more blind she'd become.

Rory shoved out a harsh breath and backed away from the pair of monsters, easing her weight onto her injured leg. It held, but the pain grew worse with each step. The cold wet spot on her jeans drooped down farther, reaching her shin now.

Somewhere nearby a finger bent with age and arthritis dialed 911.

Shit. Poor cops had no idea how to deal with demons. Some ignorant, law-abiding citizen had just sent the protect-and-serve team into the jaws of evil. Literally.

Maybe if she was out of there fast, the demons would go away and not nosh on the cops' faces. It was the only chance they had.

Before she could take so much as a step, the sight of dead brown grass filled her mind, sliding past her fast. It was lit by a bright green glow that glinted off of a blunt, shiny muzzle that looked just like those of the demons in front of her. And then the vision shifted and she saw another muzzle pointed down at a dirty street, and another lifted high to stare at the top of a chain-link fence, and another slinking under a parked semi.

Fear chilled her skin and tightened her muscles, and she had to make a conscious decision not to go into a screaming tailspin of panic. More demons were coming, getting closer. She had to get out of there—both for her sake and the cops'.

Rory took another step and her knee buckled under her weight. She nearly fell but steadied herself against a wall before she completely lost her balance.

A scratching sound warned her that something was coming. She flattened her back against the wall and split her attention between the pair of demons and whatever was coming now.

It was small—the size of a rat, but hairless and sporting a barbed scorpionlike tail that curved up over its back. Three glistening spines caught a sparkle of streetlight as its claws scrabbled over the pavement, heading straight for her. Six tiny glowing eyes lit its path.

Rory had no idea what it was, but she knew what it was going to be in a second: dead.

She aimed and fired, for once hitting where she aimed. The little demon—or whatever it was—splattered into a greasy stain. Droplets of black blood sizzled across the pavement, sending up thin tendrils of smoke.

Definitely a demon.

She felt pretty pleased and was congratulating herself for the shot when she heard more scratching coming from around the corner. Not twenty feet away, she saw a faint green glow. And then she saw what was making it.

Dozens of those barbed scorpion-tailed things came scurrying toward her, moving faster than she could run.

She didn't have enough bullets. She couldn't put weight on her fucked-up knee. The only exit was blocked by the pair of greasy black demons. Only seconds had passed since she'd looked away from them, but she didn't dare turn her attention away for long.

She needed a way out. Fast.

Rory leveled her weapon at the biggest threat. The demon she'd shot in the head was back on its feet. The hole in its skull had begun to seal shut already. The smaller demon was several feet closer to her, and she could see flashes of her own face, pale and terrified, as it stalked nearer.

She glanced up, hoping for a convenient fire escape, but there was nothing above her but clear black sky and boarded-up windows way too high to reach.

She pulled in a fortifying breath, working hard to shove out some of her fear as she exhaled. The gun bucked in her grip. The closer demon yelped and flinched but didn't go down. She fired again, and again, each shot forcing it back a bit but making no real difference. The things kept advancing, and she swore they were grinning at her, their green eyes glowing with malicious intent.

Her gun clicked. She was out of bullets. But she wasn't about to give up and let these fuckers have her. She'd survived worse odds than these.

Of course, she hadn't been bleeding then, either, calling every hairy, slimy, scaly thing nearby to come to take a bite.

Rory dropped the gun and grabbed the long board

that had stabbed her with its inconveniently placed nail. The wood was cold in her grip, but it felt solid and real. If she was going down, she was doing it Babe Ruth–style.

One of the little things hit her shoe and started crawling onto it. She tried to fling it off with a hard kick, but the pain stalled her and the thing held on. She slammed the end of the board into it, crushing its head and her own toe.

Pain sliced through her, stealing her breath for a moment.

Her attention had been shifted to the little scorpion thing for less than three seconds, but as the vision of her own head getting close filled her mind, she knew that had been too long of a distraction. The smaller demon lunged for her, and she was completely flanked—and completely fucked.

The world slowed as adrenaline flooded her body. She turned and began shifting her weight to fling herself out of the way. The jaws of the demon were wide-open, its yellow teeth only a couple of feet from her head—close enough to see black blood coating them and pulpy bits of greasy flesh stuck between them. The rotten stink of its breath made her gag.

She lifted the board to protect her face, but even as she began to move, she knew she wouldn't be fast enough. There wasn't enough time to get the board in the way before those jaws closed on her head.

This was it. This was how she was going to leave this earth—bleeding, afraid, and alone, while the rest of the world moved on as if nothing had happened. The fact that she could see them going about their routines rubbed her nose in just how small and insignificant her life really was. Now that Nana was gone, no one would miss her. As distant as she kept from people, chances were no one would even know she'd died. These things would haul her off and eat her, leaving no evidence behind.

What a sad little life she'd led, full of fear.

A metallic sound filled her ears, followed by a solid *thwack*. The open jaws careening toward her jerked down suddenly and hit her shin, but there was no force behind the blow. The muzzle simply bounced off and the head rolled away.

It had no body.

Confusion clouded her mind as she tried to figure out what she was seeing. Was this another vision? Something happening nearby? If so, then why wasn't she dead and seeing nothing?

Rory blinked, hoping to sort out reality.

A man loomed a few feet away, too big to be real. He held a wide sword in his huge hands. The gleaming blade was coated in black oil. His giant body moved quickly, muscles straining the seams of his leather jacket.

She didn't trust her eyes, and yet this all seemed quite real. It even sounded real. Her visions abated.

At the man's feet lay the body of the demon that had nearly killed her. Black blood arced out of its neck in a pulsing spray that got weaker and weaker with every spurt. In front of him was the larger demon, staying low and out of range of that lethal blade.

He'd saved her. He'd lopped off the head of the demon and saved her face from being eaten. That wasn't supposed to happen. That wasn't the way her life went these days. Things were supposed to suck, just like they always did.

And yet there he stood, not vanished like a fleeting vision.

Rory's world began to make sense again, but the shock of still being alive hadn't faded. A sense of joy filled her with her next breath. She wasn't dead. The world was still moving on, but she was moving with it.

The big man's back was to her, and he was slowly circling the demon, angling it back into a doorway for an attack. For a moment all Rory could do was stare. He was smooth, each move flowing into the next in a seamless transition of power and strength. Muscles in his thighs bulged under his jeans, and when he stepped in a shallow puddle, his boot barely made a ripple. Even the mist from his breath curled out slowly and lazily, rising into the night as if it had all the time in the world.

Graceful power radiated from his every gliding step. Shadows caressed him, holding him close in a lover's embrace. He seemed too solid—grounded as if nothing could so much as rock him. And it wasn't just his size that gave her that impression. She *felt* something sliding out of him—a heavy kind of energy that pinned her in place, mesmerizing her. She could stare at his broad back all day and never grow bored.

A sharp pain stabbed her ankle, jerking her attention back to reality. She looked down and saw that one of those little scorpion demons had stung her and was now scurrying away, its barb shining wetly with her blood.

That pain made sense. That was how her life was supposed to go. She got a beautiful visual treat in exchange for the low, low cost of being stabbed by a demon.

The board was still in her hands, and she swung at the little fucker, hoping to squash it dead. Her aim was off, and she only clipped it, sending it into a skittering spin.

The thing righted itself and sped off. The others of its kind veered around her and went straight for her savior in black leather.

"Behind you!" she called out, even as she pushed herself forward, using the board as an awkward crutch.

The man spun around in a fluid arc that was way too

graceful for someone his size. Between his big, booted feet, she saw the head of the second demon roll across the pavement into a brick wall.

Whoever he was, she was glad he was on her side. At least, he was for now.

Rory slammed her board down on one of the rat-sized things, turning it into a black stain.

The man kicked one of them into a wall hard enough to make the demon pop like a water balloon. The rest of the swarm must have seen it happen, because they moved as one, like a flock of birds, reversing direction to flee. Seconds later they were gone, back around the corner the way they'd come.

He scanned the area, searching for more signs of a threat. His wide shoulders lifted with each even breath, and that big sword was still in his grip, ready for action. Dim light gleamed off his blade, as if collecting specks of it from the inky shadows. He wasn't looking at her, but she still felt his awareness as keenly as if he'd been staring.

"You're hurt," he said. It wasn't a question.

"Only a little. I'll live."

His gaze hit her then and drove the breath from her body. His eyes were a deep, earthy green, set below thick, dark eyebrows. The bones of his face stood out, forming rigid, masculine angles. His jaw was a bold statement of strength, the muscles there bulging with determination. It wasn't his good looks that she reacted to, either, though he was a fine-looking man. There was something else in those dark eyes, something potent and stark, with a kind of desperation she'd seen only a few times in her life—usually in those who knew they were about to die. Pain radiated from him, quivering in the small lines around his eyes, so much a part of him that she wasn't even sure he was aware of how obvious his agony was to anyone who cared to see it.

She couldn't look away. His pain called out to her, making her ache in ways she didn't understand. It was as if something inside him was reaching for her, screaming in torment.

Rory shut her eyes to block out his silent pleas for help. A vision of an elderly woman's sleeping face appeared for a moment before it faded behind closing eyelids.

She pushed aside the visions, trying to concentrate on what was real and looming in front of her—all six and a half feet of him.

He took a step closer, scrutinizing her, and she felt that scrutiny glide along her body down to her cold, throbbing toes. By the time his gaze had made its path from her head to her shoes and back again, she felt stripped bare, trembling and defenseless. And that pissed her off.

She knew what he saw: the pink hair, the heavy makeup, the multiple piercings. No one ever really saw her beneath the shock factor, and that was the way she liked it.

At least until now. For some stupid reason, she wanted this man to see her—the real her—all the way down to her bones.

His gaze slid over her face, then lowered to where she was bleeding. She couldn't tell whether he was sizing up her injury because he cared or because he was looking for some weakness he could exploit. His face was about as expressive as a marble wall, so there was no way to know for sure. What she did know was that if he sent that sword sailing in her direction, there wasn't a damn thing she could think to do to stop him from slicing her in two.

His voice was low and deep, rumbling out of him like stones rolling down a mountain. "Come with me."

ALSO AVAILABLE FROM

Shannon K. Butcher

RAZOR'S EDGE
An Edge Novel

Roxanne "Razor" Haught is an expert in stealth security
for corporate espionage cases. But now she's a target.
Tanner O'Connell has no intentions of leaving Razor's
side. Despite her objections to having a "babysitter," his
orders as the newest member of the Edge are to watch her
back. With a brainwashed assassin after his partner,
Tanner cannot afford to let his desire for Razor interfere
with his duty. His special ops skills may be all that stand
between saving Razor—or losing her forever.

"Butcher is...phenomenal."
—*Affaire de Coeur*

Available wherever books are sold or at
penguin.com

facebook.com/LoveAlwaysBooks

S0422

NATIONAL BESTSELLING AUTHOR

SHANNON K. BUTCHER

They are the Sentinels: three races descended from ancient guardians of mankind, each possessing unique abilities in their battle to protect humanity against their eternal foes.

THE NOVELS OF THE SENTINEL WARS

Burning Alive
Finding the Lost
Running Scared
Living Nightmare
Blood Hunt
Dying Wish
Falling Blind
(Coming April 2013)

**"Enter the world of Shannon K. Butcher
and prepare to be spellbound."**

—*New York Times* bestselling author Sherrilyn Kenyon

Available wherever books are sold or at
penguin.com

facebook.com/ProjectParanormalBooks

S0337